STAR KNIGHTS

KAY DAVAULT

RH
GRAPHIC

NEW YORK

Star Knights was illustrated digitally with the help of Clip Studio Paint and Photoshop.

Text, cover art, and interior illustrations copyright © 2022 by Kay Davault

All rights reserved. Published in the United States by RH Graphic, an imprint of Random House Children's Books, a division of Penguin Random House LLC, New York.

RH Graphic with the book design is a trademark of Penguin Random House LLC.

Visit us on the web! RHKidsGraphic.com • @RHKidsGraphic

Educators and librarians, for a variety of teaching tools, visit us at RHTeachersLibrarians.com

Library of Congress Cataloging-in-Publication Data is available upon request.
ISBN 978-0-593-30365-8 (hardcover) — ISBN 978-0-593-30364-1 (paperback)
ISBN 978-0-593-30366-5 (lib. bdg.) — ISBN 978-0-593-30367-2 (ebook)

Designed by Patrick Crotty

MANUFACTURED IN CHINA
10 9 8 7 6 5 4 3 2 1
First Edition

A comic on every bookshelf.

To anyone who has ever made a wish

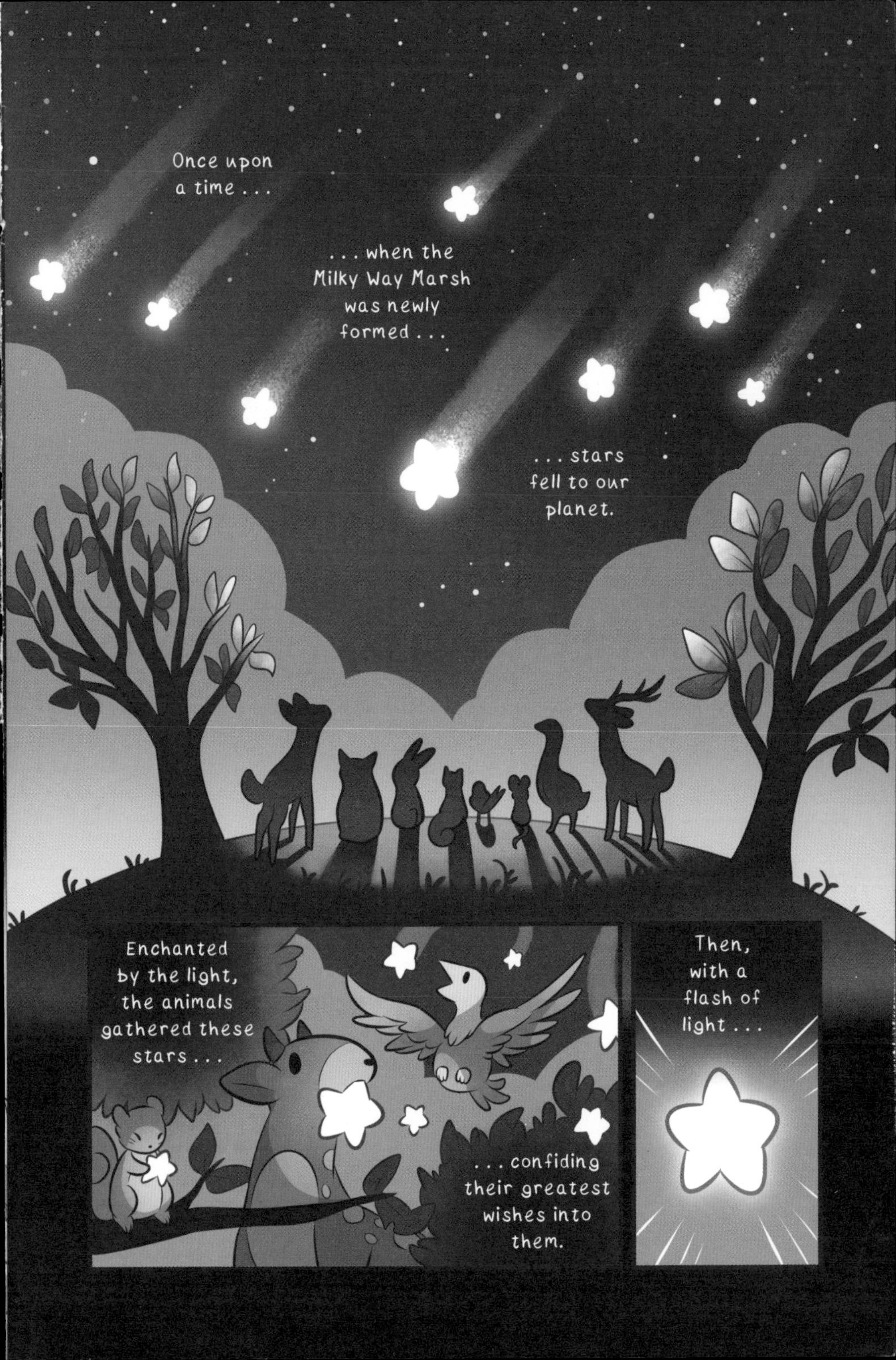
Once upon a time . . .
. . . when the Milky Way Marsh was newly formed . . .
. . . stars fell to our planet.
Enchanted by the light, the animals gathered these stars . . .
. . . confiding their greatest wishes into them.
Then, with a flash of light . . .

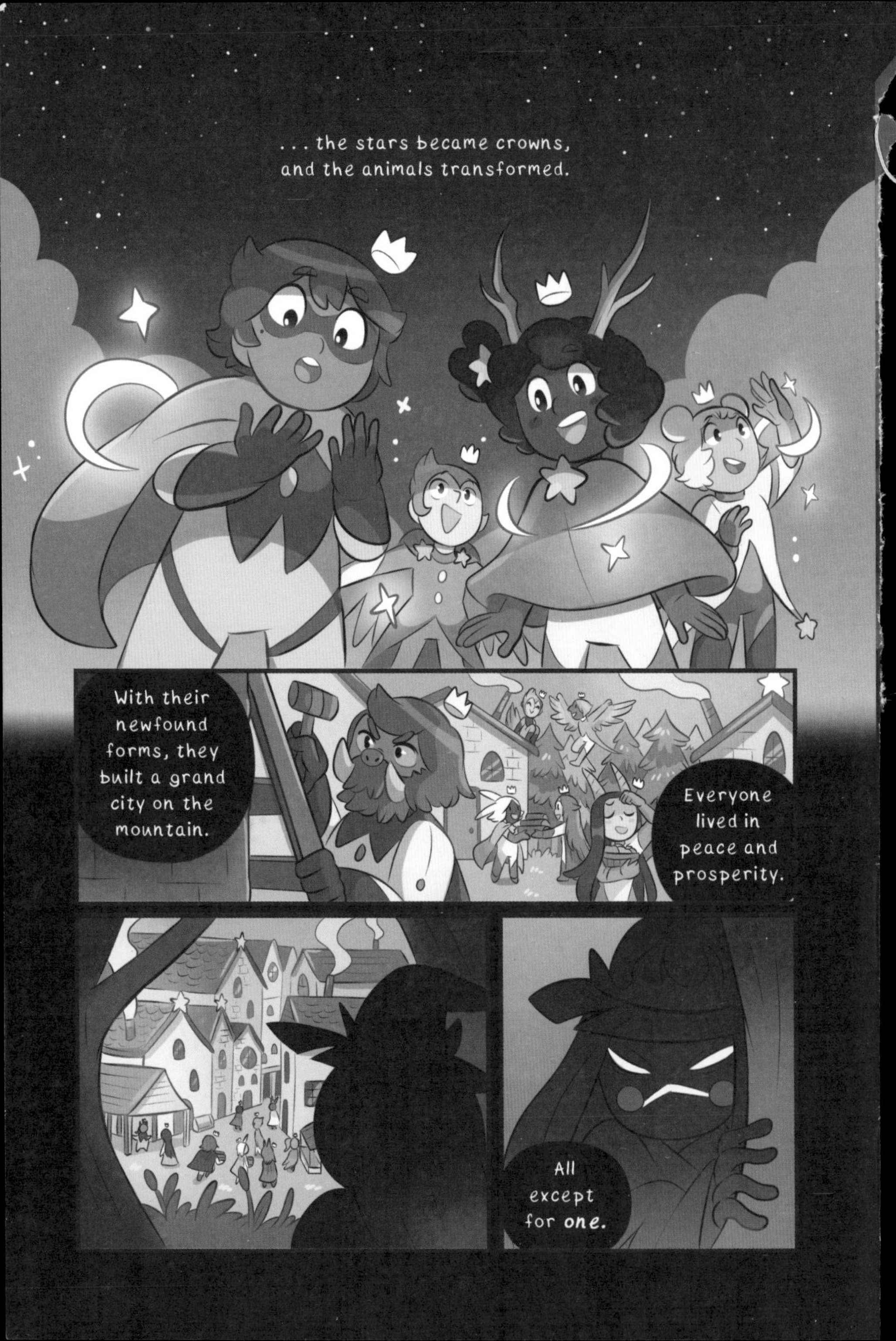
. . . the stars became crowns,
and the animals transformed.
With their newfound forms, they built a grand city on the mountain.
Everyone lived in peace and prosperity.
All except for *one*.

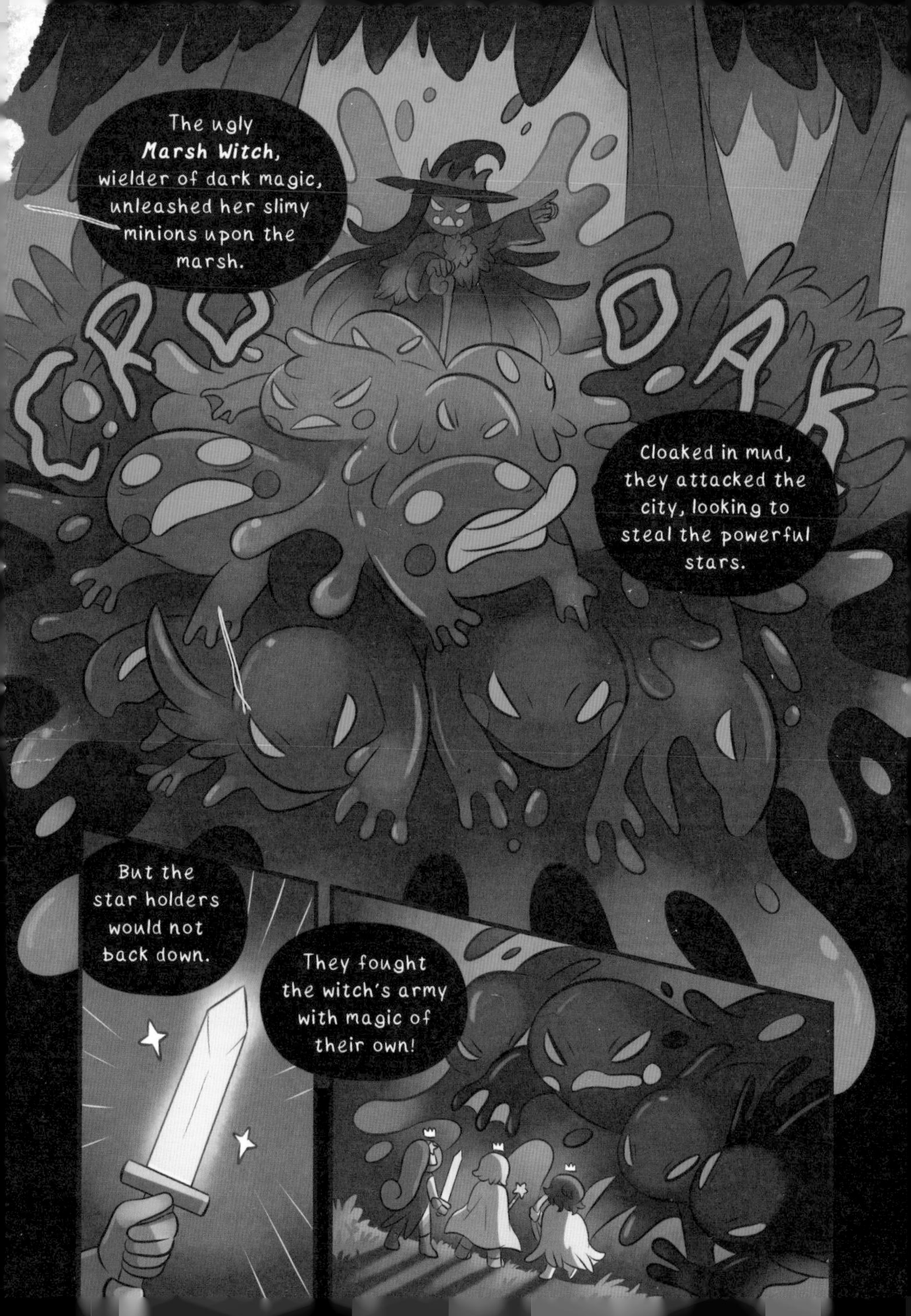
The ugly **Marsh Witch**, wielder of dark magic, unleashed her slimy minions upon the marsh.
CROAK
Cloaked in mud, they attacked the city, looking to steal the powerful stars.
But the star holders would not back down.
They fought the witch's army with magic of their own!

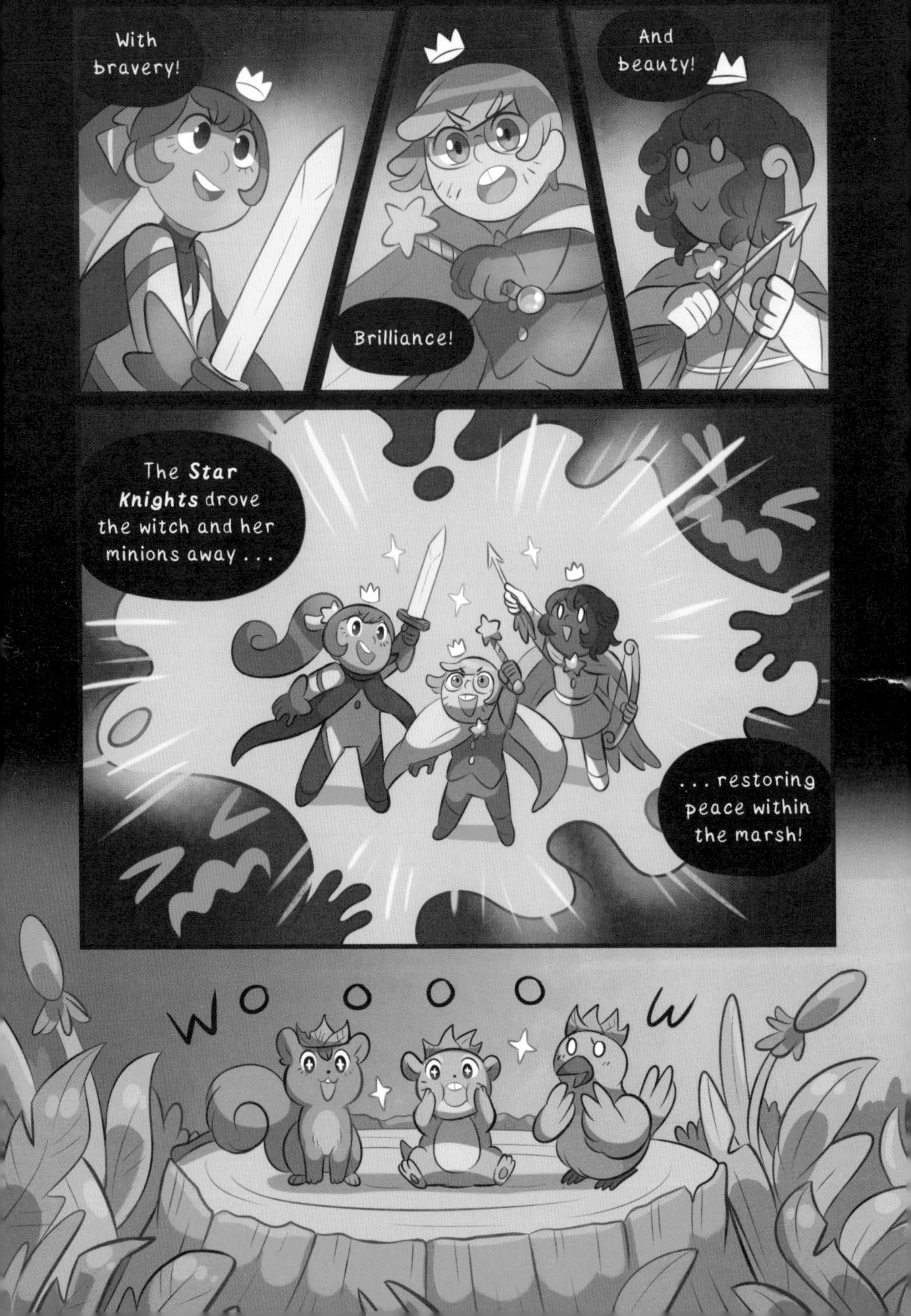
With bravery!
Brilliance!
And beauty!
The **Star Knights** drove the witch and her minions away . . .
. . . restoring peace within the marsh!
WOOOOW

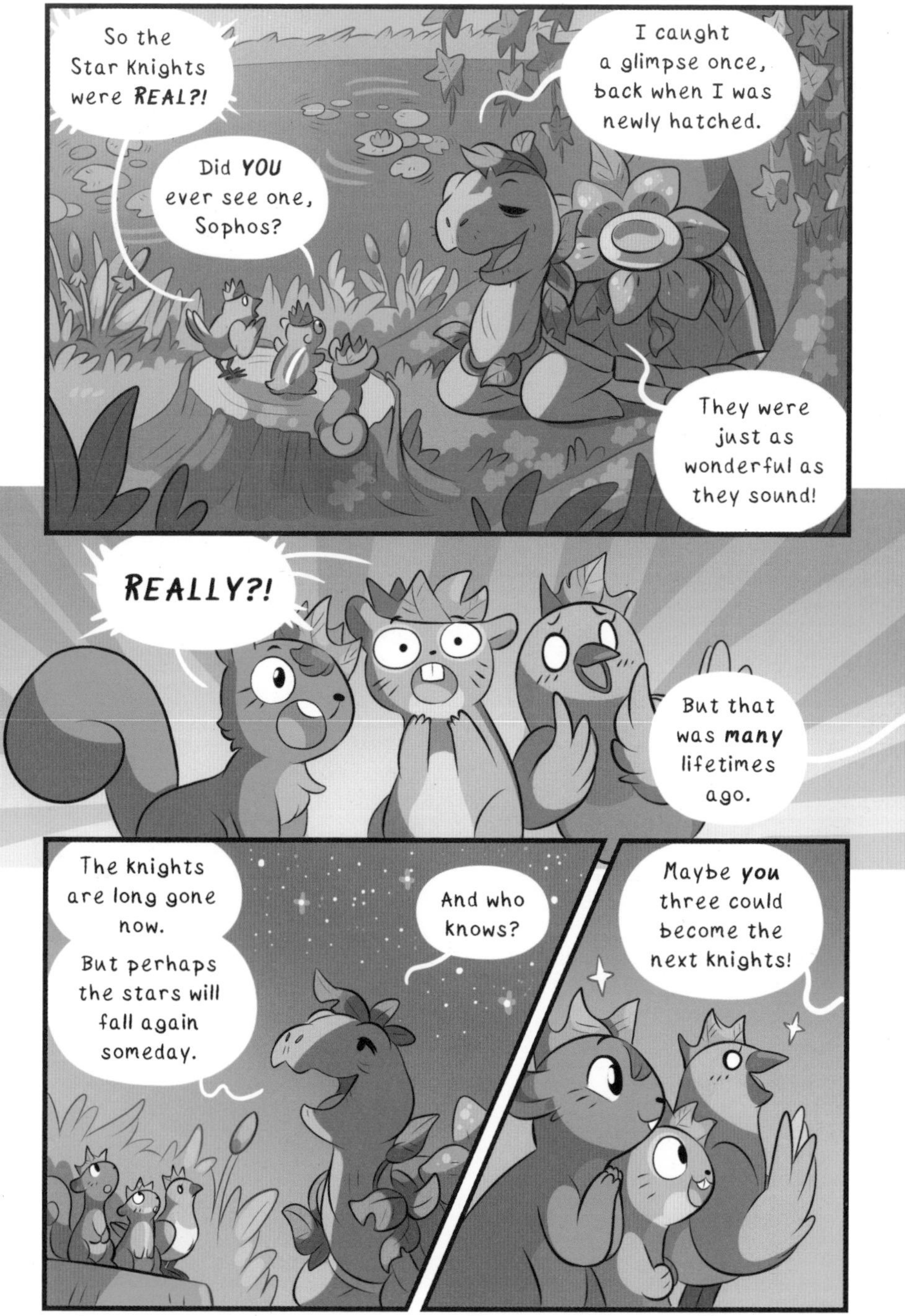

So the Star Knights were REAL?!
Did YOU ever see one, Sophos?
I caught a glimpse once, back when I was newly hatched.
They were just as wonderful as they sound!
REALLY?!
But that was many lifetimes ago.
The knights are long gone now.
But perhaps the stars will fall again someday.
And who knows?
Maybe you three could become the next knights!

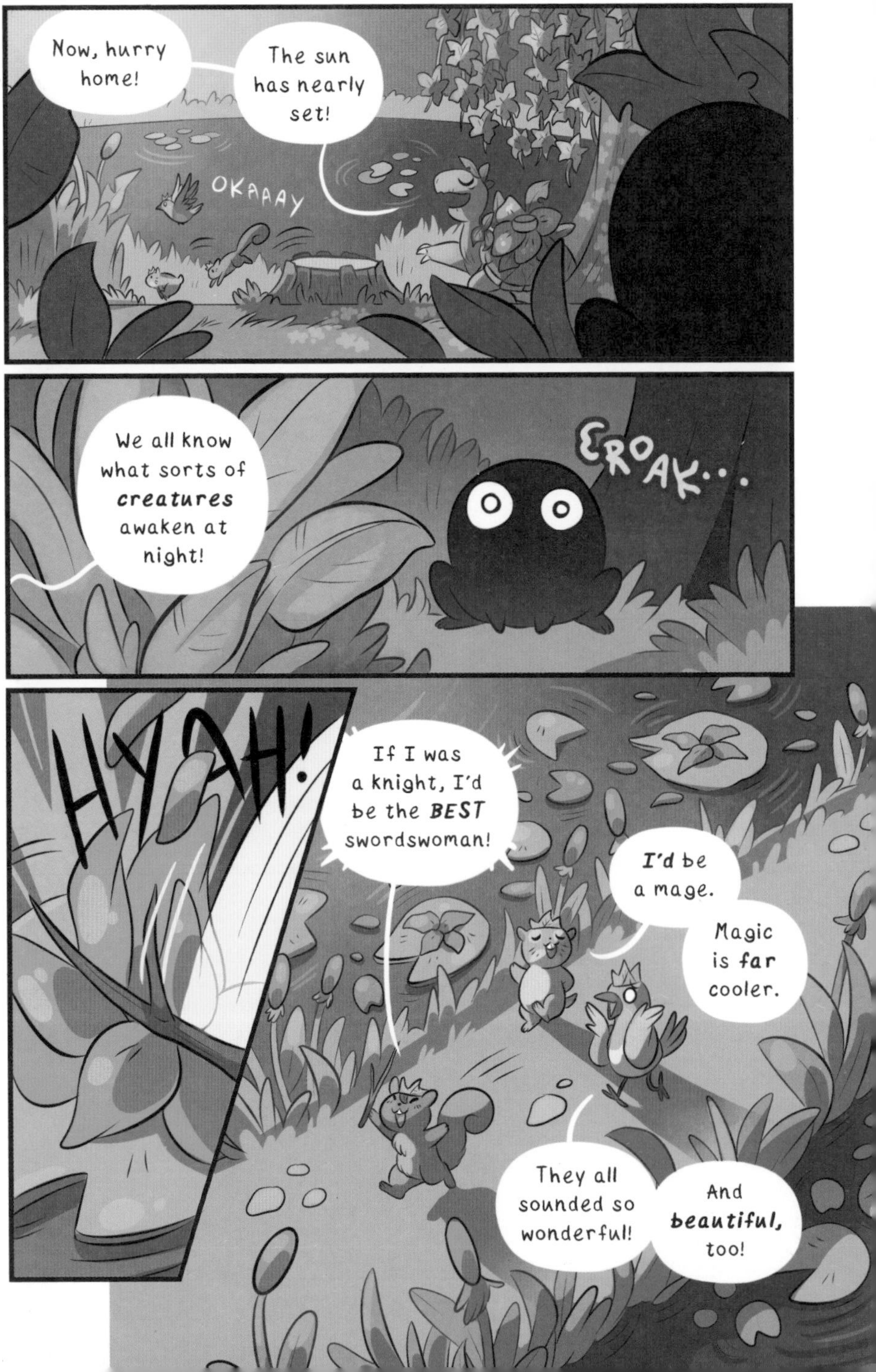
Now, hurry home!
The sun has nearly set!
OKAAAY
We all know what sorts of **creatures** awaken at night!
CROAK...
HYAH!
If I was a knight, I'd be the **BEST** swordswoman!
I'd be a mage.
Magic is **far** cooler.
They all sounded so wonderful!
And ***beautiful,*** too!

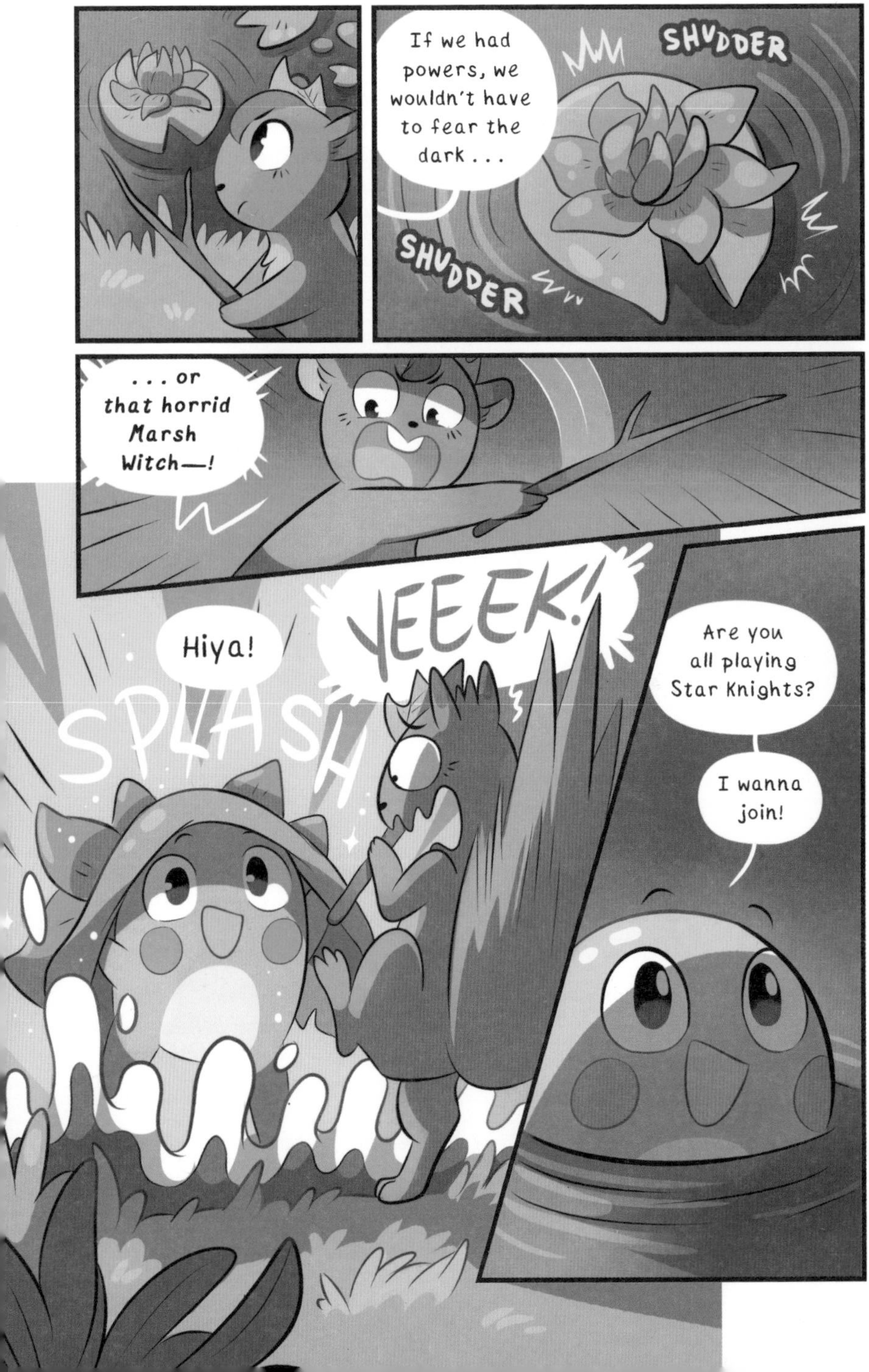

If we had powers, we wouldn't have to fear the dark . . .
SHUDDER
SHUDDER
. . . or that horrid Marsh Witch—!
Hiya!
YEEEK!
SPLASH
Are you all playing Star Knights?
I wanna join!

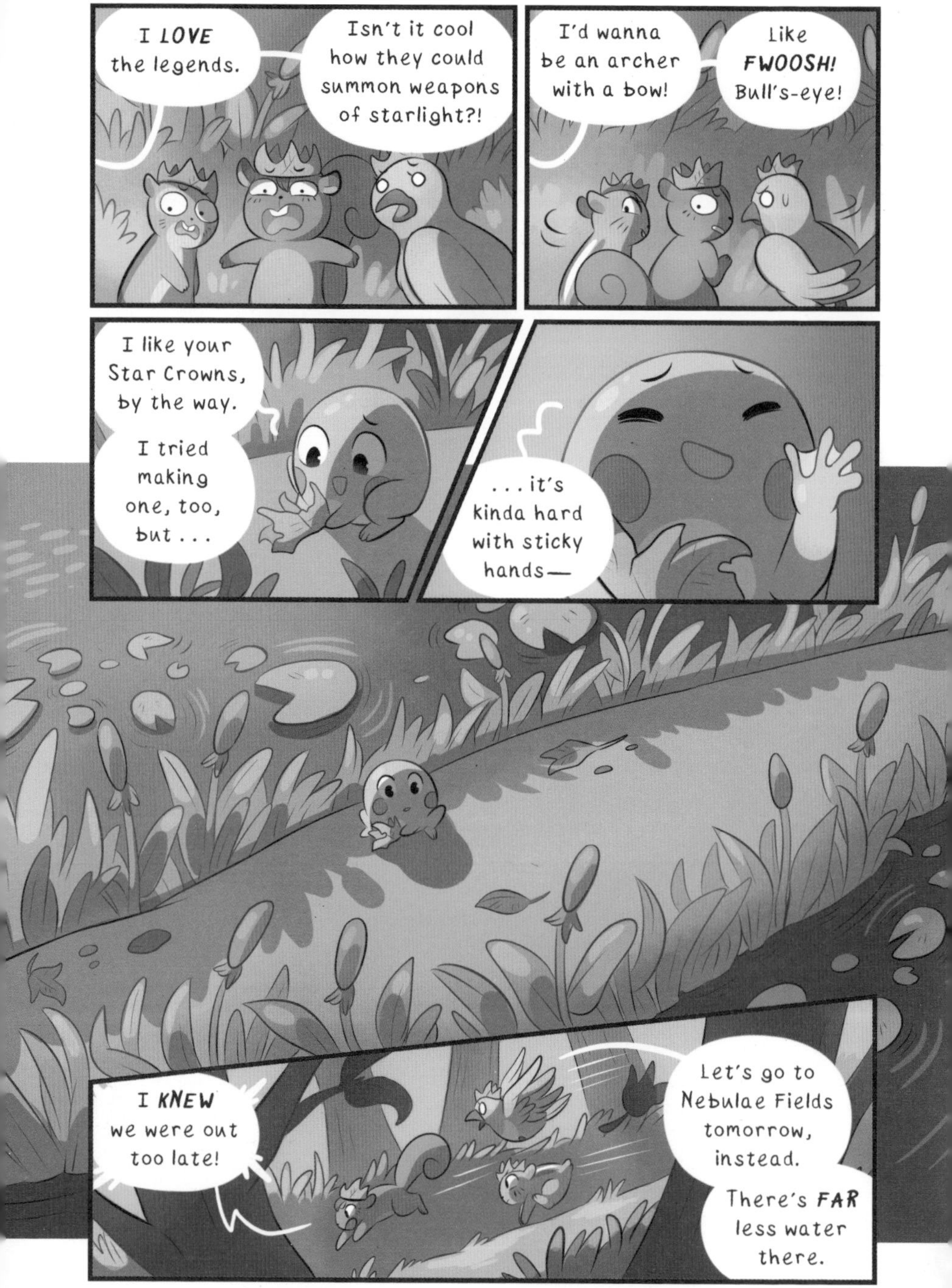
I LOVE the legends.
Isn't it cool how they could summon weapons of starlight?!
I'd wanna be an archer with a bow!
Like FWOOSH! Bull's-eye!
I like your Star Crowns, by the way.
I tried making one, too, but . . .
. . . it's kinda hard with sticky hands—
I KNEW we were out too late!
Let's go to Nebulae Fields tomorrow, instead.
There's FAR less water there.

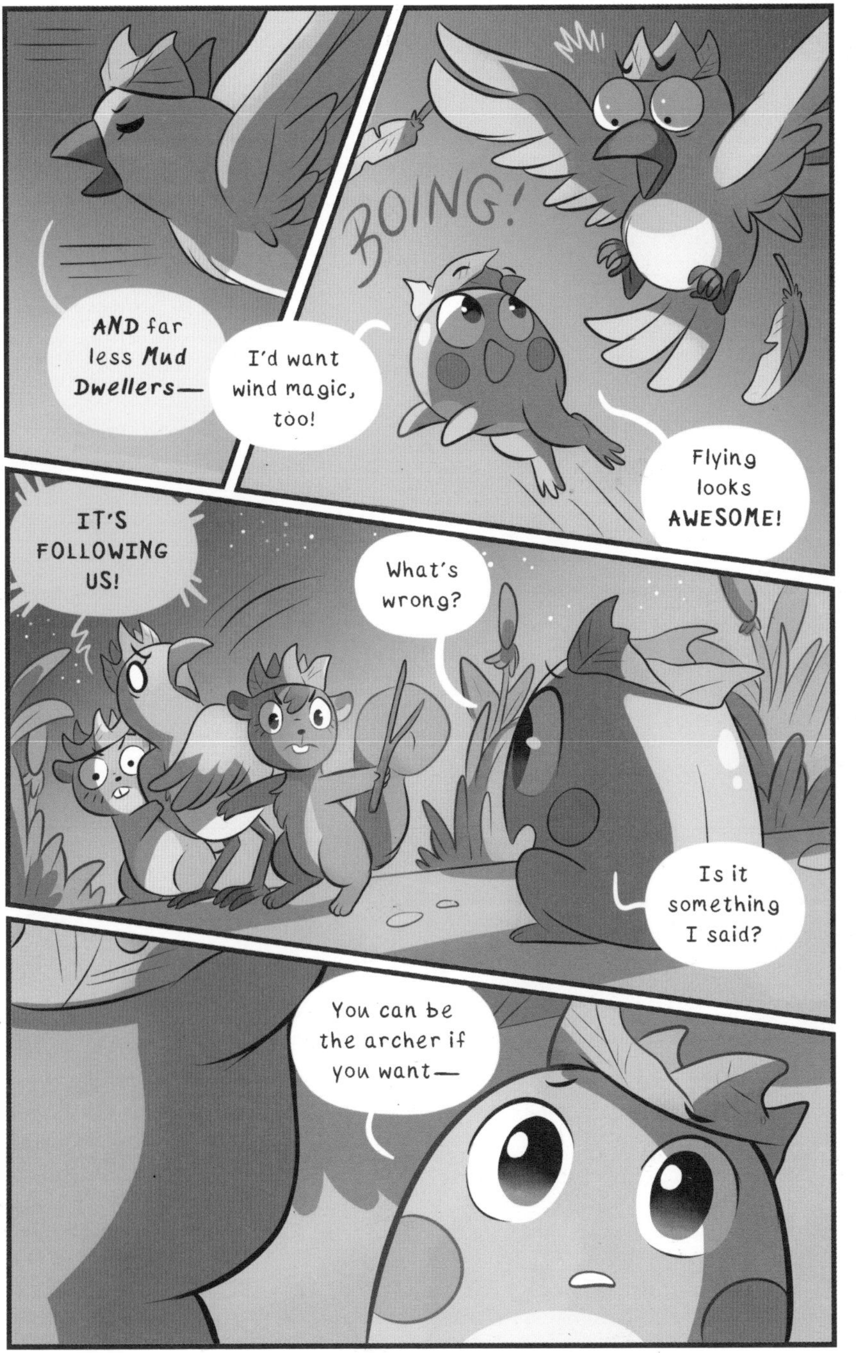
AND far less Mud Dwellers—
BOING!
I'd want wind magic, too!
Flying looks AWESOME!
IT'S FOLLOWING US!
What's wrong?
Is it something I said?
You can be the archer if you want—

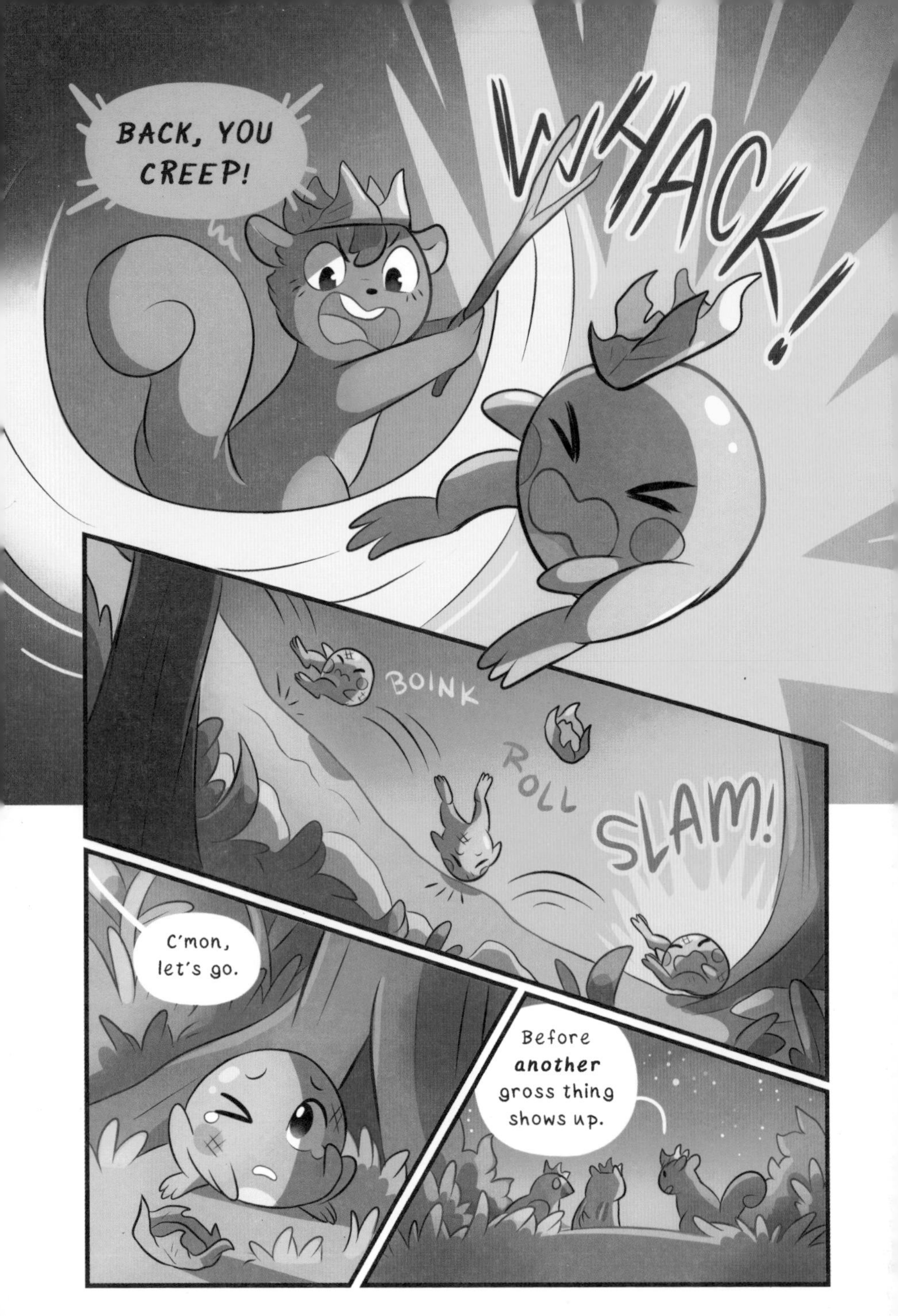

BACK, YOU CREEP!
WHACK!
BOINK
ROLL
SLAM!
C'mon, let's go.
Before **another** gross thing shows up.

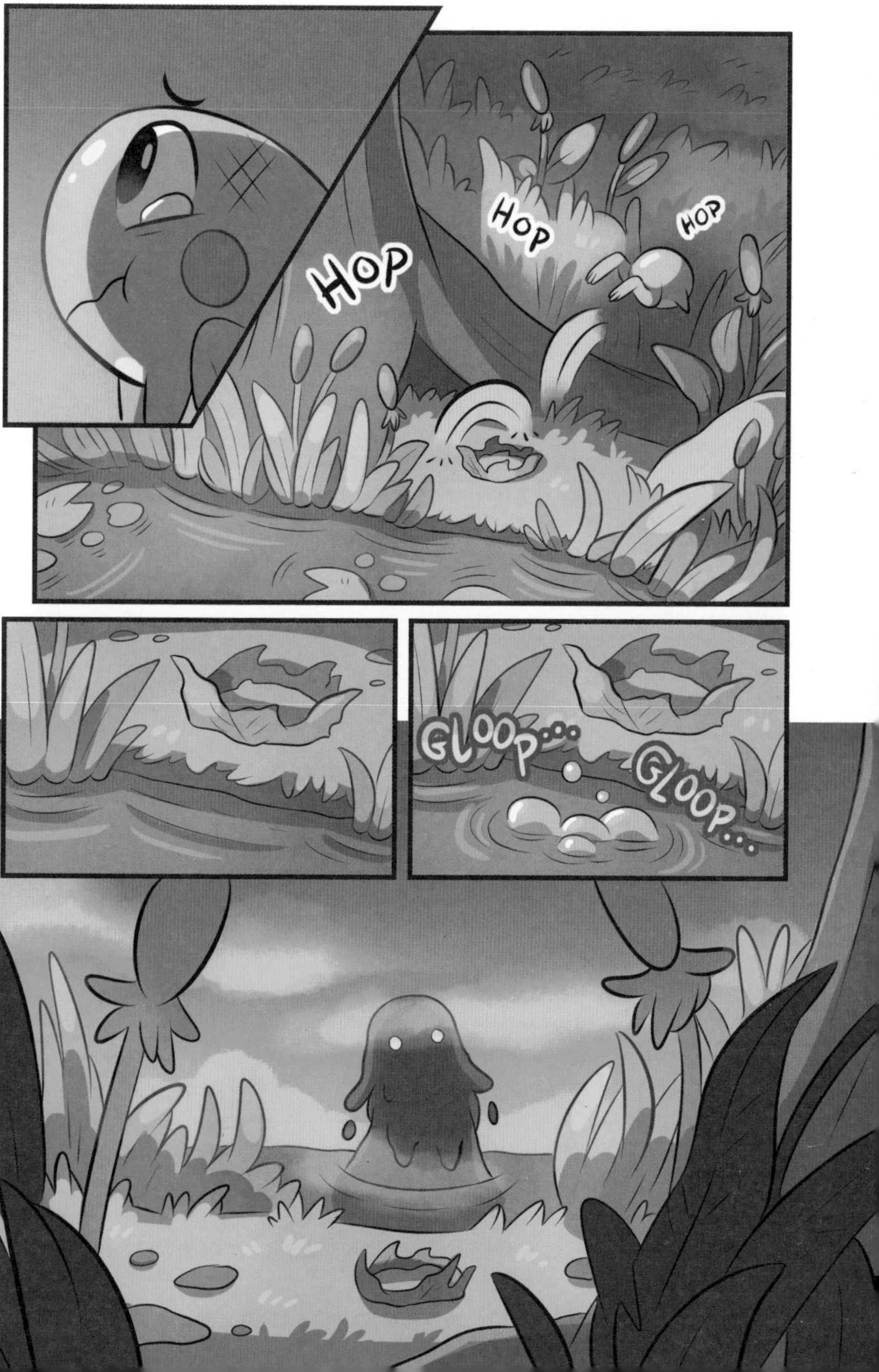
HOP
HOP
HOP
GLOOP...
GLOOP...

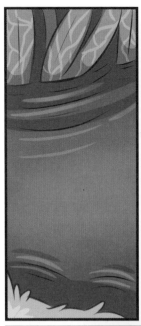

I'm **not** creepy.

Why do they always say that?

BZZZZ

VWIP!!

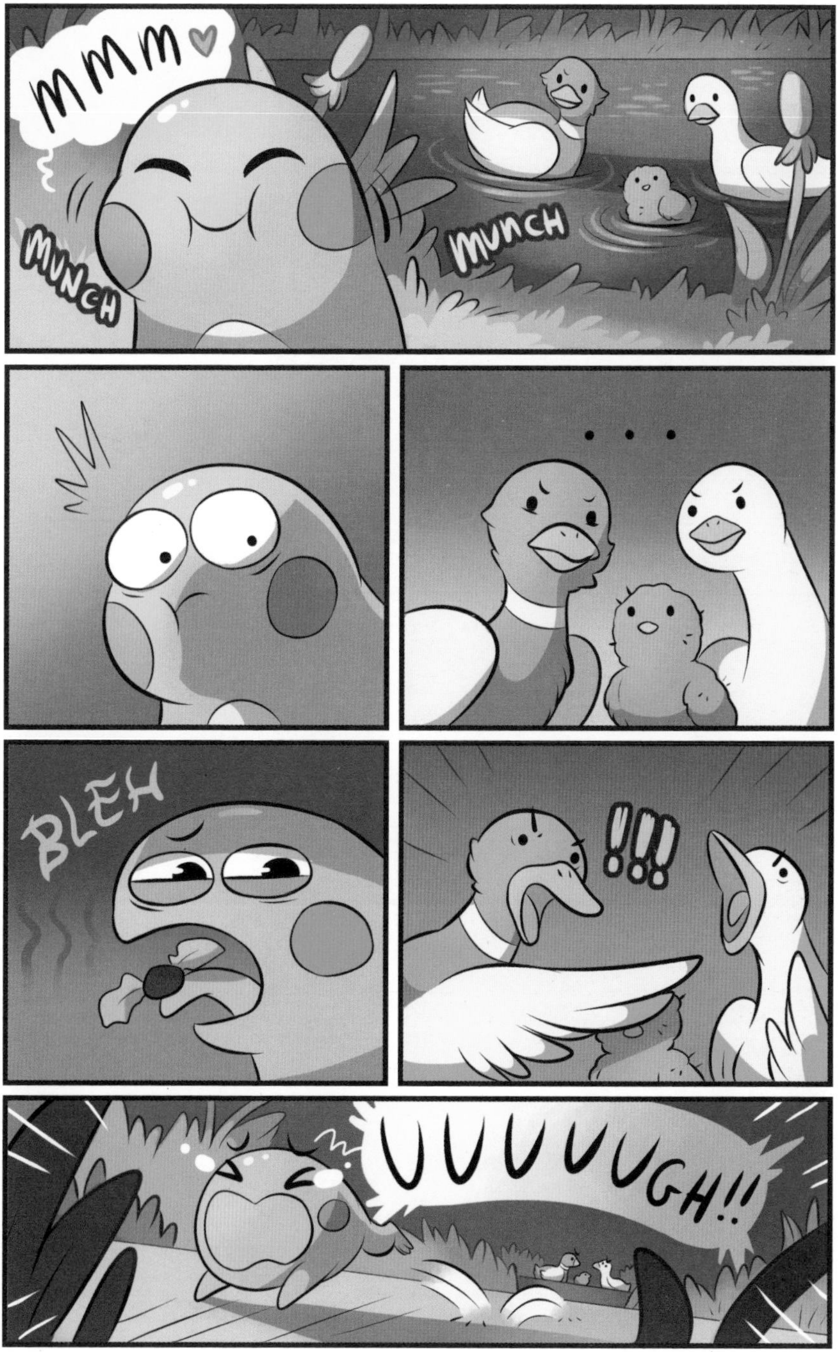
MMM
MUNCH
MUNCH
...
BLEH
!!!
UUUUUGH!!

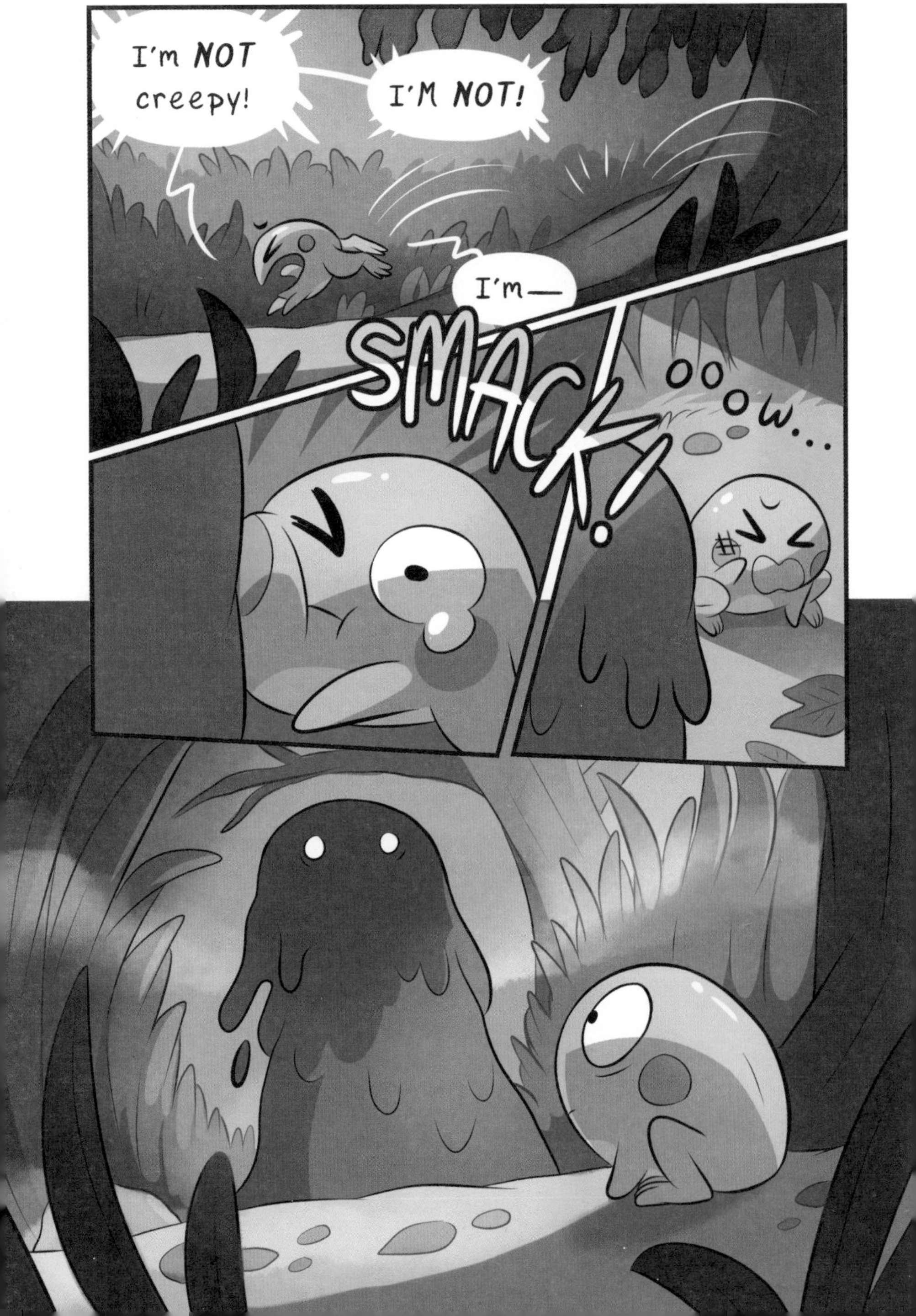
I'm NOT creepy!
I'M NOT!
I'm—
SMACK!
ooow...

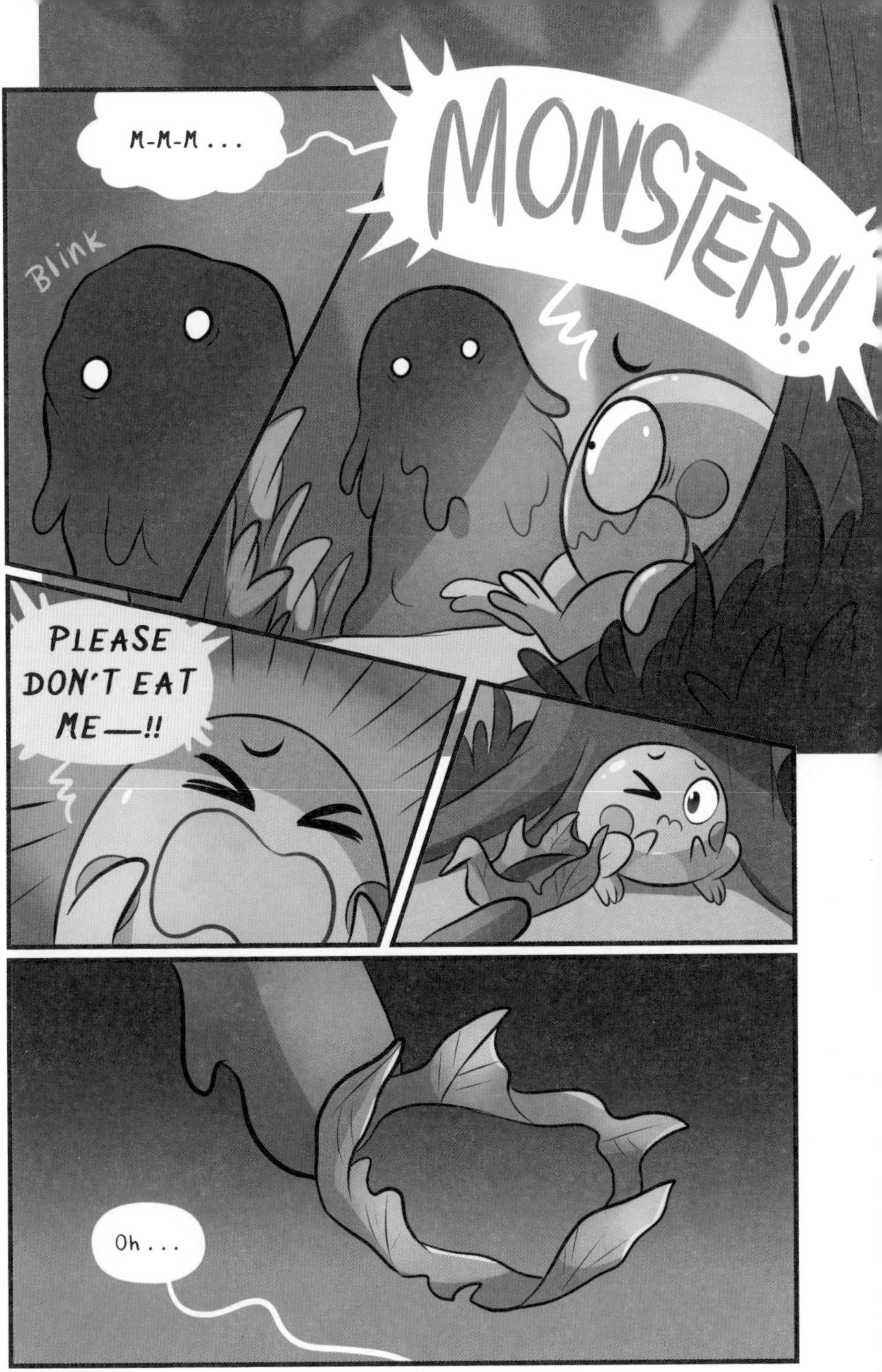
M-M-M . . .
MONSTER!!
Bliink
PLEASE DON'T EAT ME—!!
Oh . . .

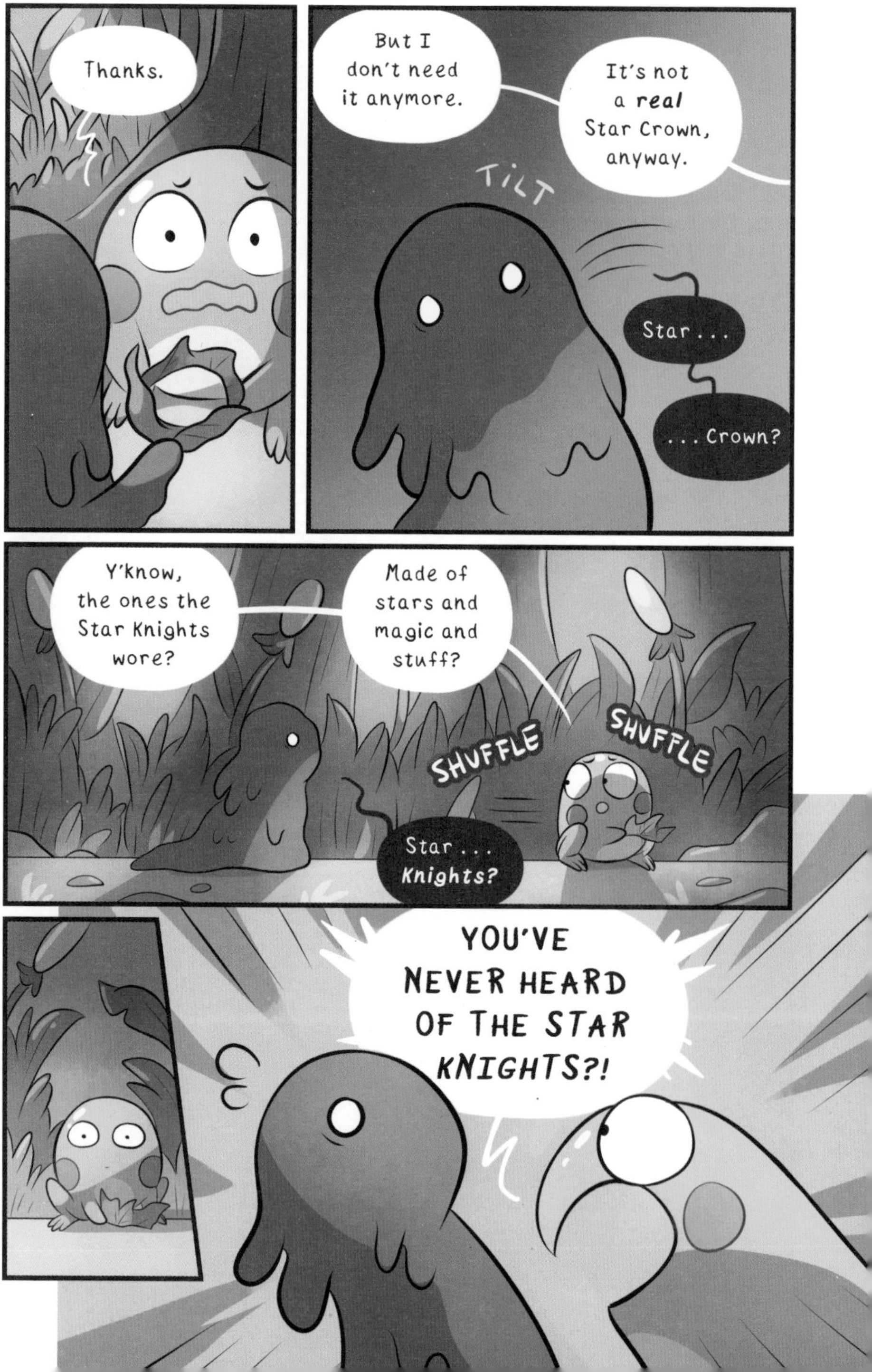
Thanks.
But I don't need it anymore.
It's not a **real** Star Crown, anyway.
TILT
Star . . .
. . . Crown?
Y'know, the ones the Star Knights wore?
Made of stars and magic and stuff?
SHUFFLE
SHUFFLE
Star . . . ***Knights?***
YOU'VE NEVER HEARD OF THE STAR *KNIGHTS?!*

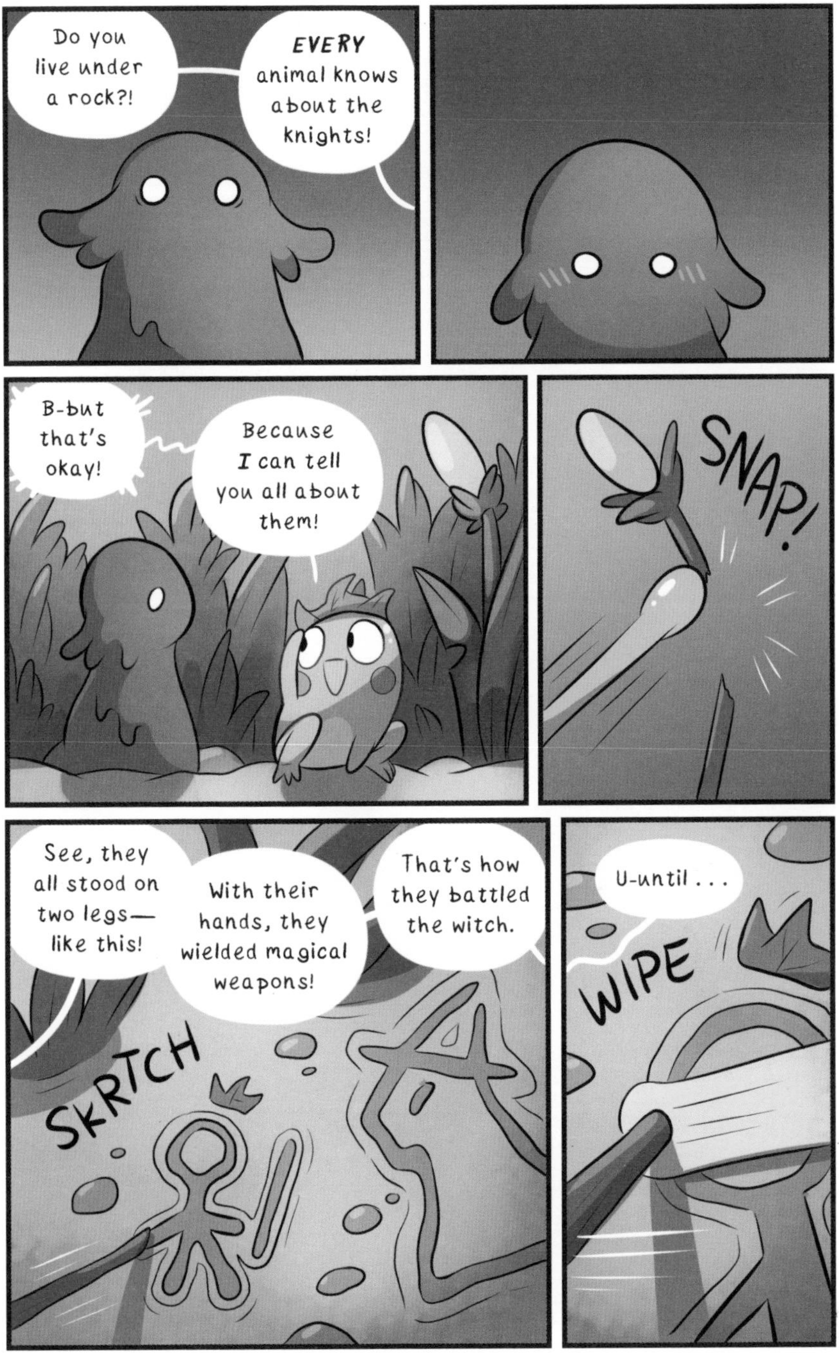
Do you live under a rock?!
EVERY animal knows about the knights!
B-but that's okay!
Because I can tell you all about them!
SNAP!
See, they all stood on two legs—like this!
With their hands, they wielded magical weapons!
That's how they battled the witch.
SKRTCH
U-until . . .
WIPE

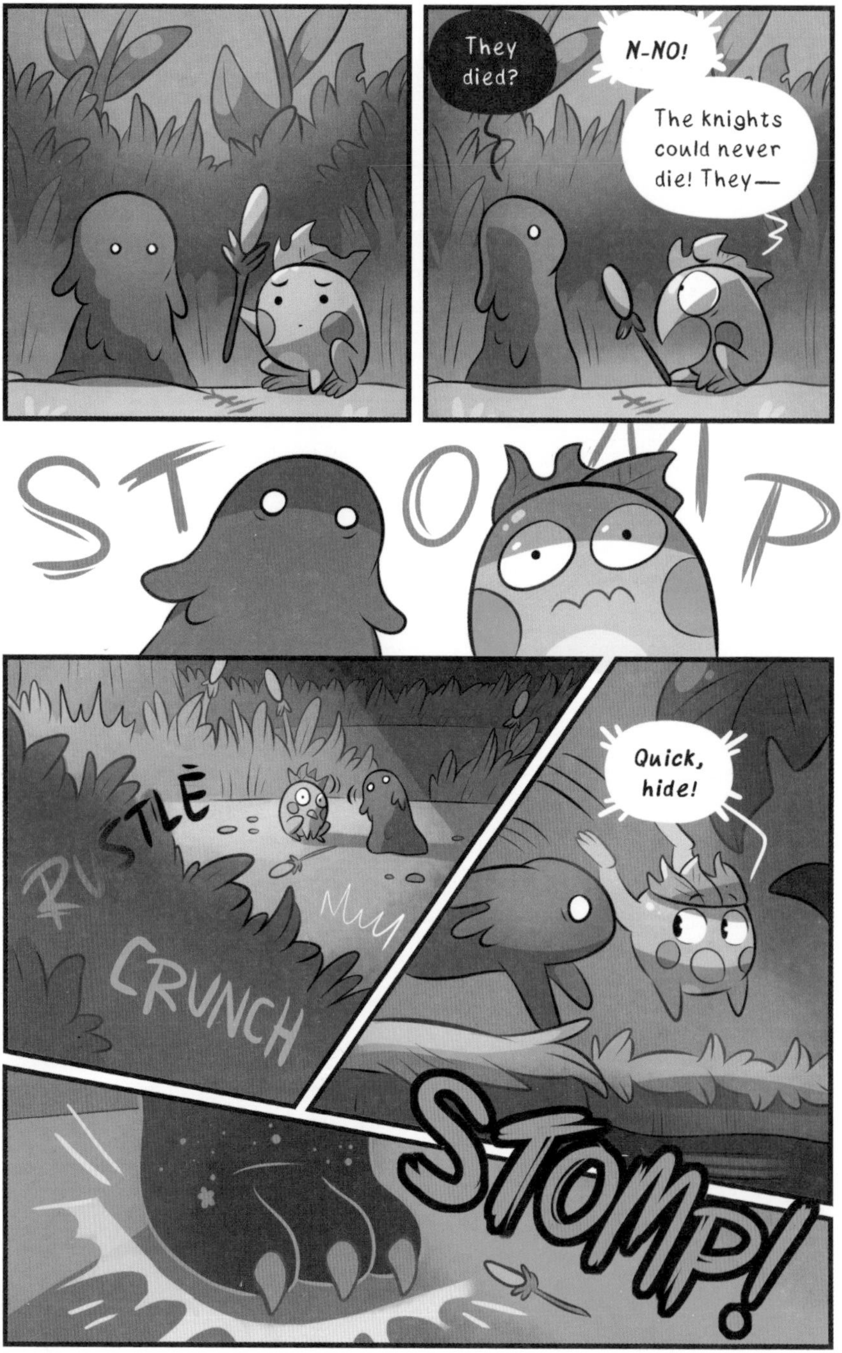
They died?
N-NO!
The knights could never die! They—
STOMP
RUSTLE
CRUNCH
Quick, hide!
STOMP!

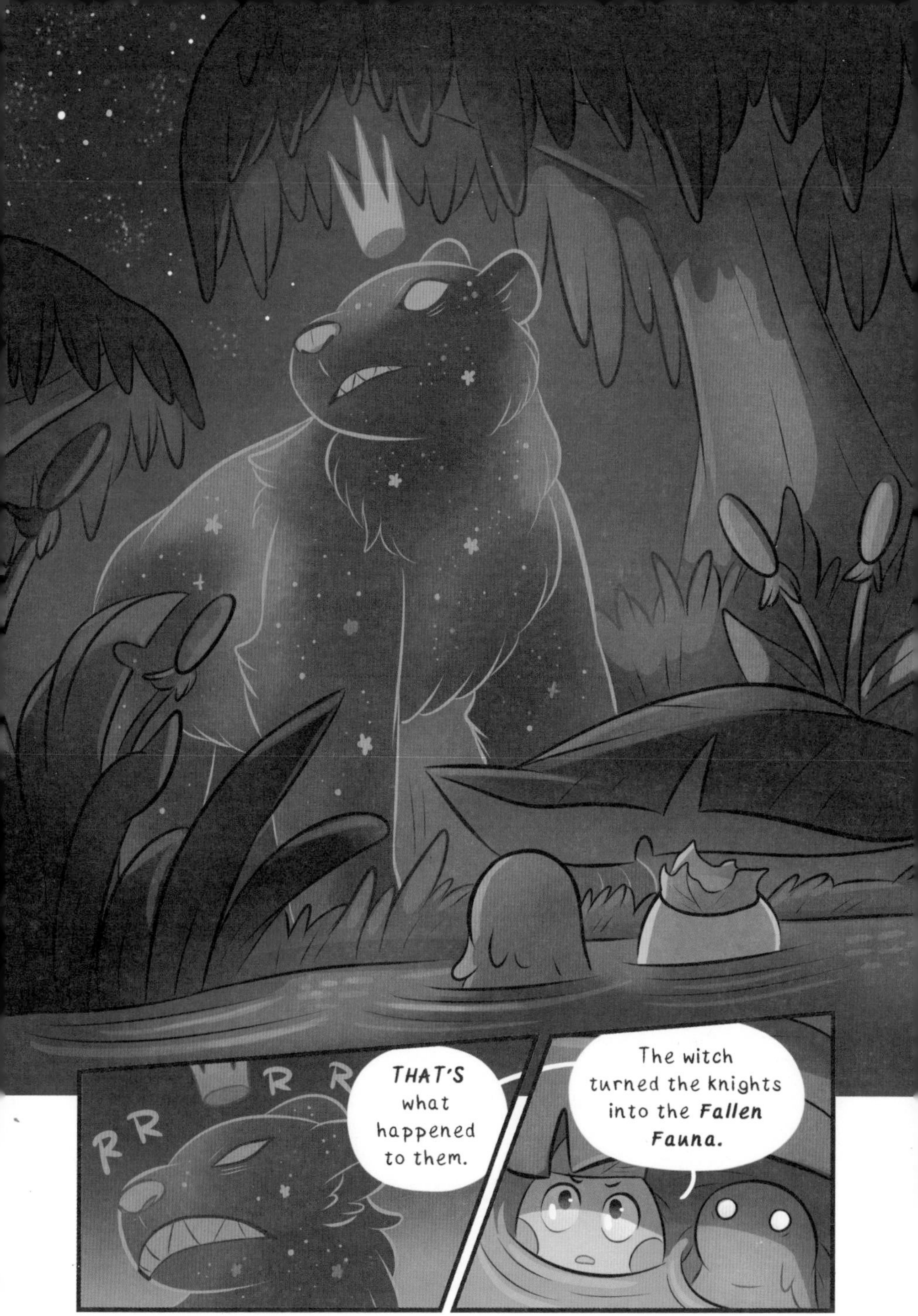
RR
R R
THAT'S what happened to them.
The witch turned the knights into the Fallen Fauna.

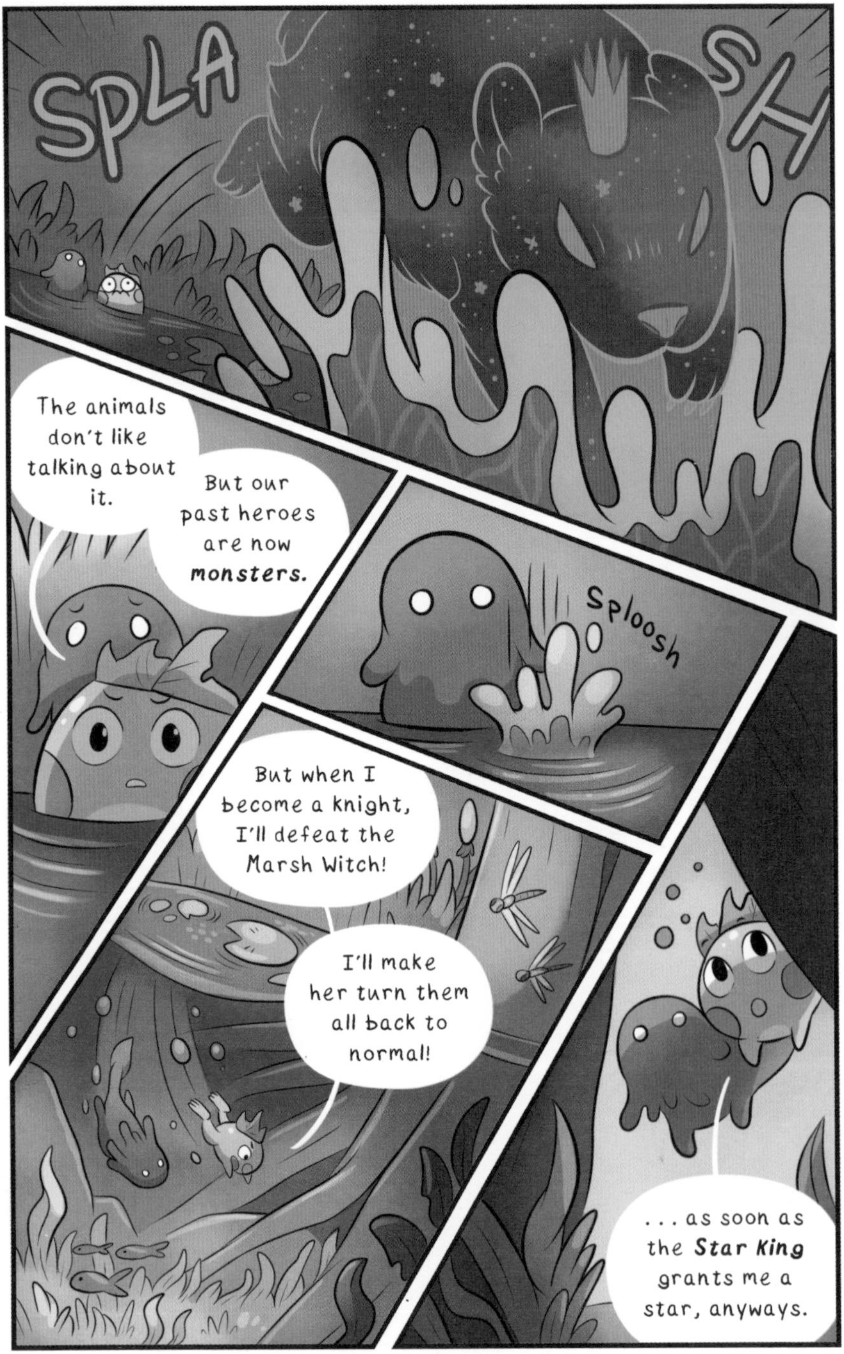
SPLASH
The animals don't like talking about it.
But our past heroes are now **monsters.**
Sploosh
But when I become a knight, I'll defeat the Marsh Witch!
I'll make her turn them all back to normal!
. . . as soon as the **Star King** grants me a star, anyways.

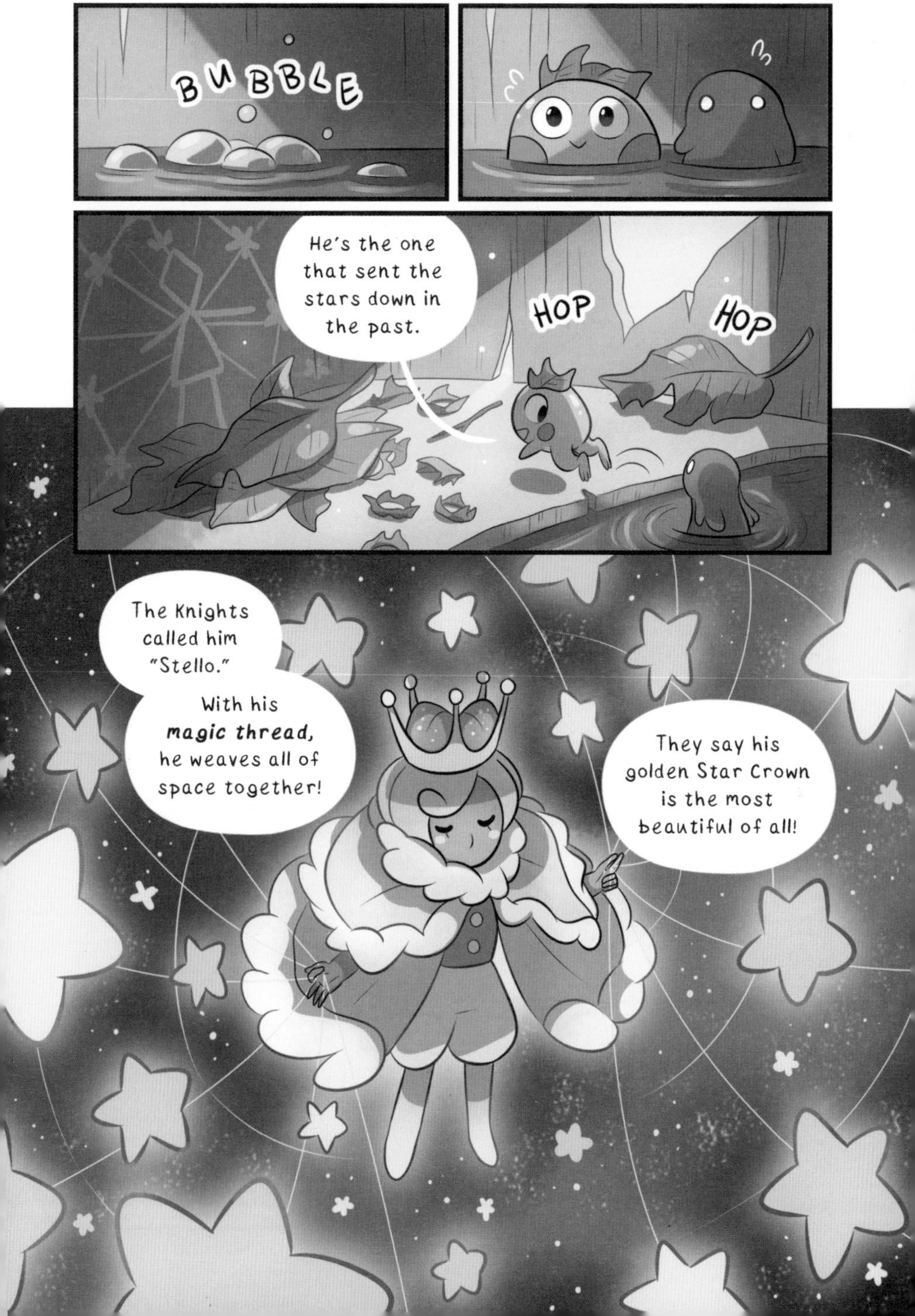
BUBBLE
He's the one that sent the stars down in the past.
HOP
HOP
The Knights called him "Stello."
With his **magic thread,** he weaves all of space together!
They say his golden Star Crown is the most beautiful of all!

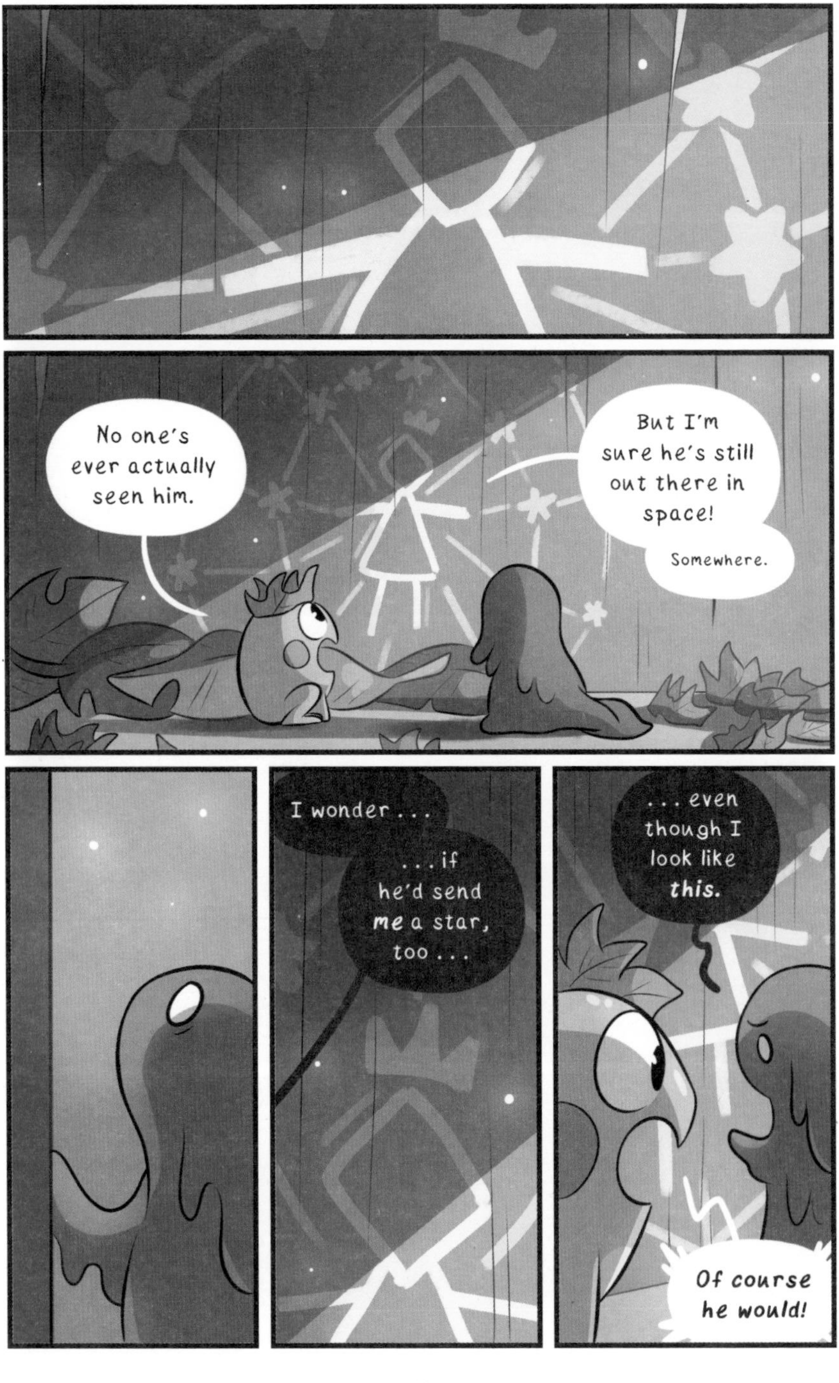

No one's ever actually seen him.
But I'm sure he's still out there in space!
Somewhere.
I wonder . . .
. . . if he'd send me a star, too . . .
. . . even though I look like this.
Of course he would!

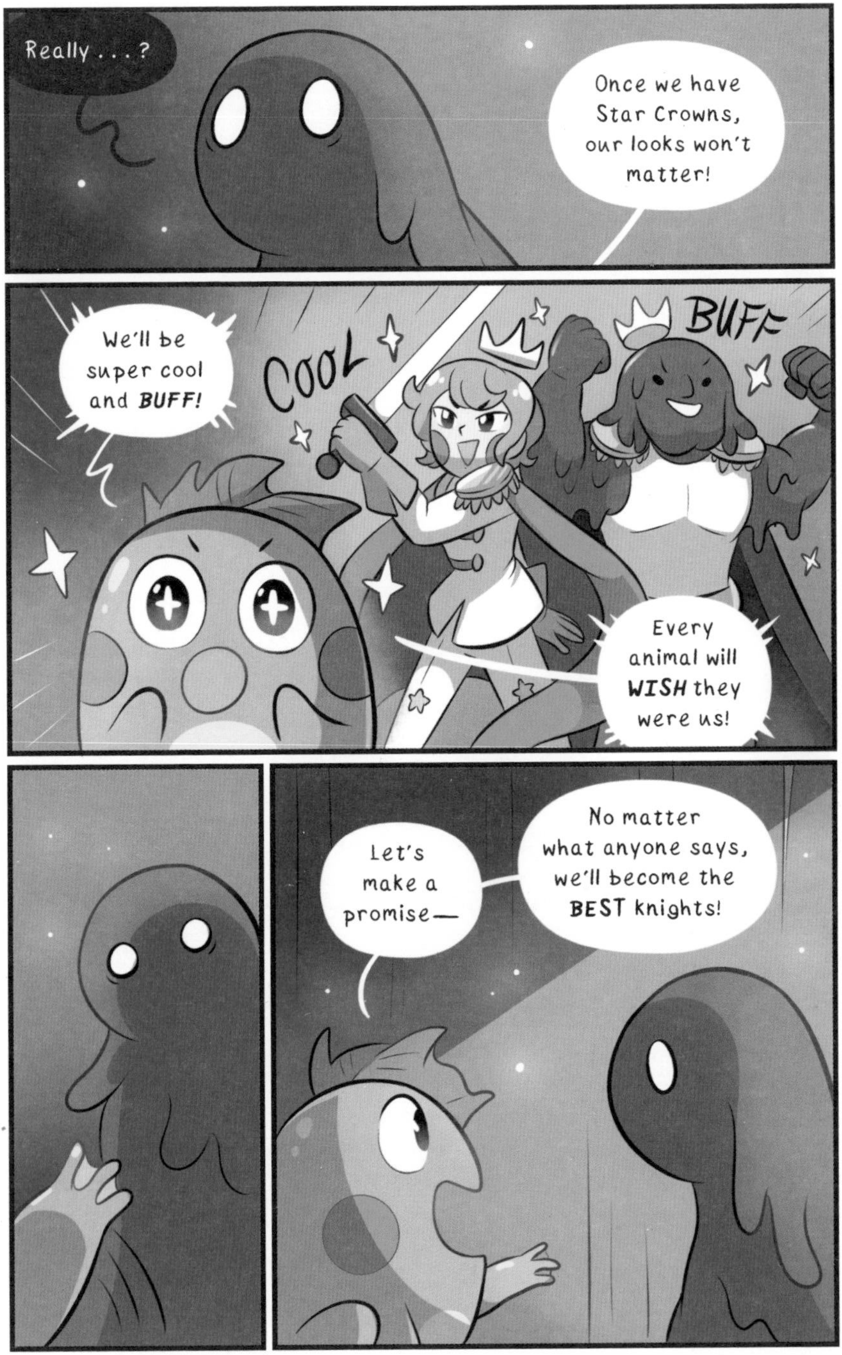
Really . . . ?
Once we have Star Crowns, our looks won't matter!
We'll be super cool and **BUFF!**
COOL
BUFF
Every animal will **WISH** they were us!
Let's make a promise—
No matter what anyone says, we'll become the **BEST** knights!

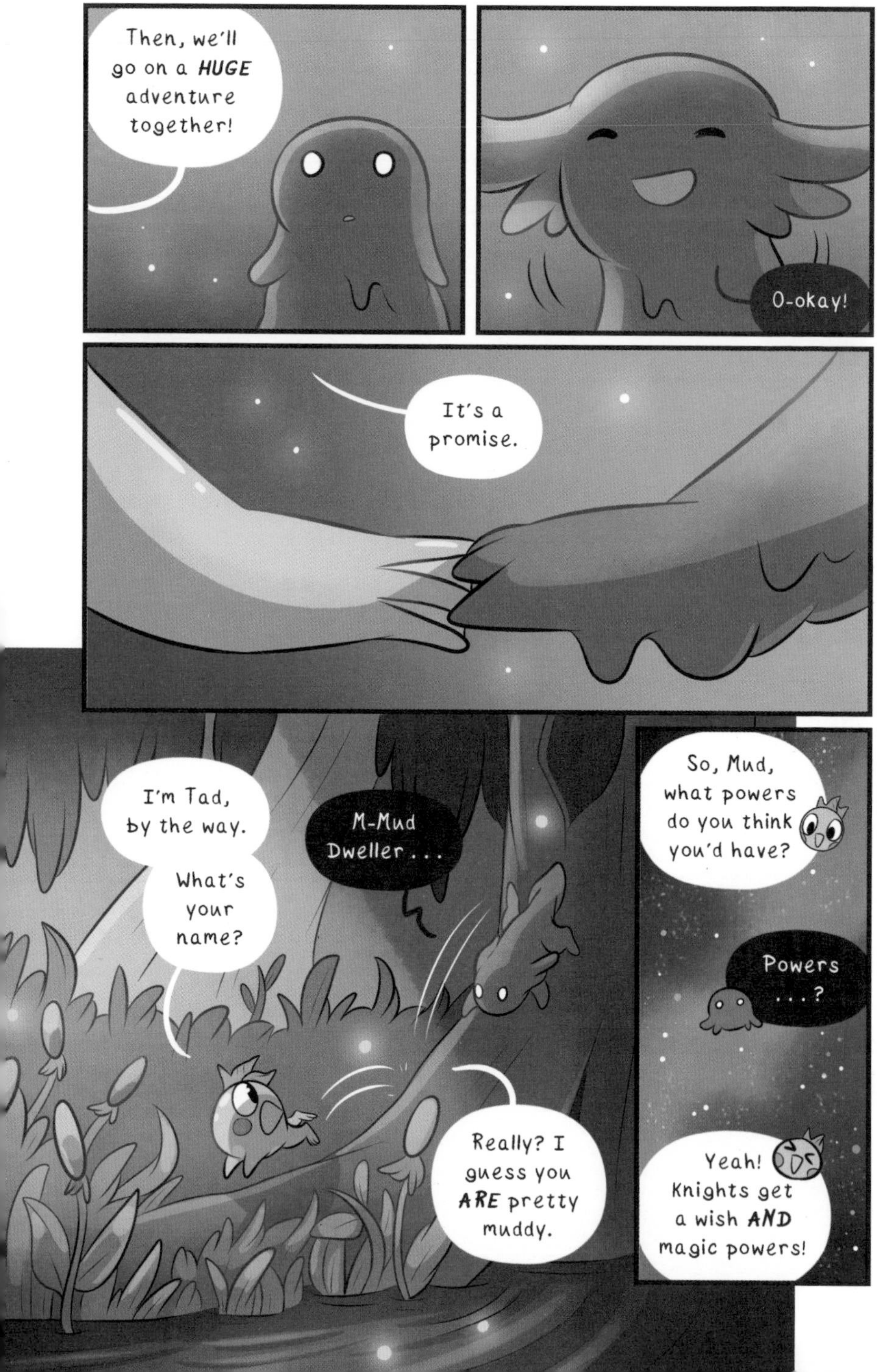

Then, we'll go on a HUGE adventure together!
O-okay!
It's a promise.
I'm Tad, by the way.
What's your name?
M-Mud Dweller . . .
Really? I guess you ARE pretty muddy.
So, Mud, what powers do you think you'd have?
Powers . . .?
Yeah! Knights get a wish AND magic powers!

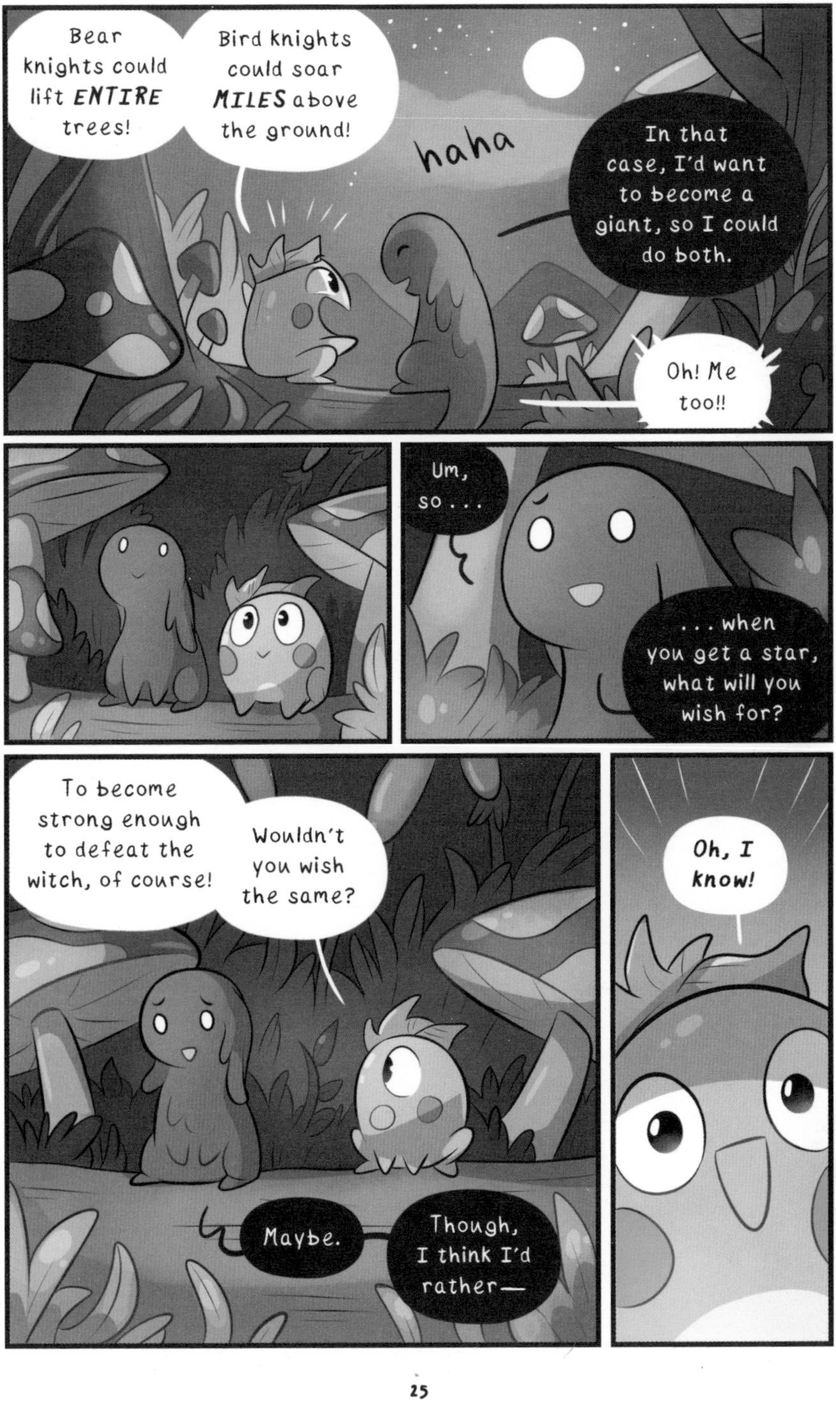
Bear knights could lift ENTIRE trees!
Bird knights could soar MILES above the ground!
haha
In that case, I'd want to become a giant, so I could do both.
Oh! Me too!!
Um, so . . .
. . . when you get a star, what will you wish for?
To become strong enough to defeat the witch, of course!
Wouldn't you wish the same?
Maybe.
Though, I think I'd rather—
Oh, I know!

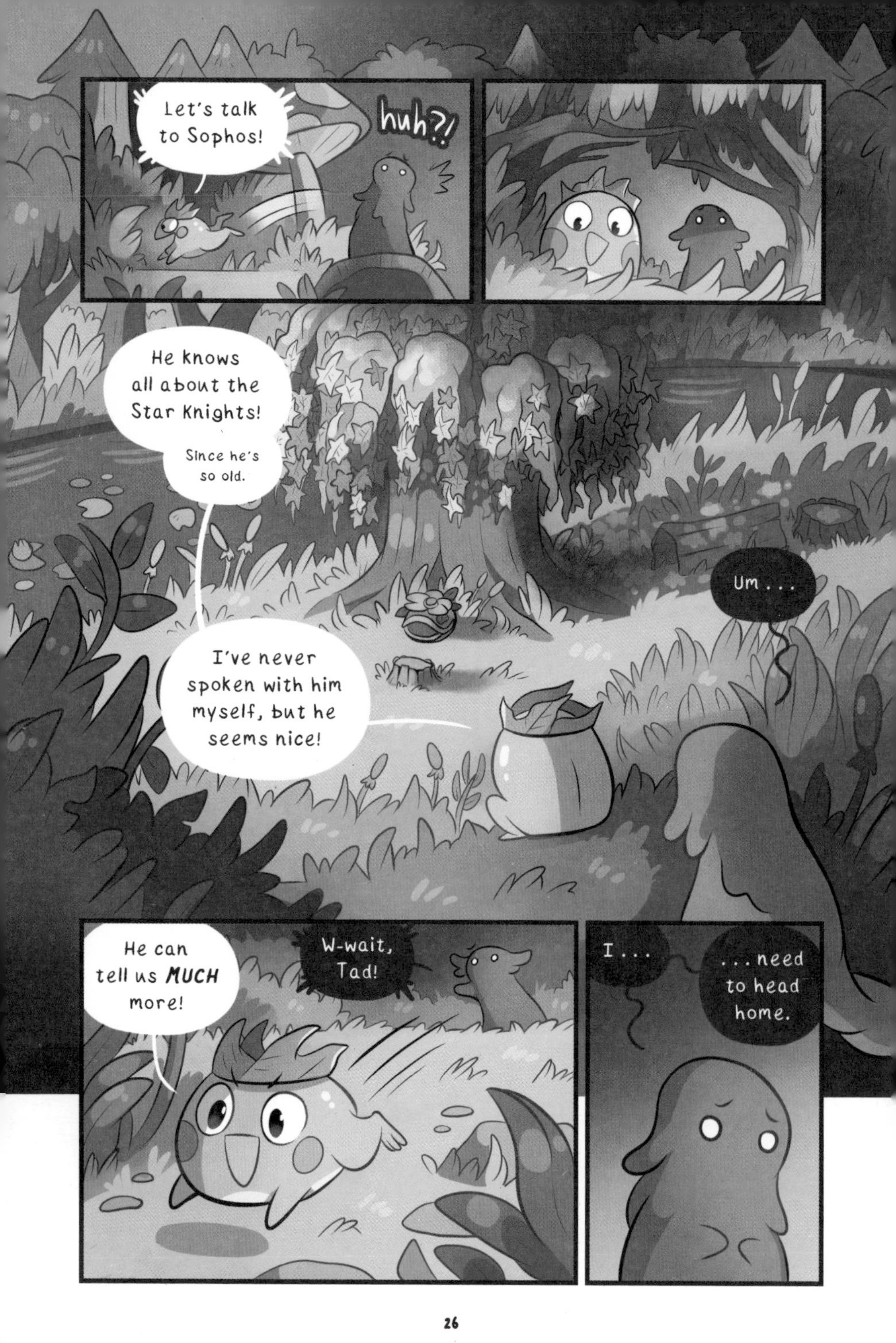
Let's talk to Sophos!
huh?!
He knows all about the Star Knights!
Since he's so old.
I've never spoken with him myself, but he seems nice!
Um . . .
He can tell us **MUCH** more!
W-wait, Tad!
I . . .
. . . need to head home.

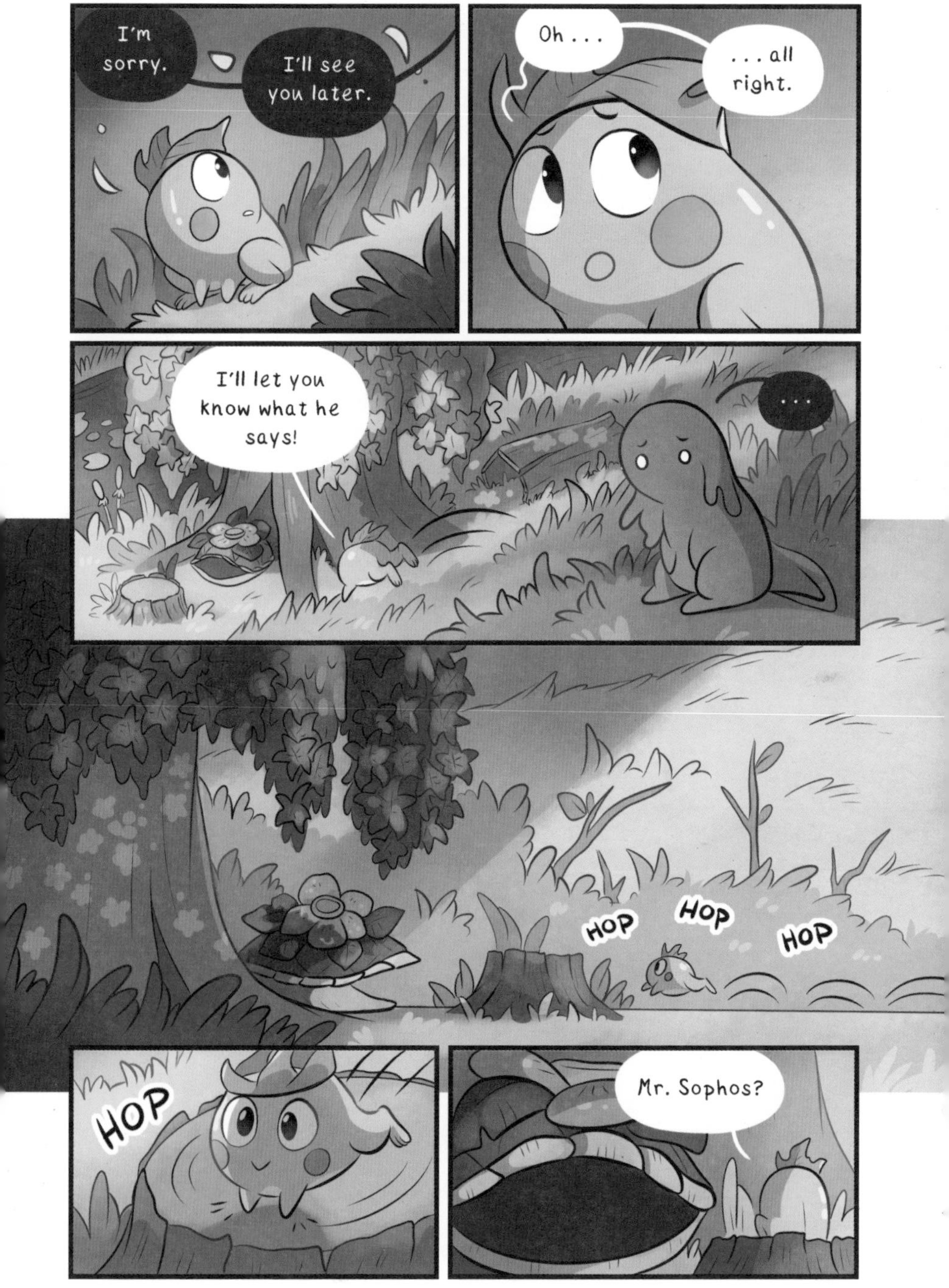
I'm sorry.
I'll see you later.
Oh . . .
. . . all right.
I'll let you know what he says!
. . .
HOP
HOP
HOP
HOP
Mr. Sophos?

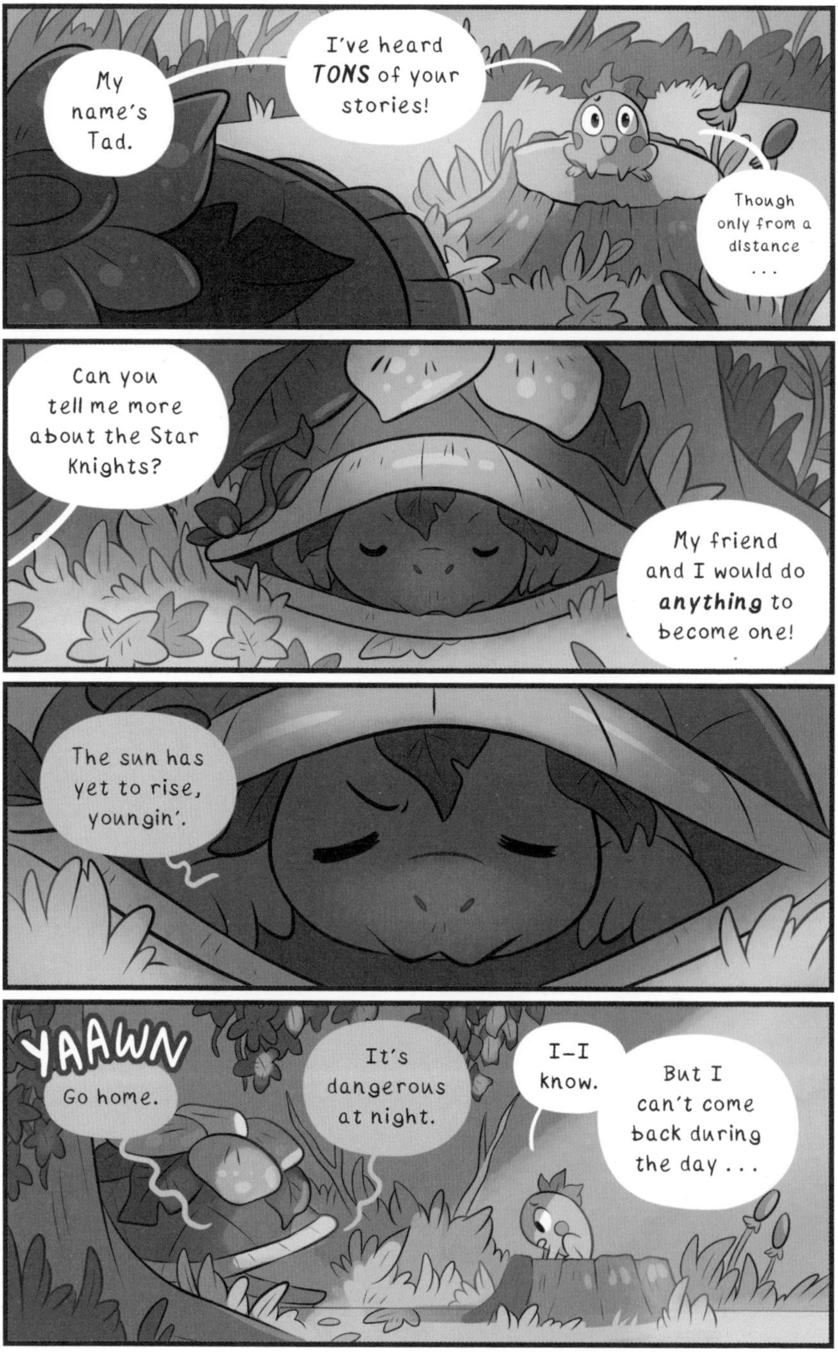
My name's Tad.
I've heard **TONS** of your stories!
Though only from a distance . . .
Can you tell me more about the Star Knights?
My friend and I would do ***anything*** to become one!
The sun has yet to rise, youngin'.
YAAWN
Go home.
It's dangerous at night.
I-I know.
But I can't come back during the day . . .

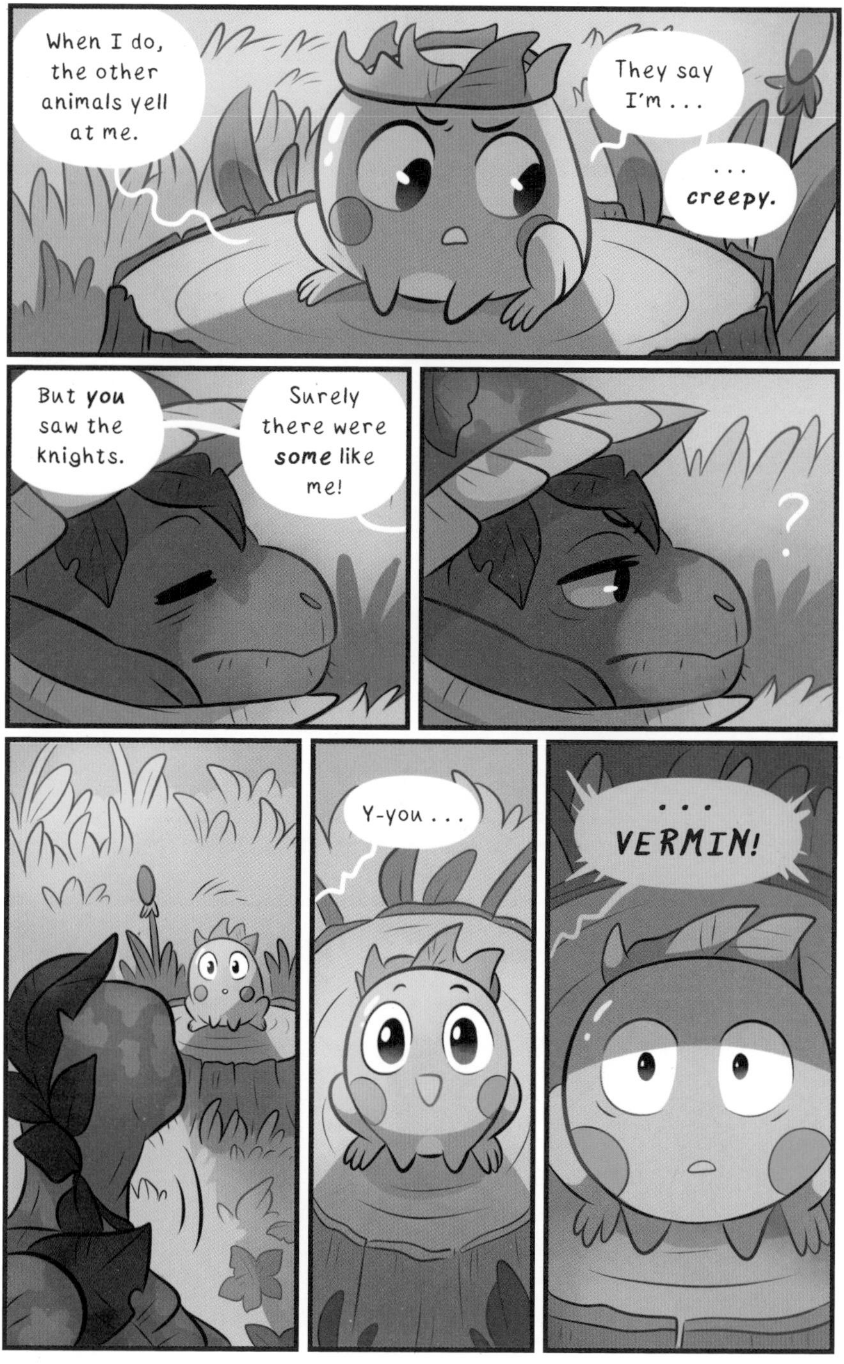
When I do, the other animals yell at me.
They say I'm . . .
. . . creepy.
But you saw the knights.
Surely there were some like me!
?
Y-you . . .
. . . VERMIN!

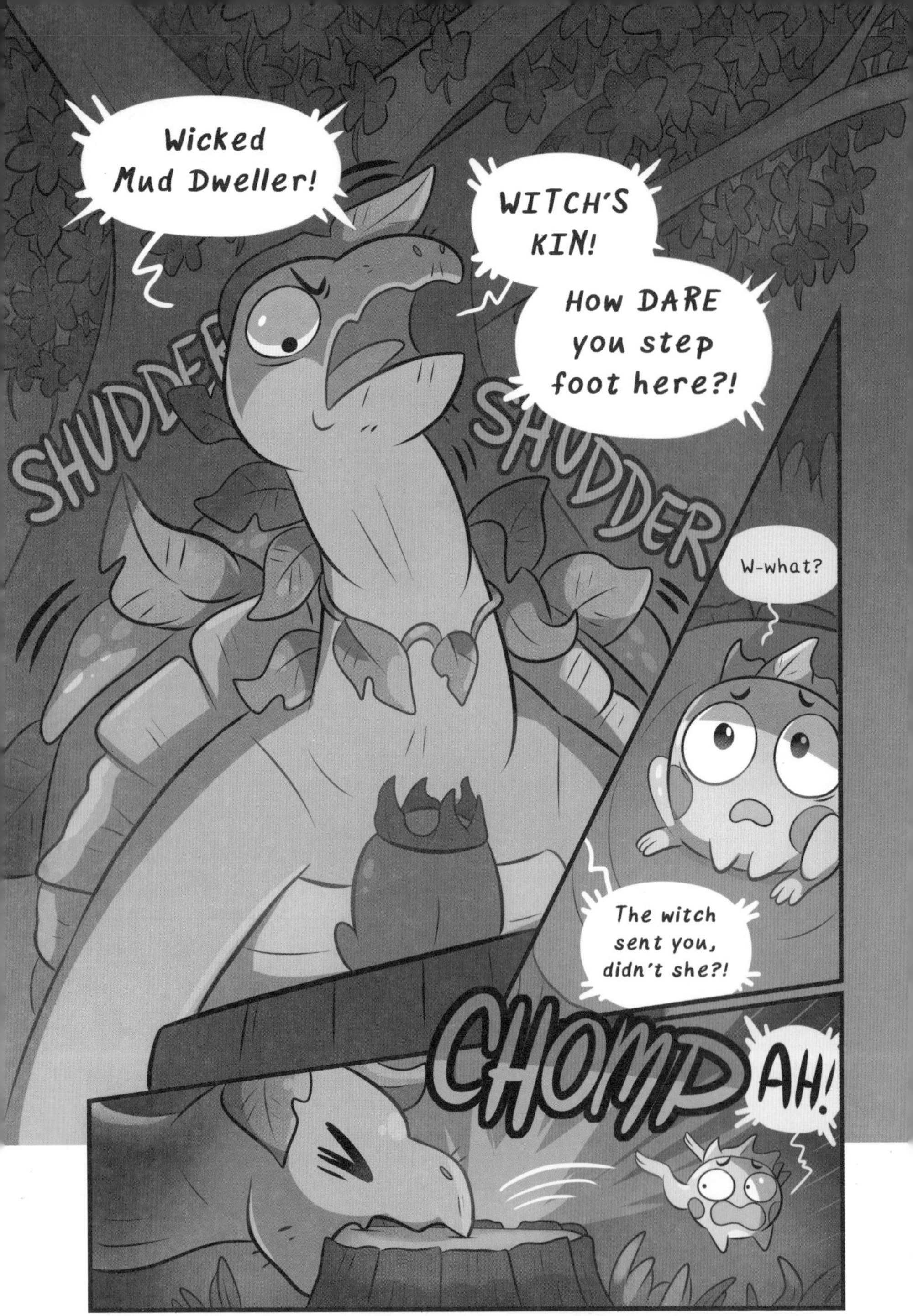
Wicked Mud Dweller!
WITCH'S KIN!
How DARE you step foot here?!
SHUDDER SHUDDER
W-what?
The witch sent you, didn't she?!
CHOMP
AH!

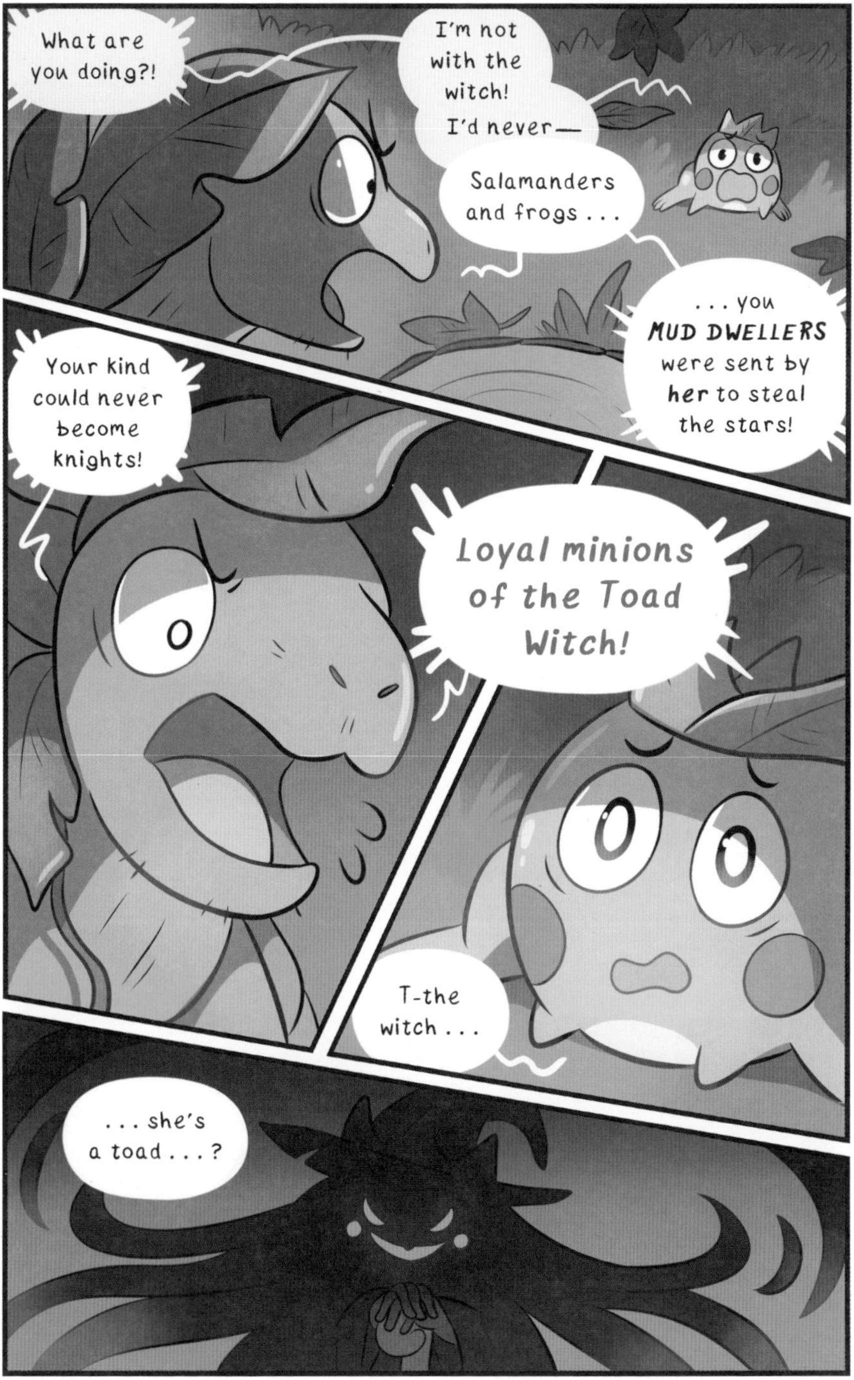
What are you doing?!
I'm not with the witch! I'd never—
Salamanders and frogs . . .
. . . you MUD DWELLERS were sent by her to steal the stars!
Your kind could never become knights!
Loyal minions of the Toad Witch!
T-the witch . . .
. . . she's a toad . . . ?

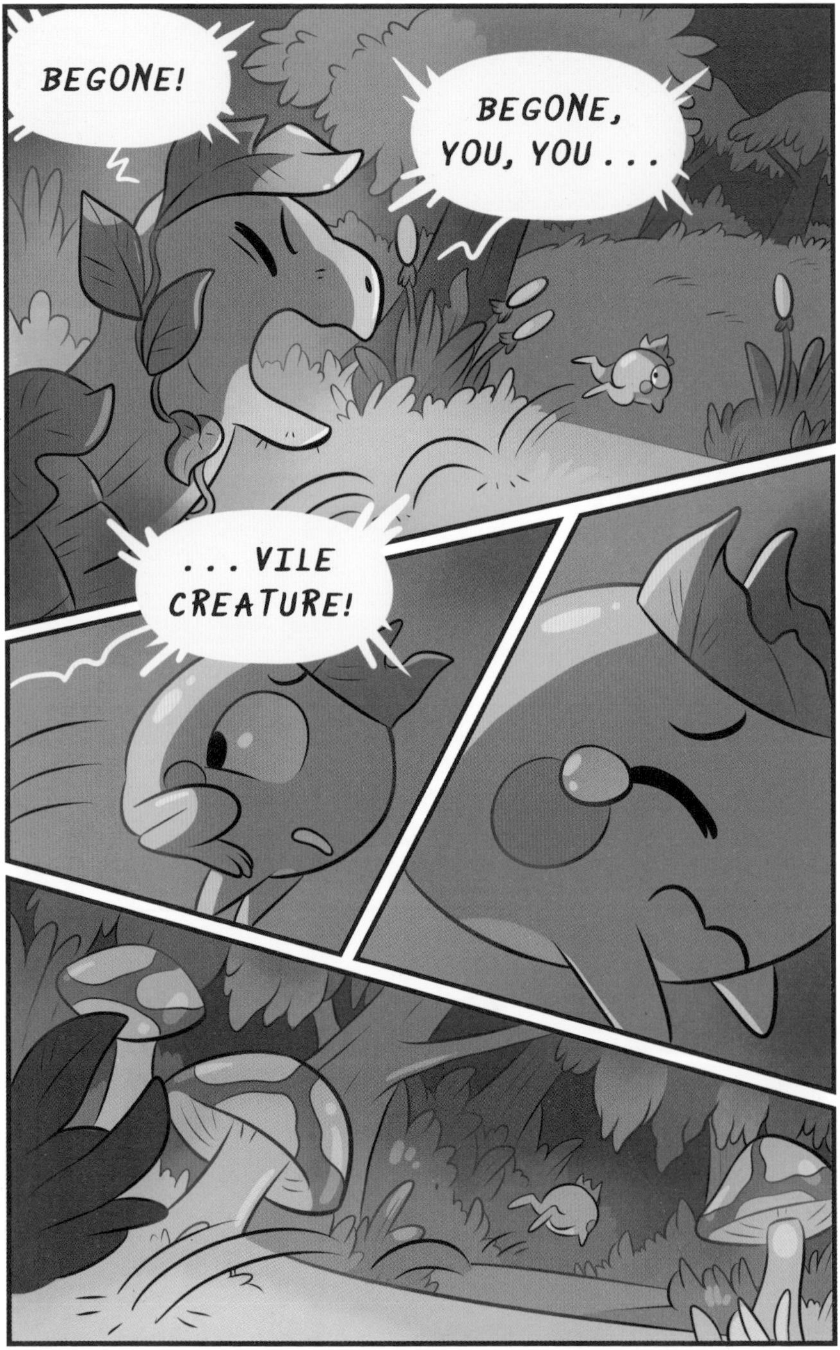
BEGONE!
BEGONE, YOU, YOU . . .
. . . VILE CREATURE!

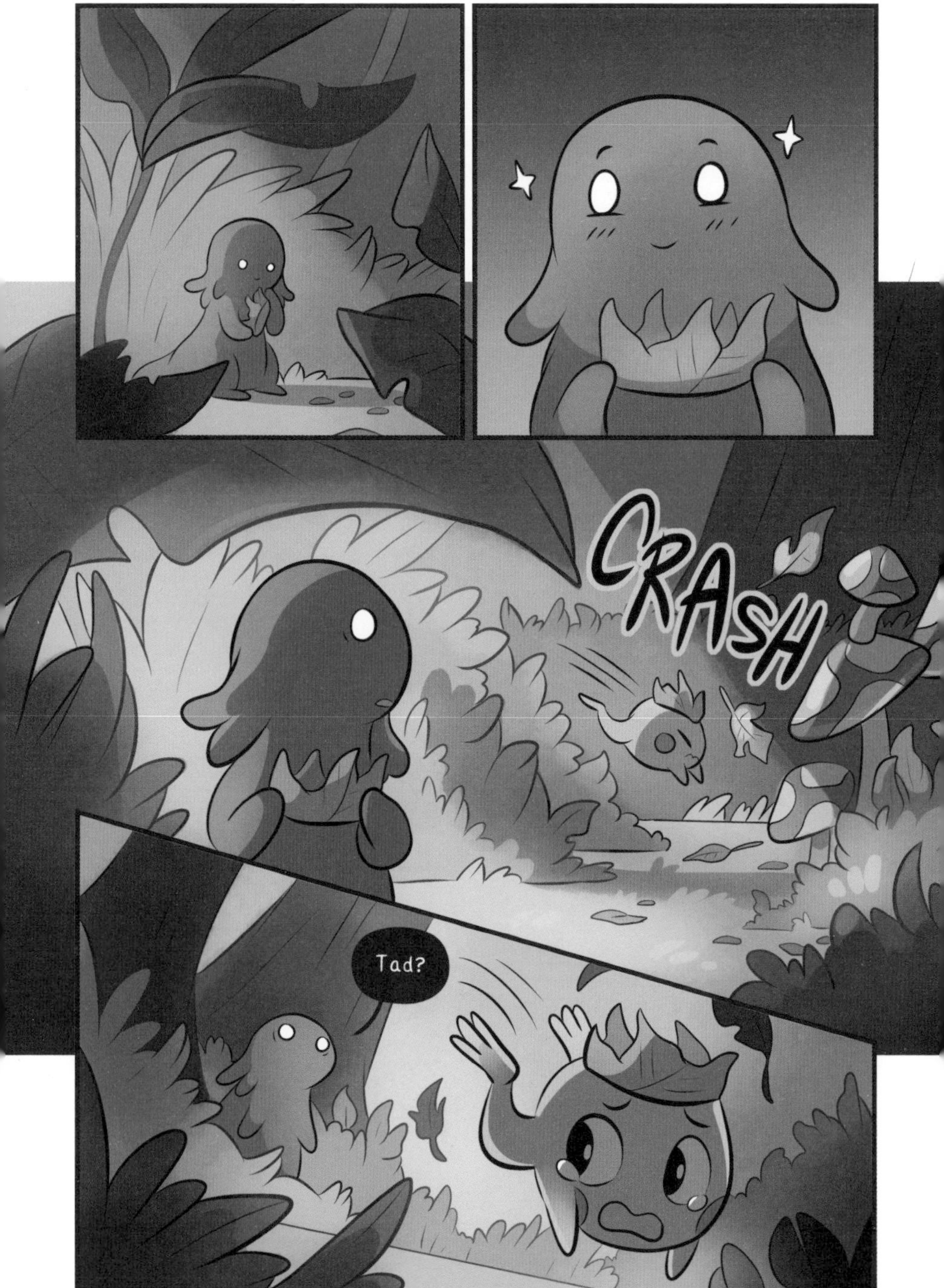
CRASH
Tad?

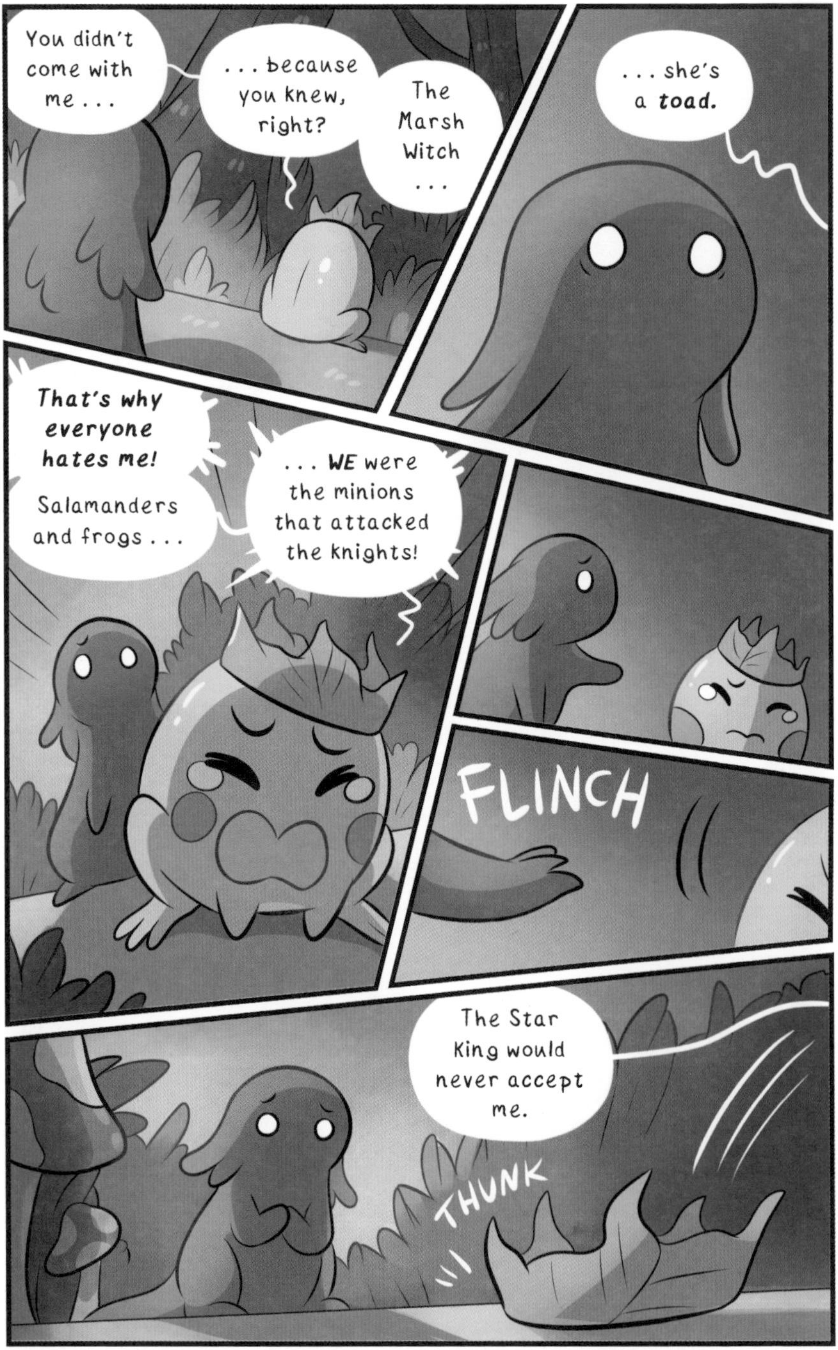
You didn't come with me . . .
. . . because you knew, right?
The Marsh Witch . . .
. . . she's a **toad.**
That's why everyone hates me!
Salamanders and frogs . . .
. . . **WE** were the minions that attacked the knights!
FLINCH
The Star King would never accept me.
THUNK

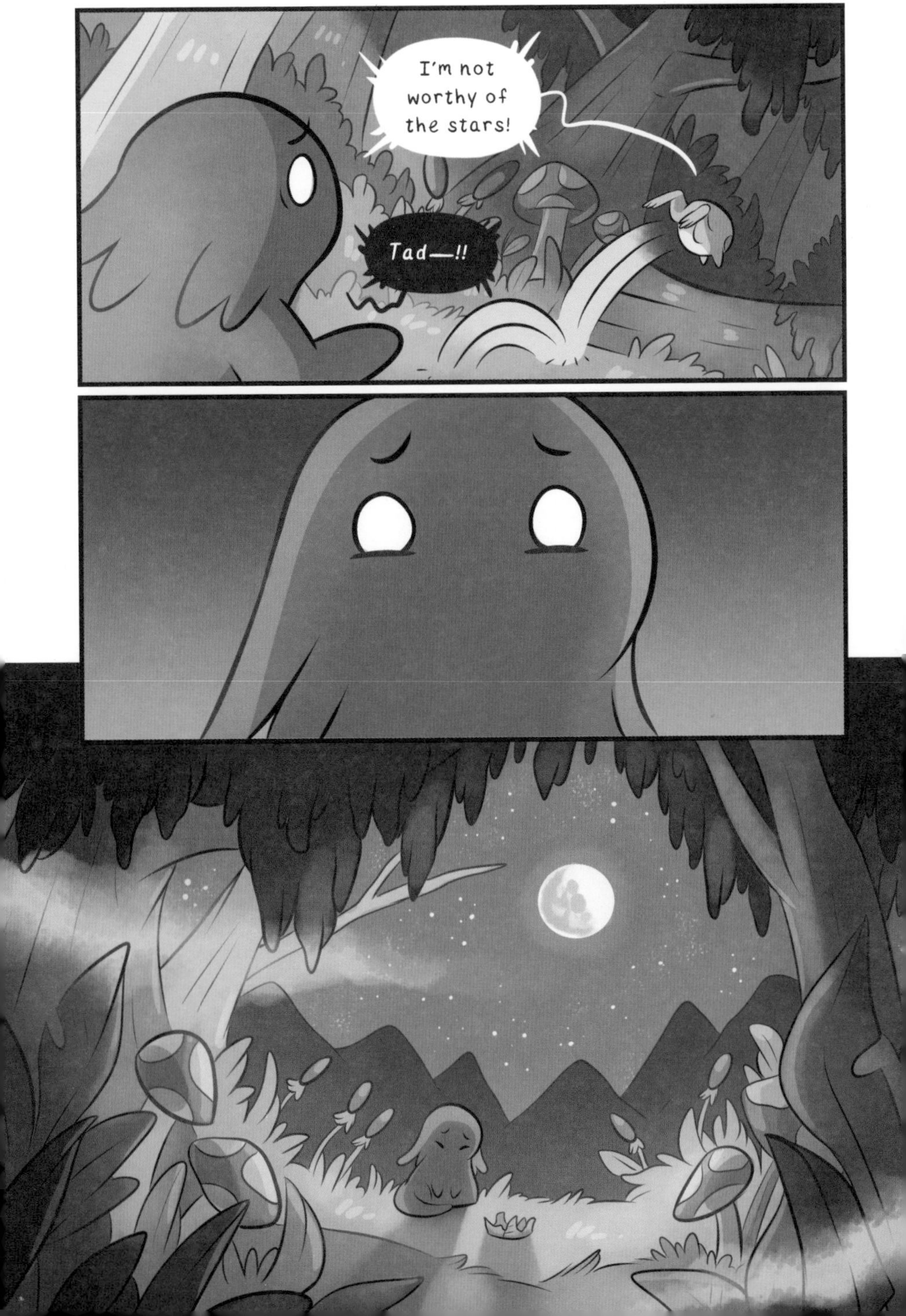
I'm not worthy of the stars!
Tad—!!

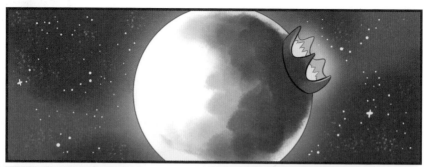

Lady Cygnus!

Lady Cygnus!

CLick

CLACK

BAM!

A bright light has appeared above the Milky Way Marsh!

It's the Star King.

He's returned to our galaxy . . .

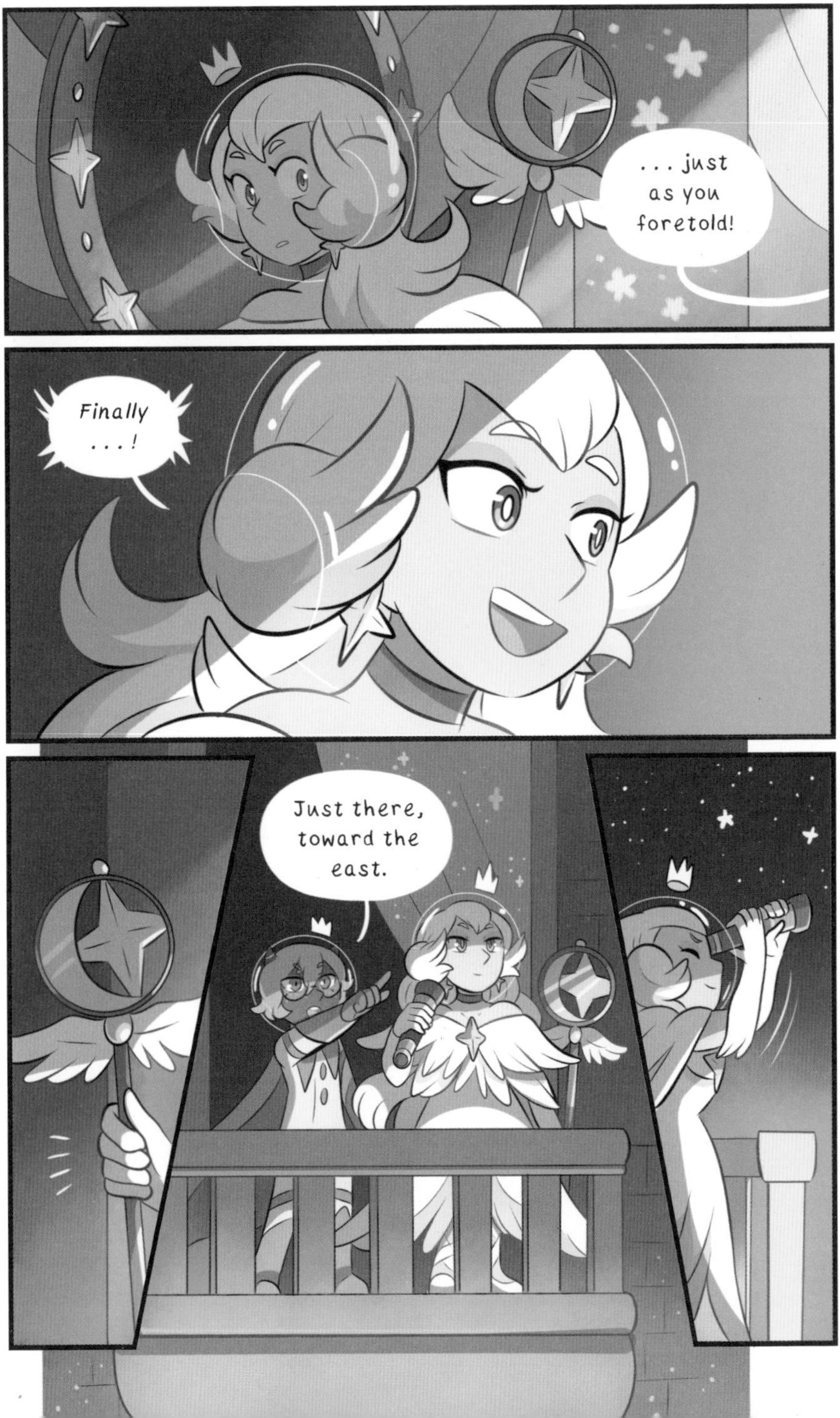
. . . just as you foretold!
Finally . . . !
Just there, toward the east.

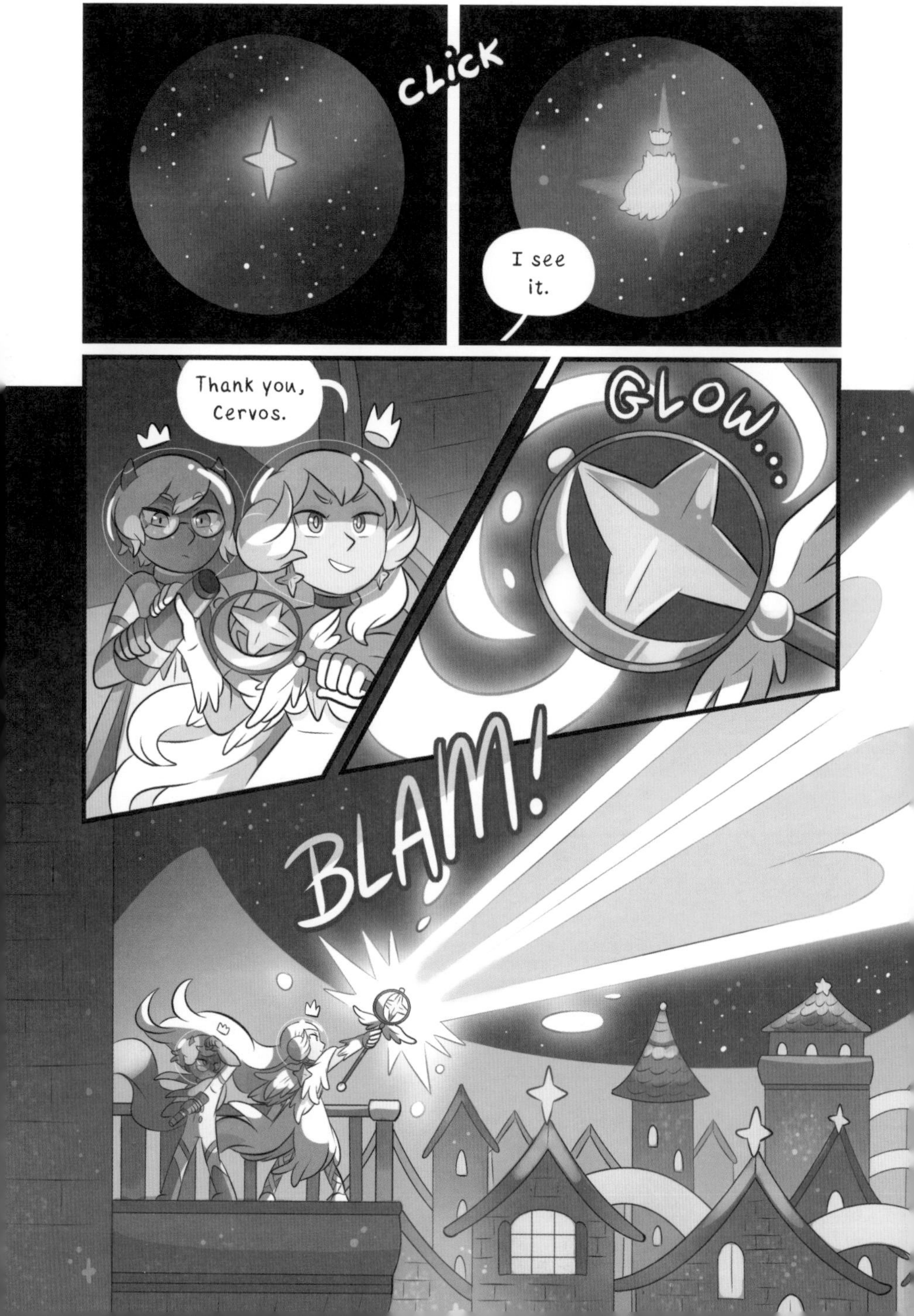
CLICK
I see it.
Thank you, Cervos.
GLOW...
BLAM!

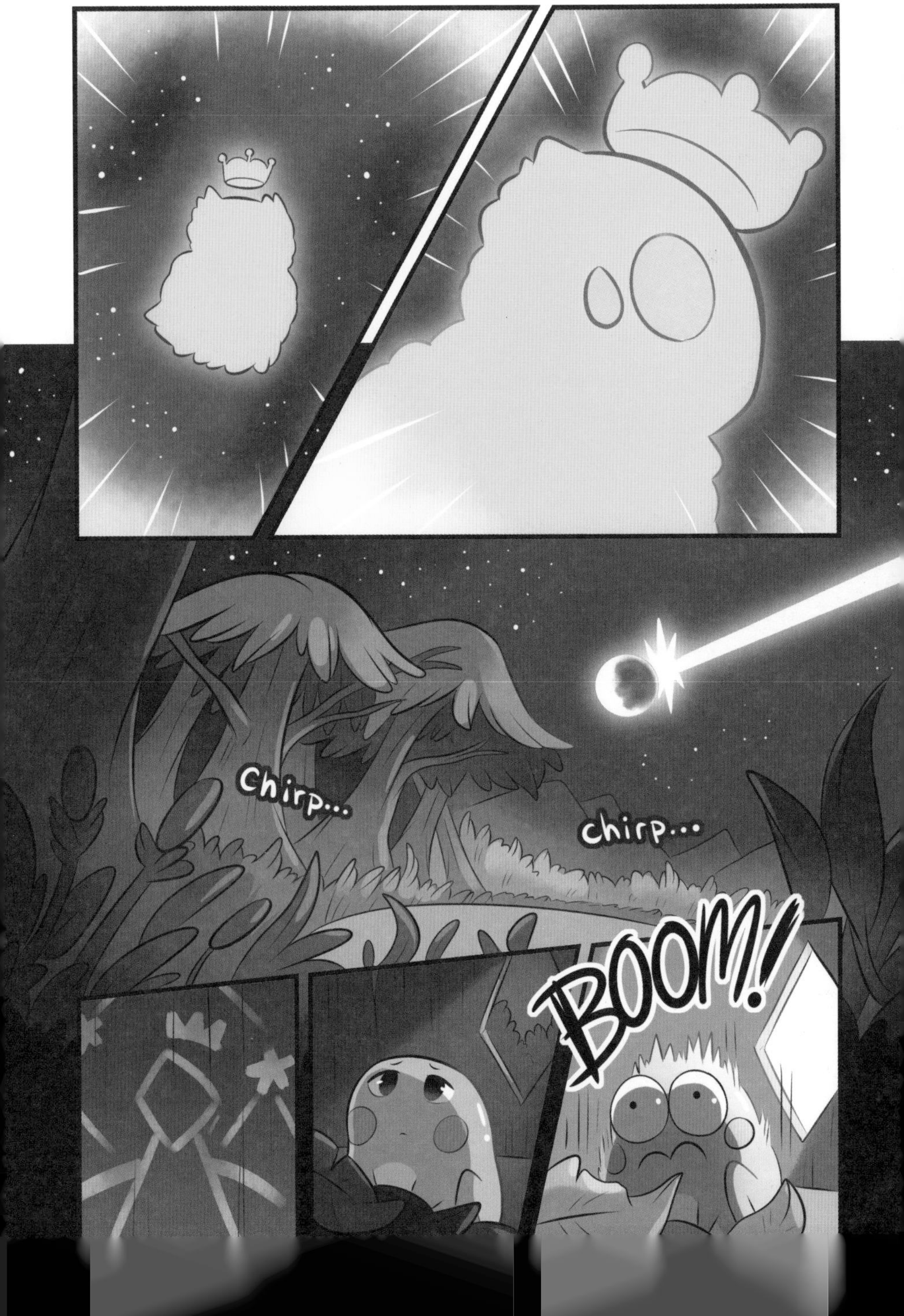
chirp...
chirp...
BOOM!

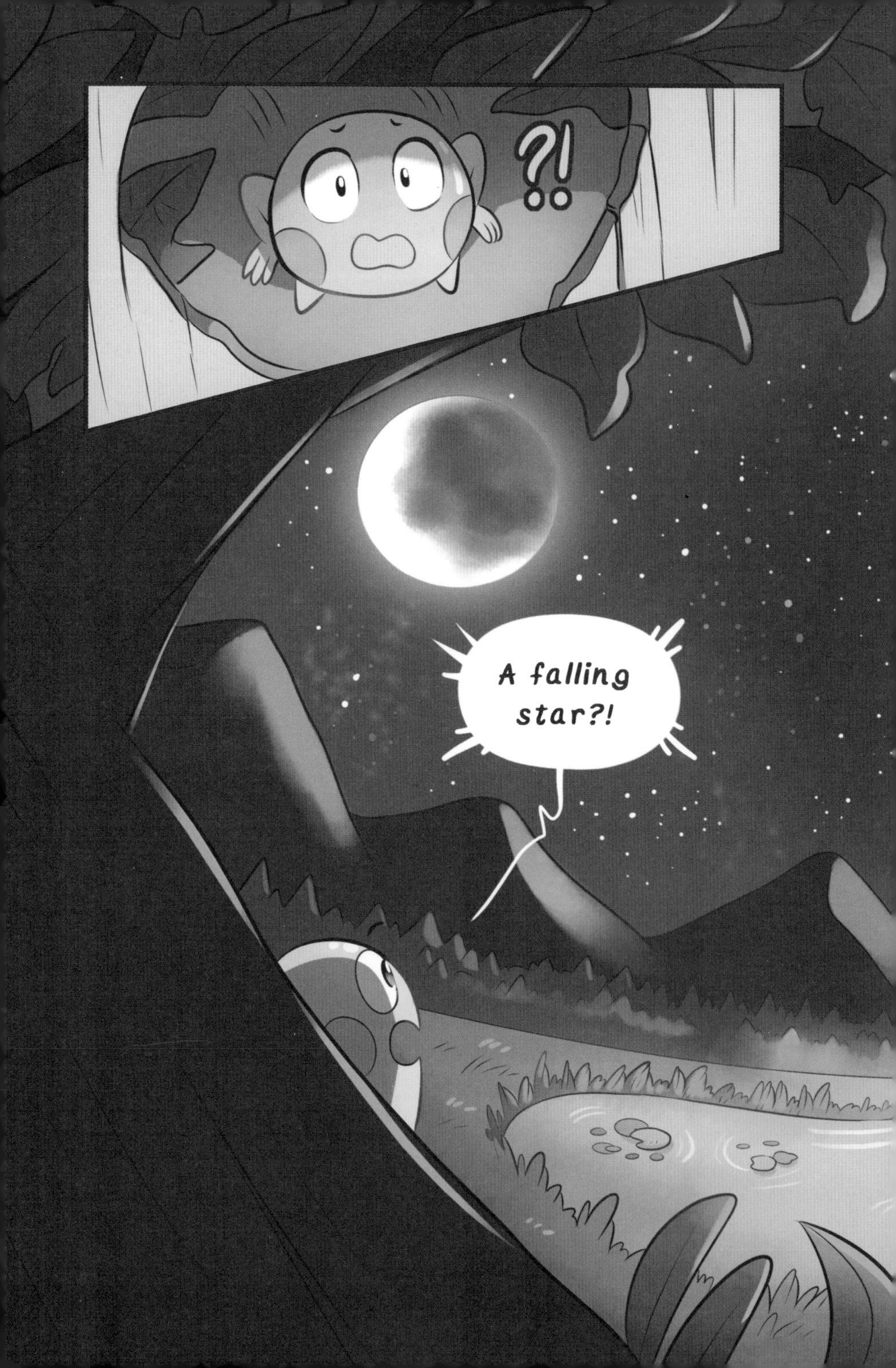
?!
A falling star?!

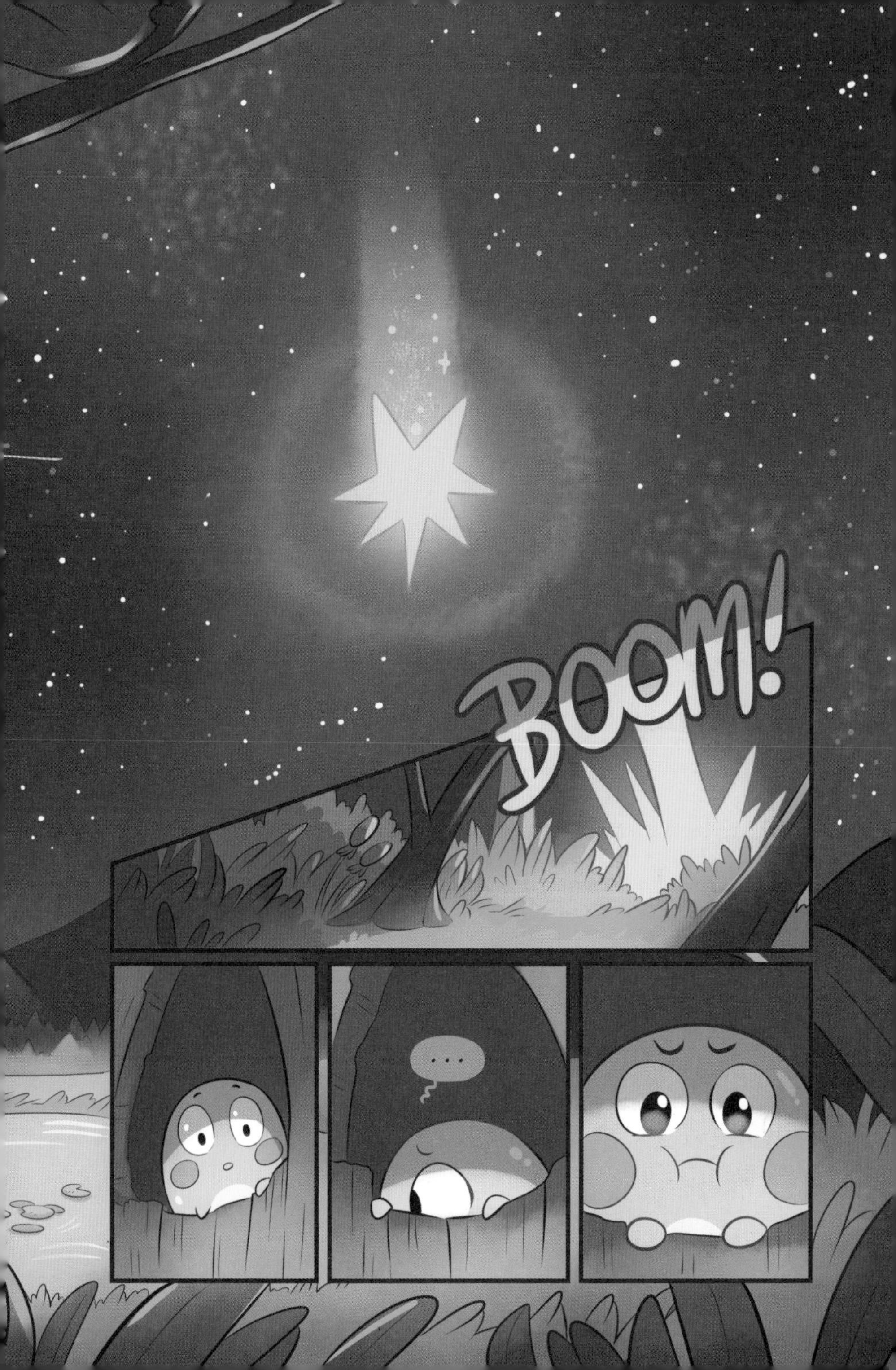
BOOM!
...

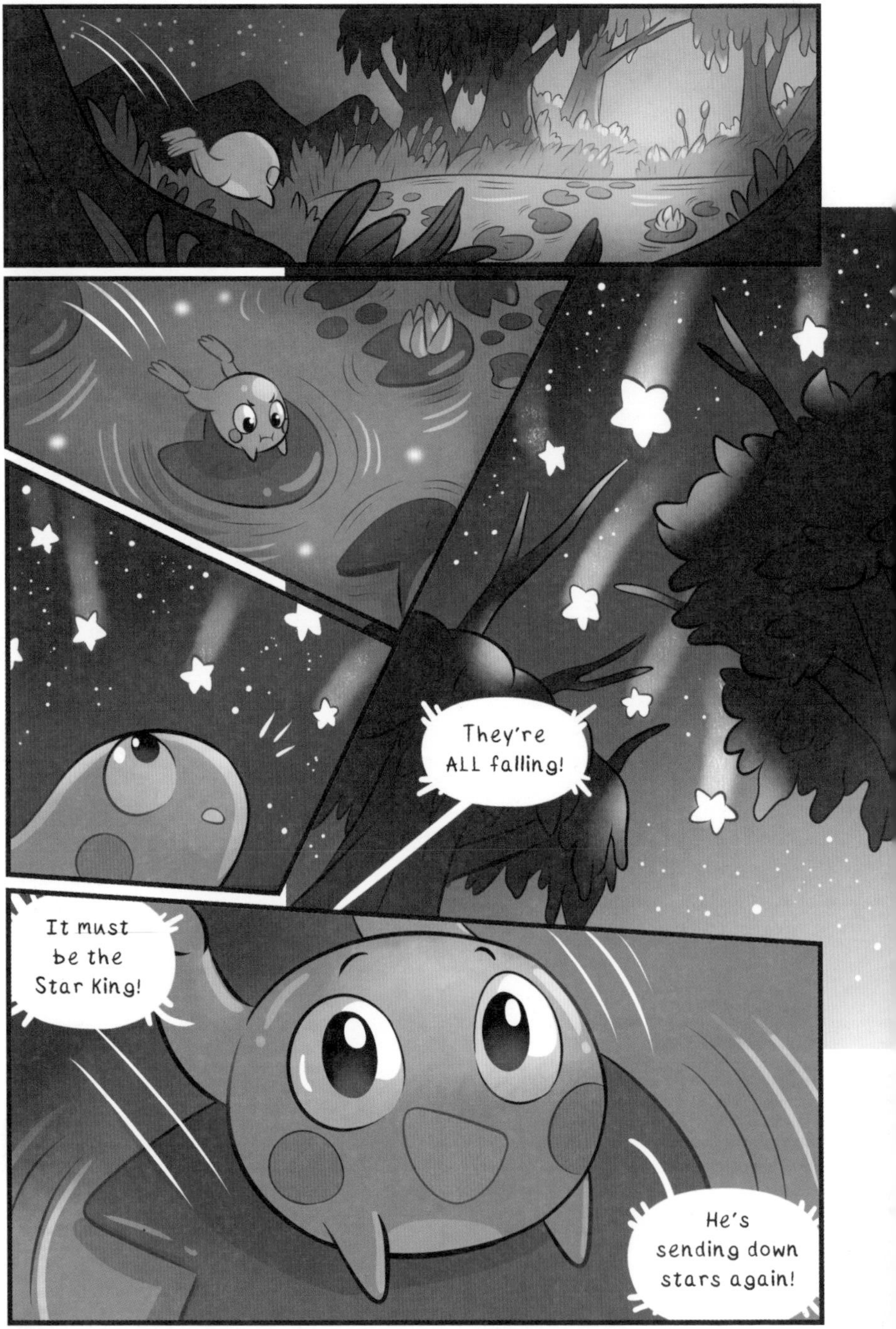
They're ALL falling!
It must be the Star King!
He's sending down stars again!

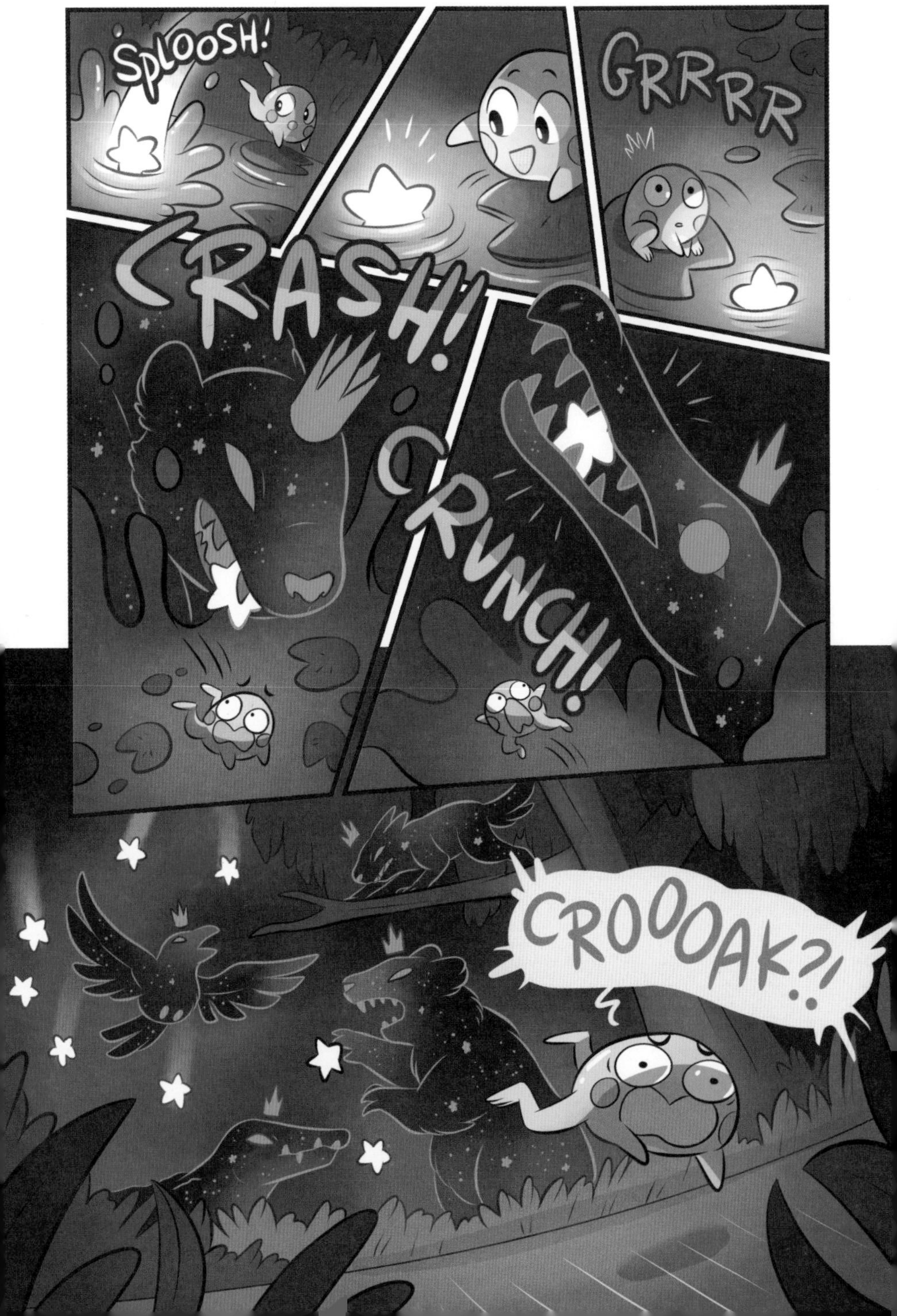
SPLOOSH!
GRRRRR
CRASH!
CRUNCH!
CROOOAK?!

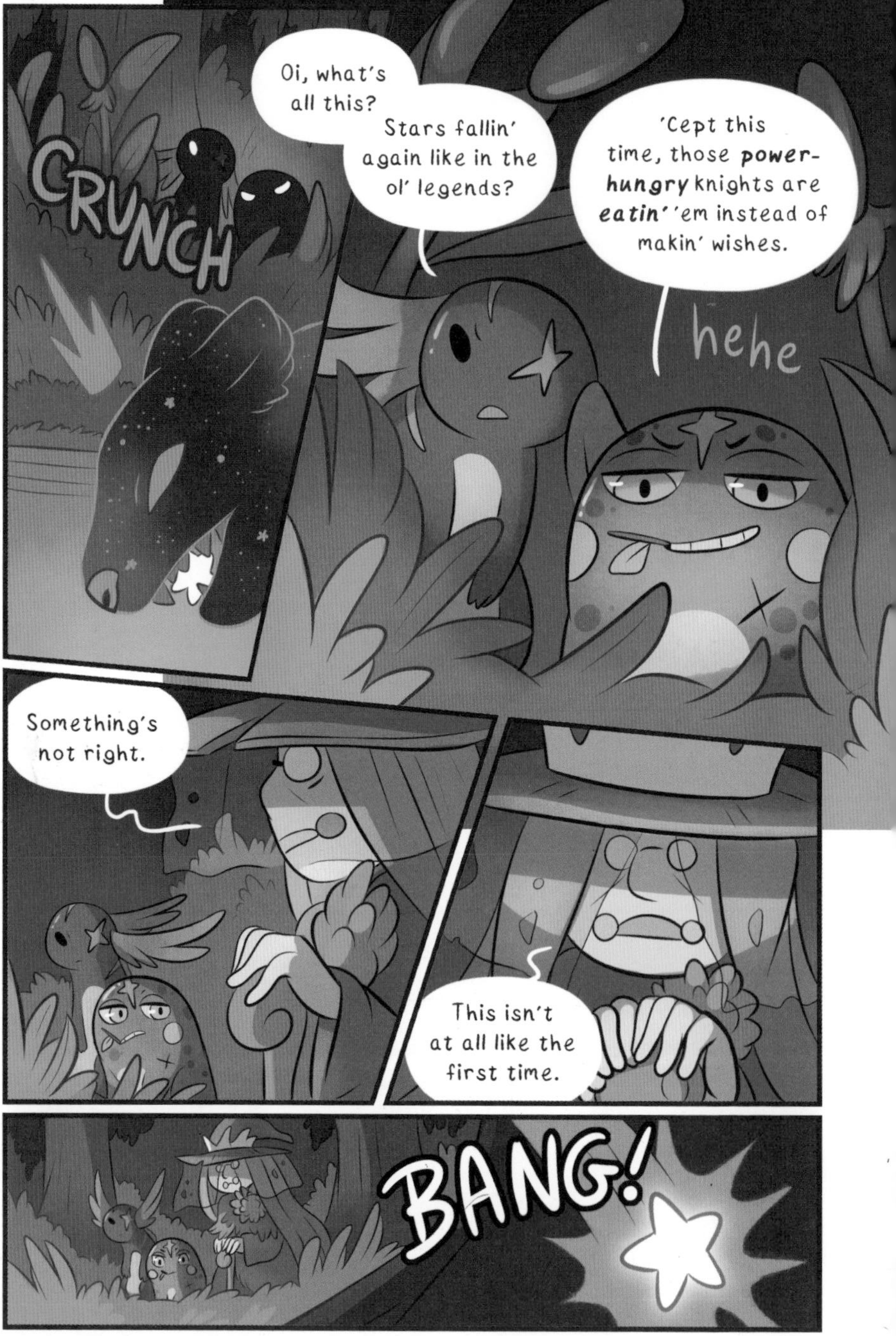
CRUNCH
Oi, what's all this?
Stars fallin' again like in the ol' legends?
'Cept this time, those power-hungry knights are eatin' 'em instead of makin' wishes.
hehe
Something's not right.
This isn't at all like the first time.
BANG!

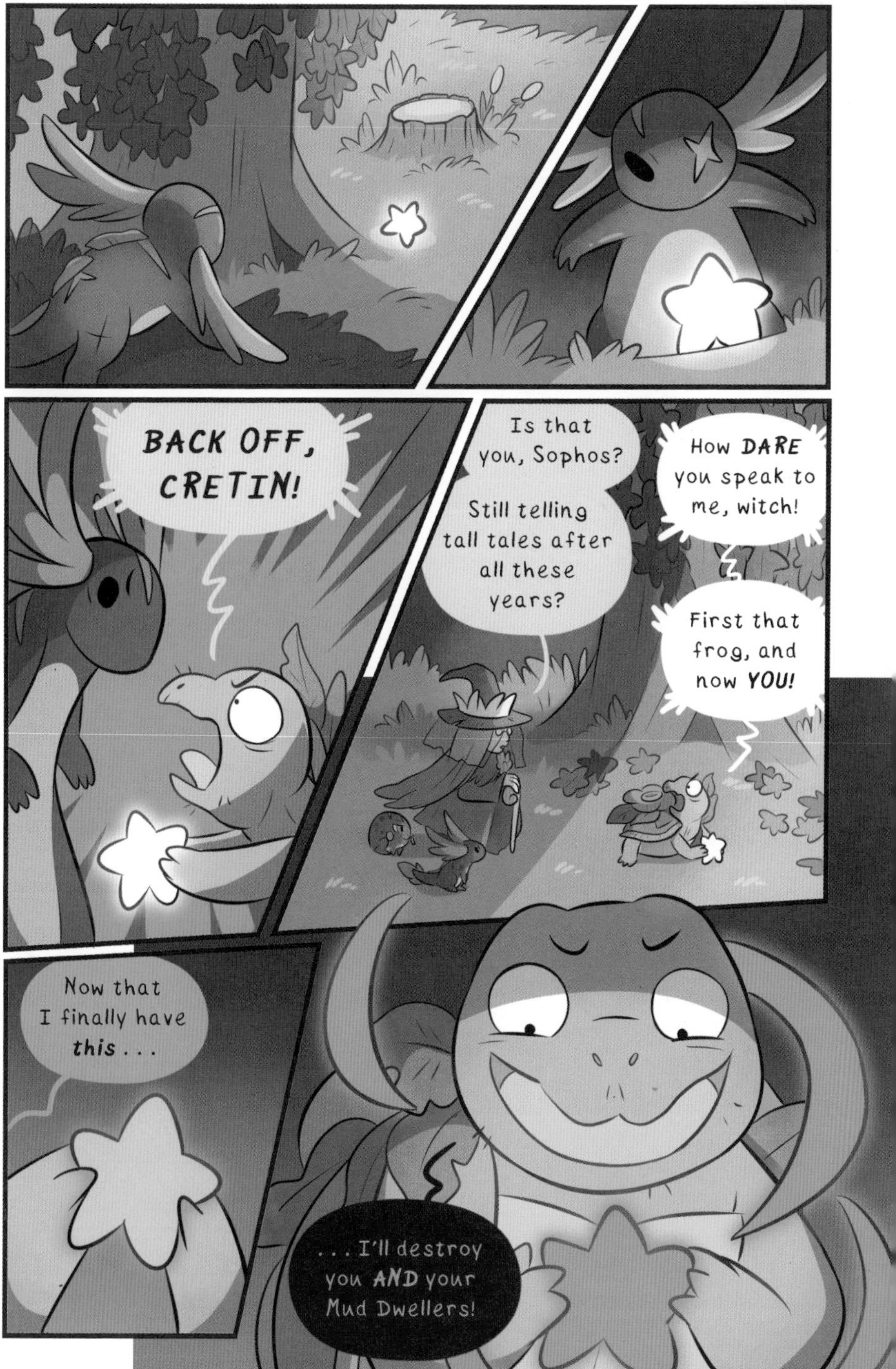
BACK OFF, CRETIN!
Is that you, Sophos?
Still telling tall tales after all these years?
How DARE you speak to me, witch!
First that frog, and now YOU!
Now that I finally have this . . .
. . . I'll destroy you AND your Mud Dwellers!

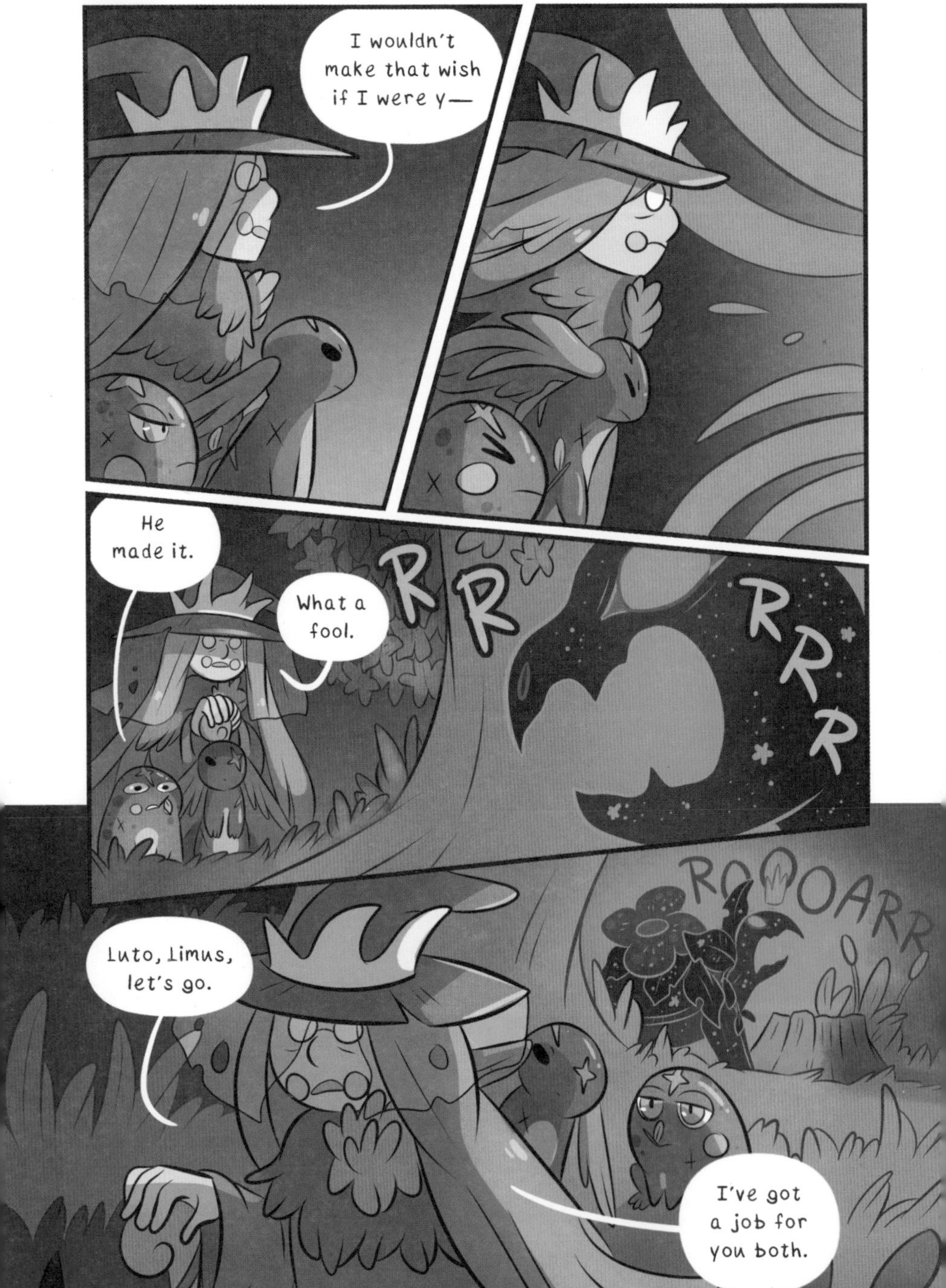

I wouldn't make that wish if I were y—
He made it.
What a fool.
RR
RRRR
ROOOARR
Luto, Limus, let's go.
I've got a job for you both.

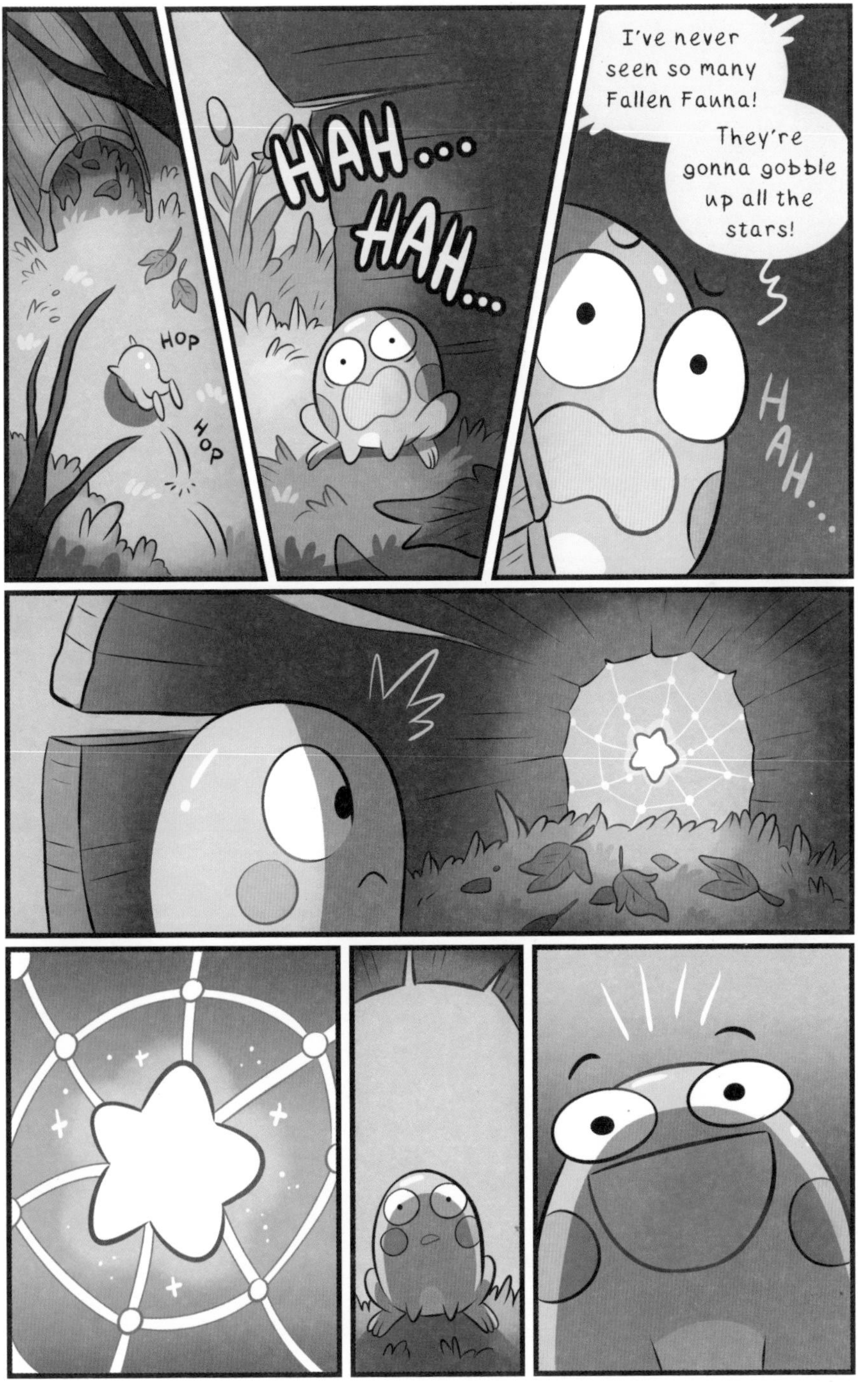
HOP
HOP
HAH...
HAH...
I've never seen so many Fallen Fauna!
They're gonna gobble up all the stars!
HAH...

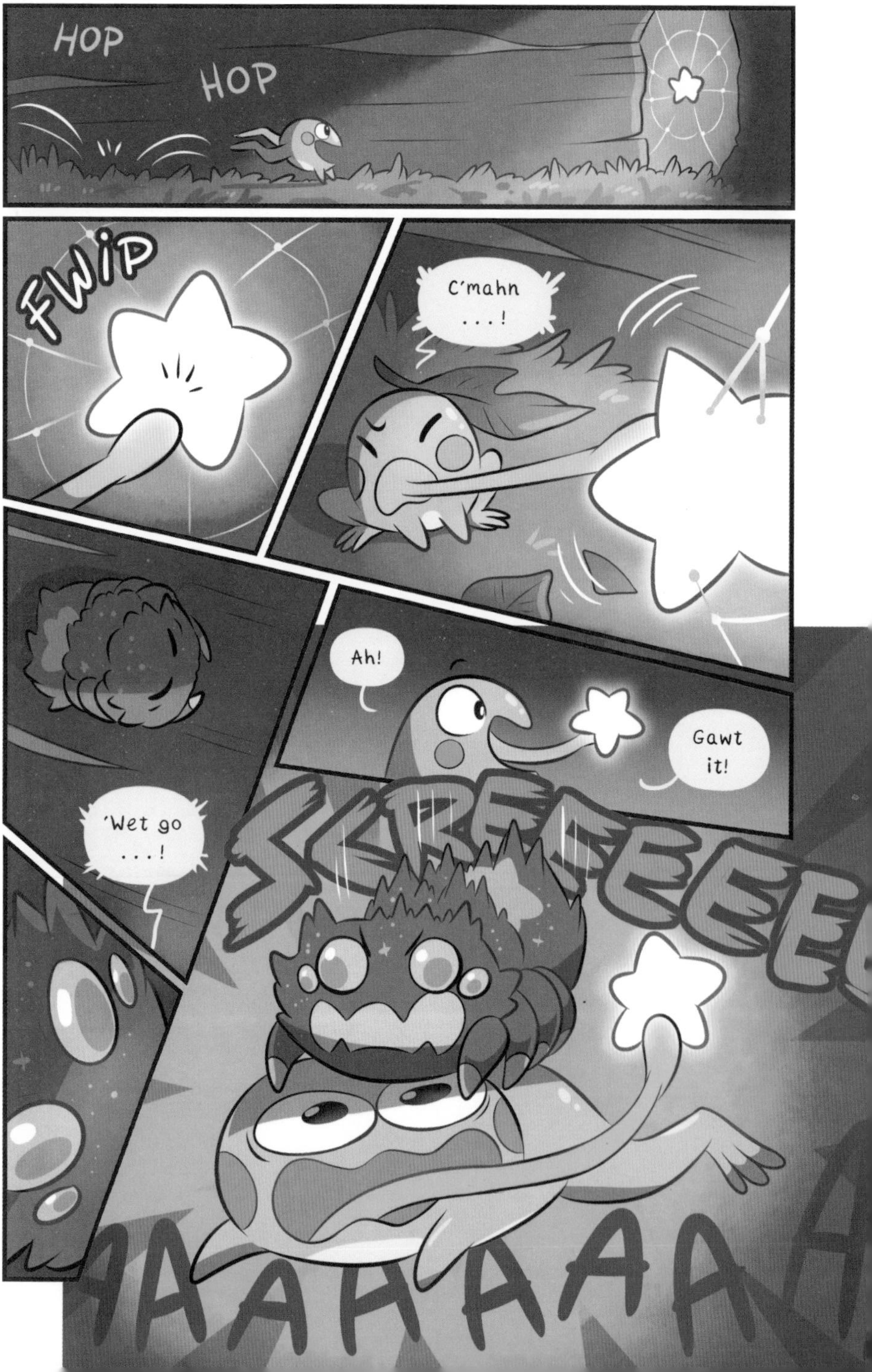
HOP
HOP
FWIP
C'mahn ...!
Ah!
Gawt it!
'Wet go ...!

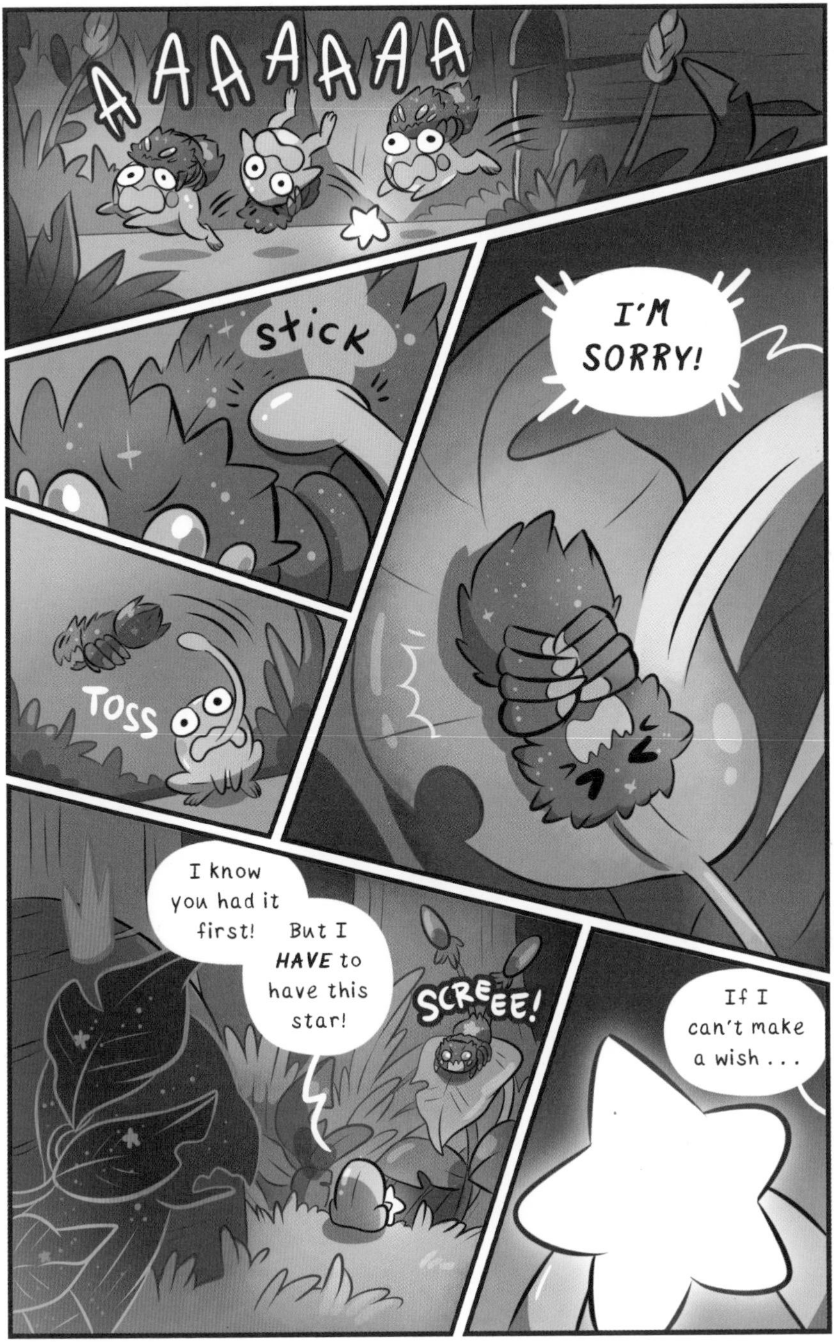
AAAAAAA
stick
I'M SORRY!
TOSS
I know you had it first!
But I HAVE to have this star!
SCREEE!
If I can't make a wish . . .

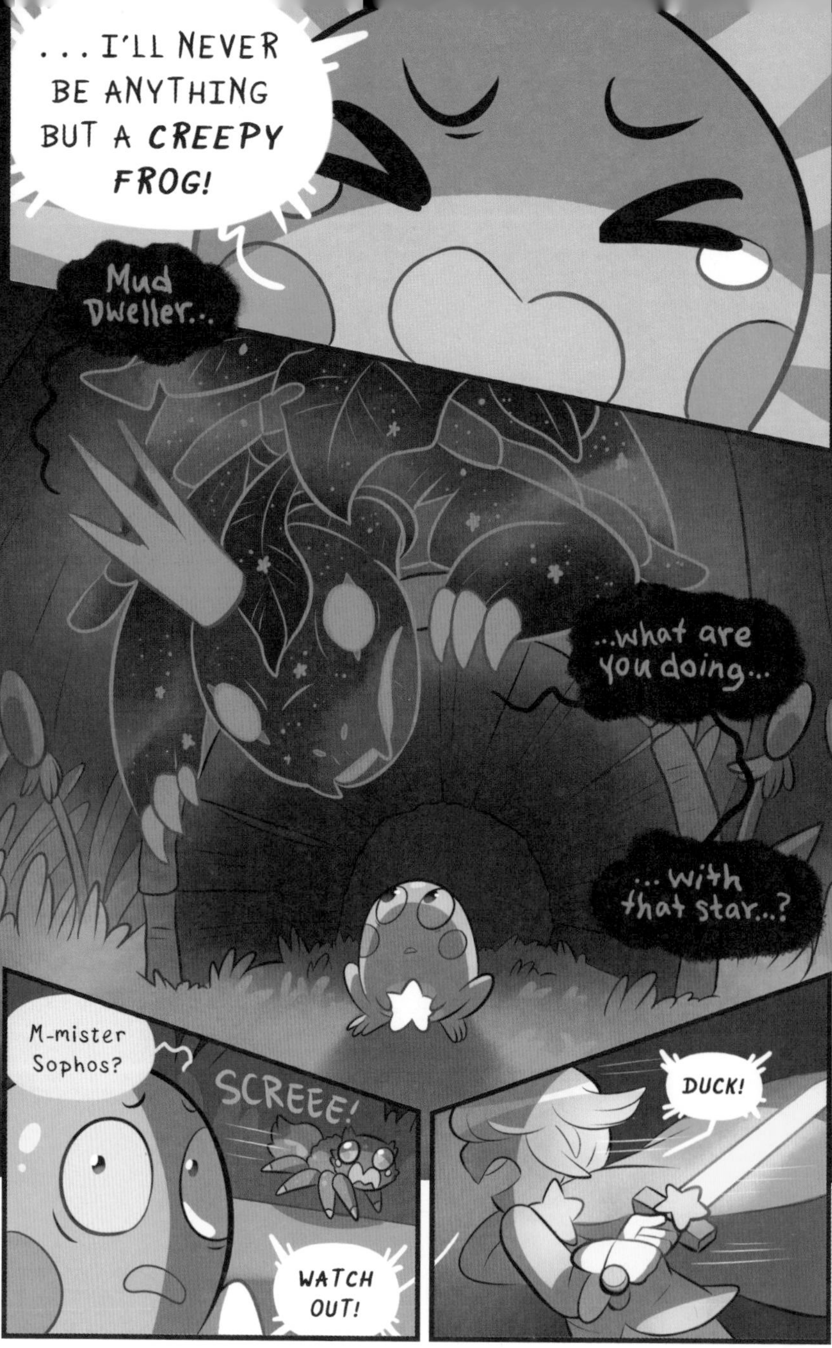
. . . I'LL NEVER BE ANYTHING BUT A CREEPY FROG!
Mud Dweller...
...what are you doing...
...with that star...?
M-mister Sophos?
SCREEE!
WATCH OUT!
DUCK!

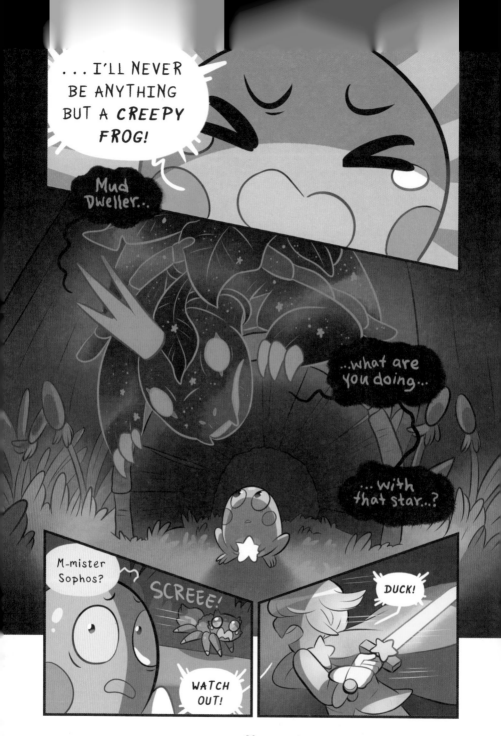

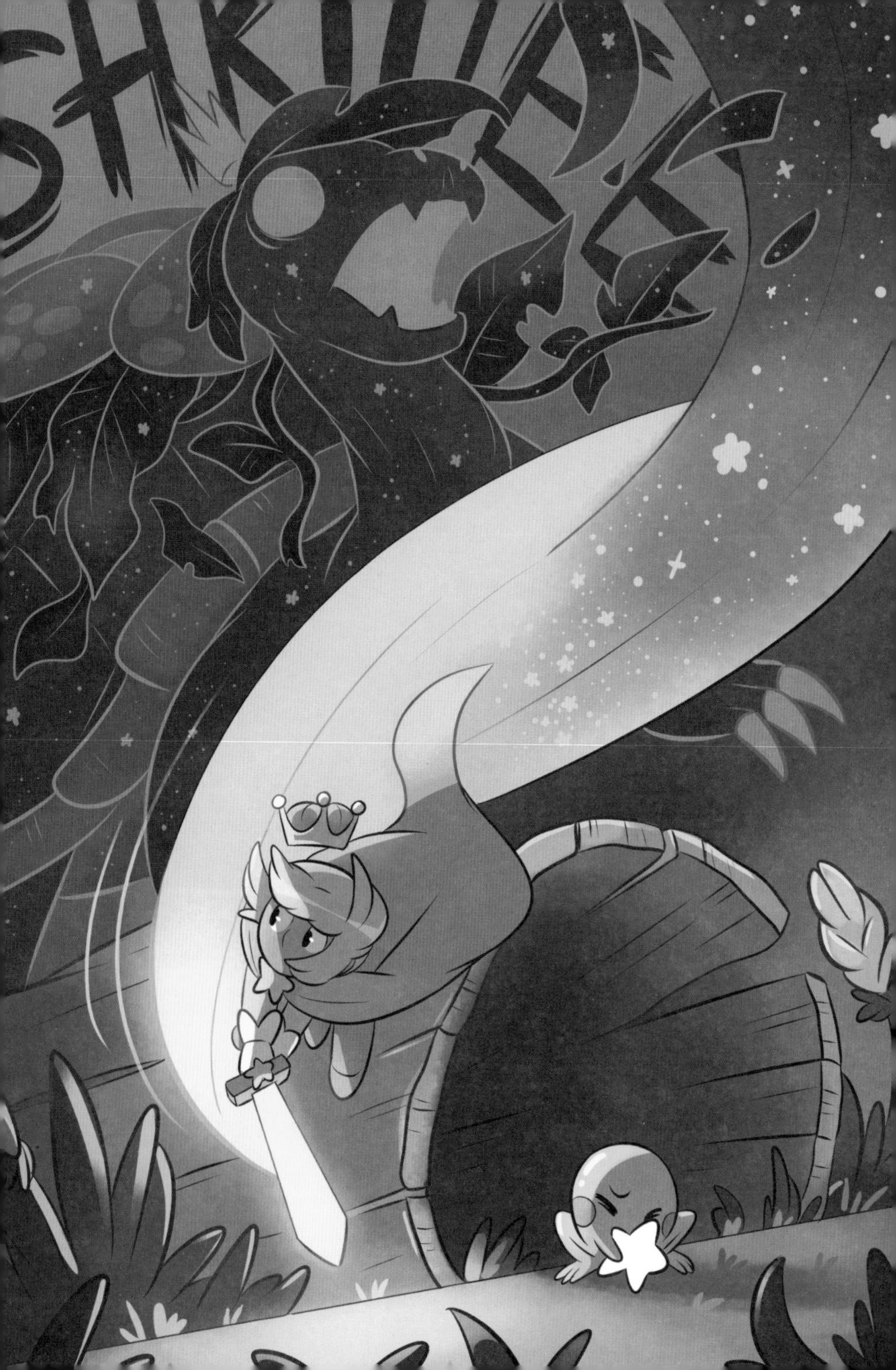

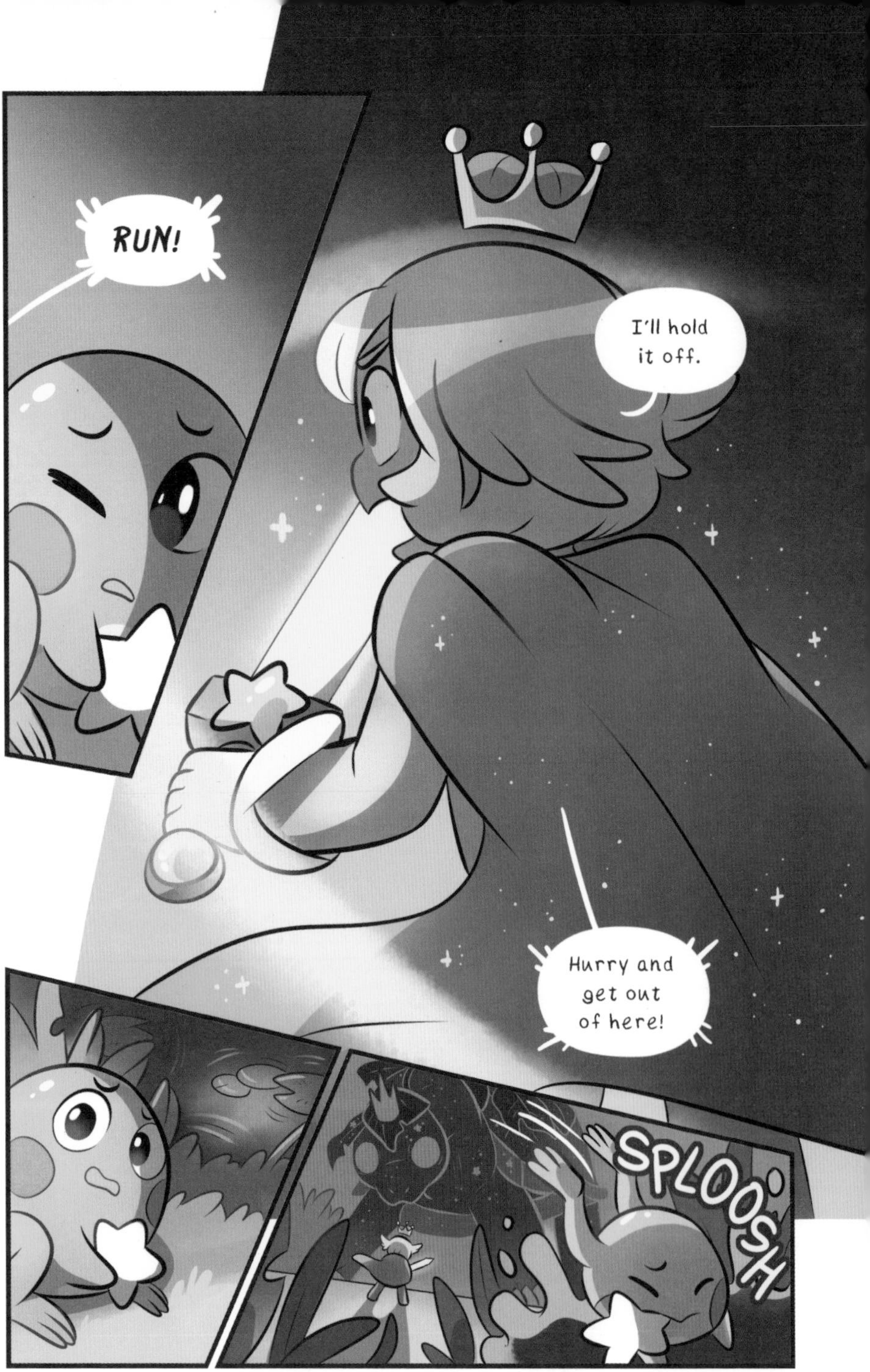
RUN!
I'll hold it off.
Hurry and get out of here!
SPLOOSH

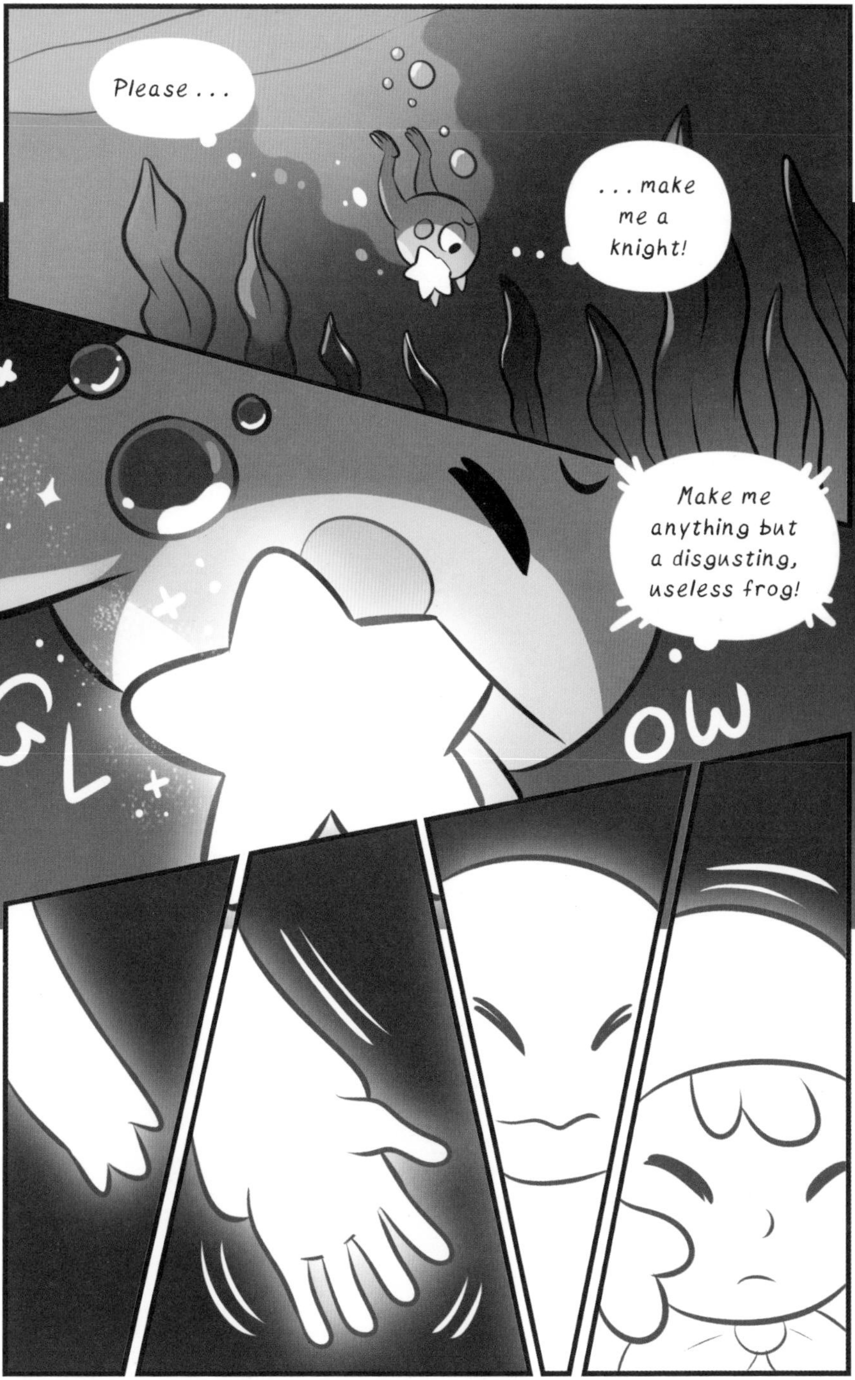

Please . . .
. . . make me a knight!
Make me anything but a disgusting, useless frog!
GLOW

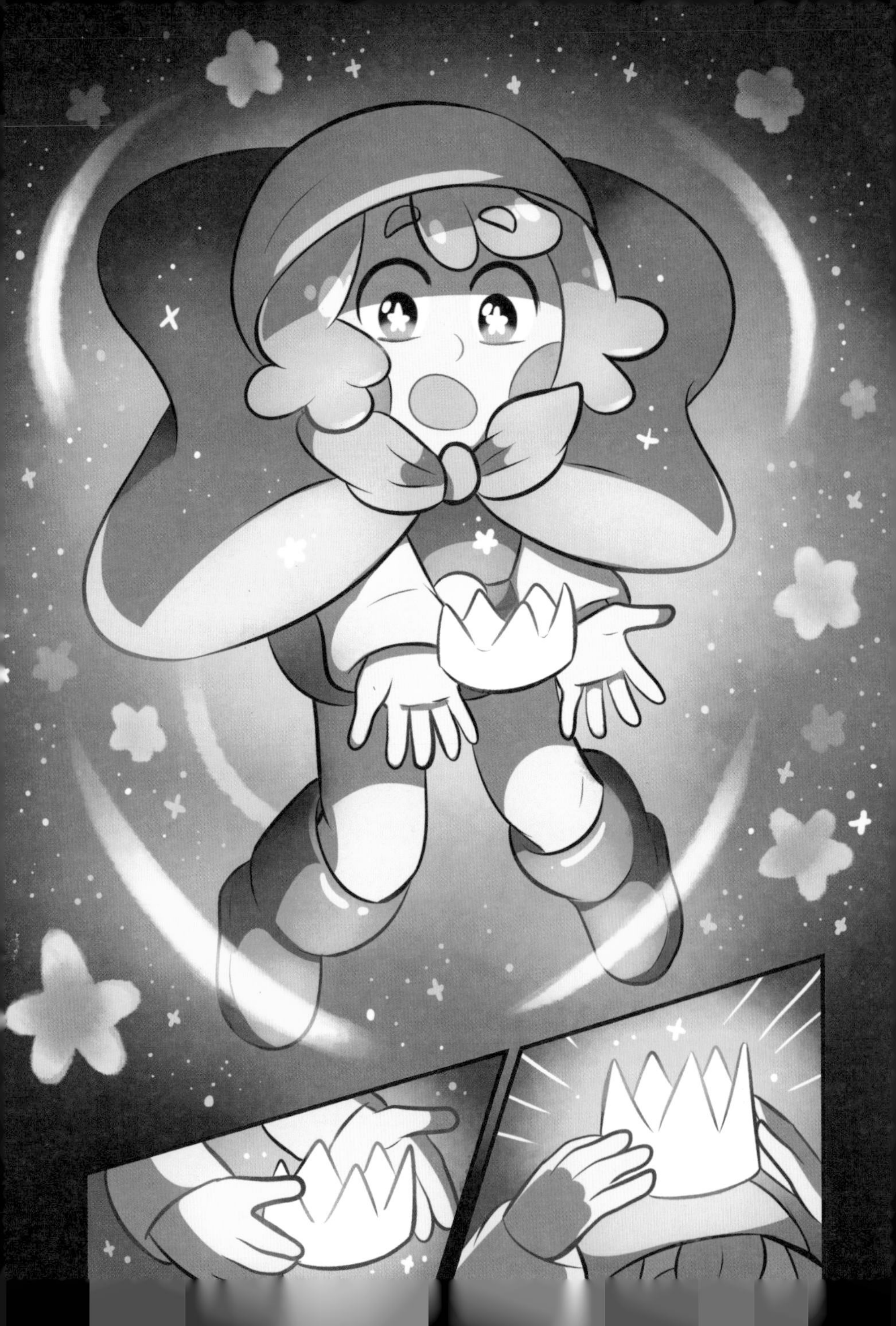

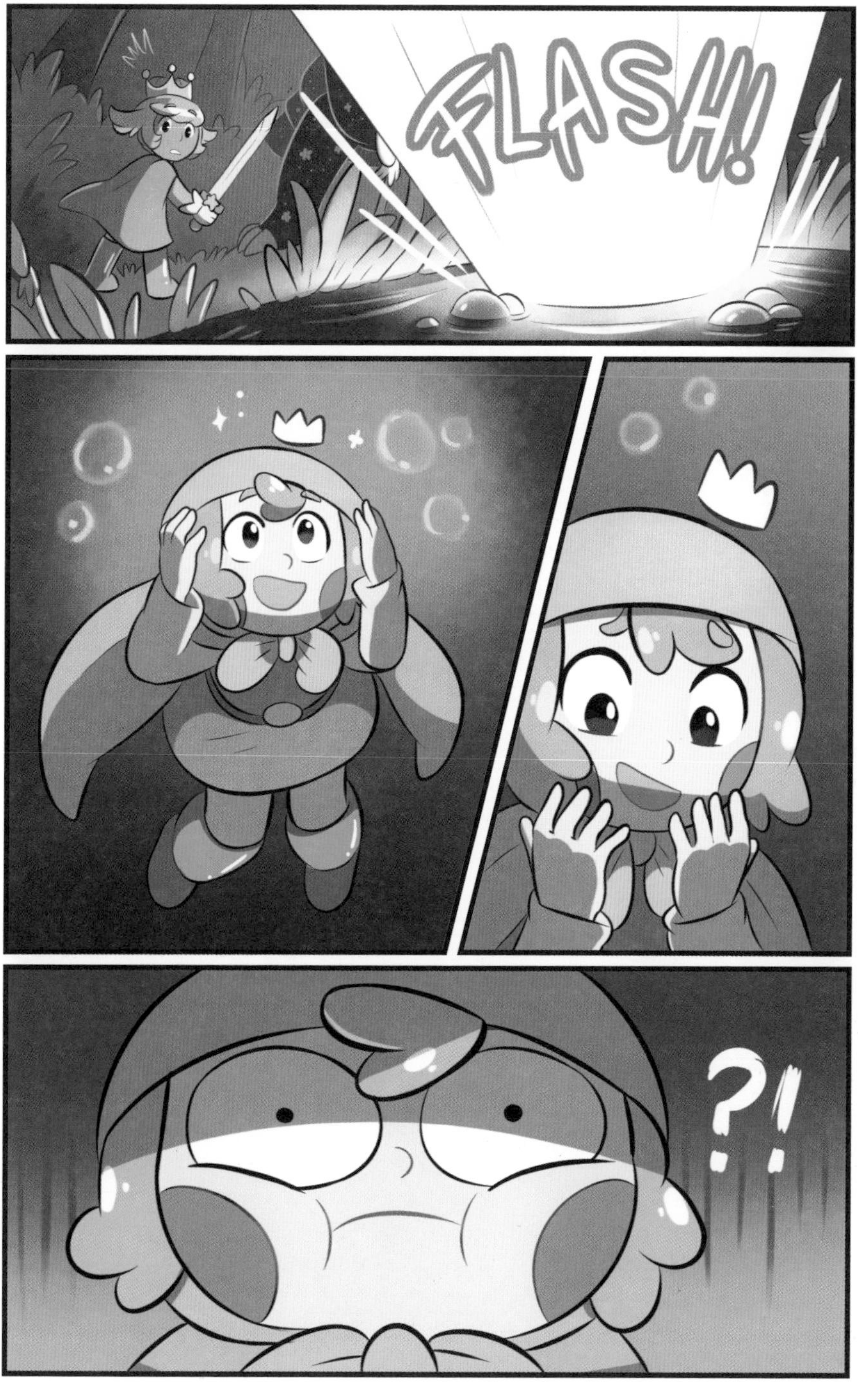
FLASH!
?!

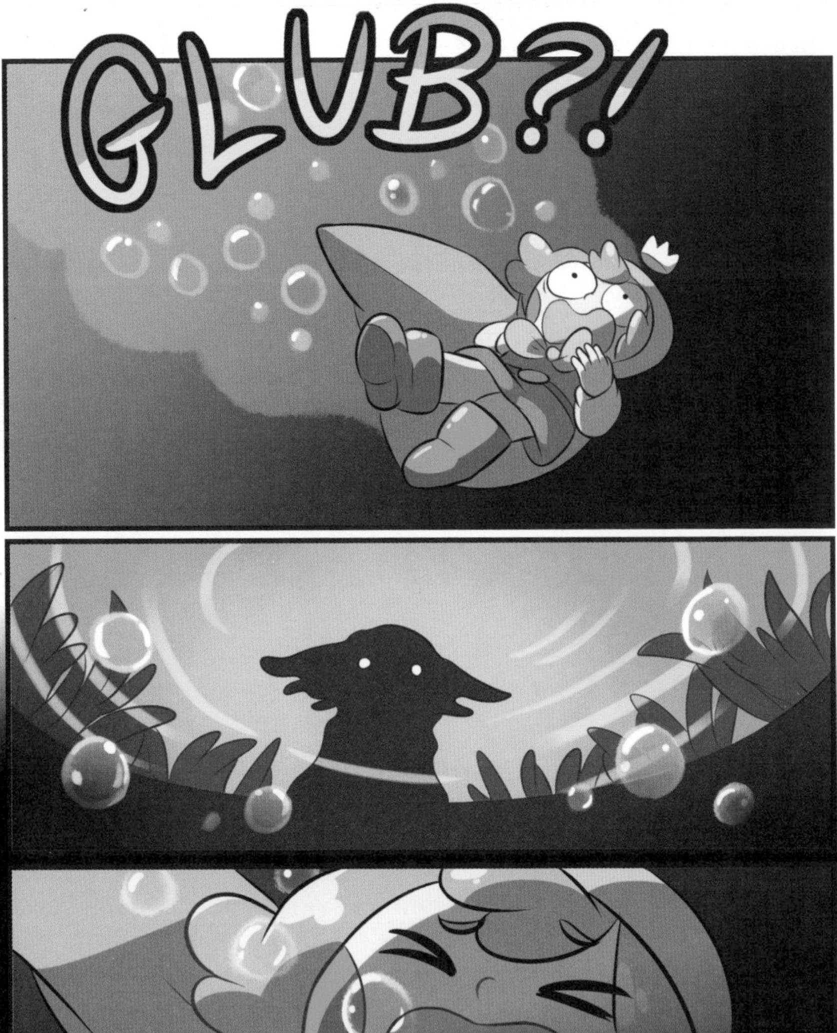
GLUB?!

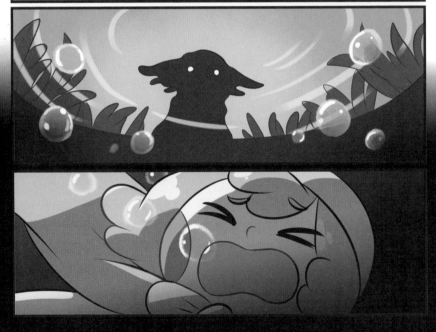

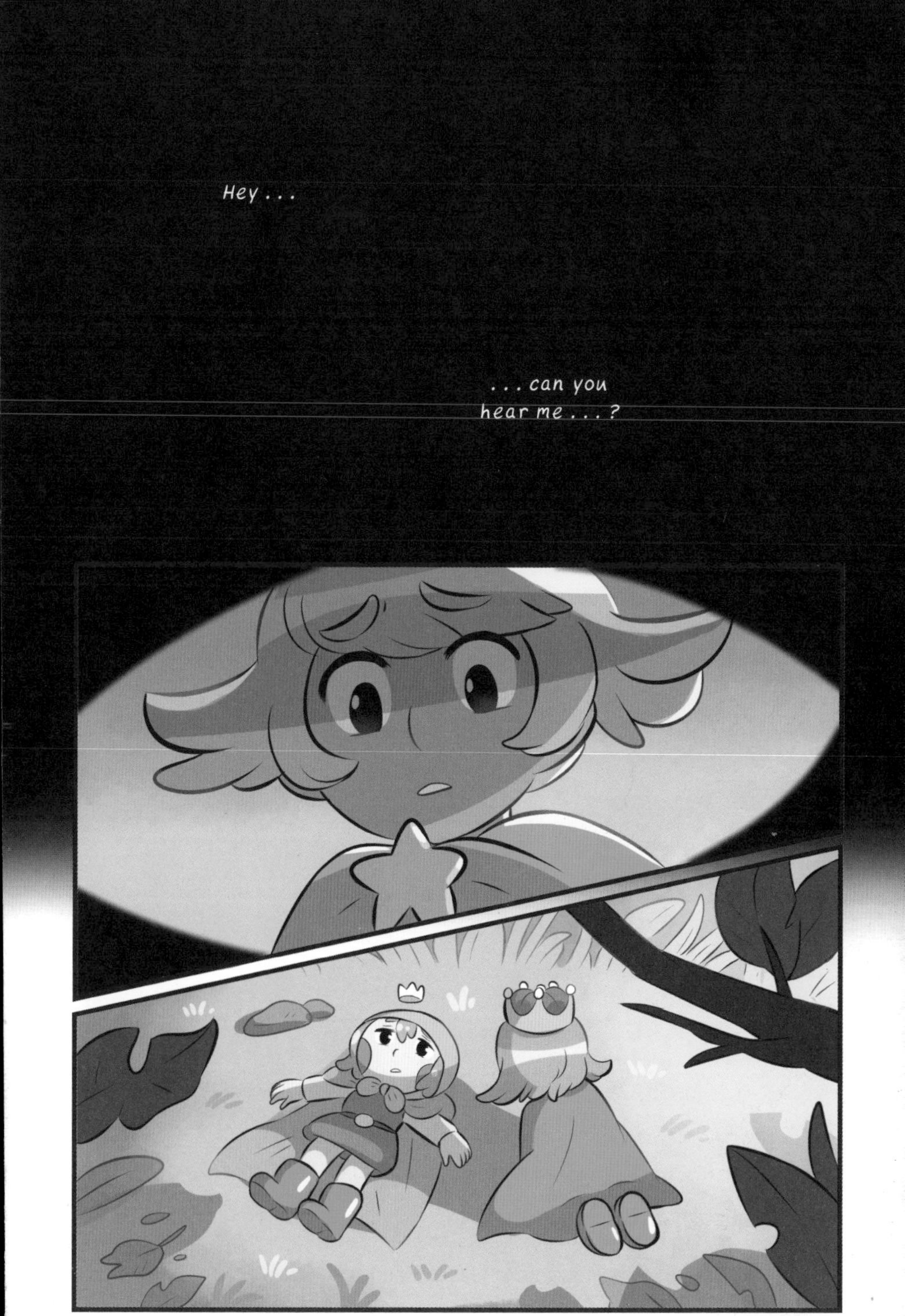
Hey . . .
. . . can you
hear me . . . ?

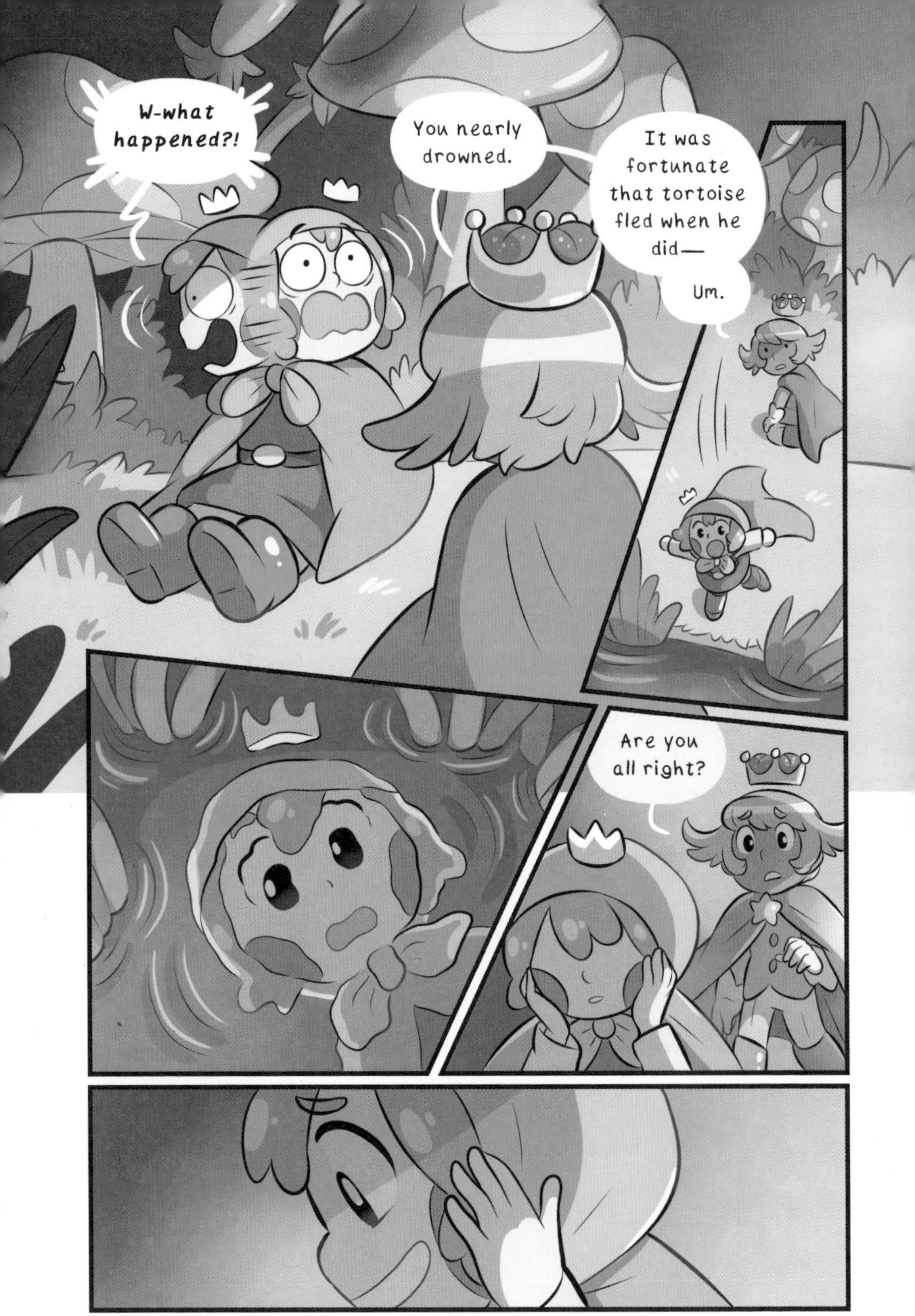
W-what happened?!
You nearly drowned.
It was fortunate that tortoise fled when he did—
Um.
Are you all right?

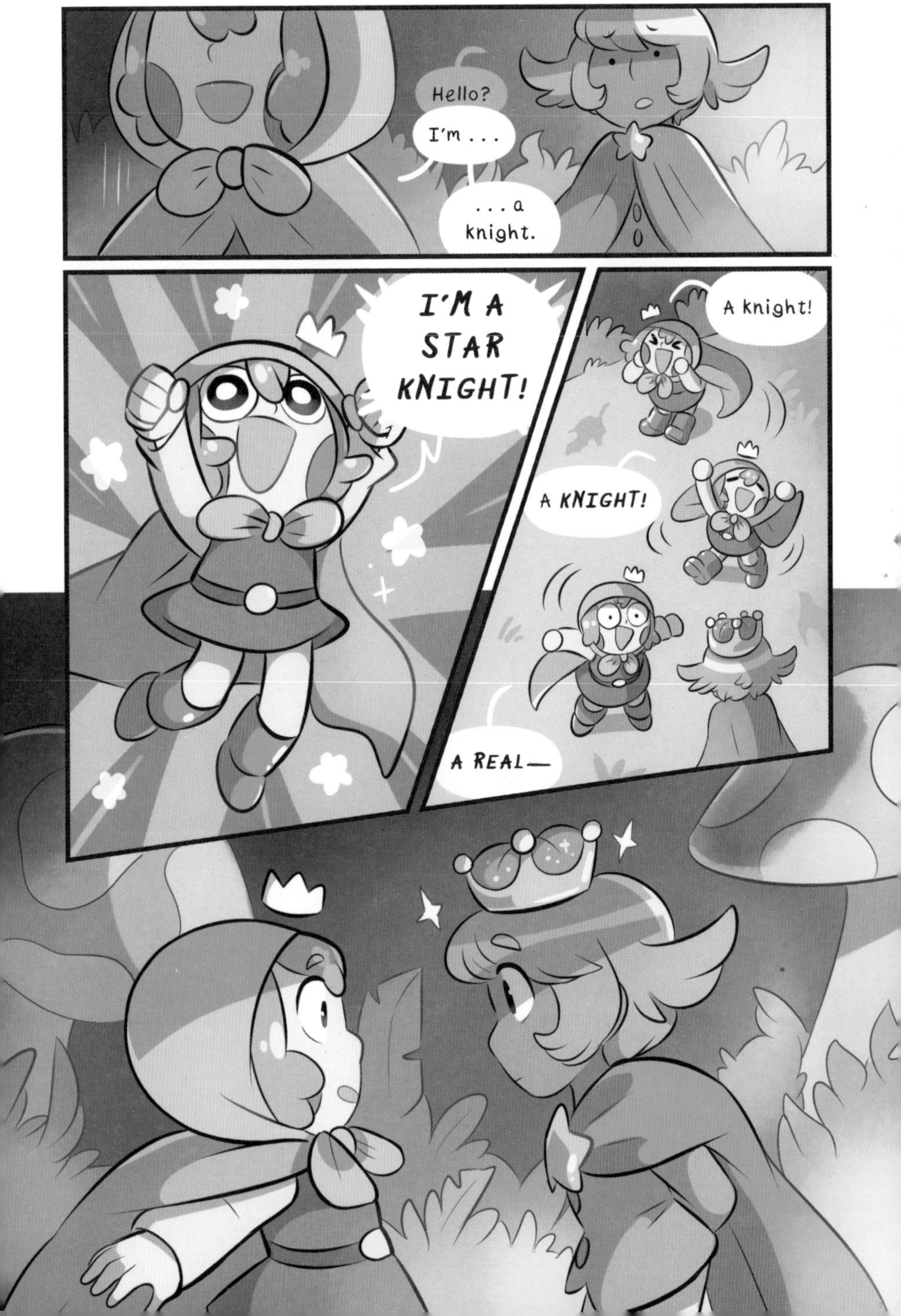
Hello?
I'm . . .
. . . a knight.
I'M A STAR KNIGHT!
A knight!
A KNIGHT!
A REAL—

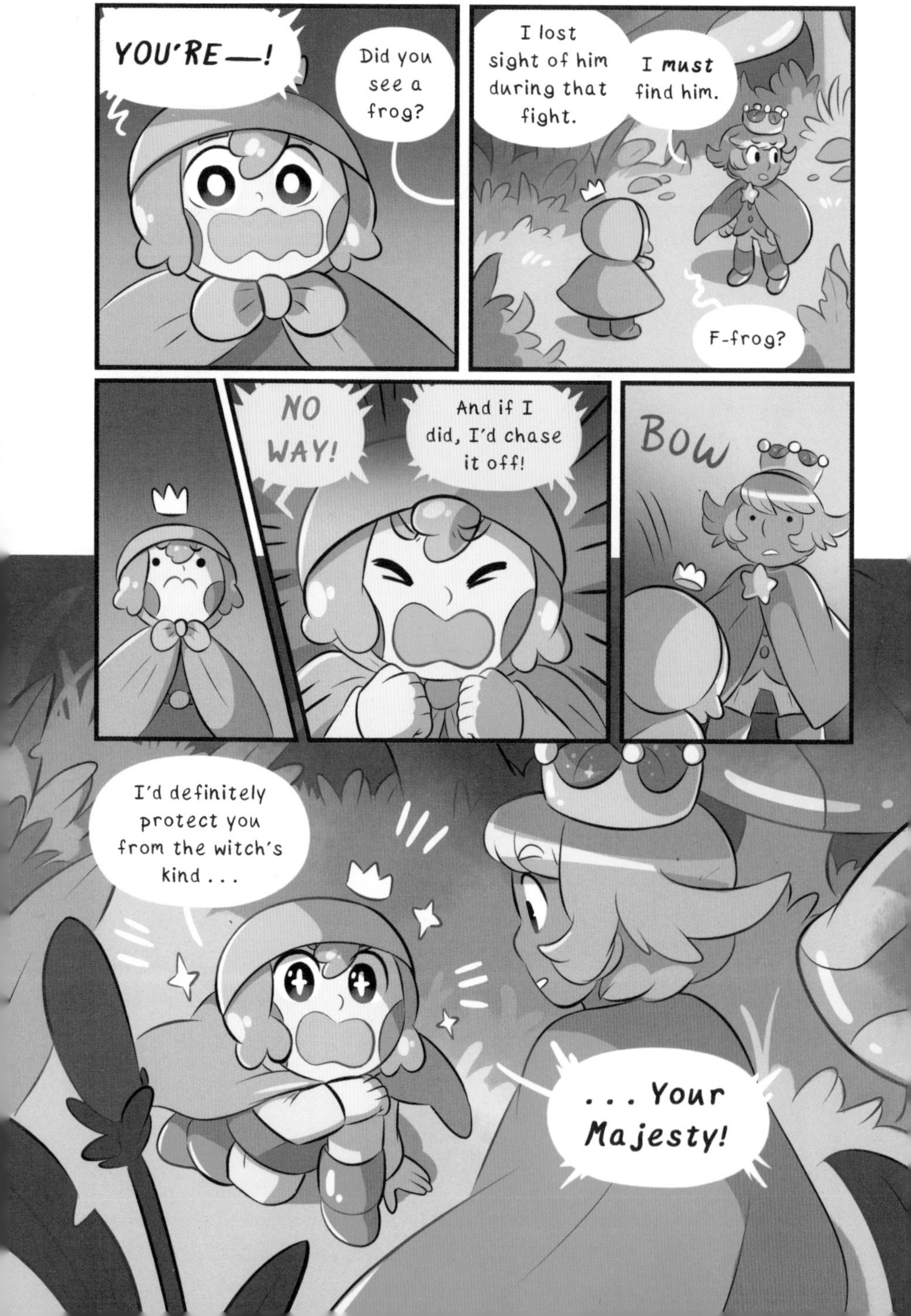
YOU'RE—!
Did you see a frog?
I lost sight of him during that fight.
I must find him.
F-frog?
NO WAY!
And if I did, I'd chase it off!
BOW
I'd definitely protect you from the witch's kind . . .
. . . Your Majesty!

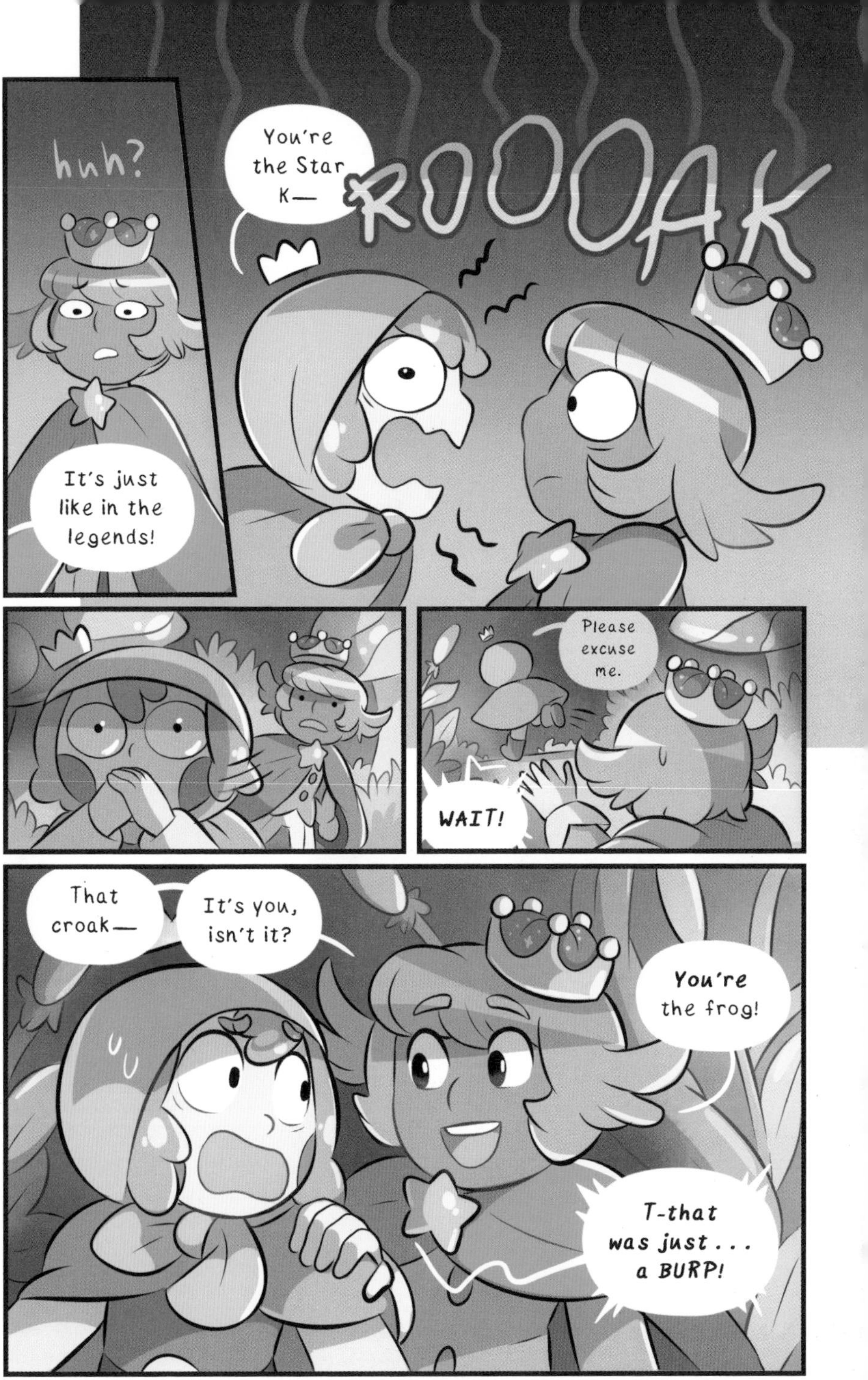
huh?
It's just like in the legends!
You're the Star K—
ROOOAK
Please excuse me.
WAIT!
That croak—
It's you, isn't it?
You're the frog!
T-that was just . . . a BURP!

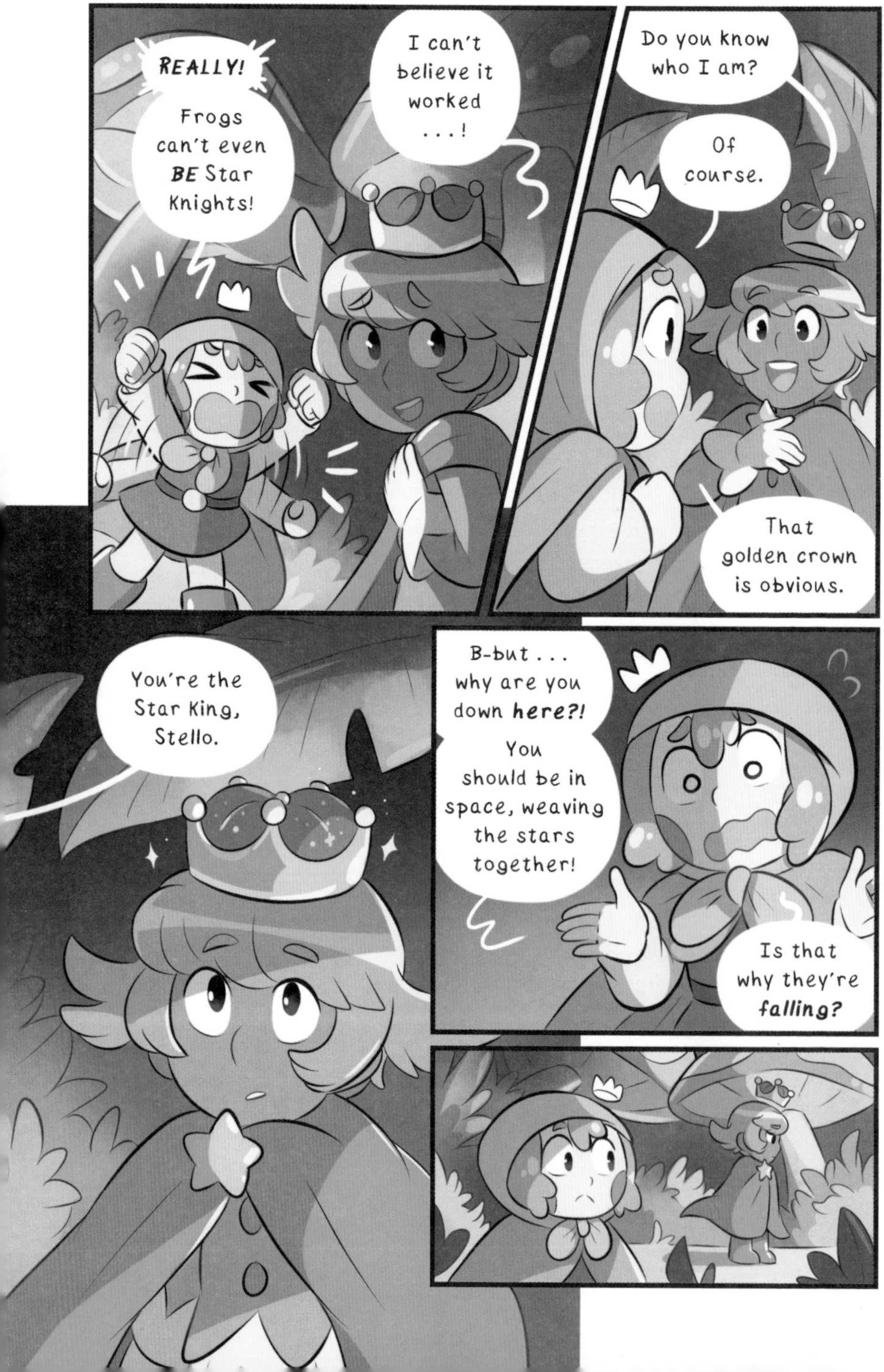
REALLY!
Frogs can't even BE Star Knights!
I can't believe it worked . . . !
Do you know who I am?
Of course.
That golden crown is obvious.
You're the Star King, Stello.
B-but . . . why are you down here?!
You should be in space, weaving the stars together!
Is that why they're falling?

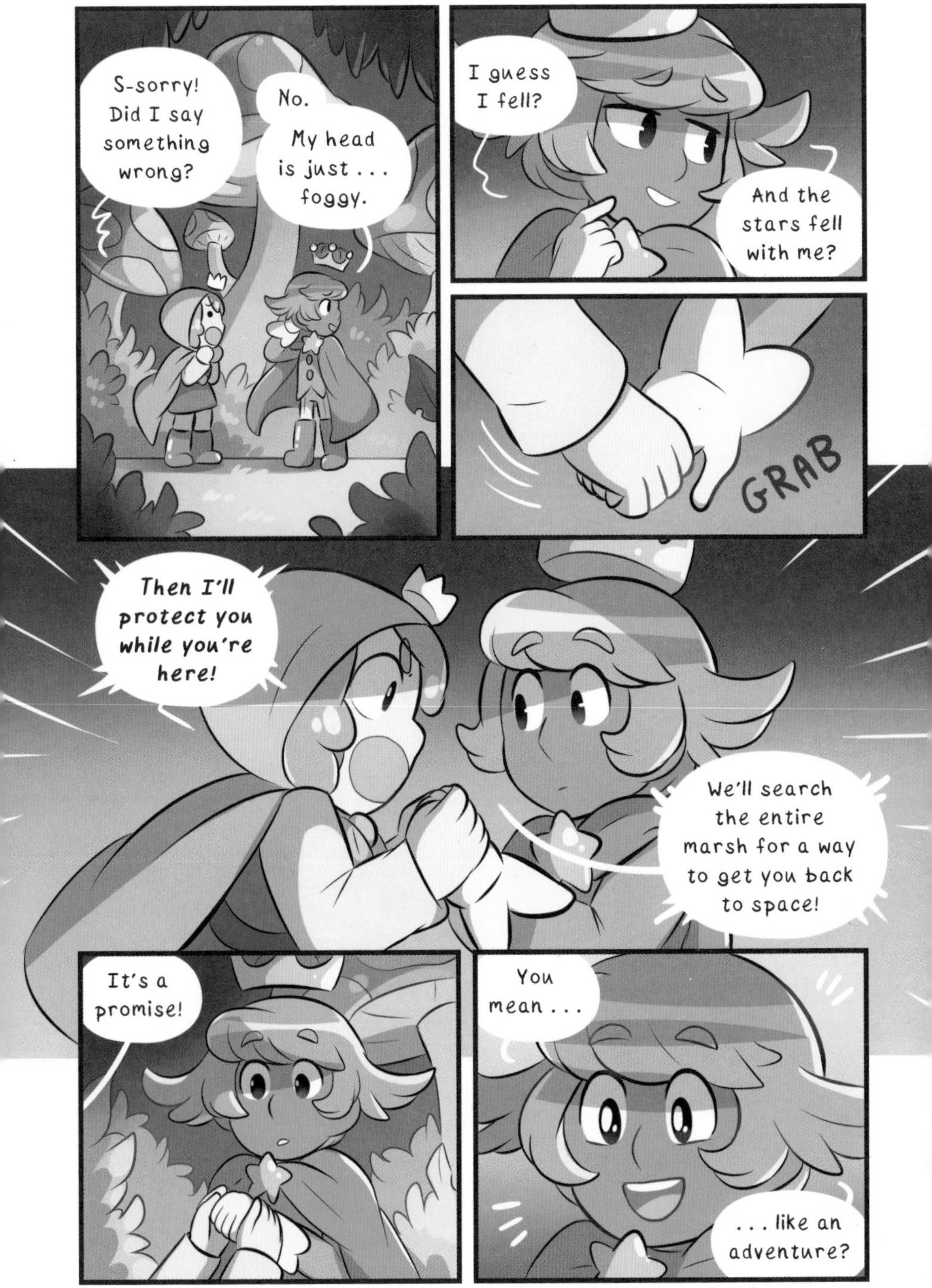
S-sorry! Did I say something wrong?
No.
My head is just . . . foggy.
I guess I fell?
And the stars fell with me?
GRAB
Then I'll protect you while you're here!
We'll search the entire marsh for a way to get you back to space!
It's a promise!
You mean . . .
. . . like an adventure?

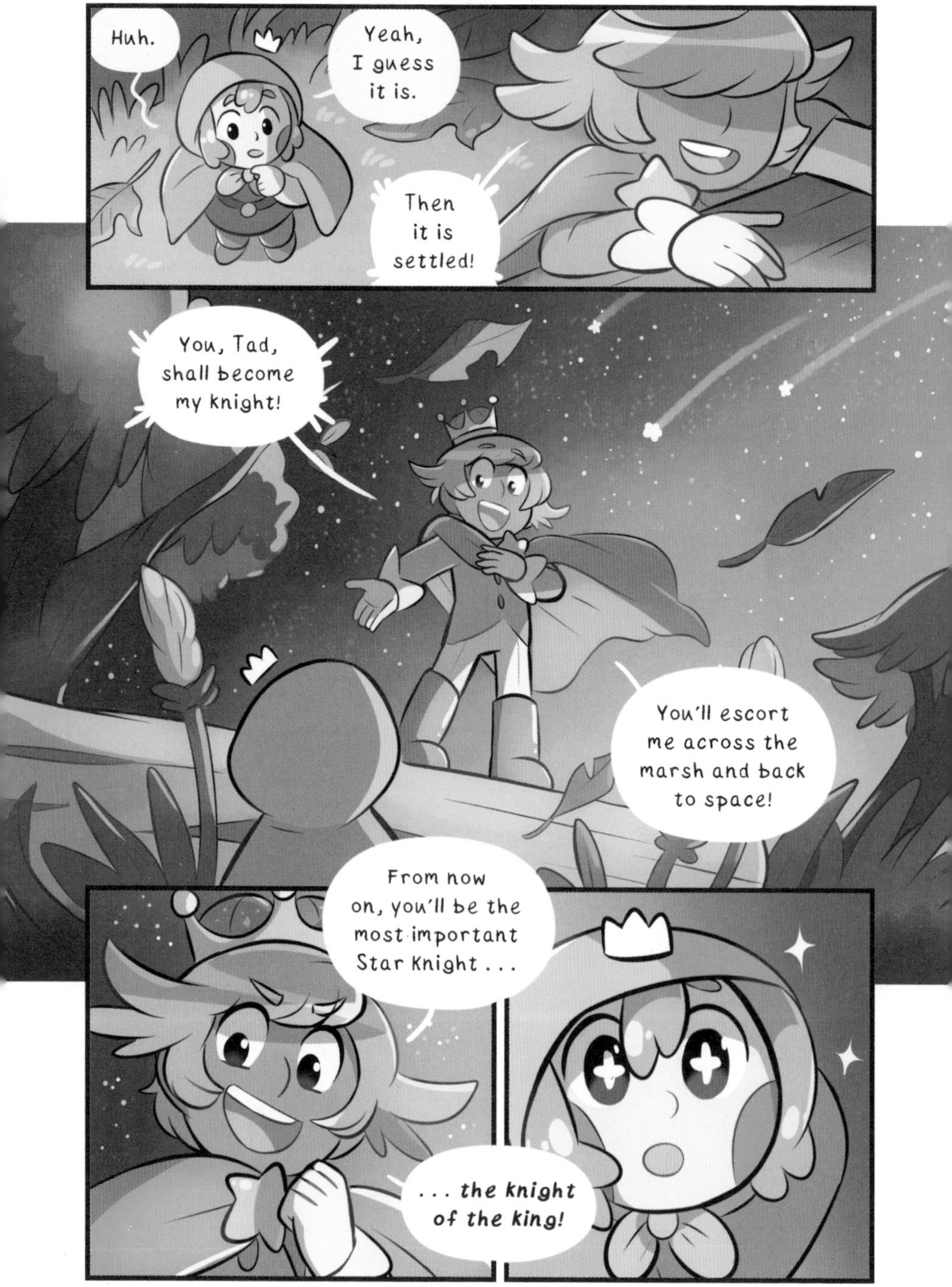
Huh.
Yeah, I guess it is.
Then it is settled!
You, Tad, shall become my knight!
You'll escort me across the marsh and back to space!
From now on, you'll be the most important Star Knight . . .
. . . the knight of the king!

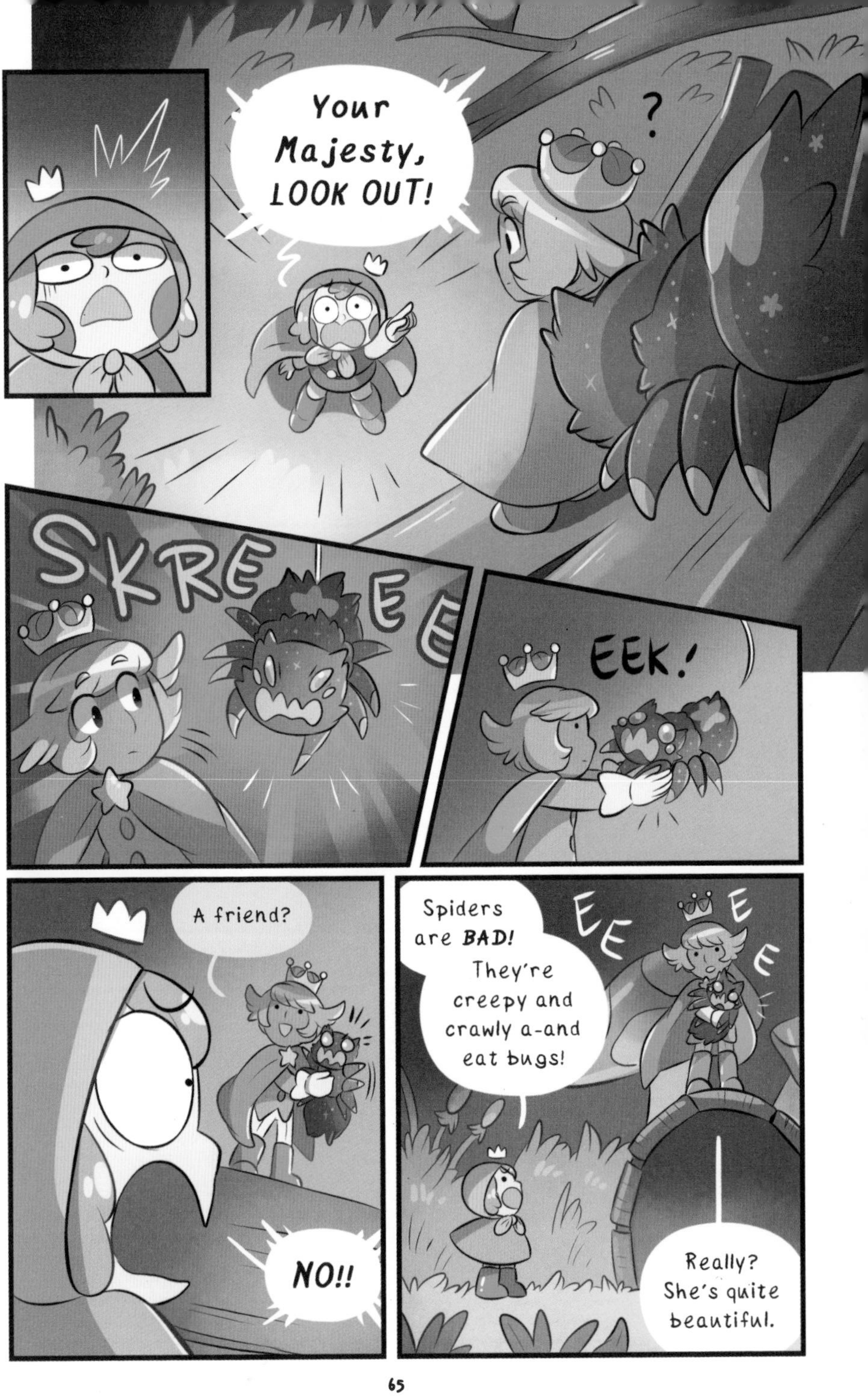
Your Majesty, LOOK OUT!
?
SKREEEE
EEK!
A friend?
NO!!
Spiders are BAD!
They're creepy and crawly a-and eat bugs!
EEE
Really? She's quite beautiful.

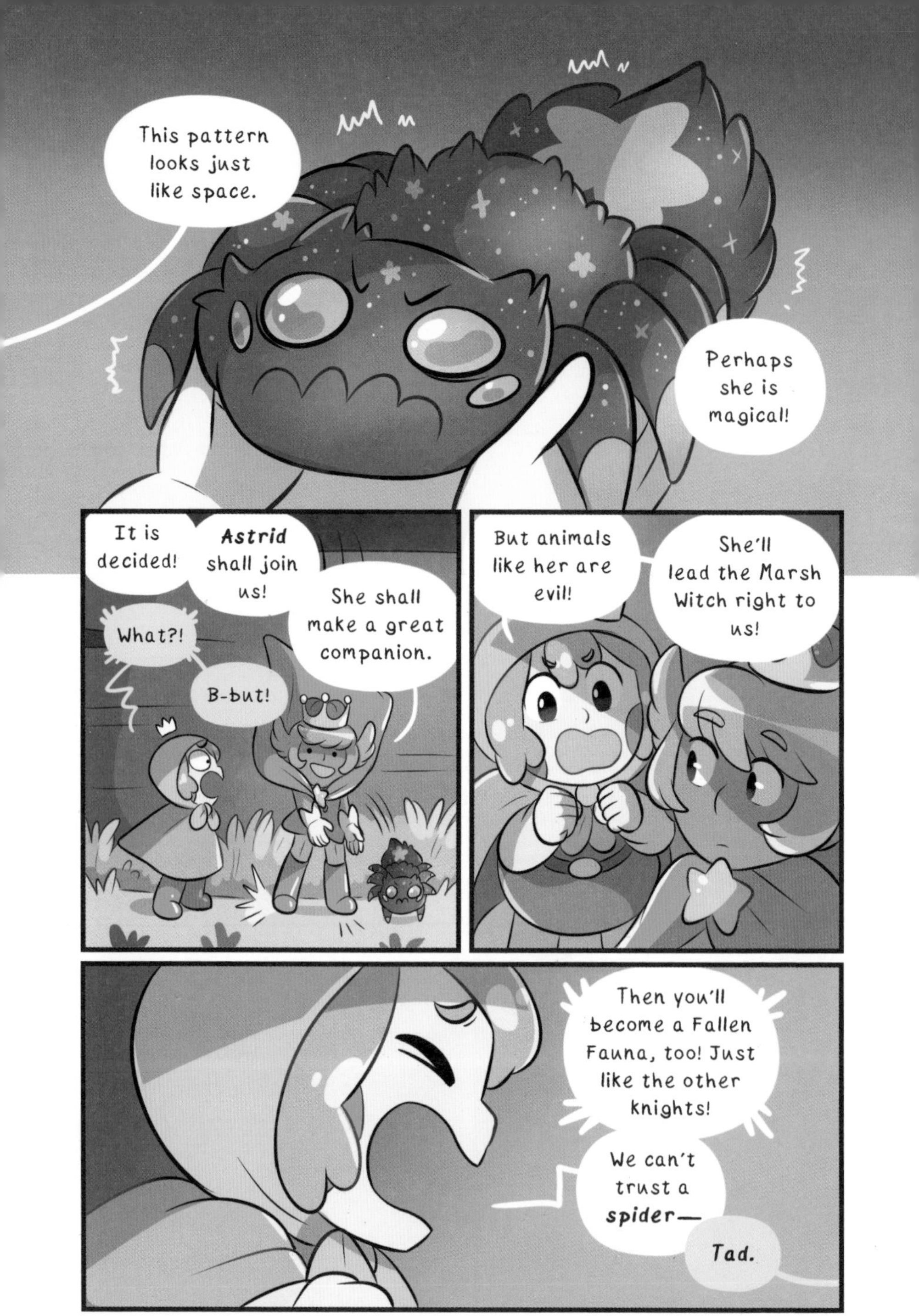
This pattern looks just like space.
Perhaps she is magical!
It is decided!
Astrid shall join us!
What?!
B-but!
She shall make a great companion.
But animals like her are evil!
She'll lead the Marsh Witch right to us!
Then you'll become a Fallen Fauna, too! Just like the other knights!
We can't trust a **spider**—
Tad.

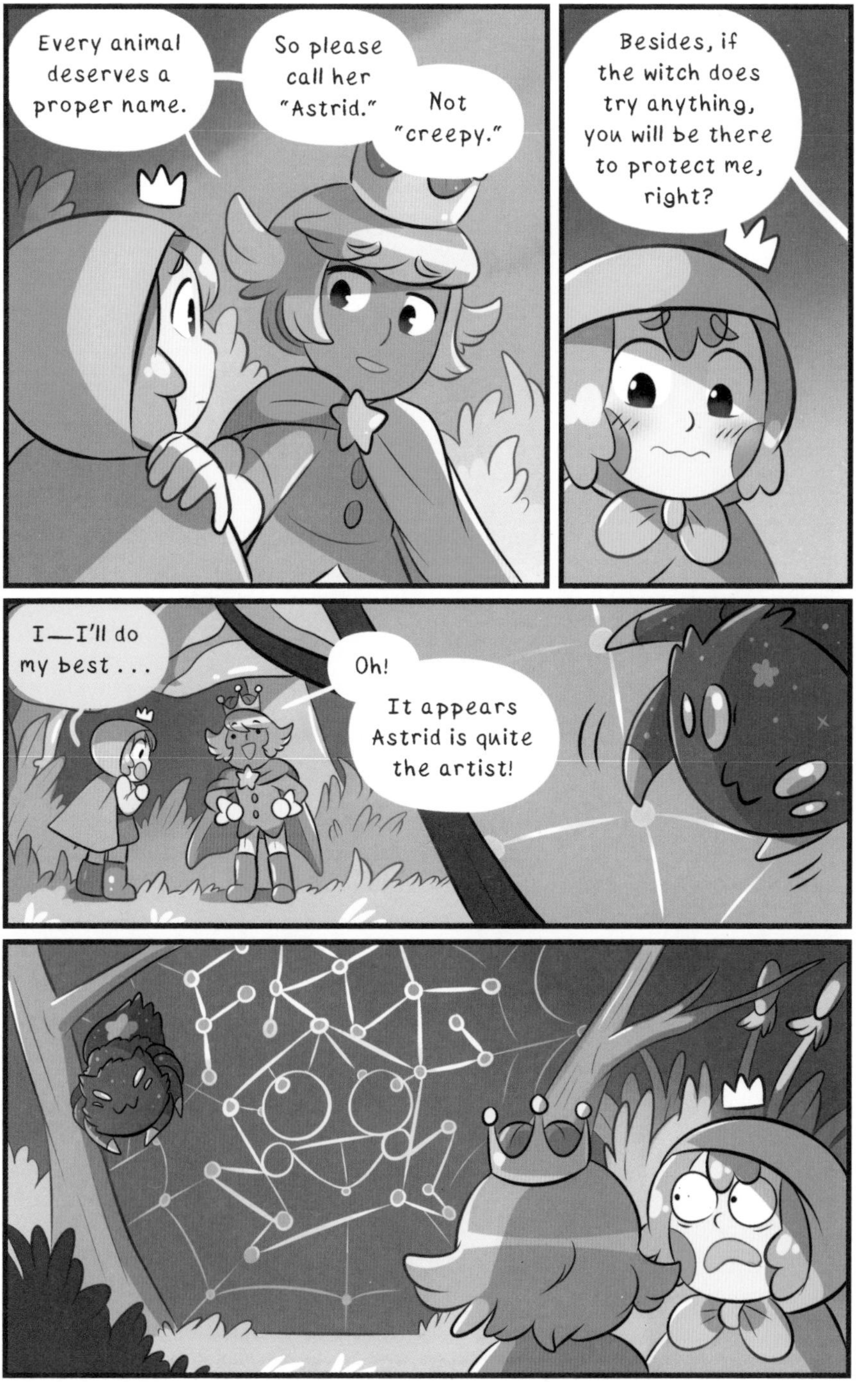
Every animal deserves a proper name.
So please call her "Astrid."
Not "creepy."
Besides, if the witch does try anything, you will be there to protect me, right?
I—I'll do my best . . .
Oh!
It appears Astrid is quite the artist!

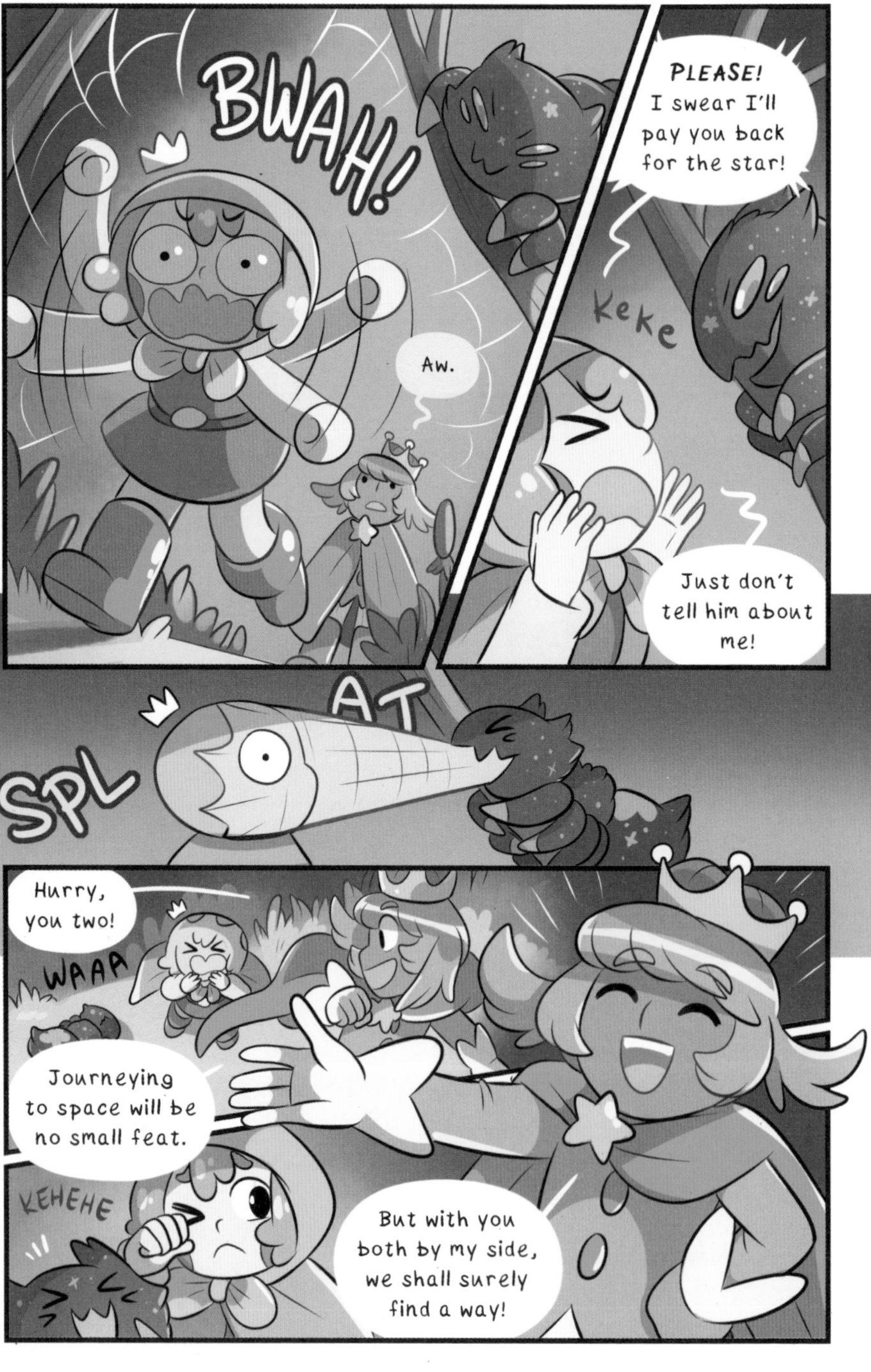
BWAH!
Aw.
PLEASE! I swear I'll pay you back for the star!
Keke
Just don't tell him about me!
SPL
AT
Hurry, you two!
WAAA
Journeying to space will be no small feat.
KEHEHE
But with you both by my side, we shall surely find a way!

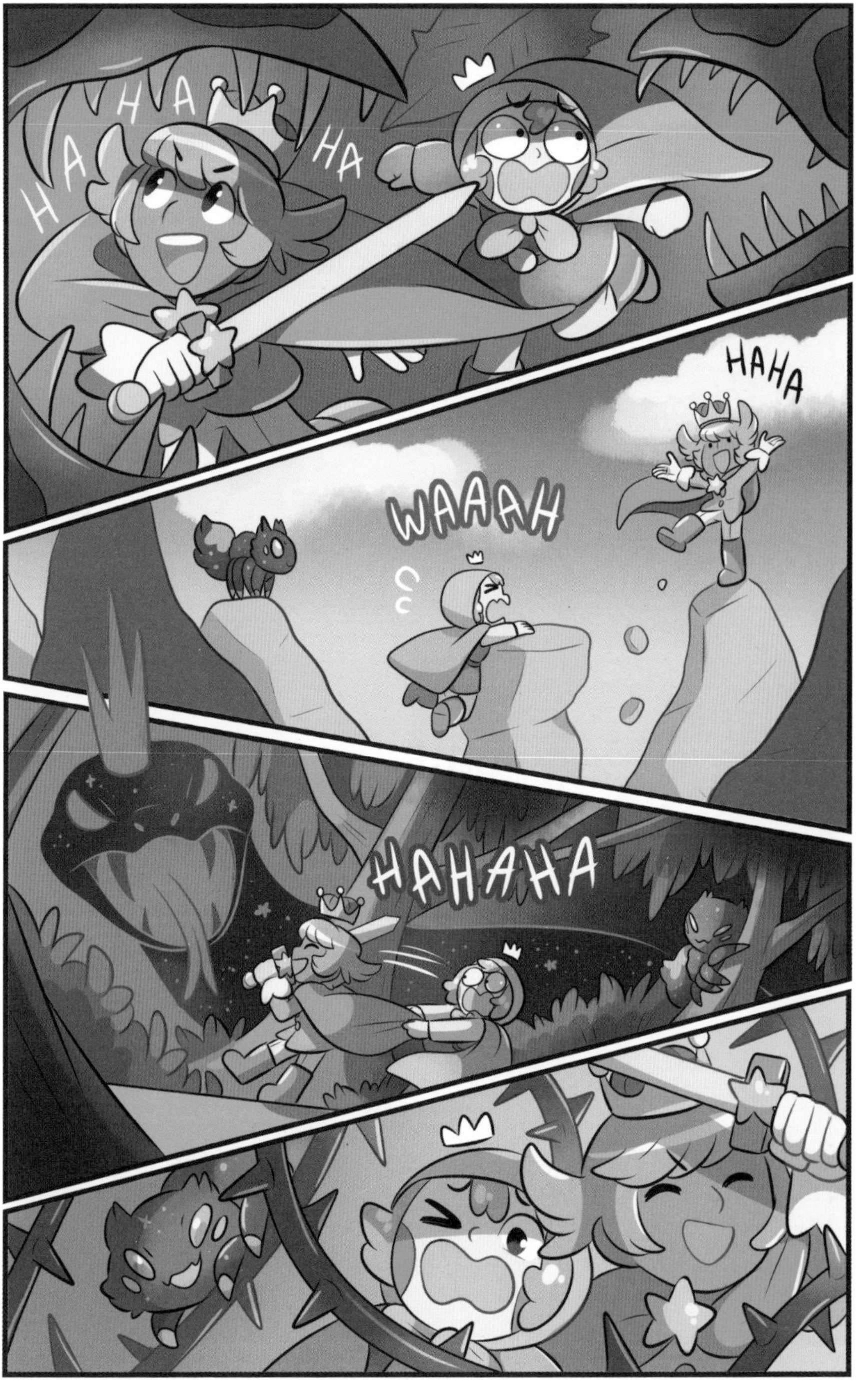
HA HA HA HA HA
HAHA
WAAAH
HAHAHA

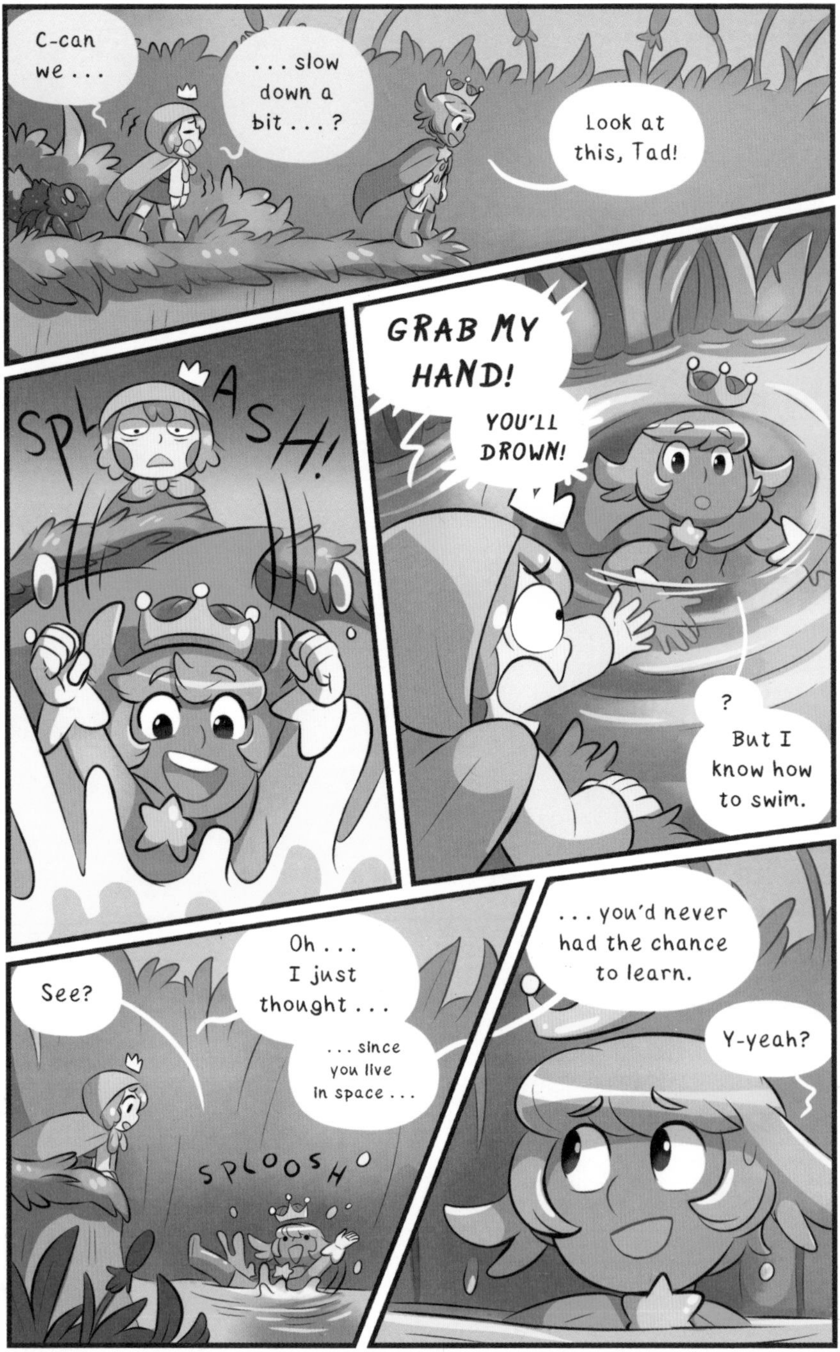
C-can we . . .
. . . slow down a bit . . . ?
Look at this, Tad!
SPLASH!
GRAB MY HAND!
YOU'LL DROWN!
?
But I know how to swim.
See?
SPLOOSH
Oh . . . I just thought . . .
. . . since you live in space . . .
. . . you'd never had the chance to learn.
Y-yeah?

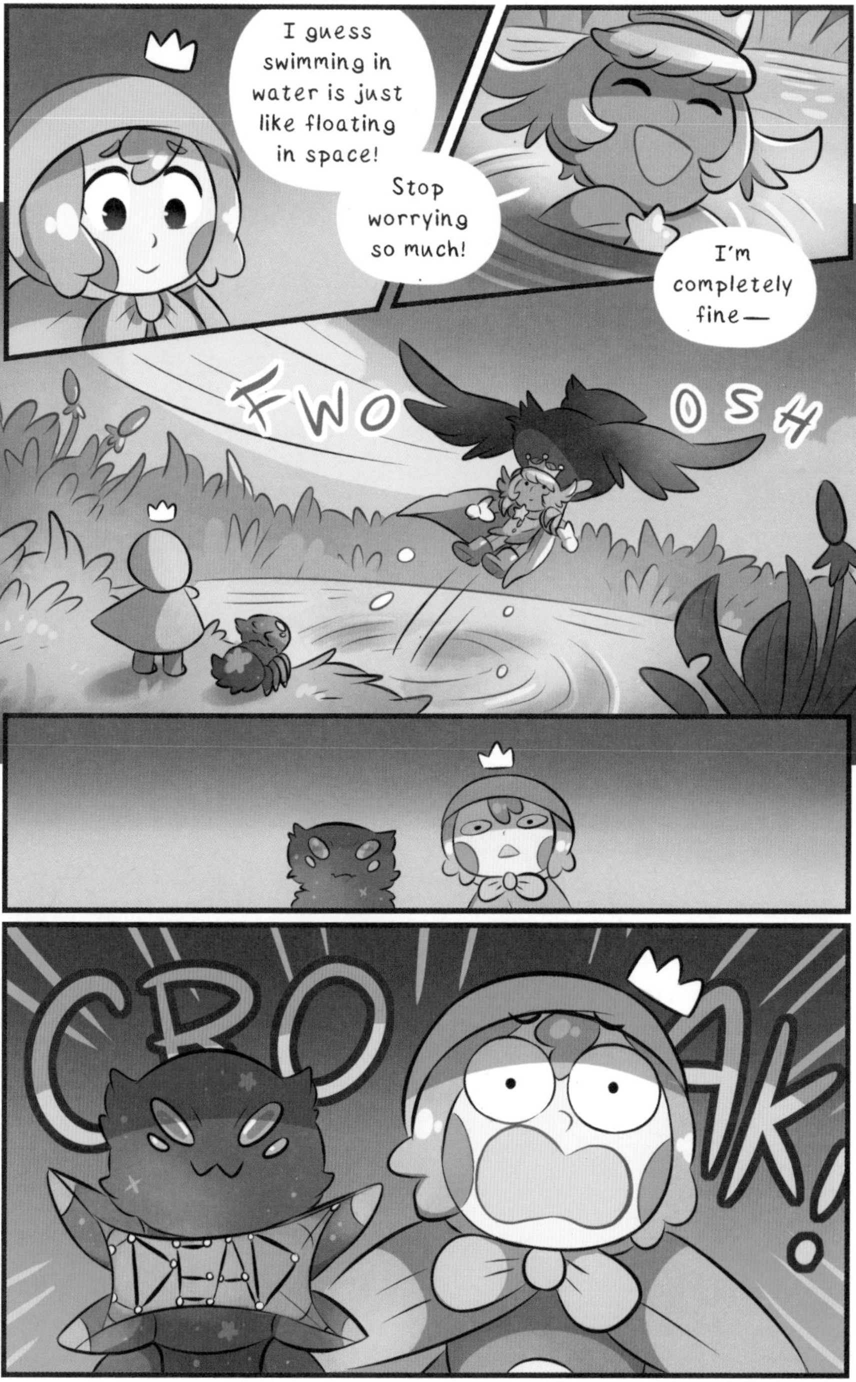

I guess swimming in water is just like floating in space!
Stop worrying so much!
I'm completely fine—
FWOOSH
CROAK!

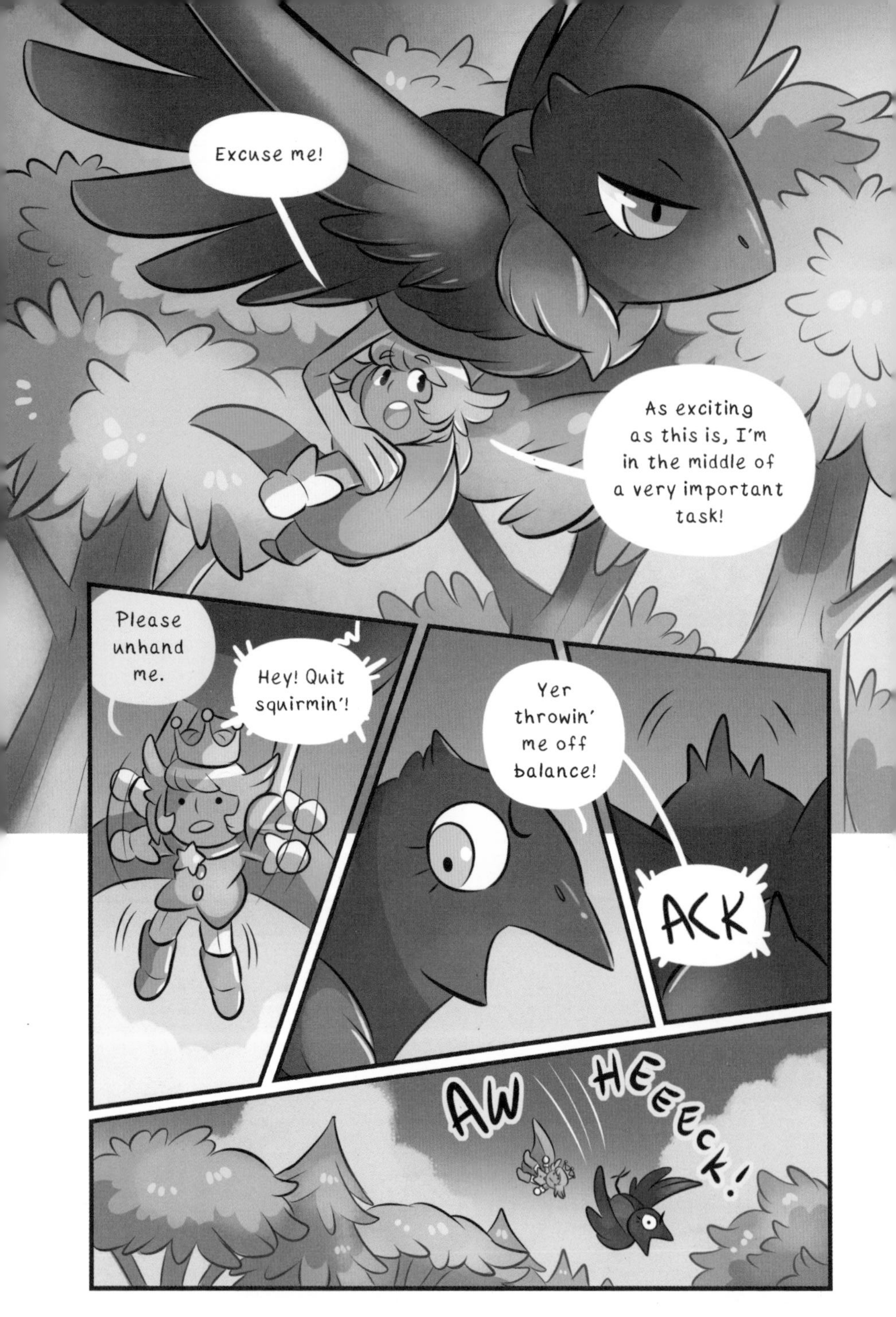
Excuse me!
As exciting as this is, I'm in the middle of a very important task!
Please unhand me.
Hey! Quit squirmin'!
Yer throwin' me off balance!
ACK
AW HEEECK!

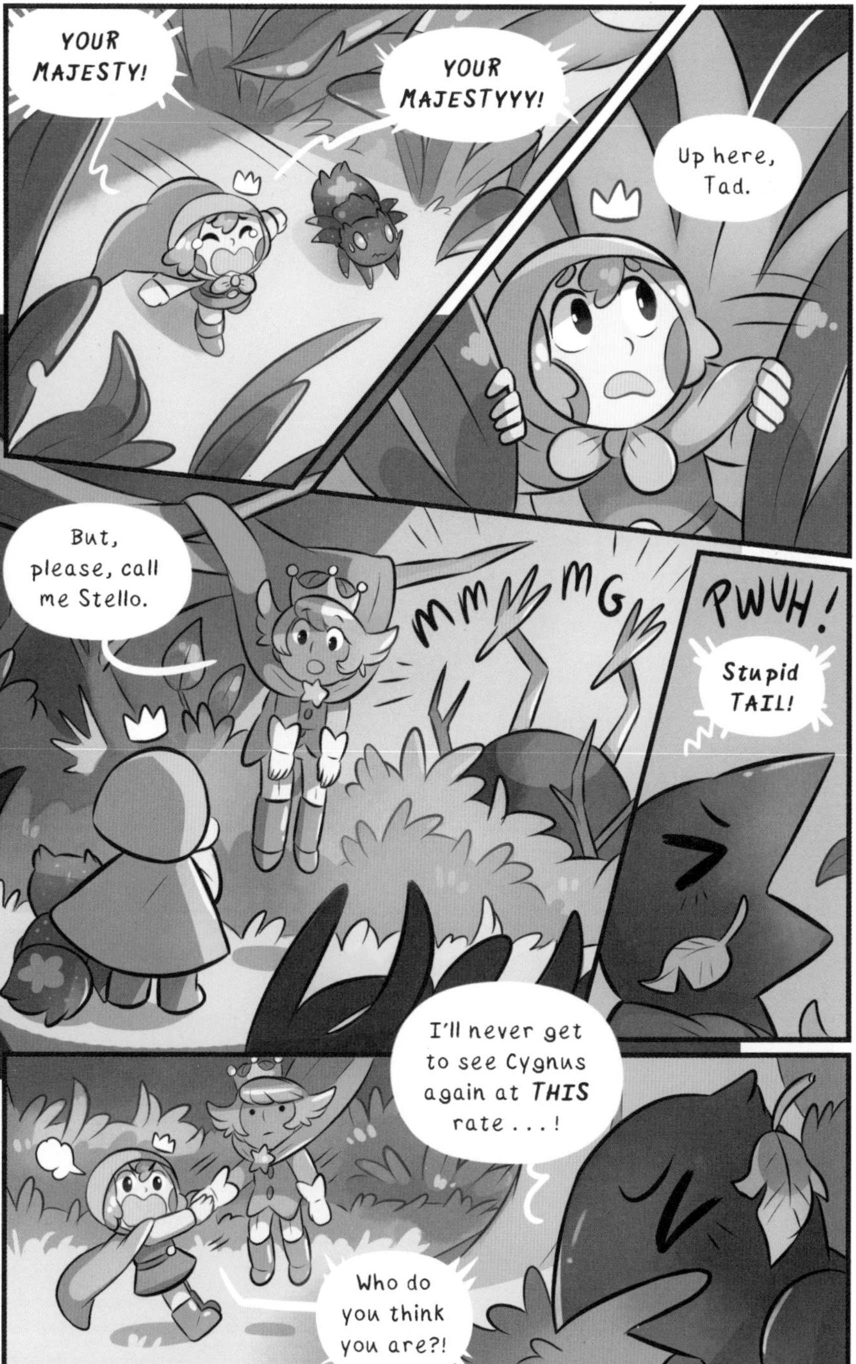
YOUR MAJESTY!
YOUR MAJESTYYY!
Up here, Tad.
But, please, call me Stello.
MMMMG
PWUH!
Stupid TAIL!
I'll never get to see Cygnus again at THIS rate . . . !
Who do you think you are?!

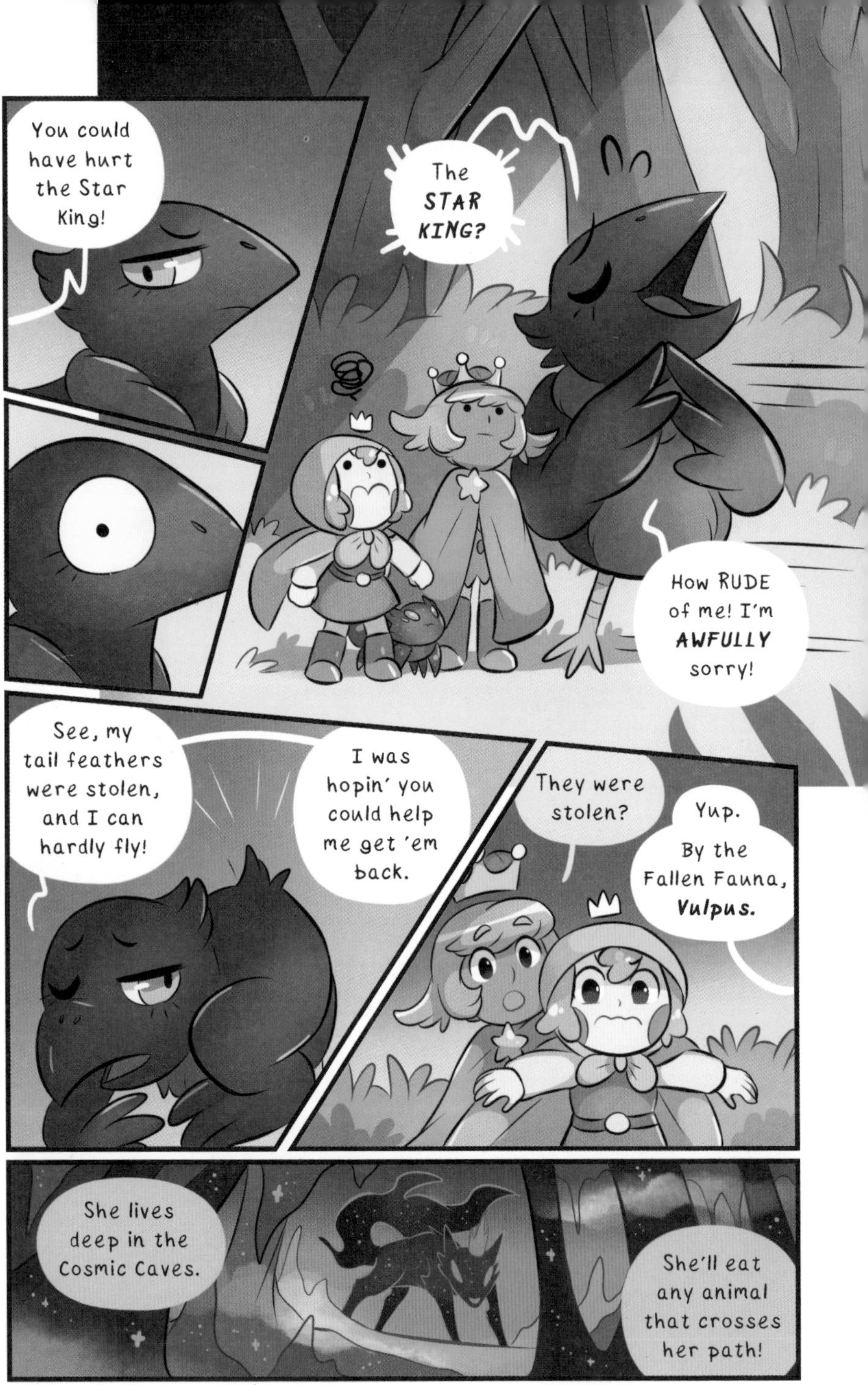
You could have hurt the Star King!
The STAR KING?
How RUDE of me! I'm AWFULLY sorry!
See, my tail feathers were stolen, and I can hardly fly!
I was hopin' you could help me get 'em back.
They were stolen?
Yup.
By the Fallen Fauna, Vulpus.
She lives deep in the Cosmic Caves.
She'll eat any animal that crosses her path!

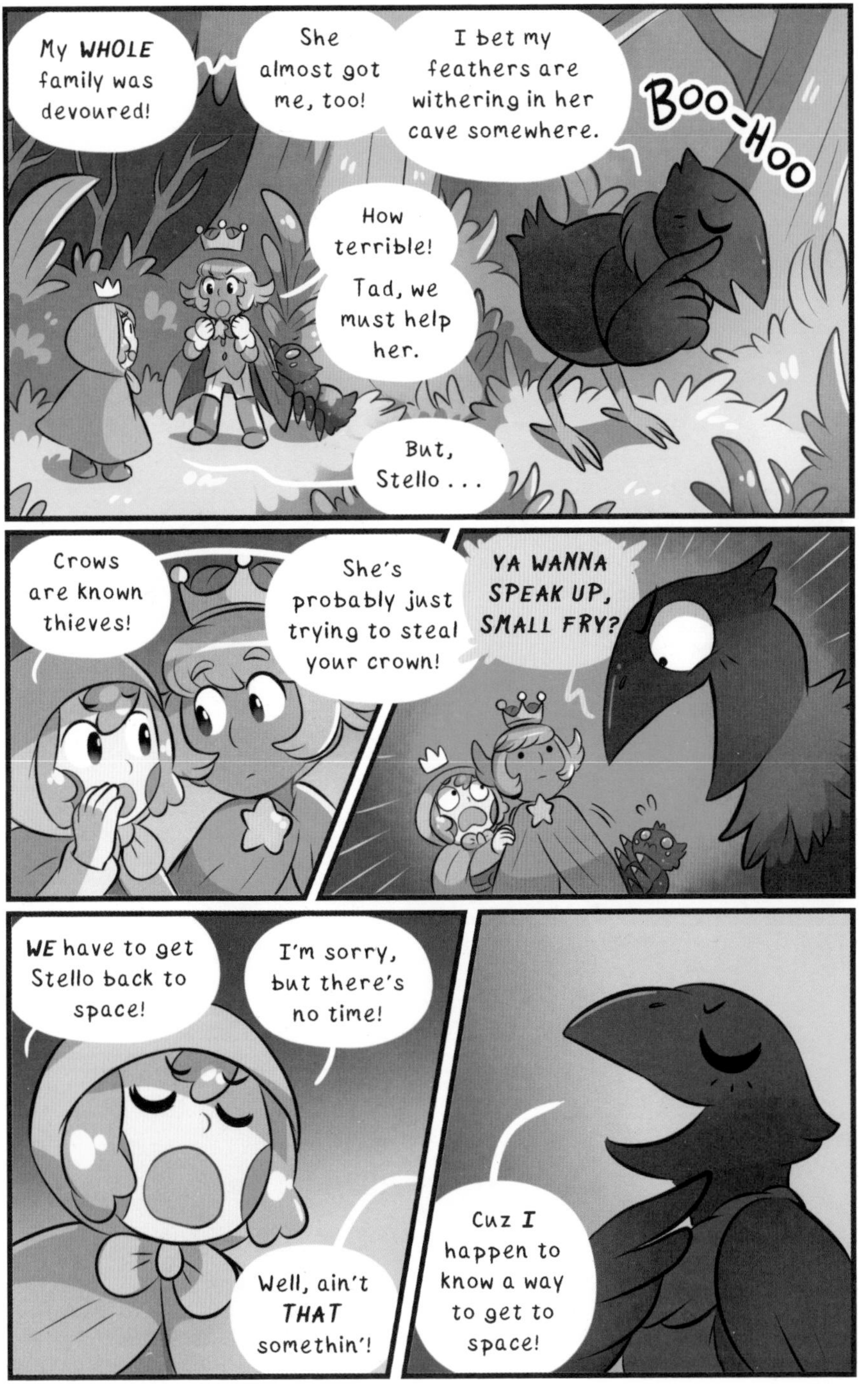
My WHOLE family was devoured!
She almost got me, too!
I bet my feathers are withering in her cave somewhere.
BOO-HOO
How terrible!
Tad, we must help her.
But, Stello . . .
Crows are known thieves!
She's probably just trying to steal your crown!
YA WANNA SPEAK UP, SMALL FRY?
WE have to get Stello back to space!
I'm sorry, but there's no time!
Well, ain't THAT somethin'!
Cuz I happen to know a way to get to space!

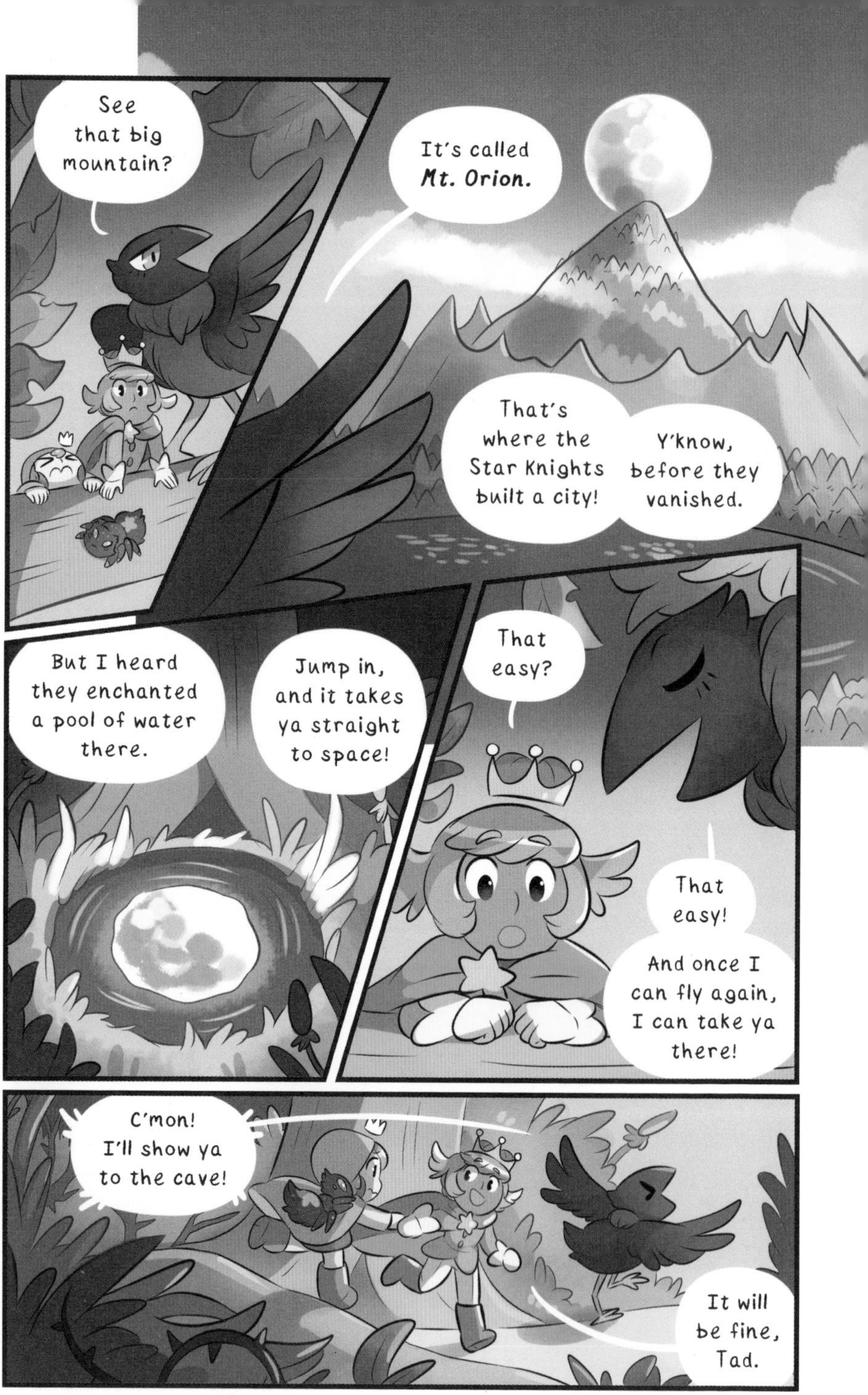

See that big mountain?
It's called **Mt. Orion.**
That's where the Star Knights built a city!
Y'know, before they vanished.
But I heard they enchanted a pool of water there.
Jump in, and it takes ya straight to space!
That easy?
That easy!
And once I can fly again, I can take ya there!
C'mon! I'll show ya to the cave!
It will be fine, Tad.

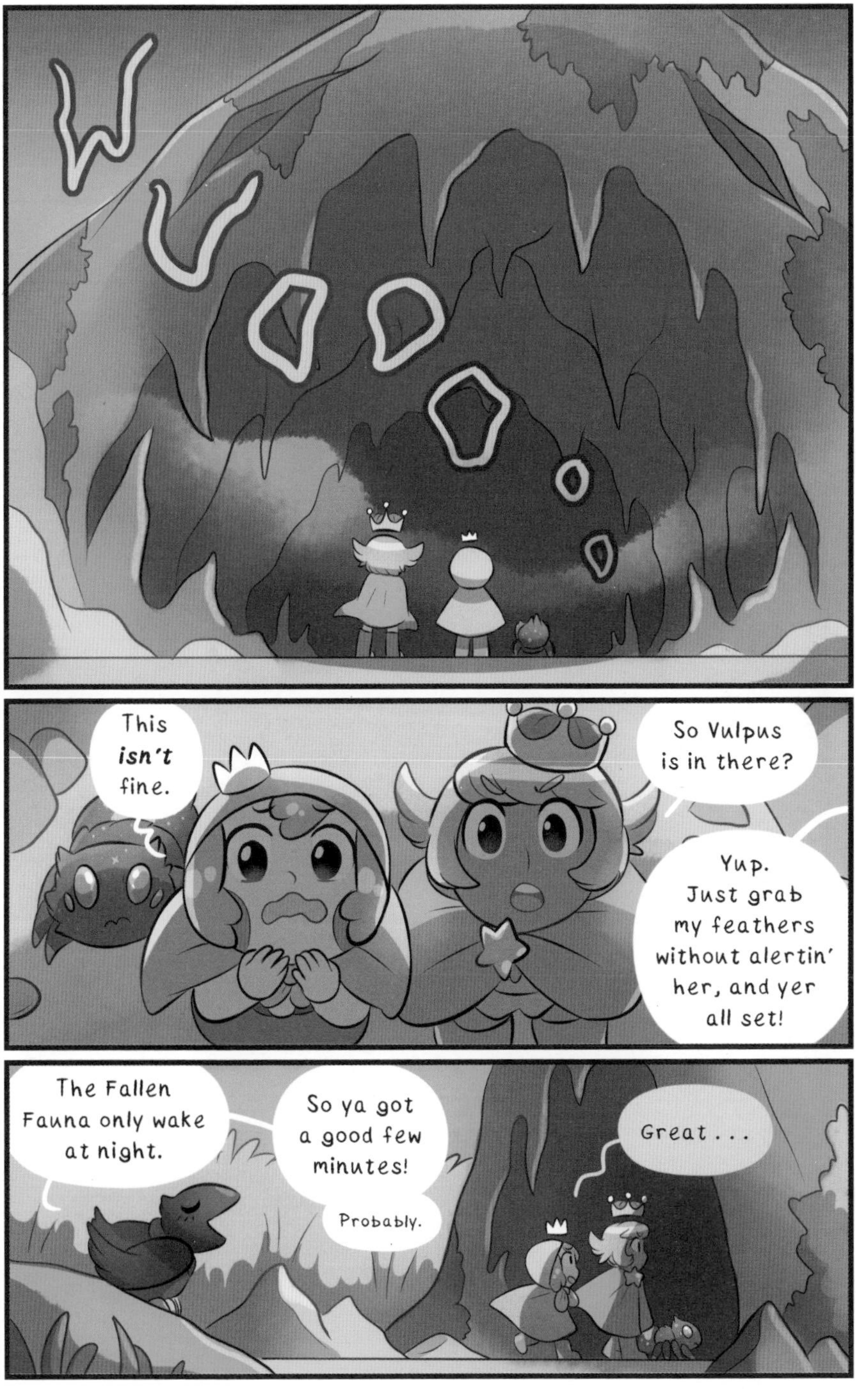
WUOOOOO
This *isn't* fine.
So Vulpus is in there?
Yup. Just grab my feathers without alertin' her, and yer all set!
The Fallen Fauna only wake at night.
So ya got a good few minutes!
Probably.
Great . . .

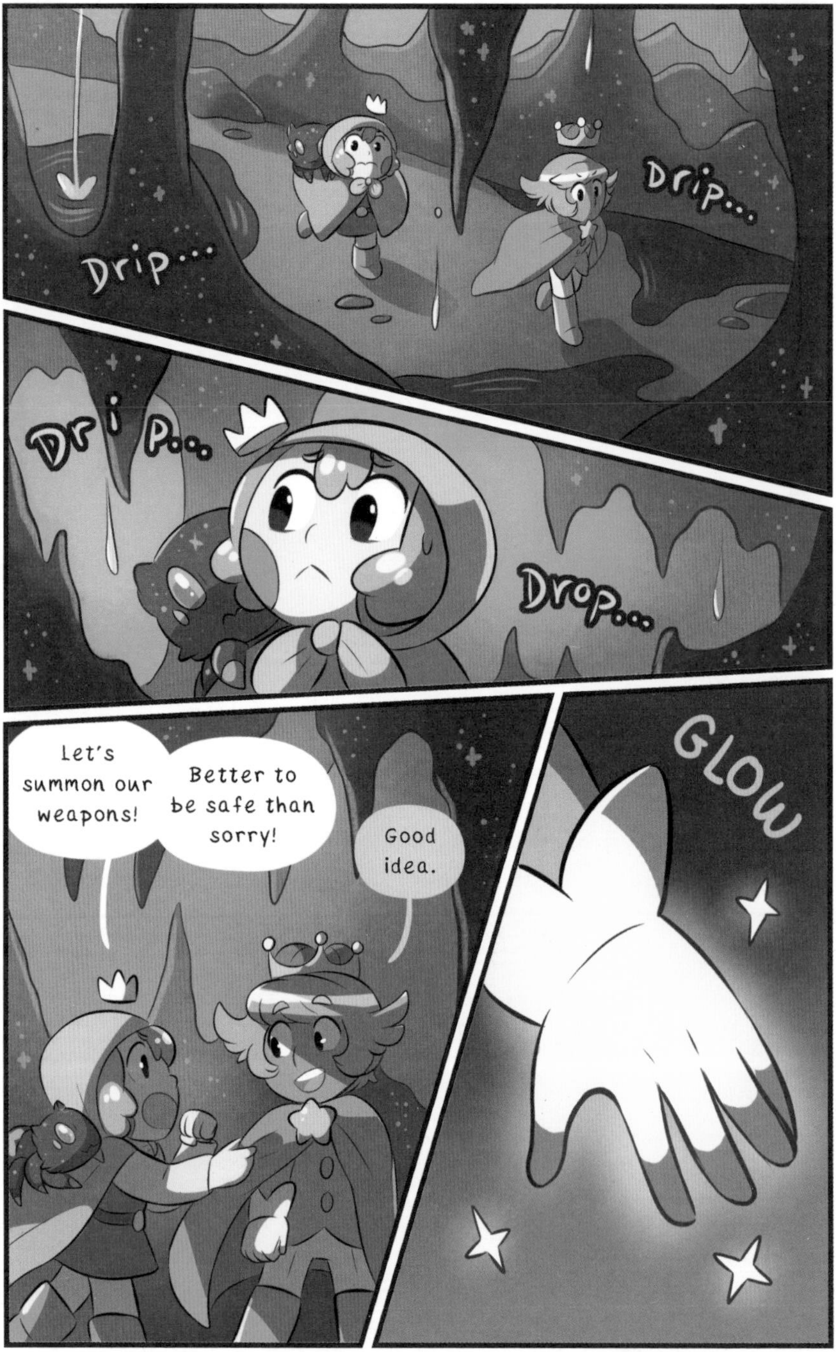
Drip...
Drip...
Dri p...
Drop...
Let's summon our weapons!
Better to be safe than sorry!
Good idea.
GLOW

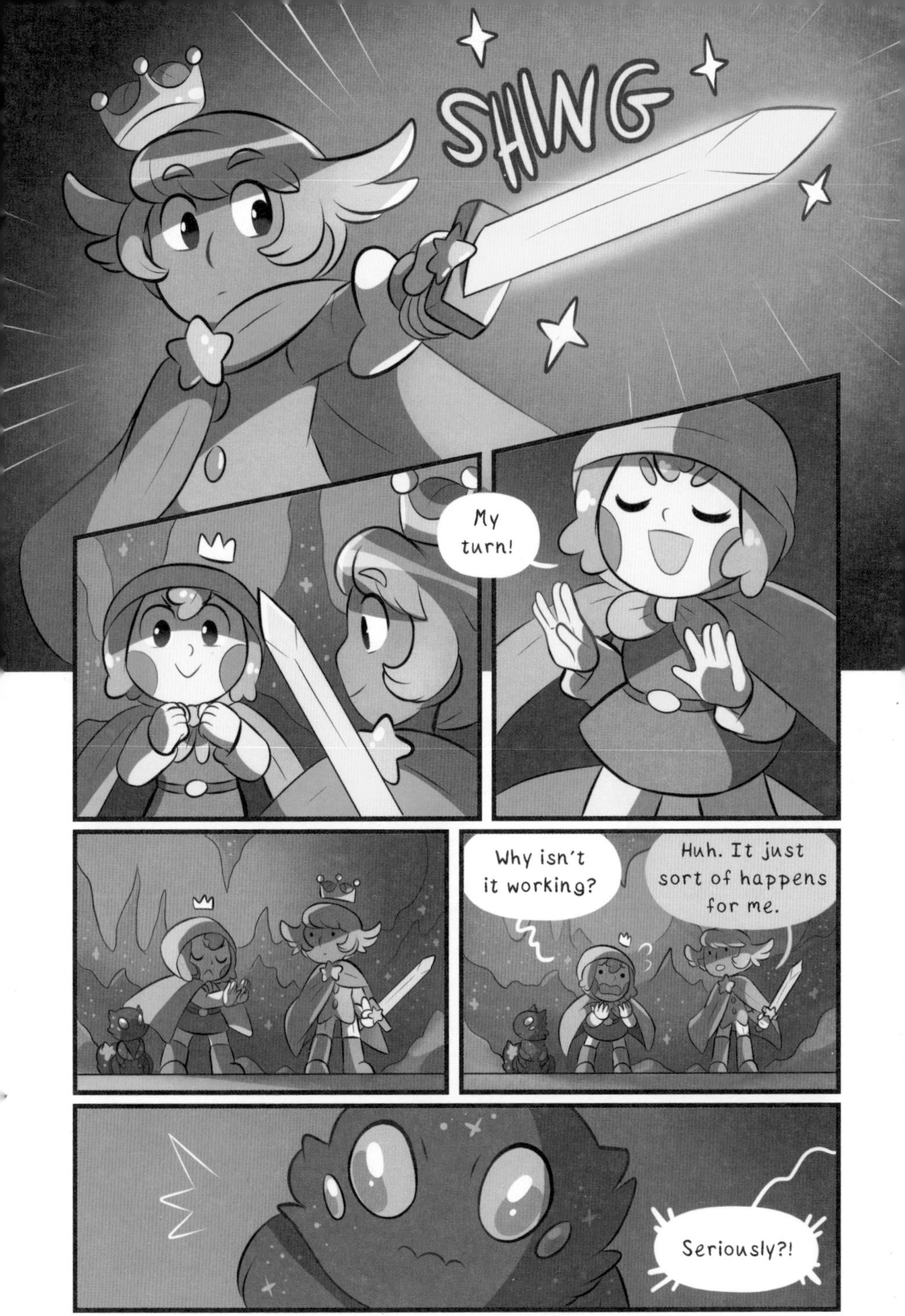
SHING
My turn!
Why isn't it working?
Huh. It just sort of happens for me.
Seriously?!

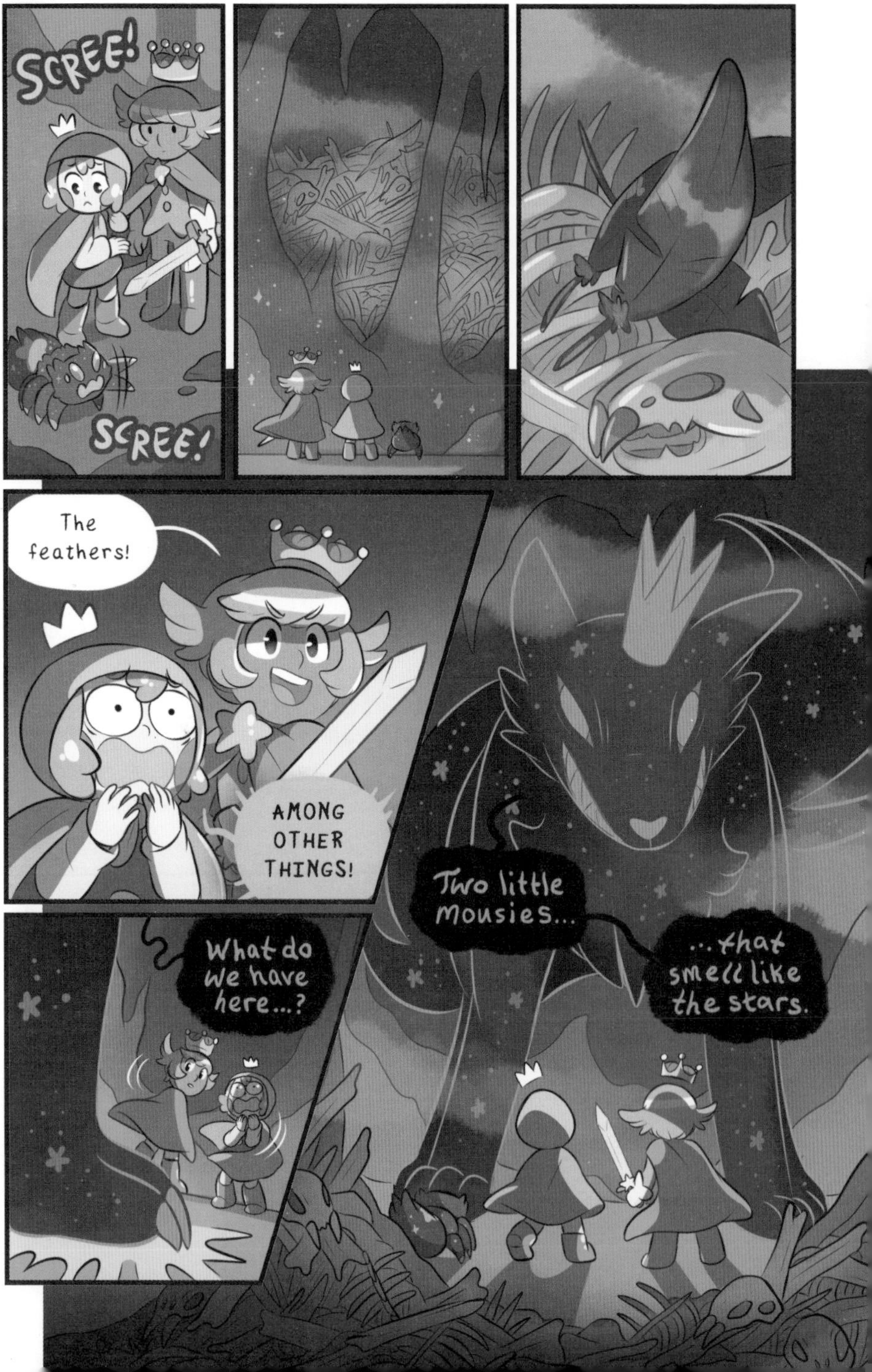
SCREE!
SCREE!
The feathers!
AMONG OTHER THINGS!
What do we have here...?
Two little mousies...
...that smell like the stars.

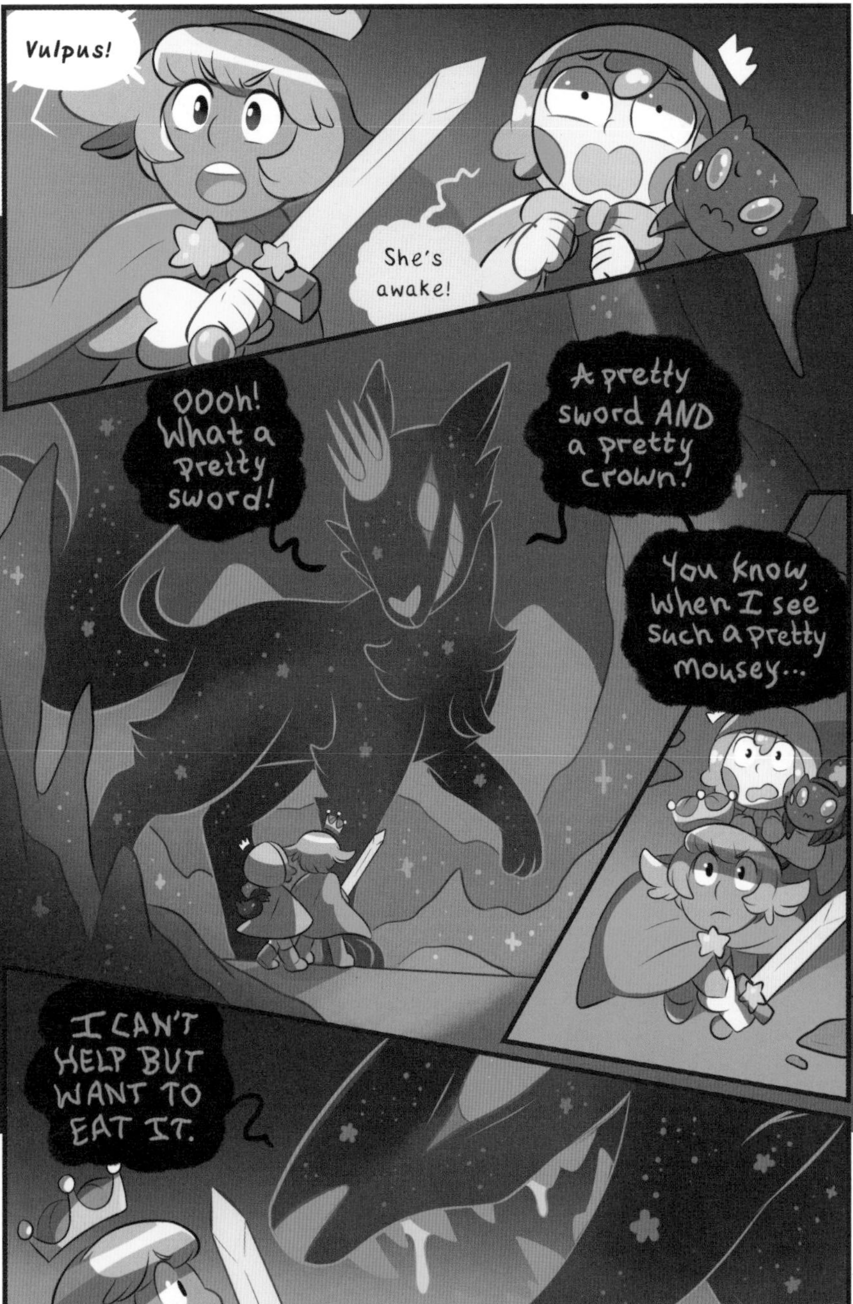
Vulpus!
She's awake!
OOOh! What a pretty sword!
A pretty sword AND a pretty crown!
You know, when I see such a pretty mousey...
I CAN'T HELP BUT WANT TO EAT IT.

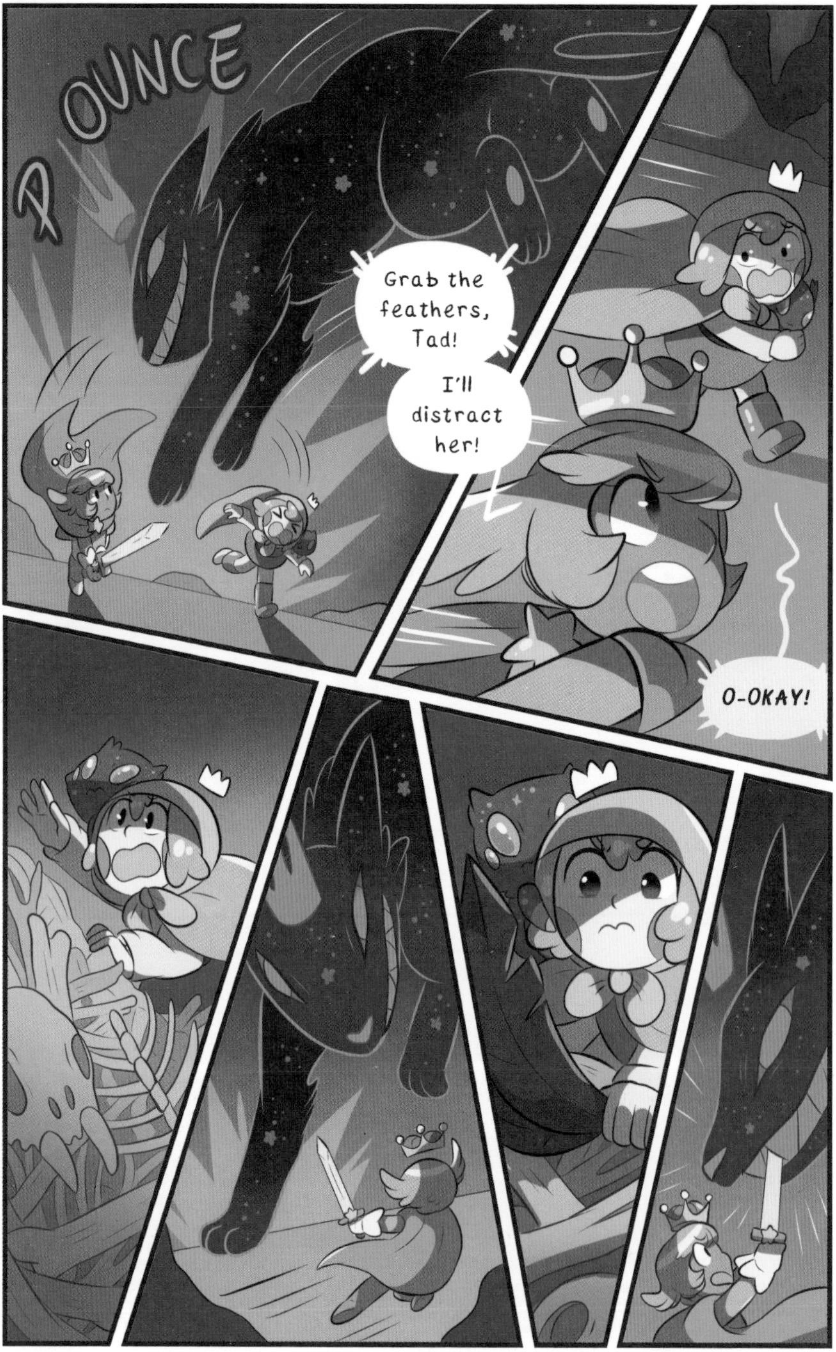
POUNCE
Grab the feathers, Tad!
I'll distract her!
O-OKAY!

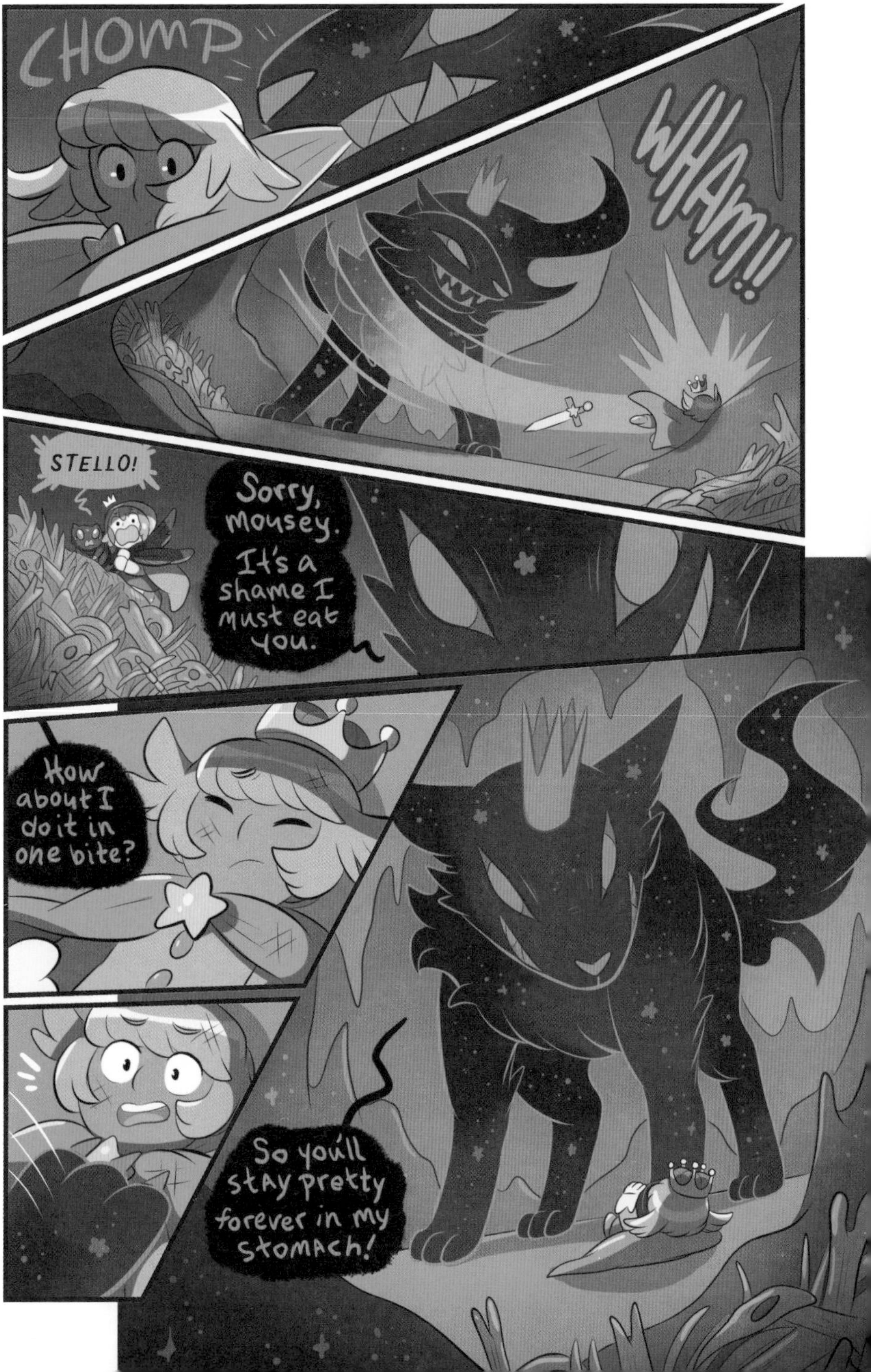
CHOMP
WHAM!!
STELLO!
Sorry, mousey.
It's a shame I must eat you.
How about I do it in one bite?
So you'll stay pretty forever in my stomach!

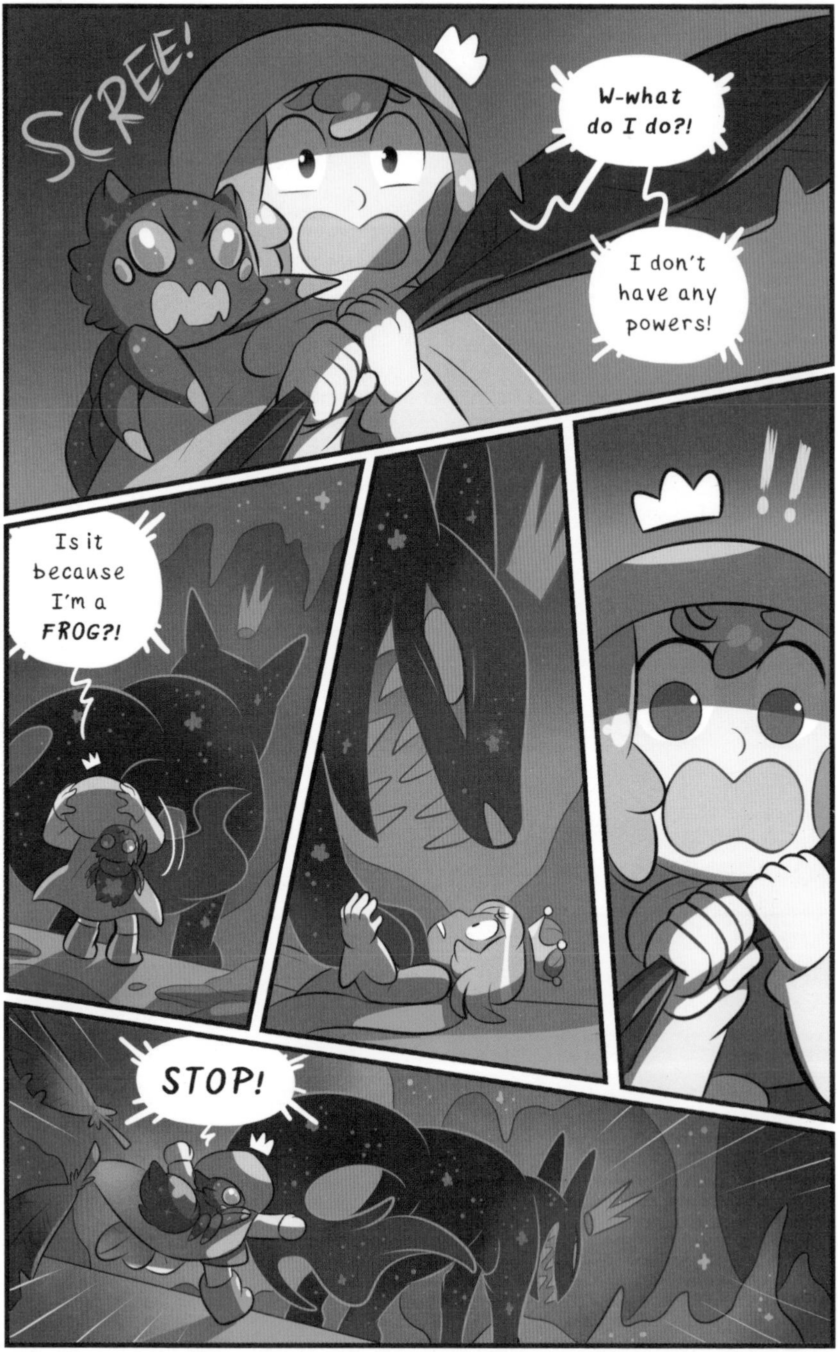
SCREE!
W-what do I do?!
I don't have any powers!
Is it because I'm a FROG?!
!!
STOP!

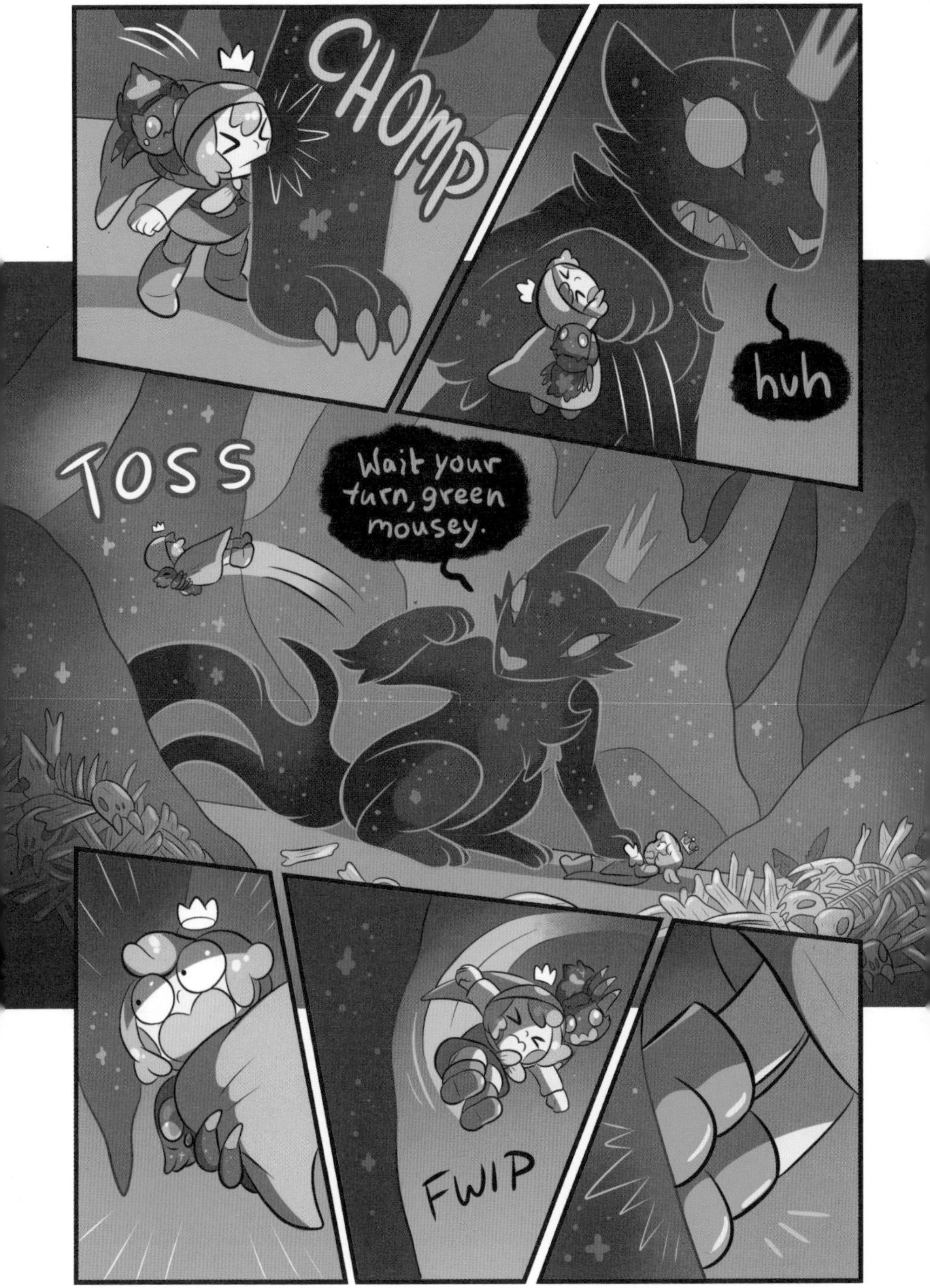
CHOMP
huh
TOSS
Wait your turn, green mousey.
FWIP

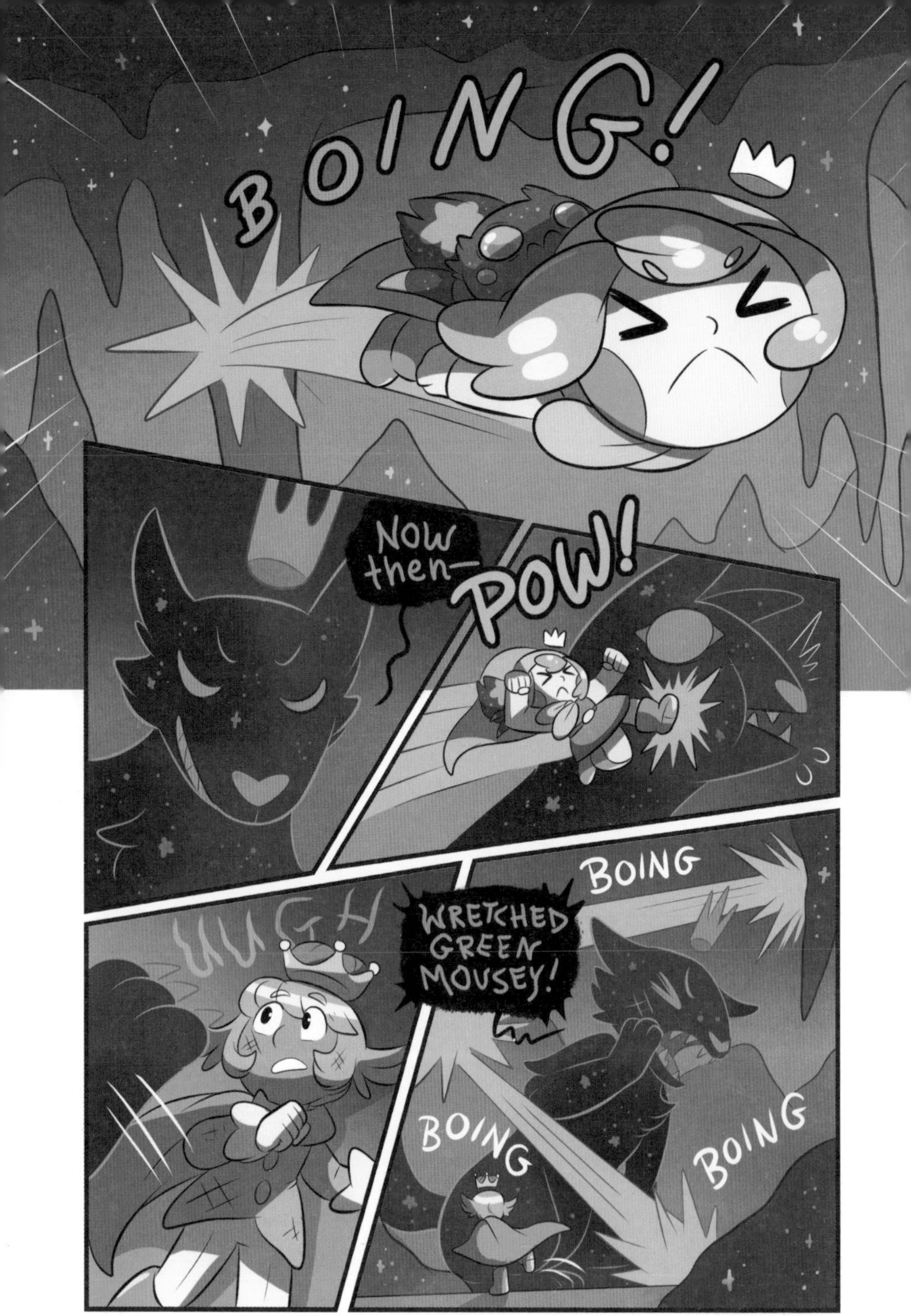
BOING!
Now then—
POW!
BOING
UUGH
WRETCHED GREEN MOUSEY!
BOING
BOING

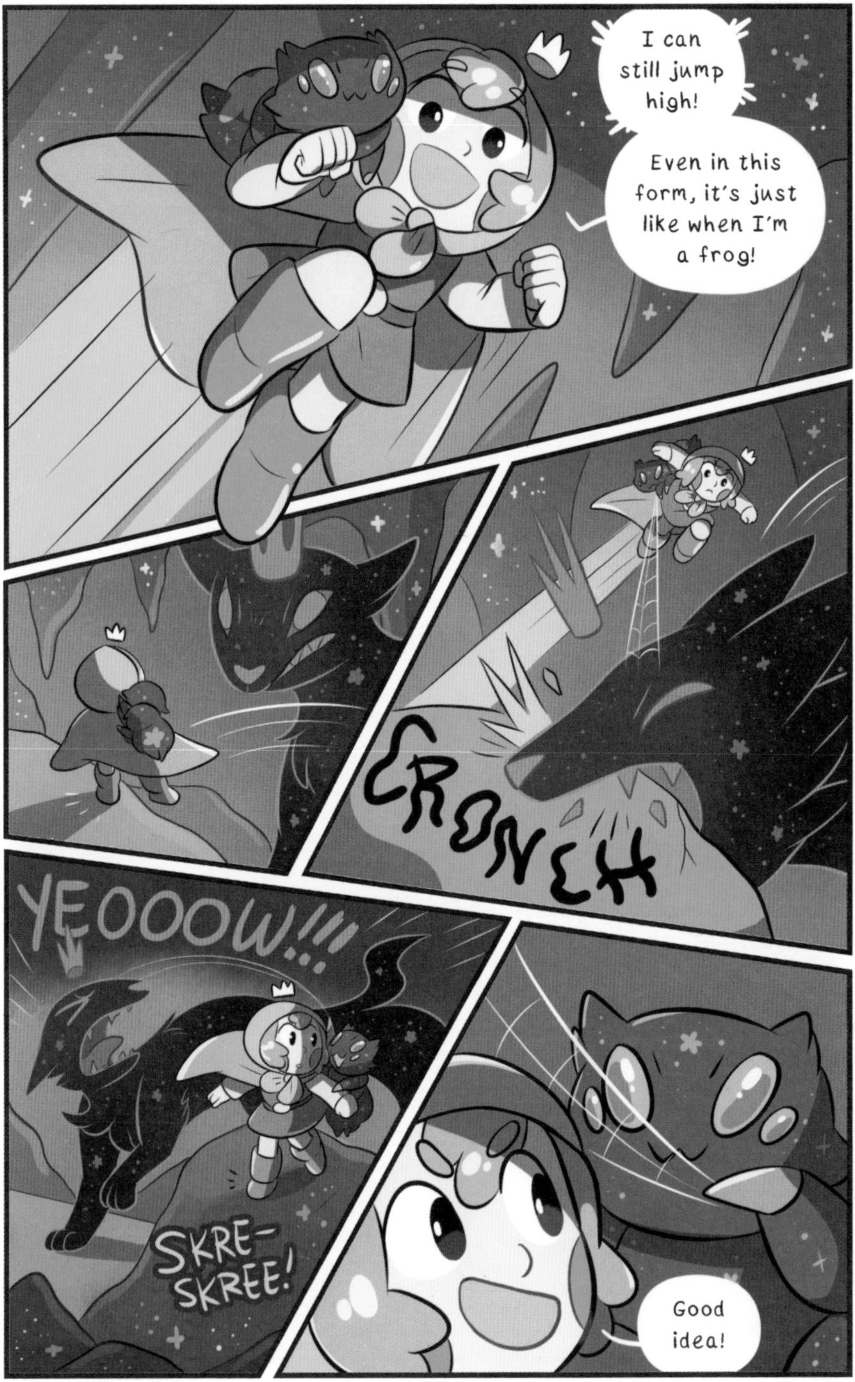
I can still jump high!
Even in this form, it's just like when I'm a frog!
CRONCH
YEOOOW!!!
SKRE-SKREE!
Good idea!

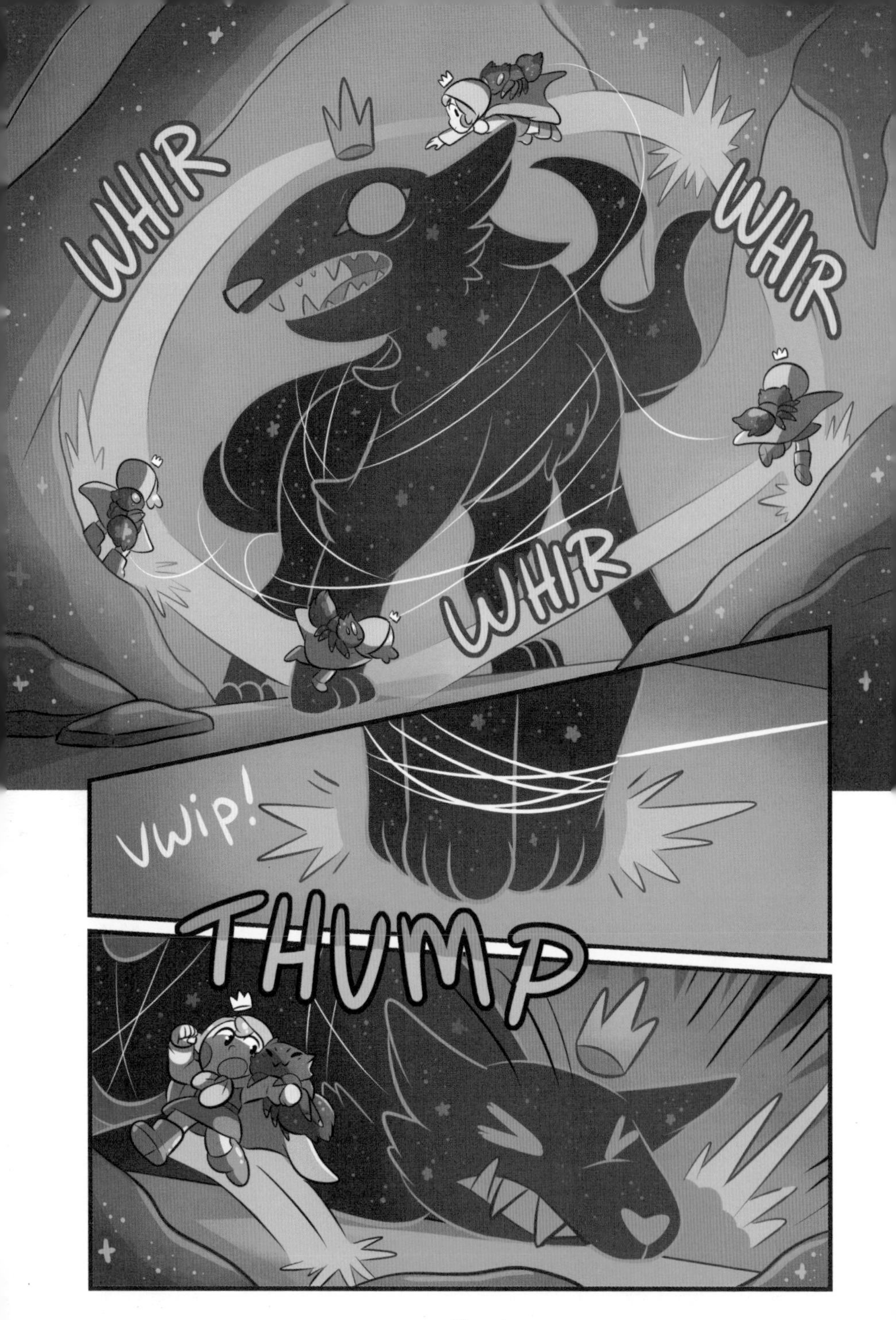
WHIR
WHIR
WHIR
VWIP!
THUMP

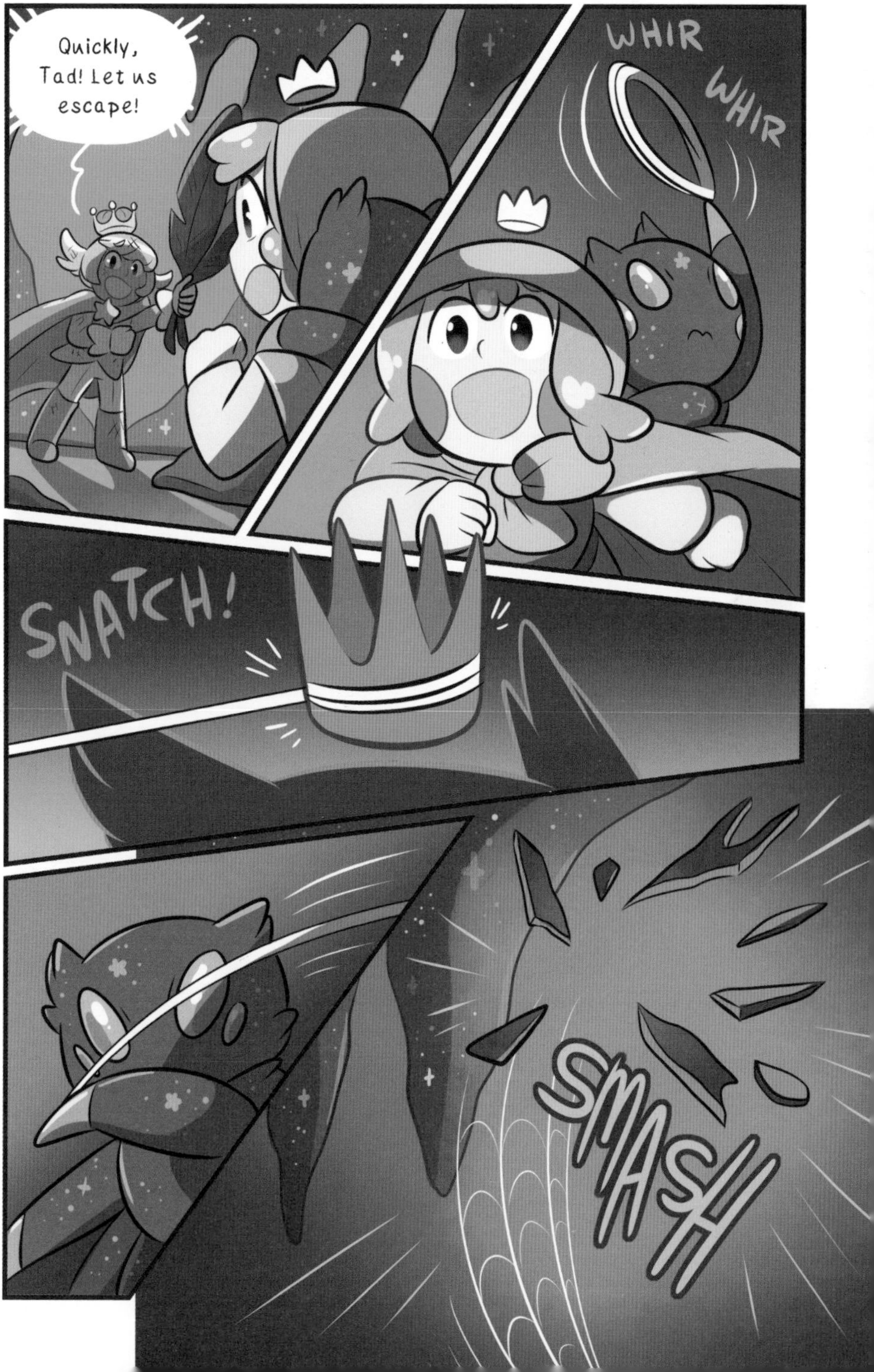
Quickly, Tad! Let us escape!
WHIR
WHIR
WHIR
SNATCH!
SMASH

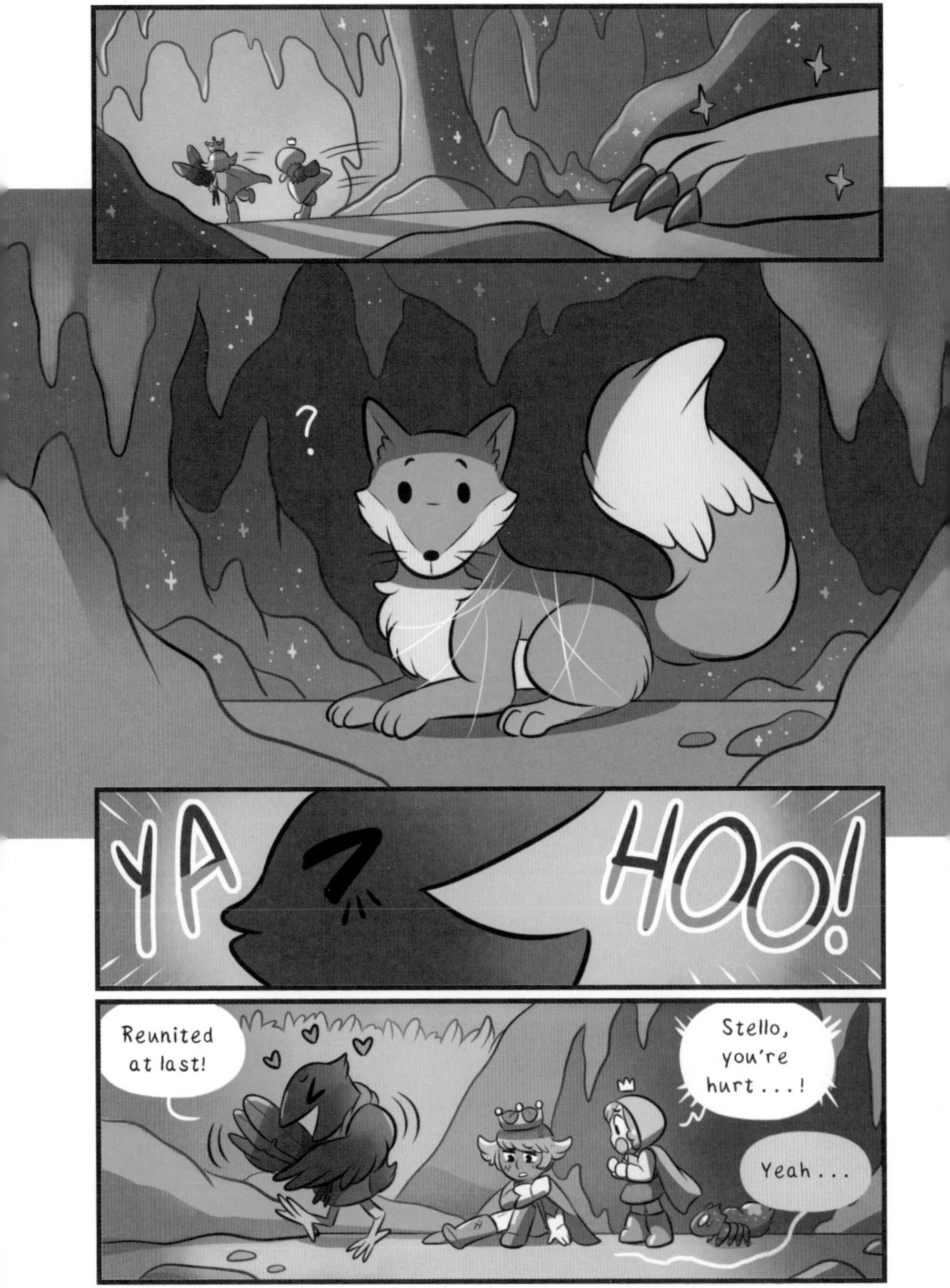
?
YA
HOO!
Reunited at last!
Stello, you're hurt . . . !
Yeah . . .

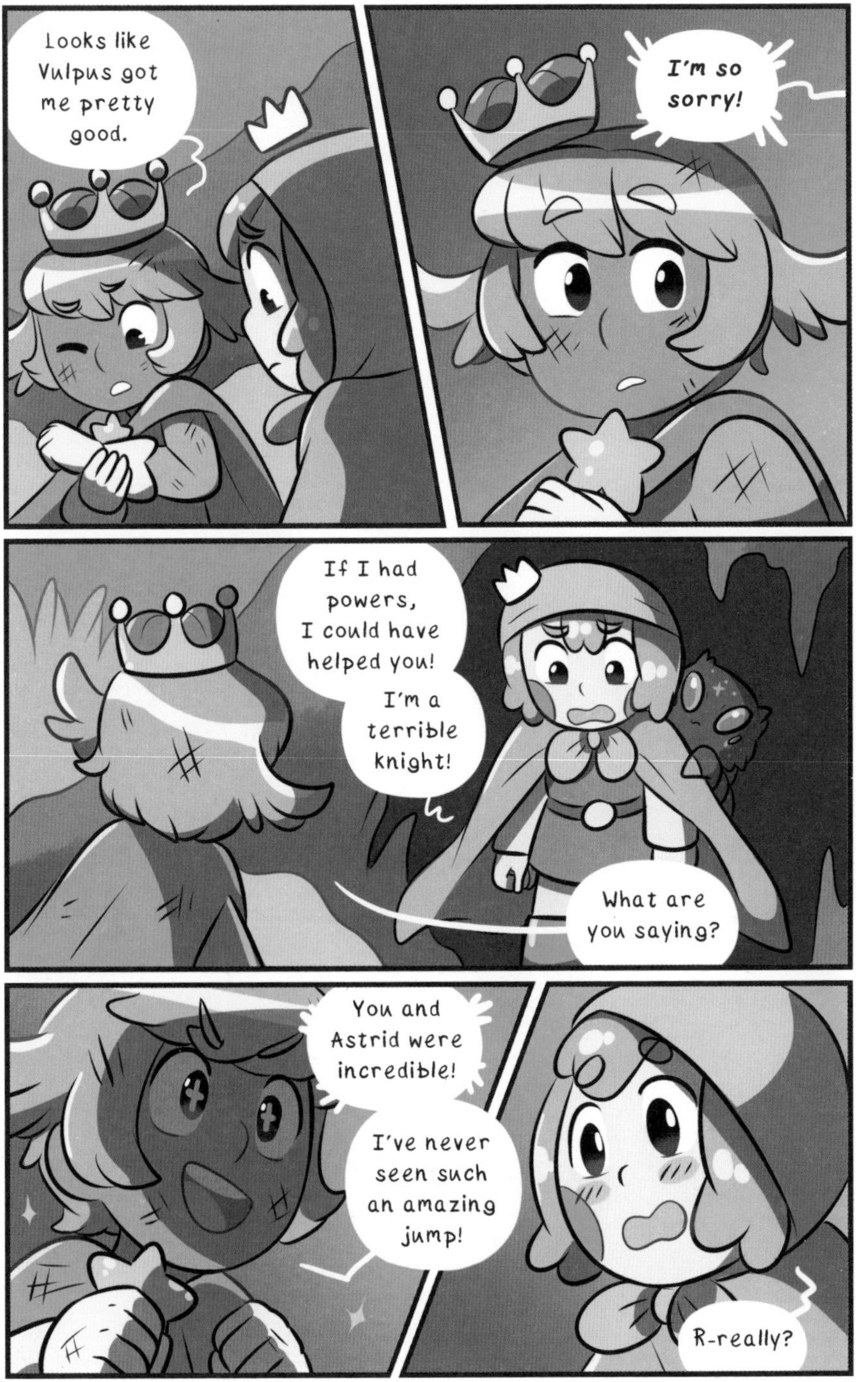
Looks like Vulpus got me pretty good.
I'm so sorry!
If I had powers, I could have helped you!
I'm a terrible knight!
What are you saying?
You and Astrid were incredible!
I've never seen such an amazing jump!
R-really?

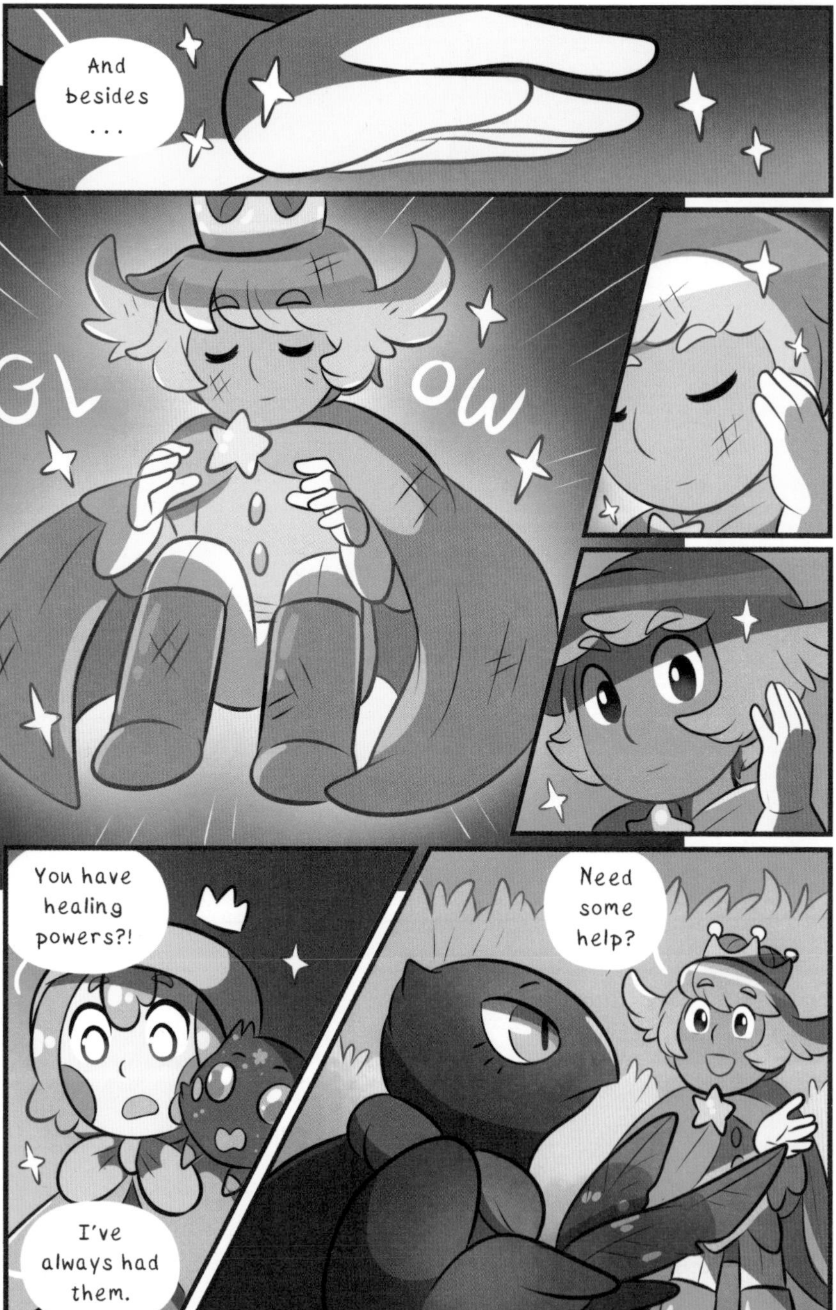
And besides . . .
GL
OW
You have healing powers?!
I've always had them.
Need some help?

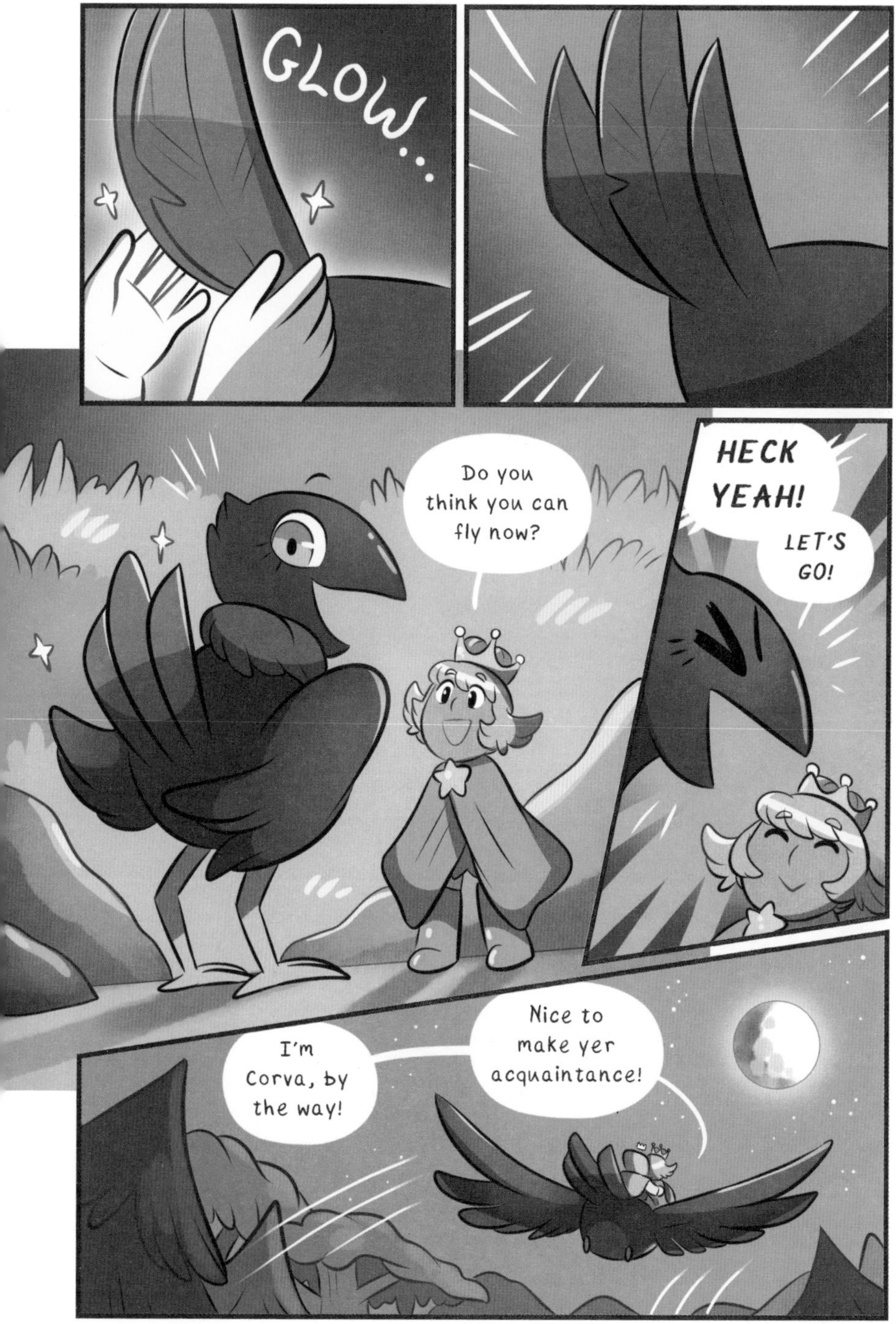
GLOW...
Do you think you can fly now?
HECK YEAH!
LET'S GO!
I'm Corva, by the way!
Nice to make yer acquaintance!

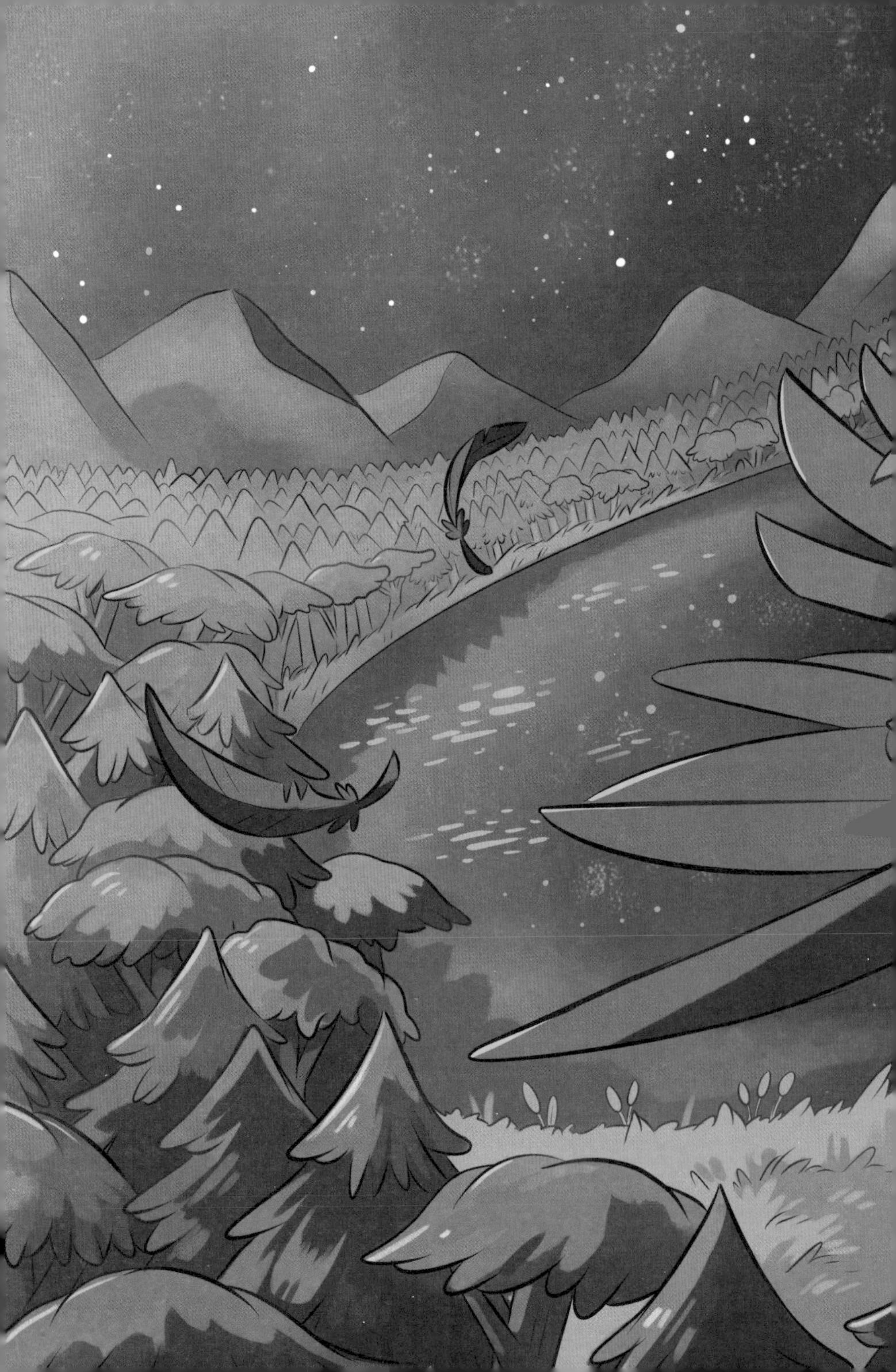

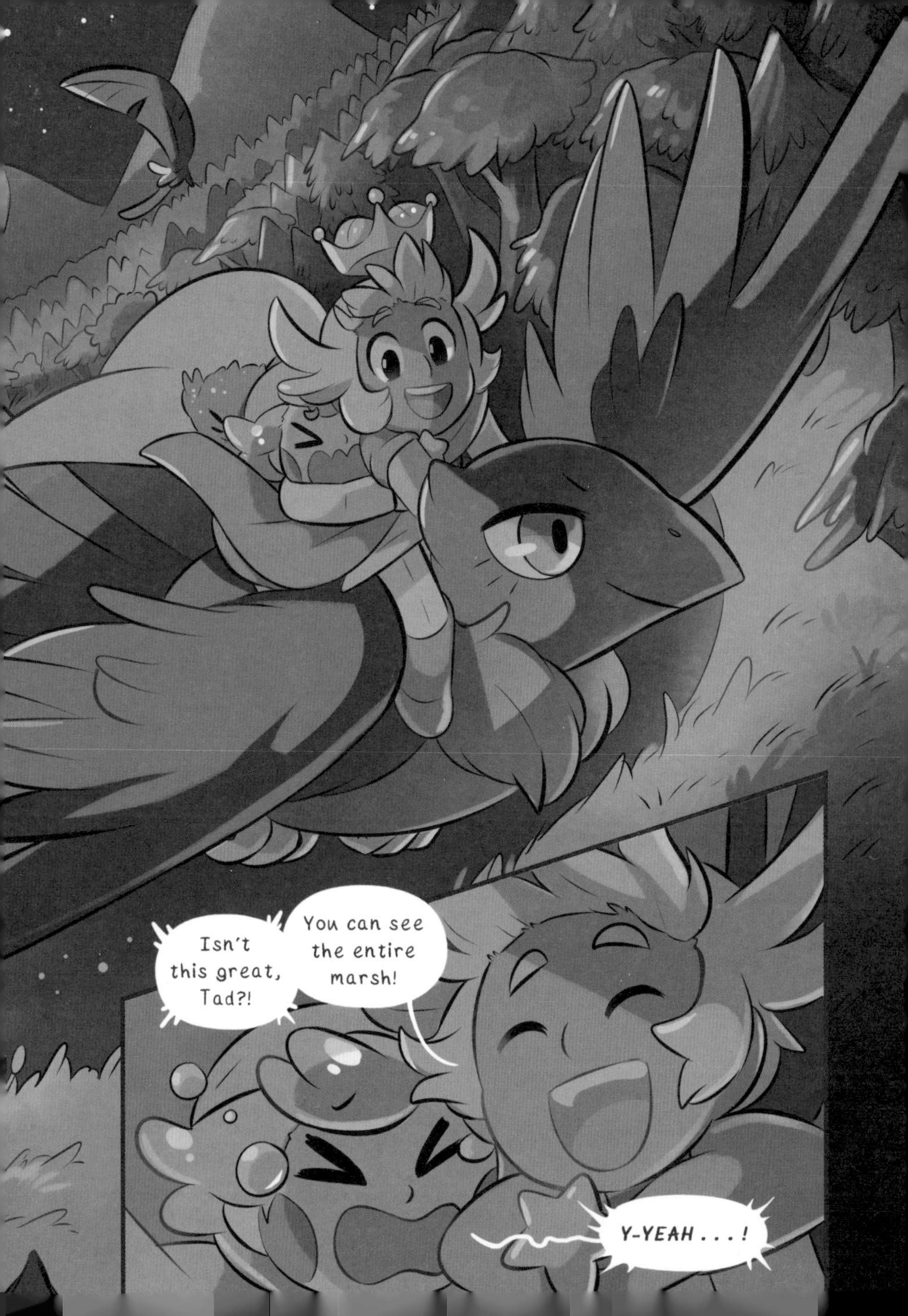
Isn't this great, Tad?!
You can see the entire marsh!
Y-YEAH . . . !

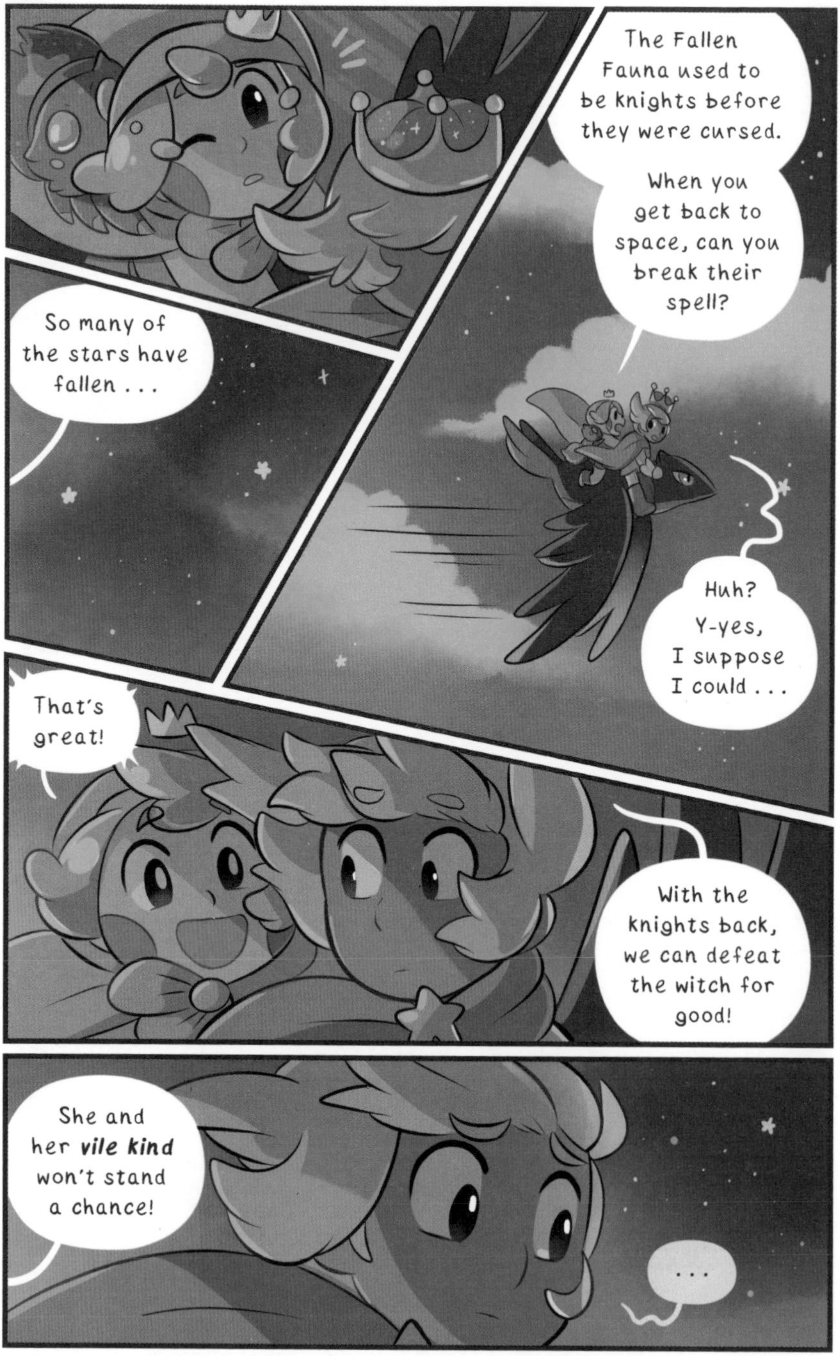

So many of the stars have fallen . . .
The Fallen Fauna used to be knights before they were cursed.
When you get back to space, can you break their spell?
Huh? Y-yes, I suppose I could . . .
That's great!
With the knights back, we can defeat the witch for good!
She and her **vile kind** won't stand a chance!
. . .

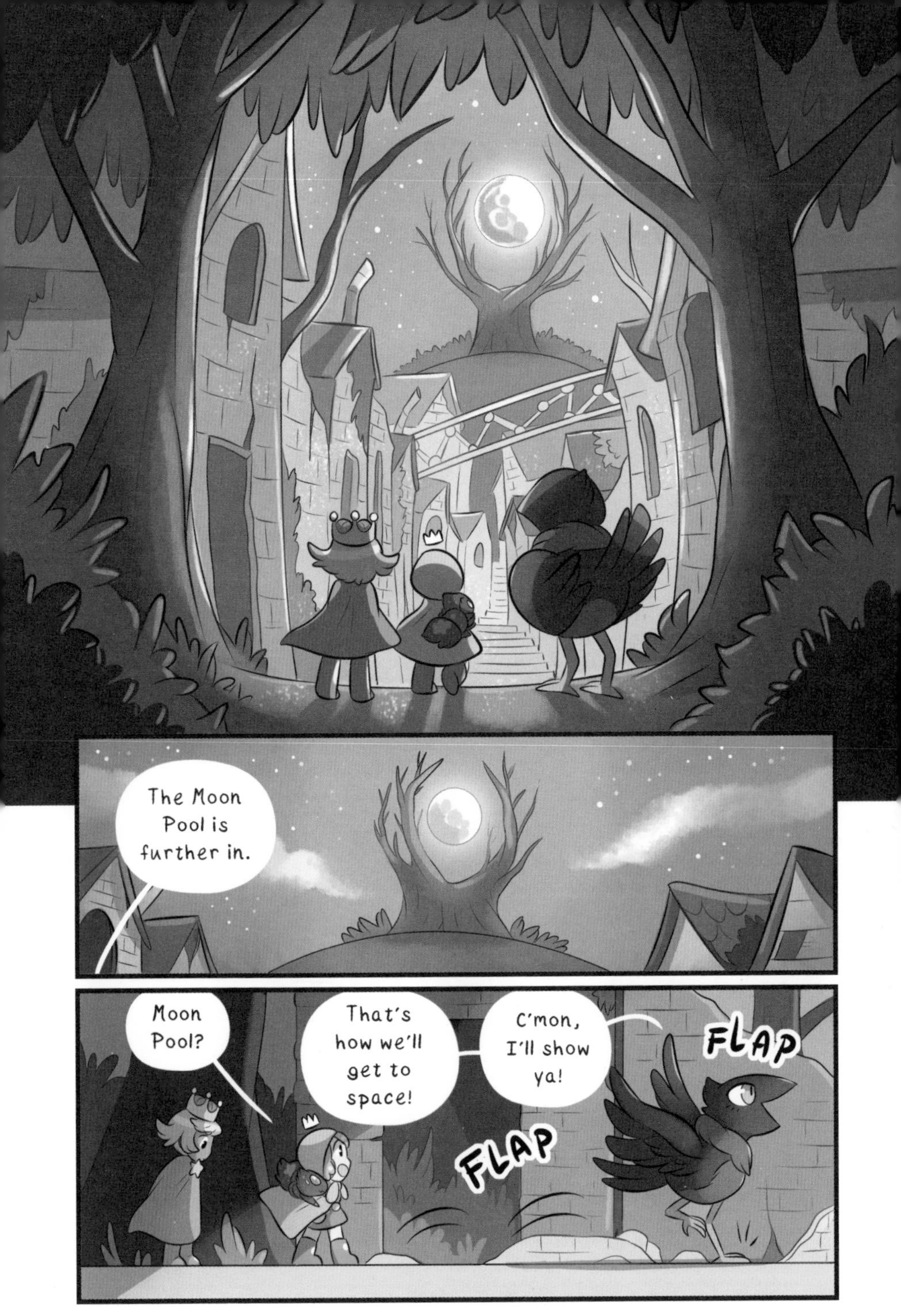
The Moon Pool is further in.
Moon Pool?
That's how we'll get to space!
C'mon, I'll show ya!
FLAP
FLAP

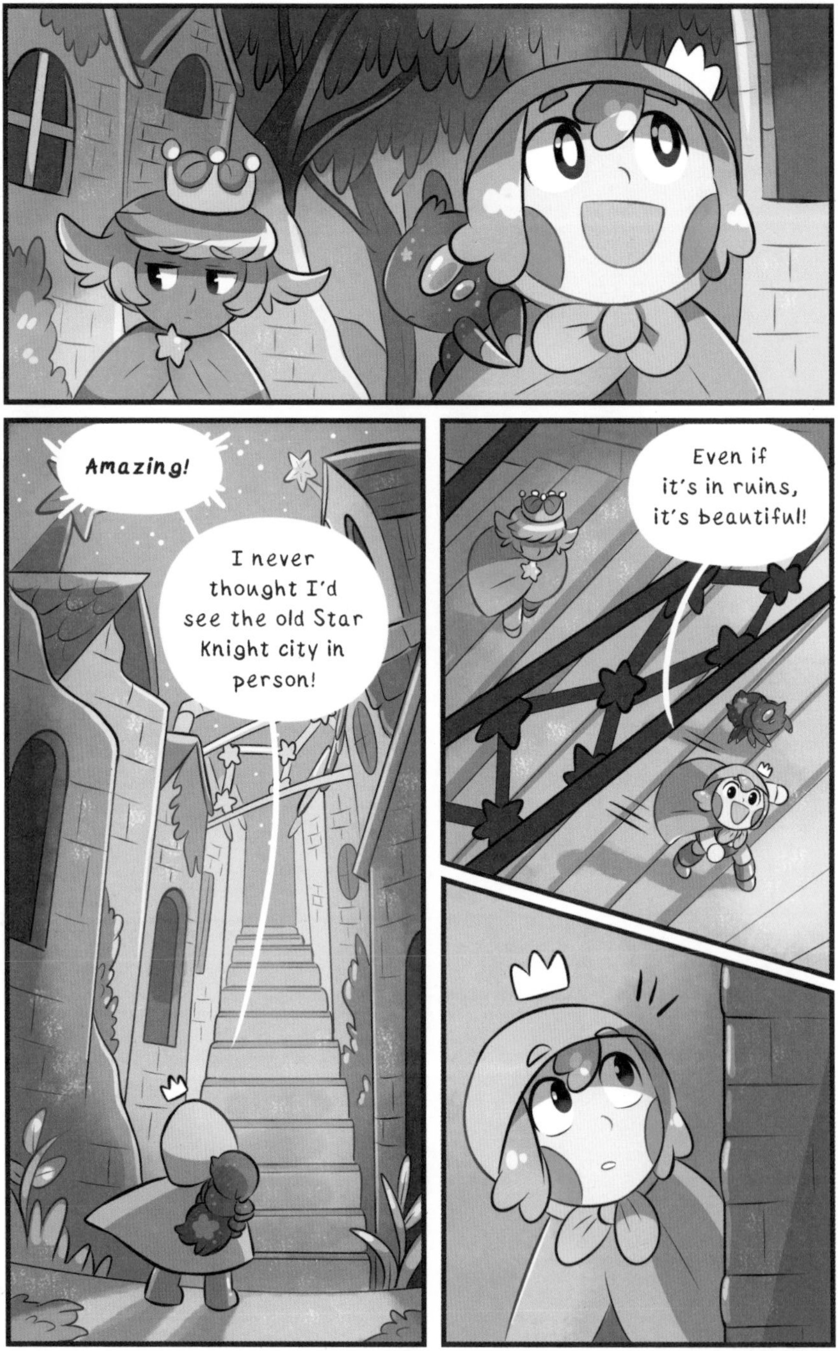
Amazing!
I never thought I'd see the old Star Knight city in person!
Even if it's in ruins, it's beautiful!

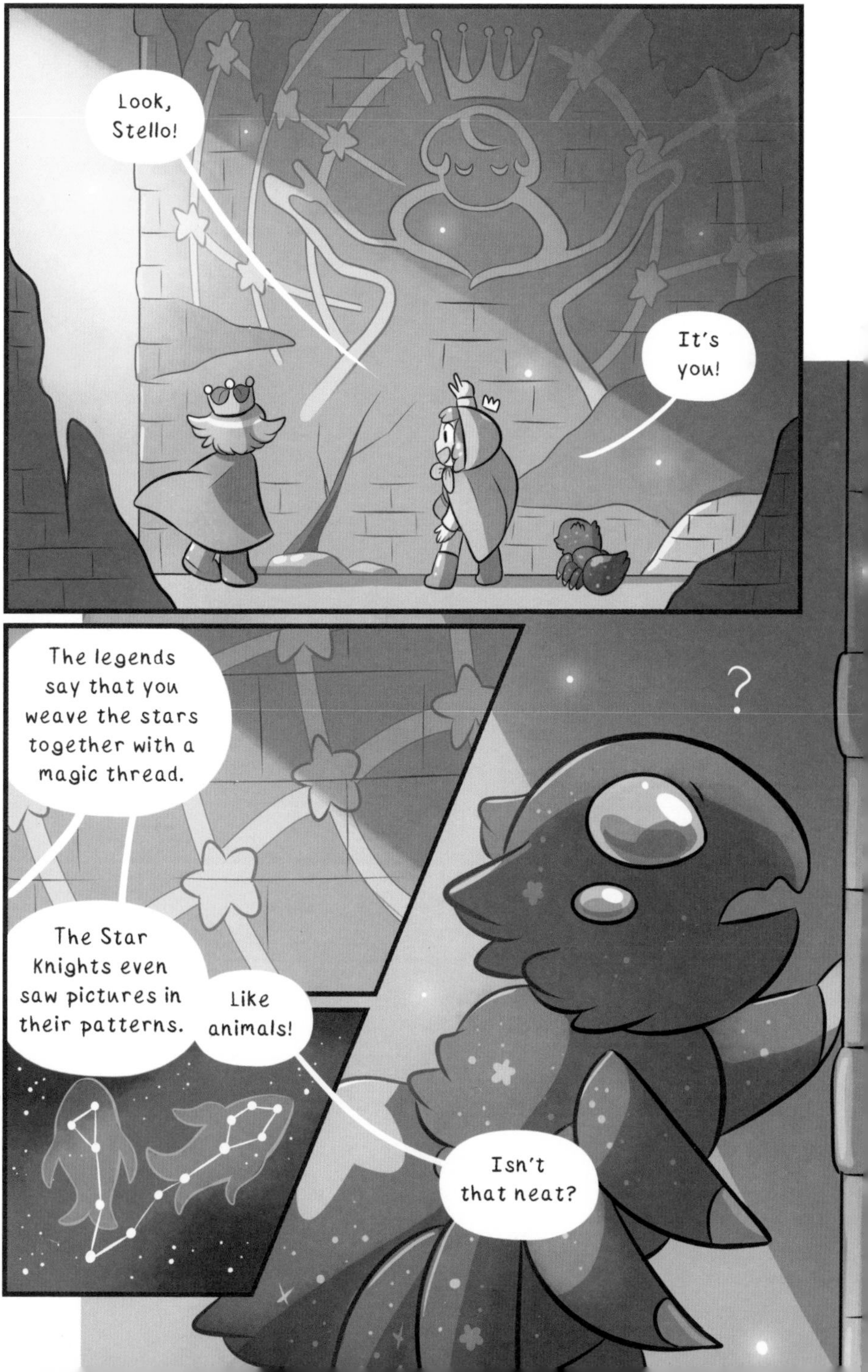

Look, Stello!
It's you!
The legends say that you weave the stars together with a magic thread.
?
The Star Knights even saw pictures in their patterns.
Like animals!
Isn't that neat?

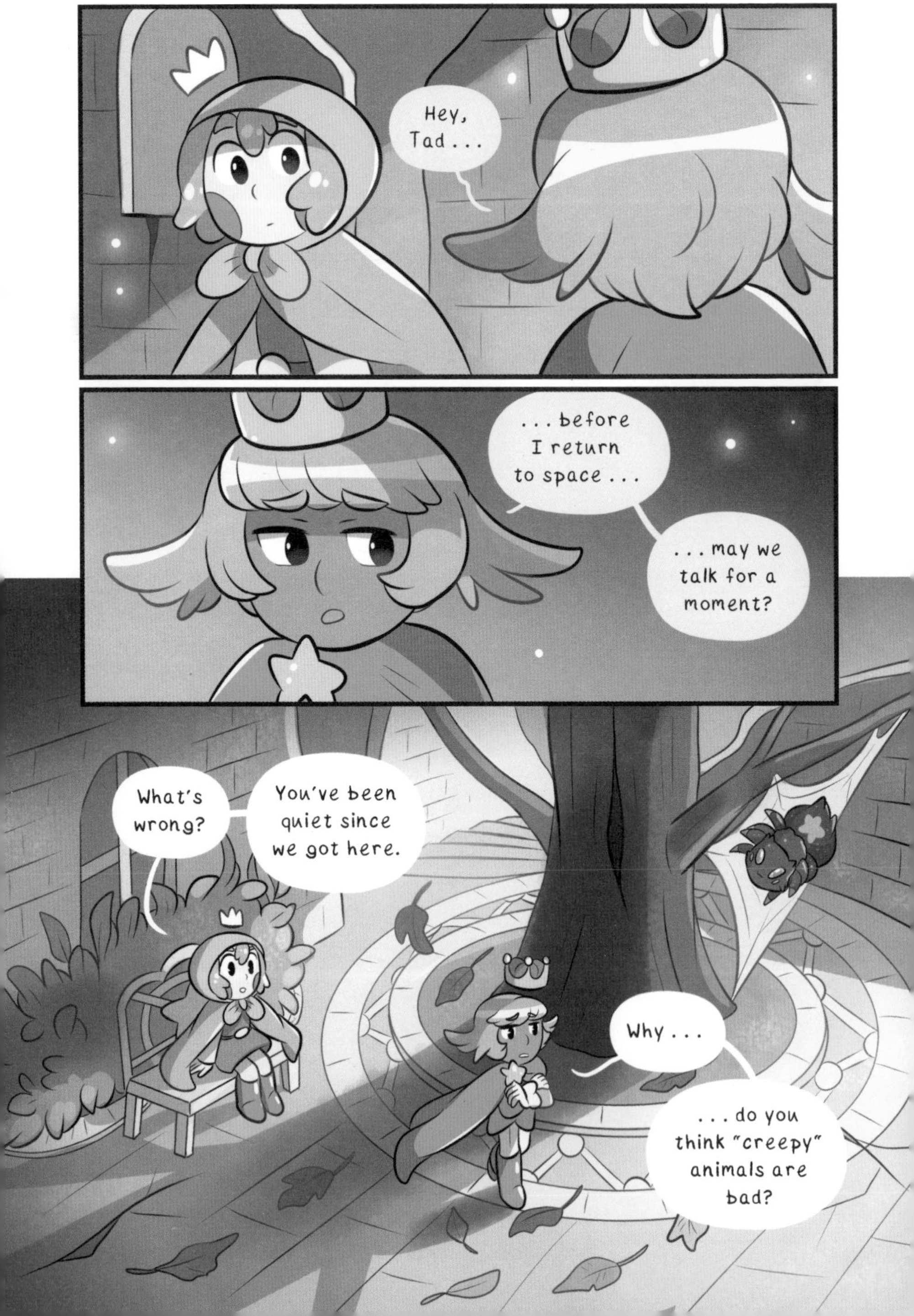
Hey, Tad . . .
. . . before I return to space . . .
. . . may we talk for a moment?
What's wrong?
You've been quiet since we got here.
Why . . .
. . . do you think "creepy" animals are bad?

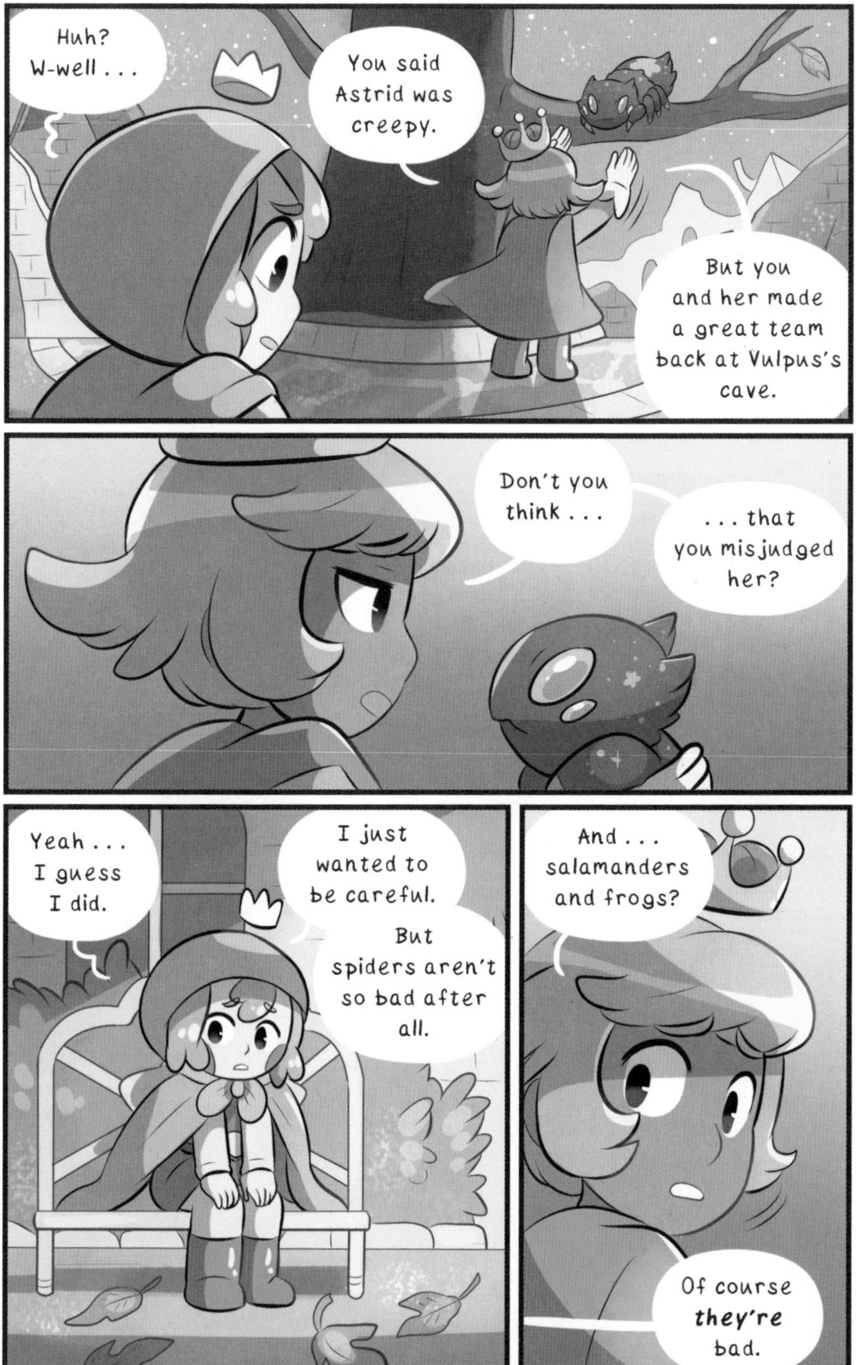
Huh?
W-well . . .
You said Astrid was creepy.
But you and her made a great team back at Vulpus's cave.
Don't you think . . .
. . . that you misjudged her?
Yeah . . . I guess I did.
I just wanted to be careful.
But spiders aren't so bad after all.
And . . . salamanders and frogs?
Of course *they're* bad.

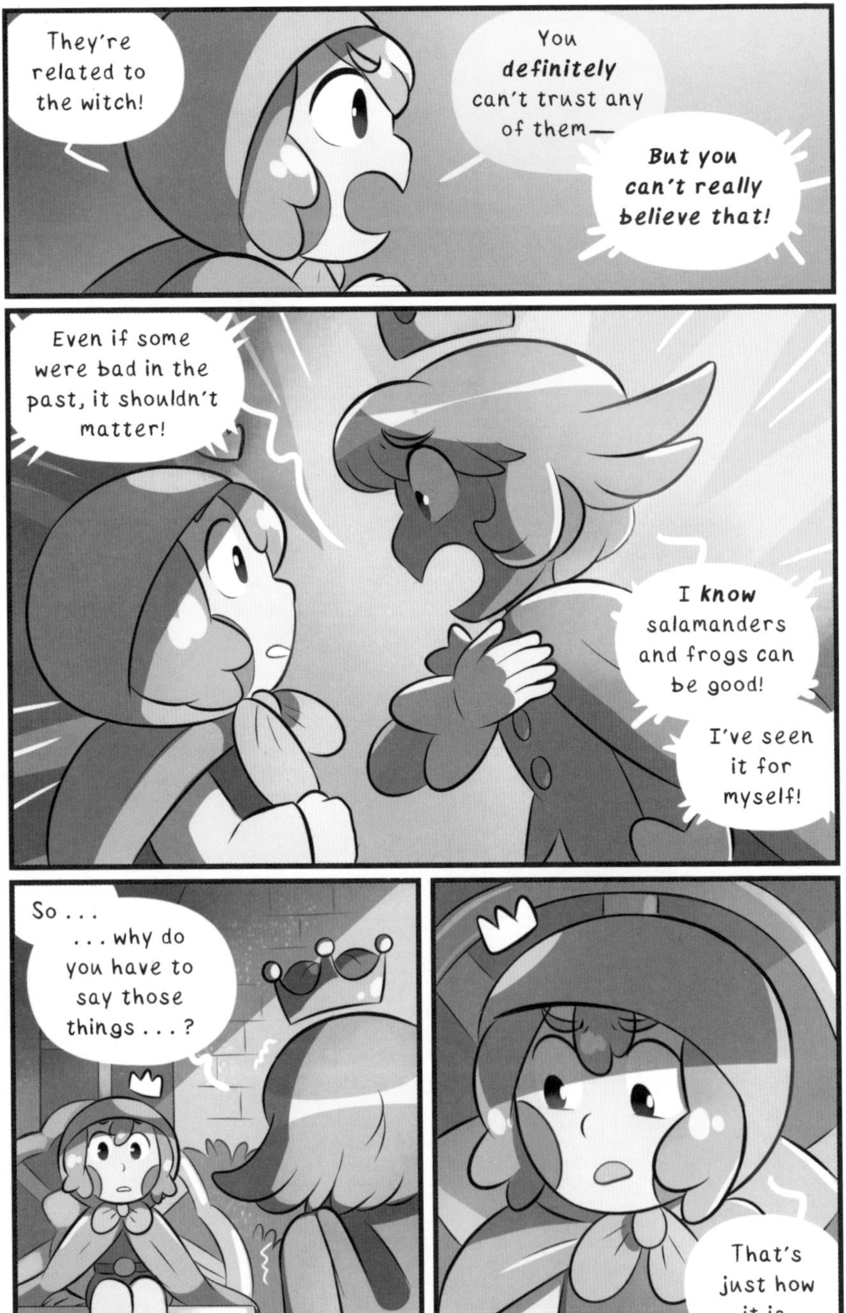
They're related to the witch!
You definitely can't trust any of them—
But you can't really believe that!
Even if some were bad in the past, it shouldn't matter!
I know salamanders and frogs can be good!
I've seen it for myself!
So . . .
. . . why do you have to say those things . . . ?
That's just how it is.

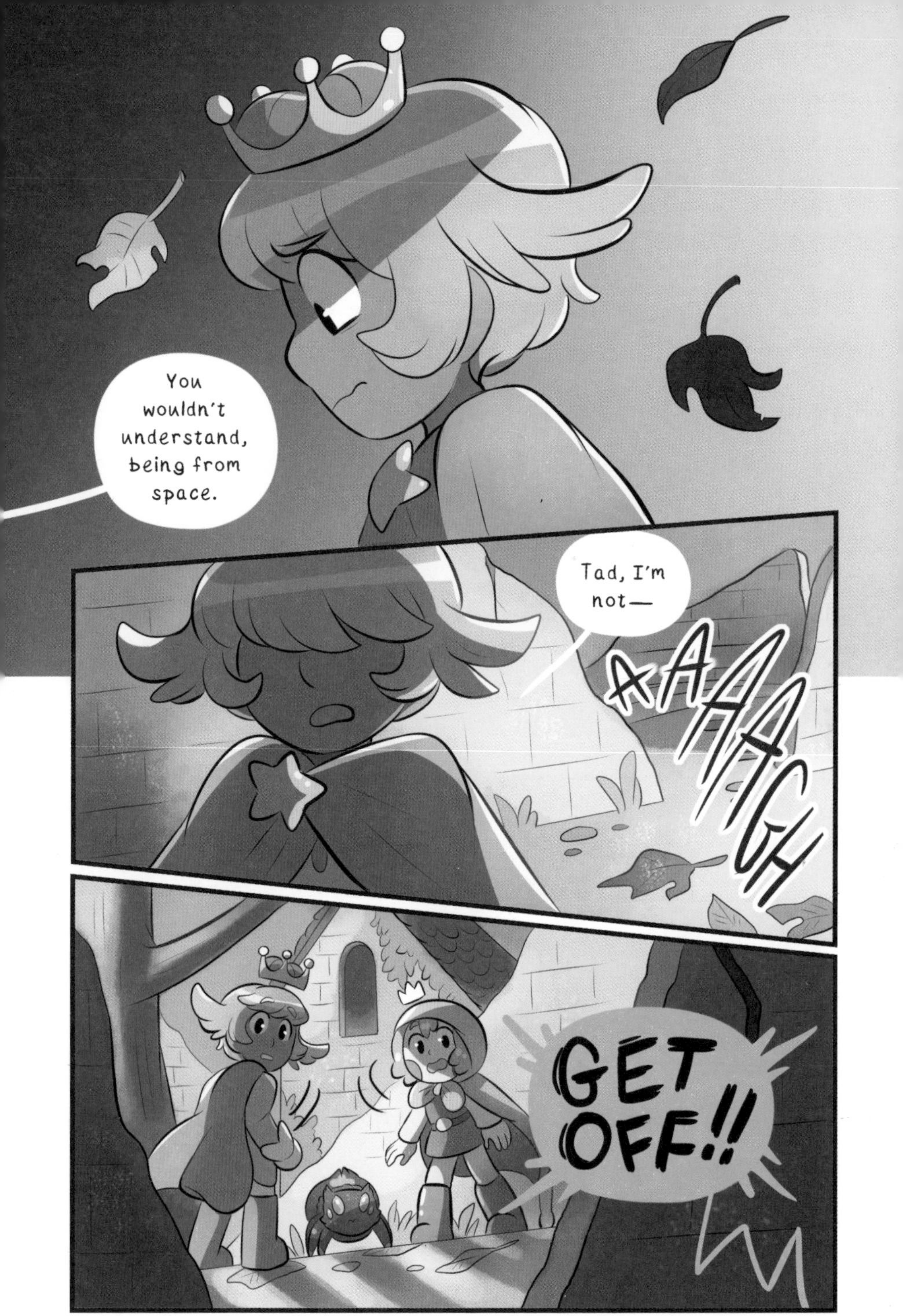
You wouldn't understand, being from space.
Tad, I'm not—
AAAAGH
GET OFF!!

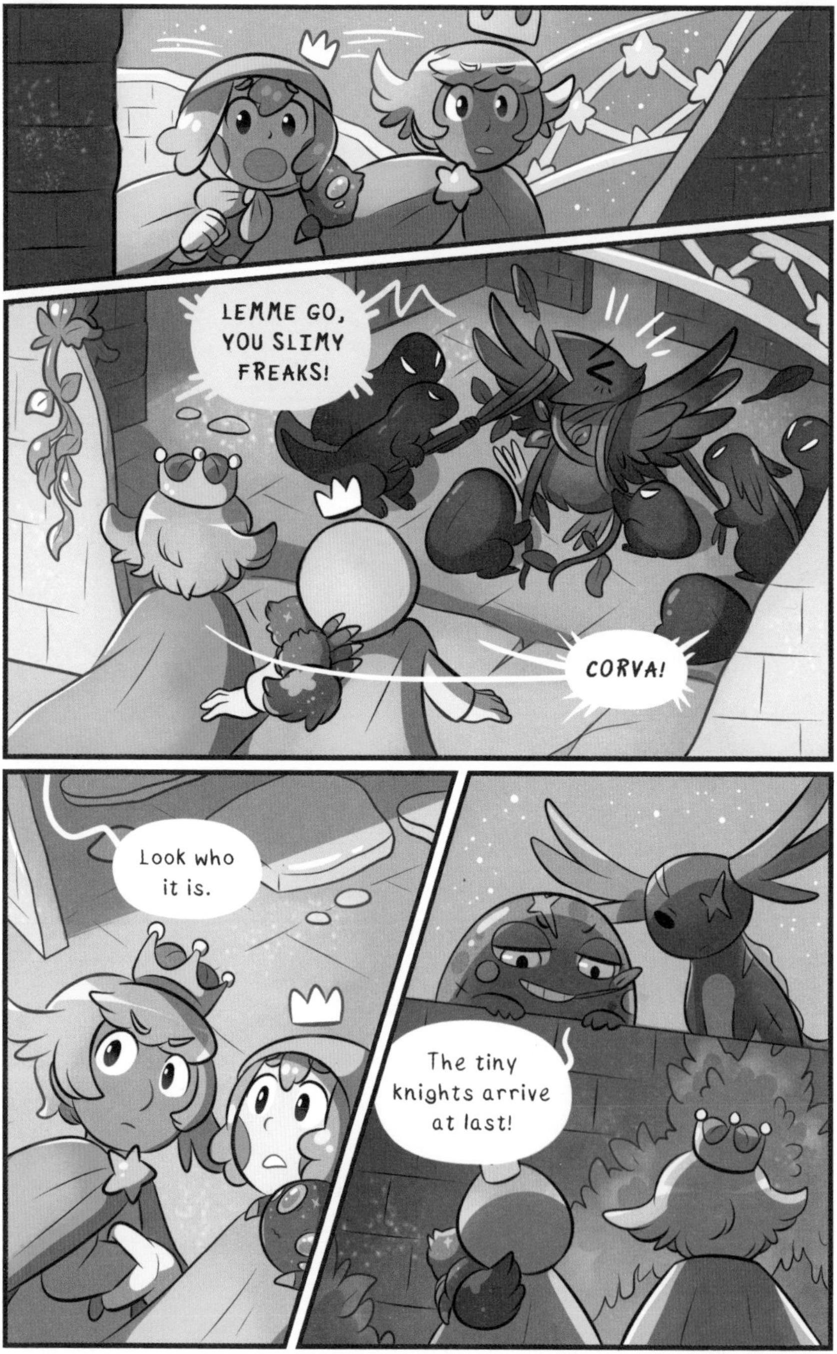
LEMME GO, YOU SLIMY FREAKS!
CORVA!
Look who it is.
The tiny knights arrive at last!

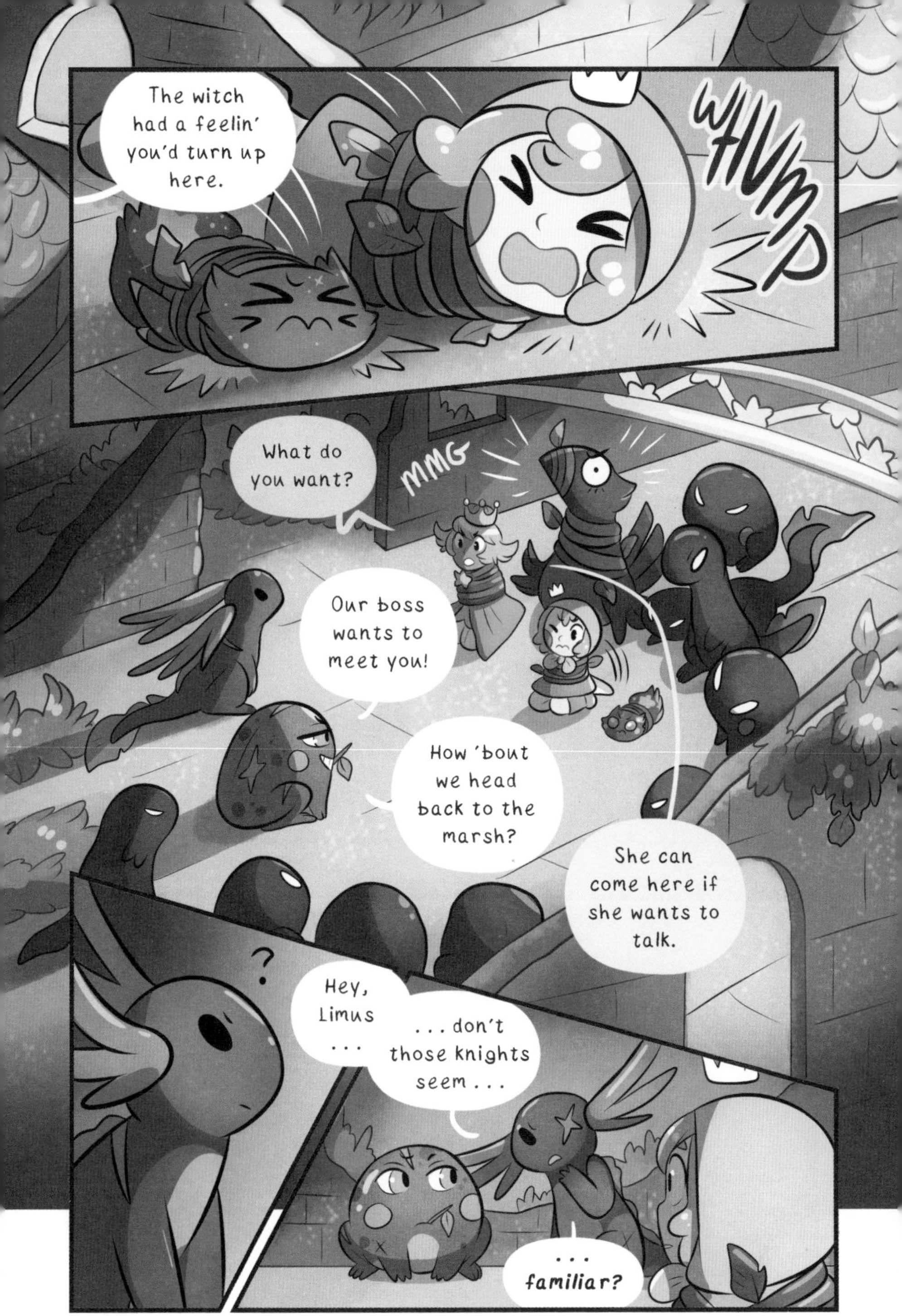
The witch had a feelin' you'd turn up here.
WHUMP
What do you want?
MMG
Our boss wants to meet you!
How 'bout we head back to the marsh?
She can come here if she wants to talk.
?
Hey, Limus . . .
. . . don't those knights seem . . .
. . . familiar?

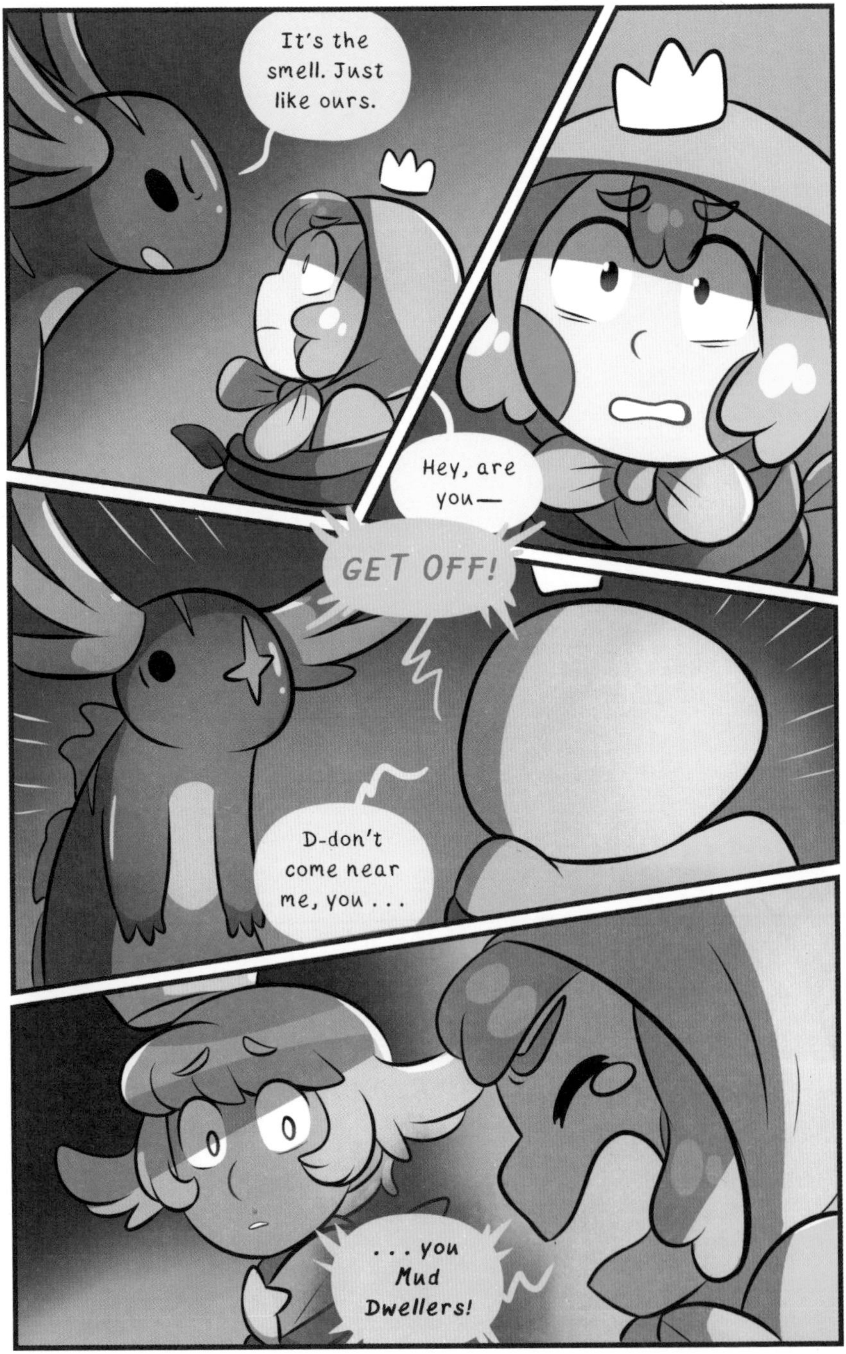
It's the smell. Just like ours.
Hey, are you—
GET OFF!
D-don't come near me, you . . .
. . . you Mud Dwellers!

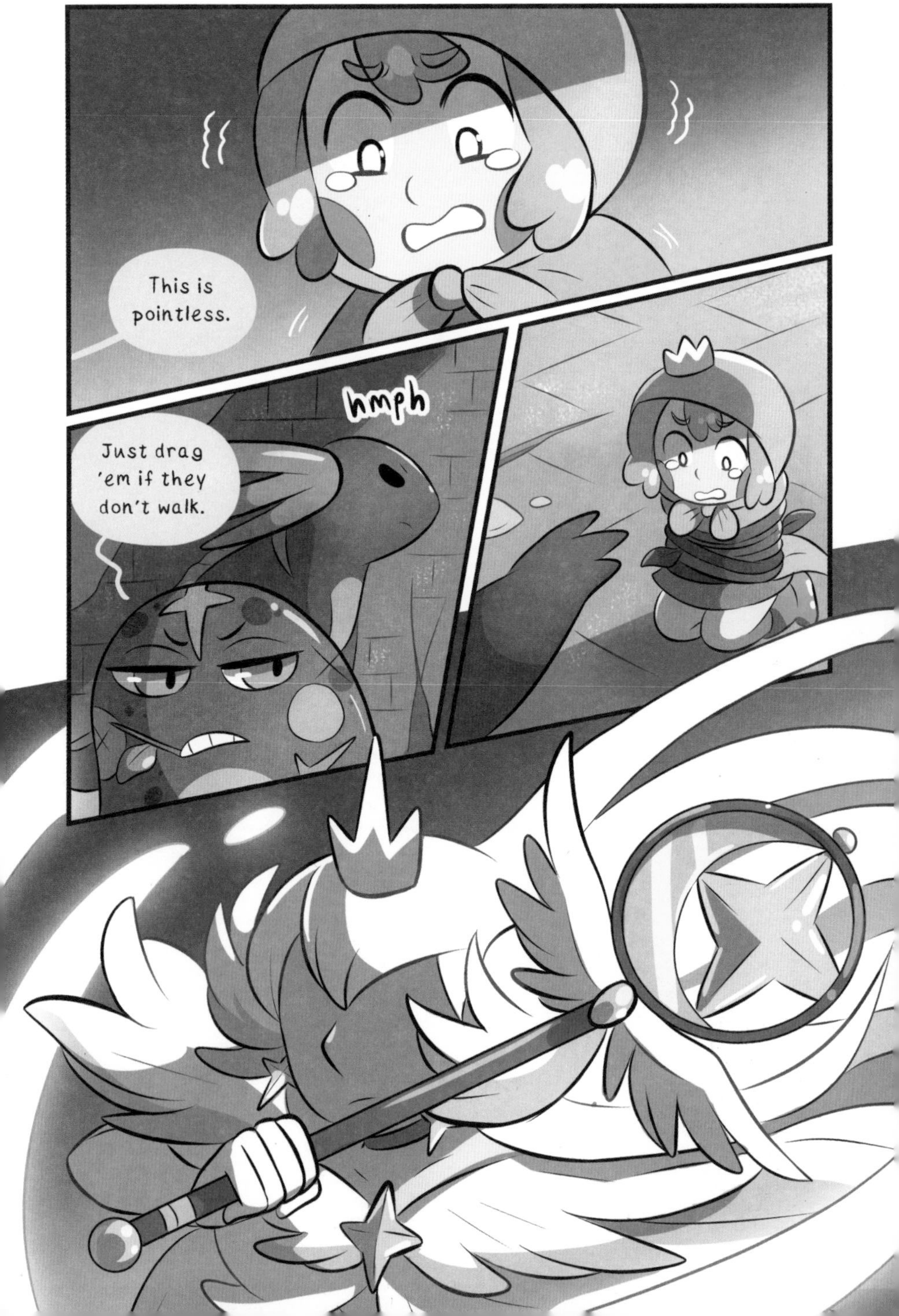
This is pointless.
hmph
Just drag 'em if they don't walk.

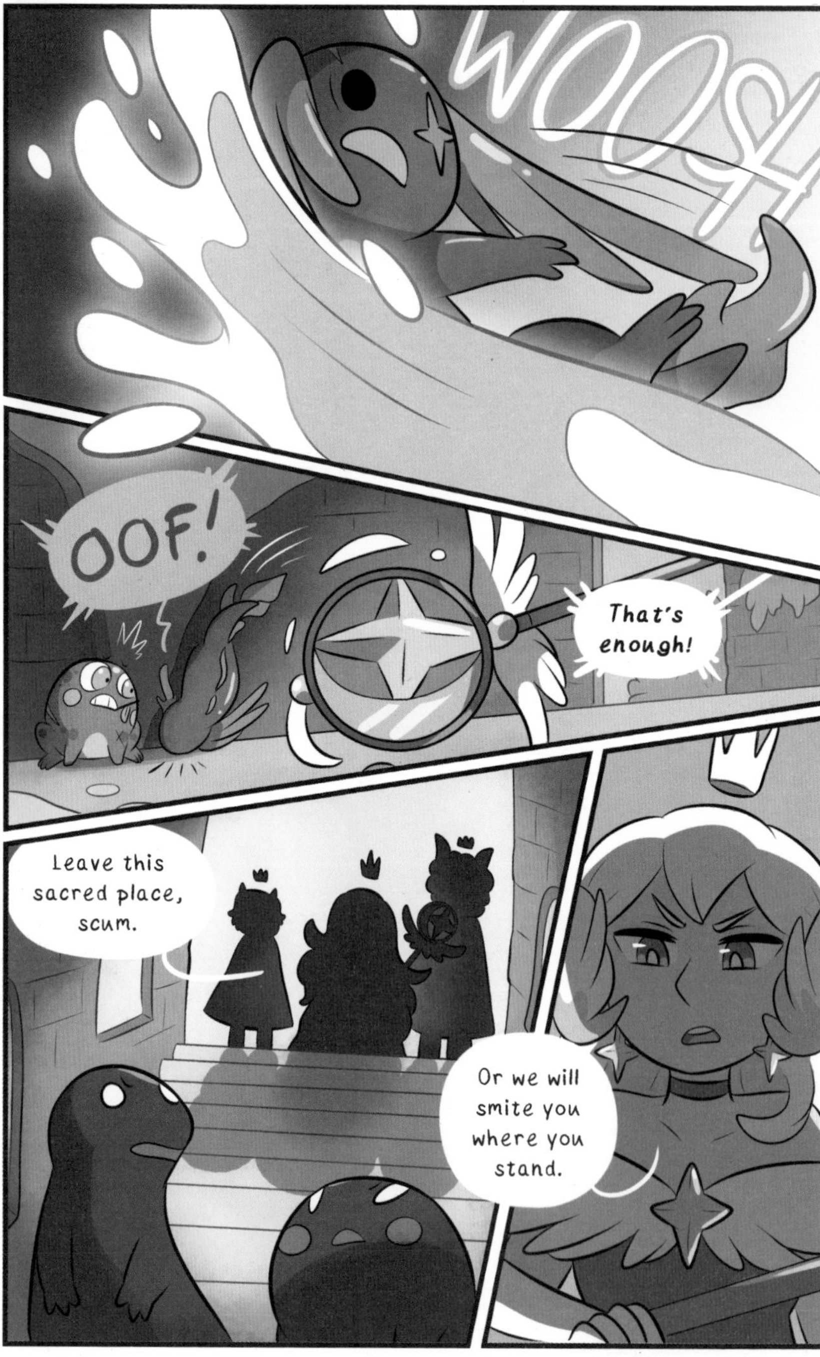
WOOSH
OOF!
That's enough!
Leave this sacred place, scum.
Or we will smite you where you stand.

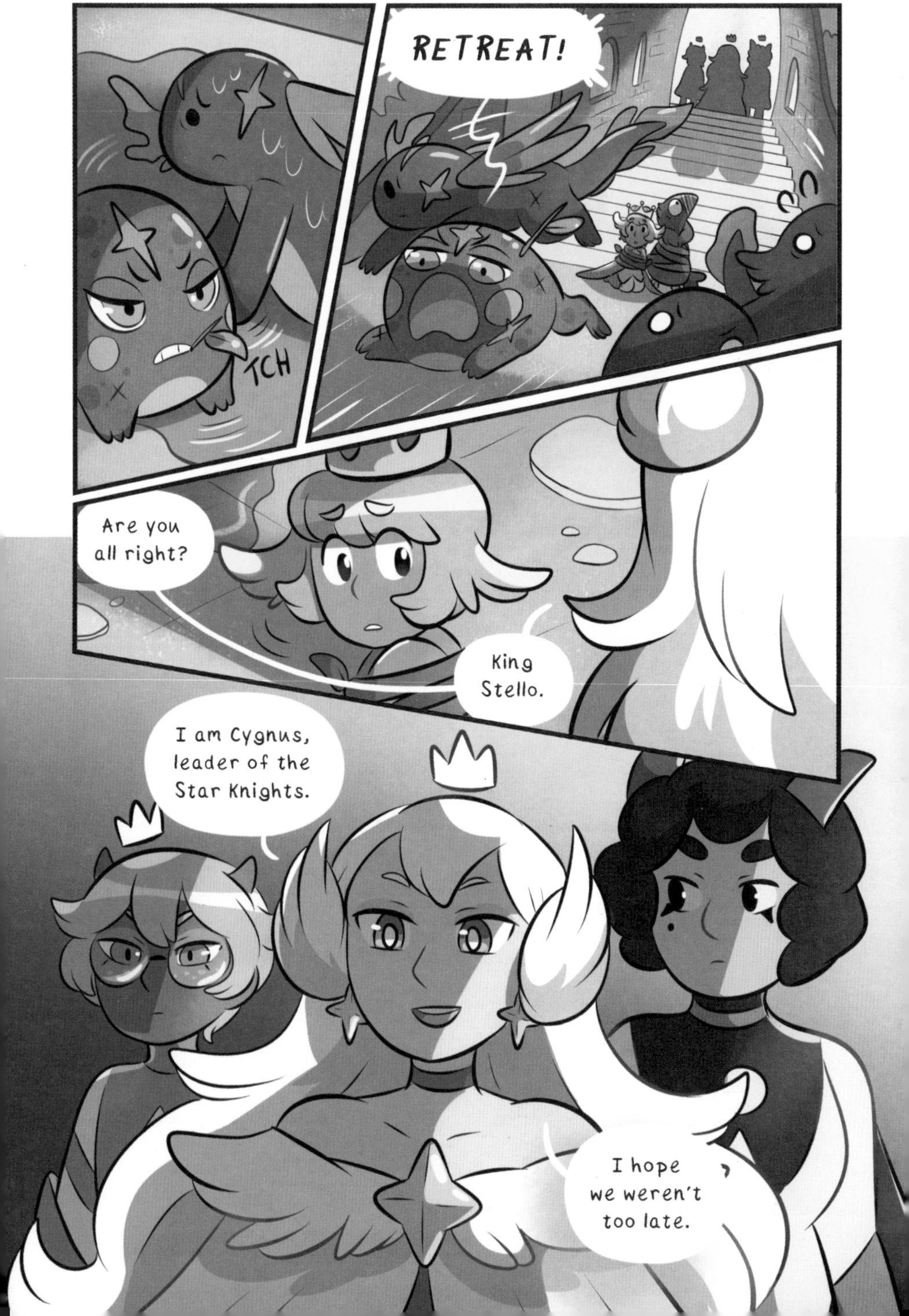
TCH
RETREAT!
Are you all right?
King Stello.
I am Cygnus, leader of the Star Knights.
I hope we weren't too late.

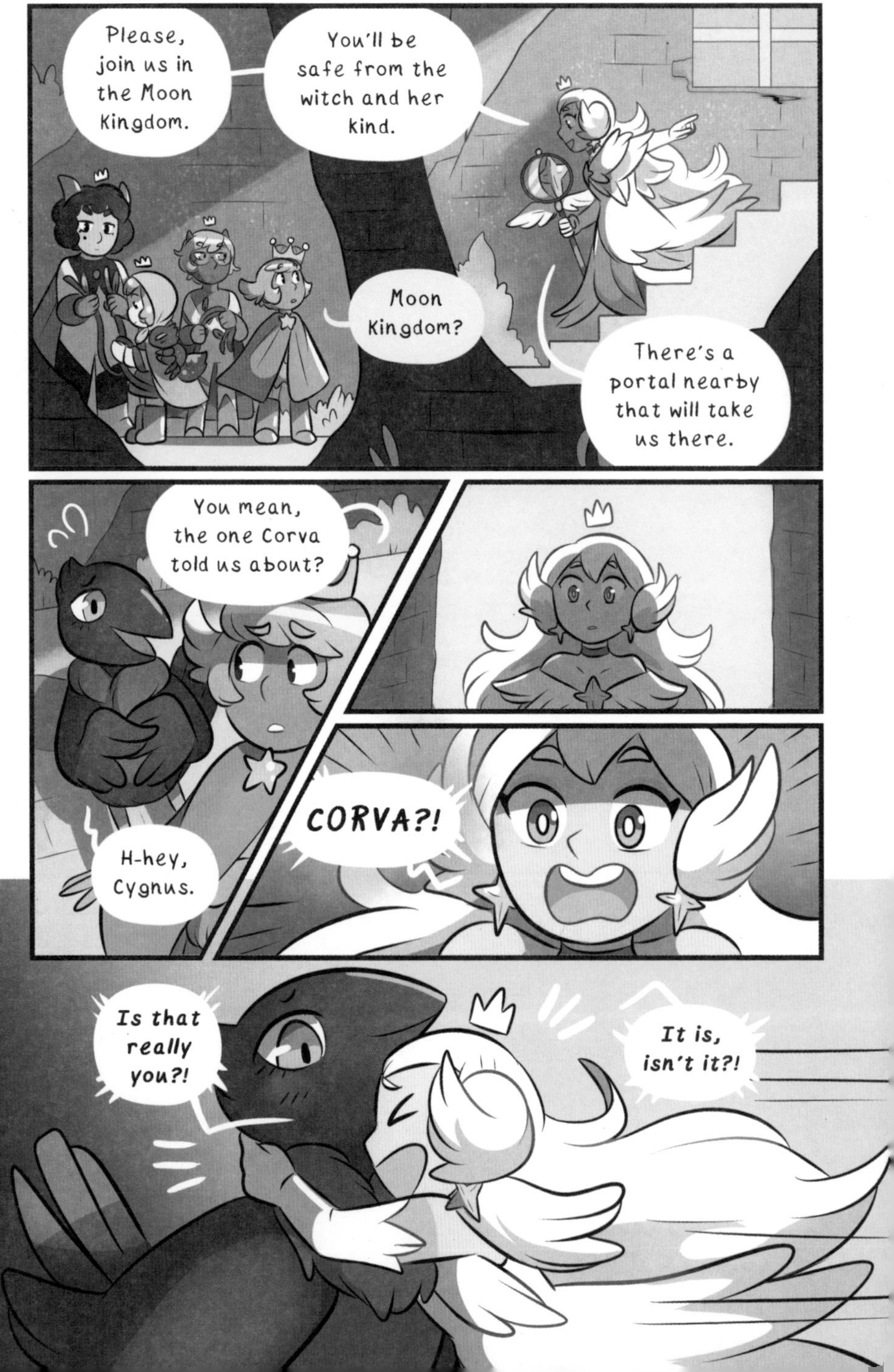

Please, join us in the Moon Kingdom.
You'll be safe from the witch and her kind.
Moon Kingdom?
There's a portal nearby that will take us there.
You mean, the one Corva told us about?
H-hey, Cygnus.
CORVA?!
Is that really you?!
It is, isn't it?!

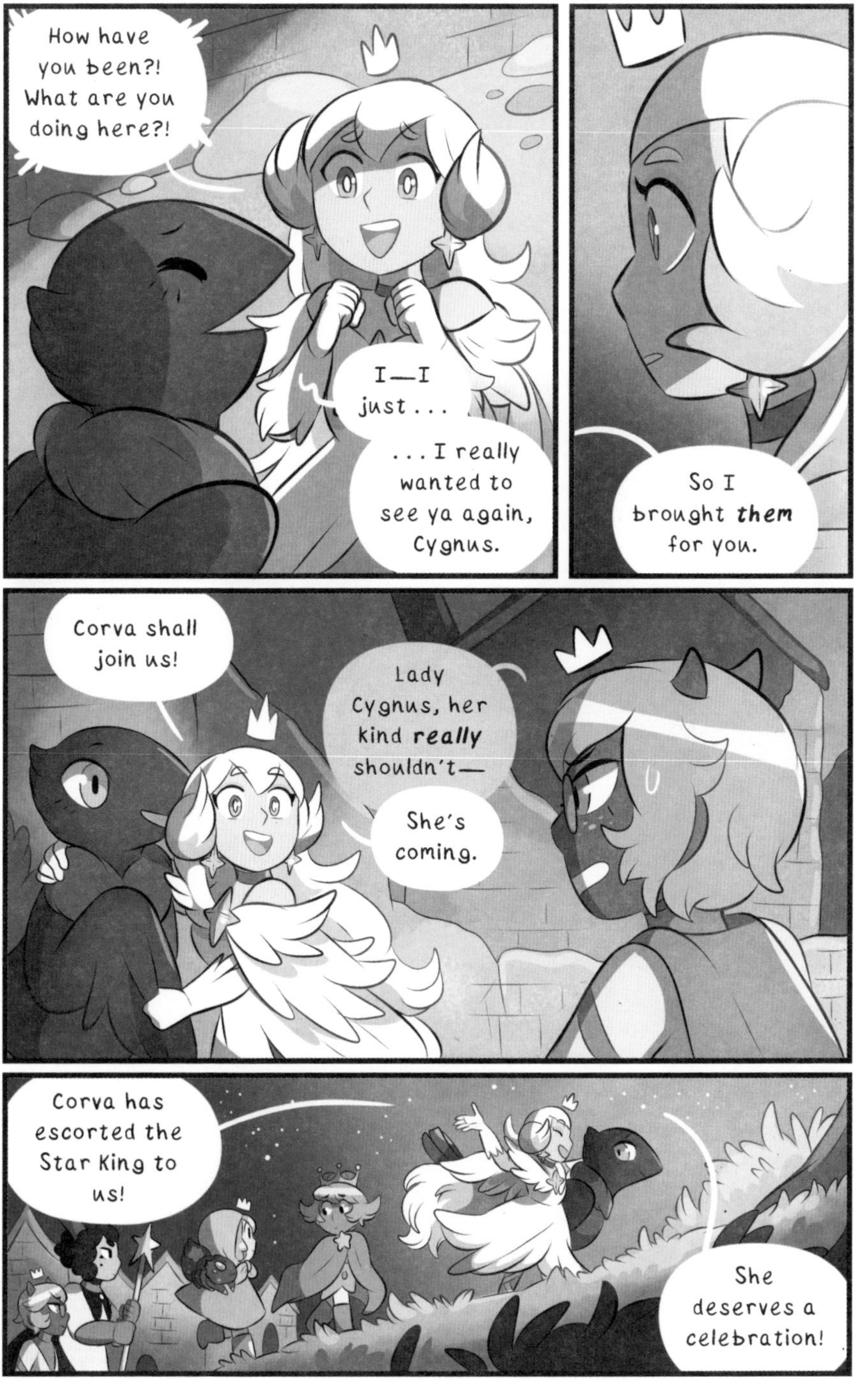
How have you been?! What are you doing here?!
I—I just . . .
. . . I really wanted to see ya again, Cygnus.
So I brought **them** for you.
Corva shall join us!
Lady Cygnus, her kind **really** shouldn't—
She's coming.
Corva has escorted the Star King to us!
She deserves a celebration!

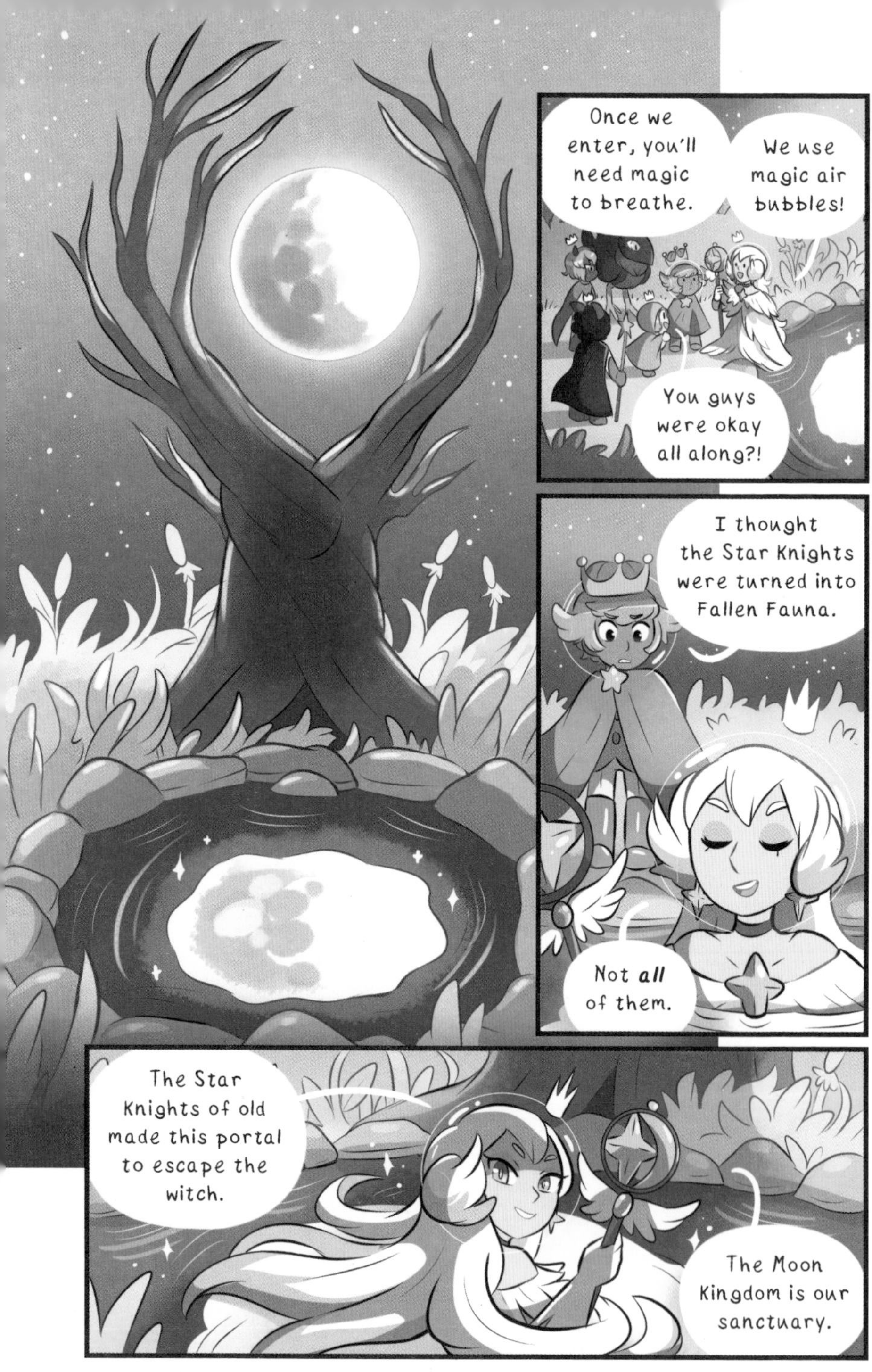

Once we enter, you'll need magic to breathe.
We use magic air bubbles!
You guys were okay all along?!
I thought the Star Knights were turned into Fallen Fauna.
Not *all* of them.
The Star Knights of old made this portal to escape the witch.
The Moon Kingdom is our sanctuary.

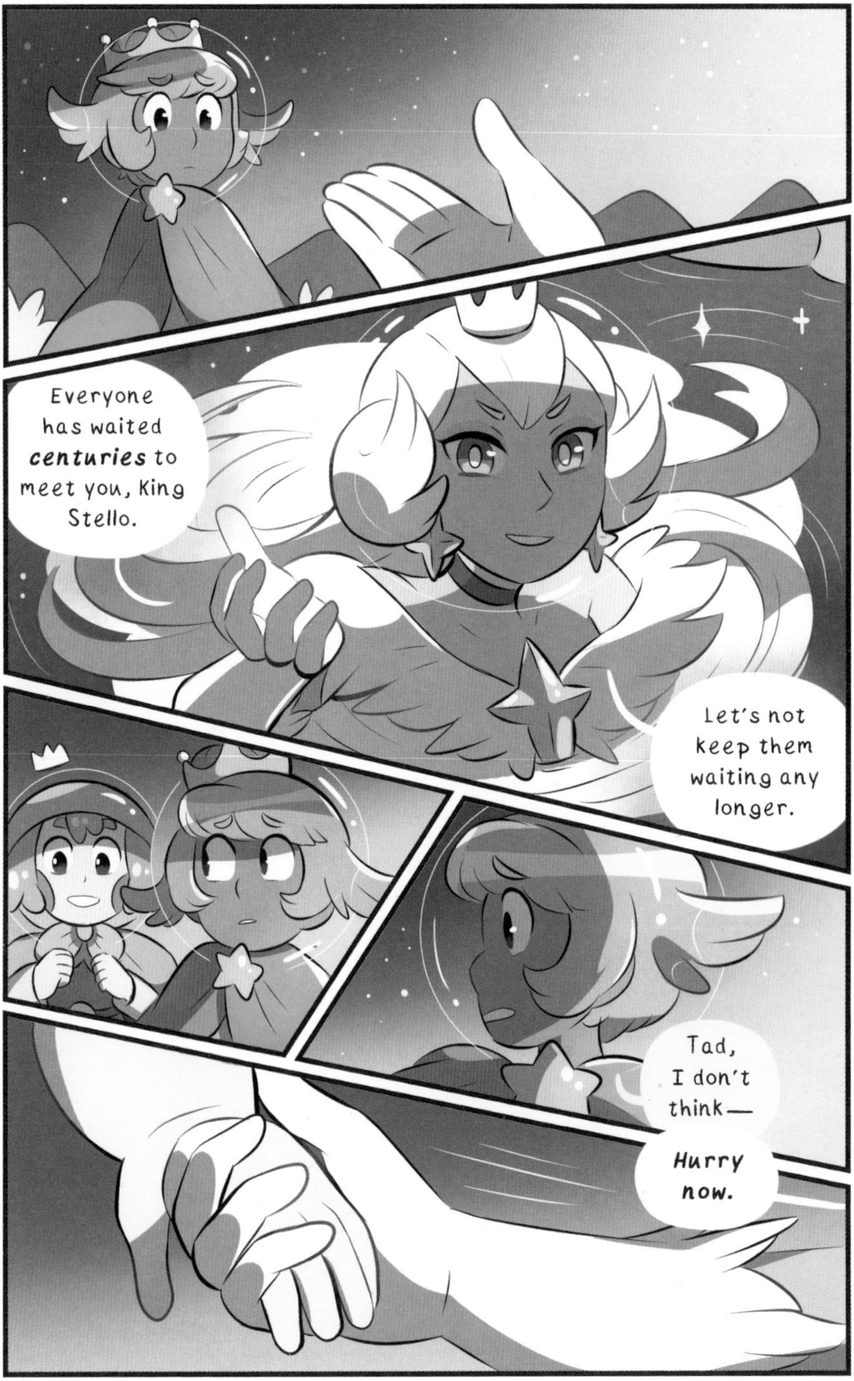

Everyone has waited **centuries** to meet you, King Stello.
Let's not keep them waiting any longer.
Tad, I don't think—
Hurry now.

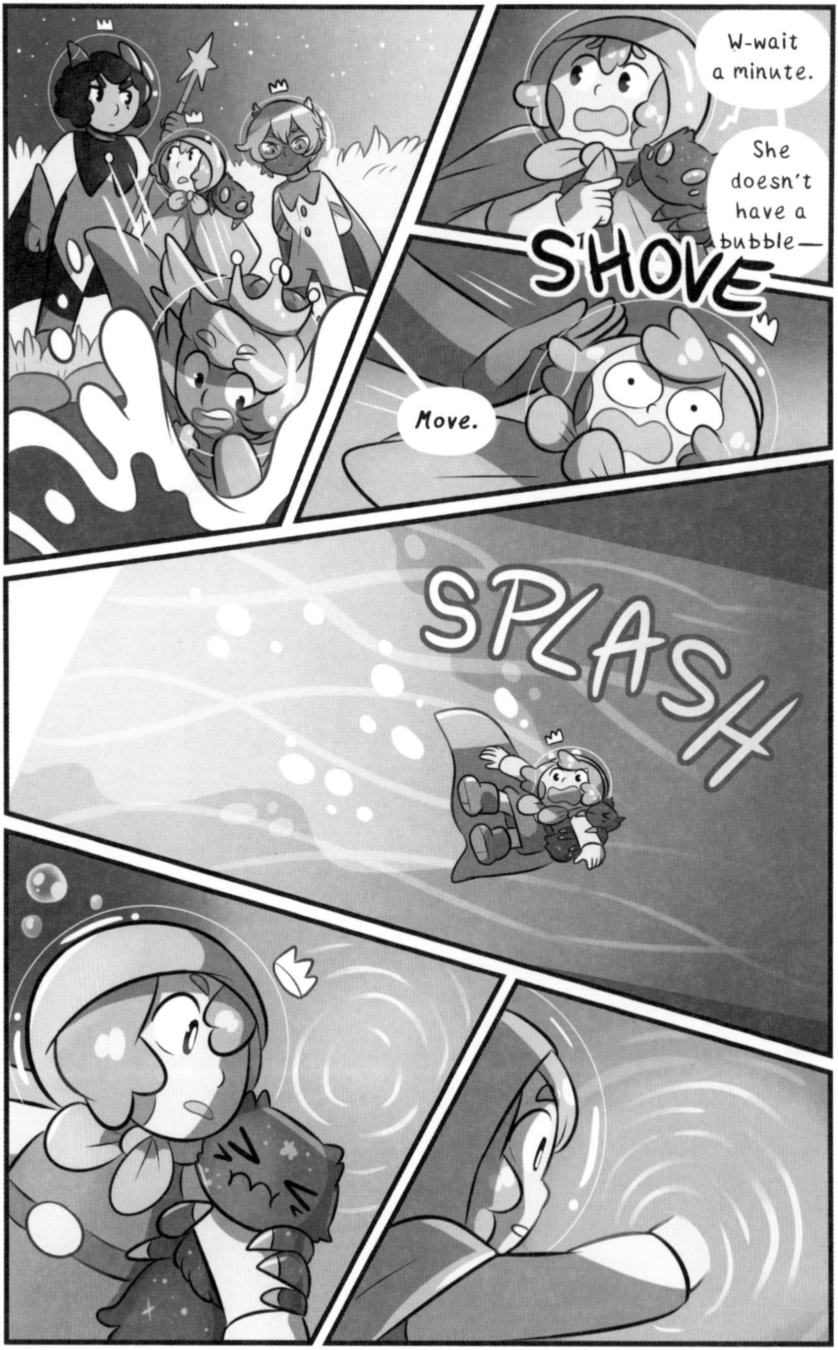
W-wait a minute.
She doesn't have a bubble—
SHOVE
Move.
SPLASH

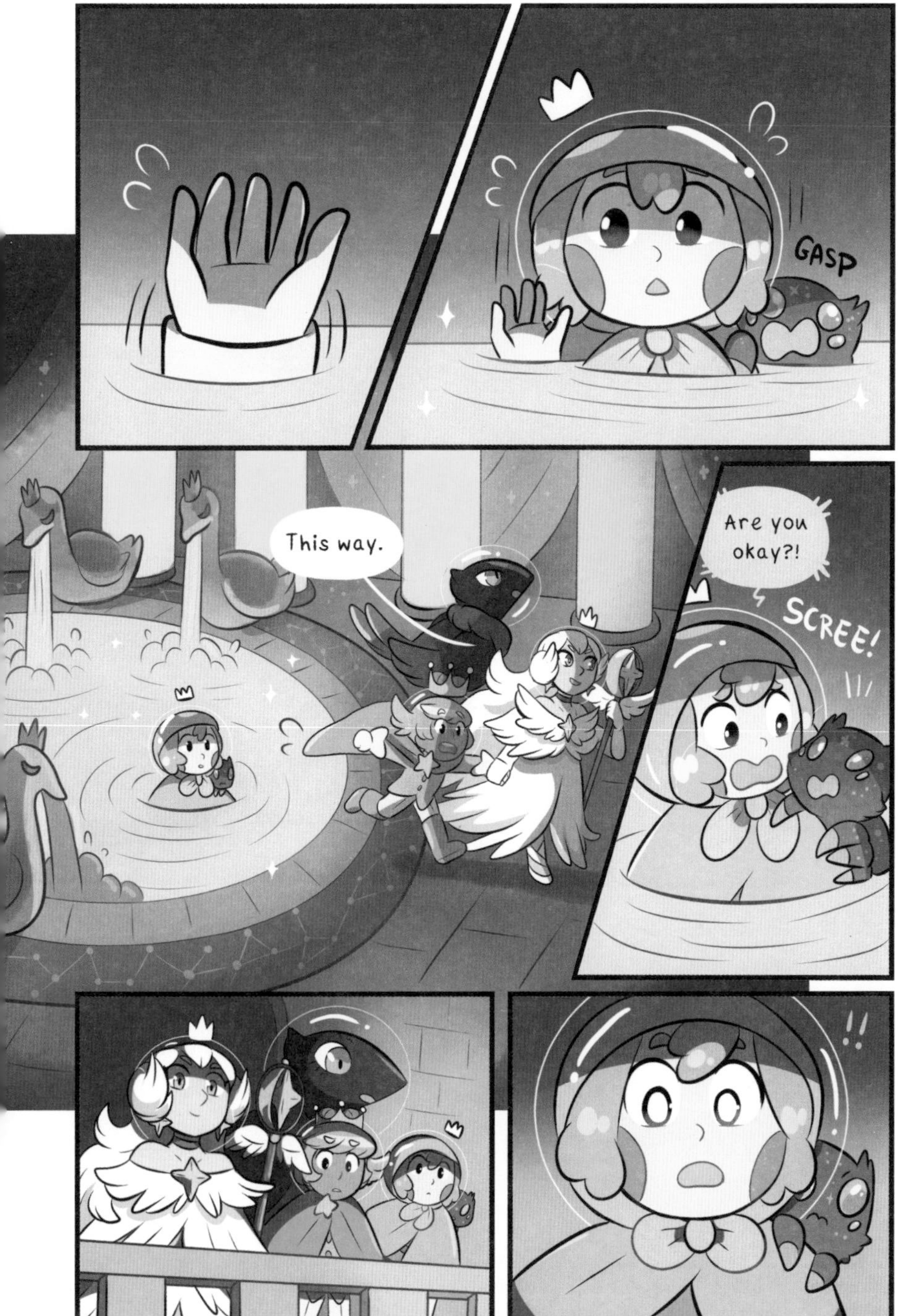
GASP
This way.
Are you okay?!
SCREE!
!!

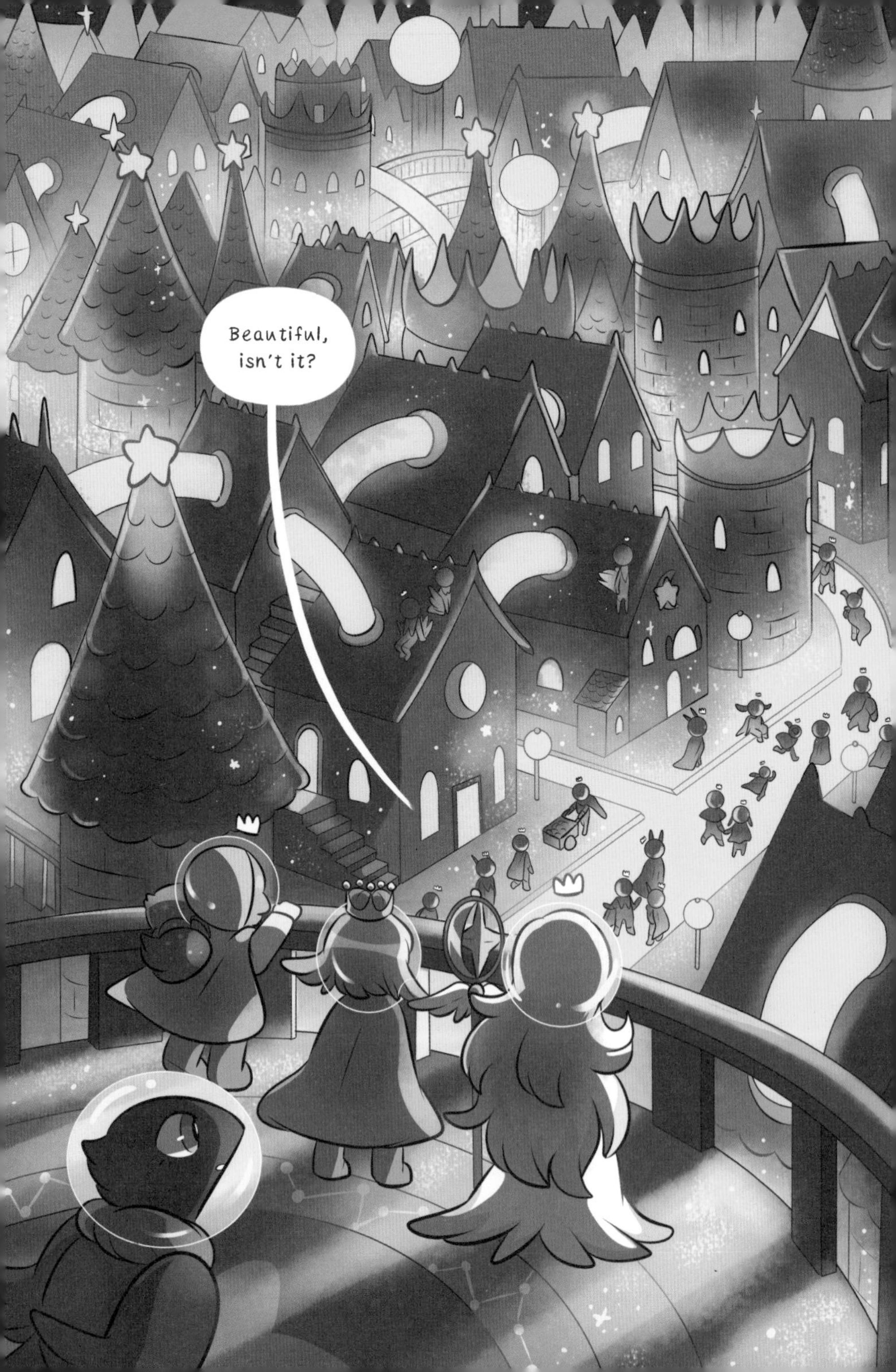
Beautiful, isn't it?

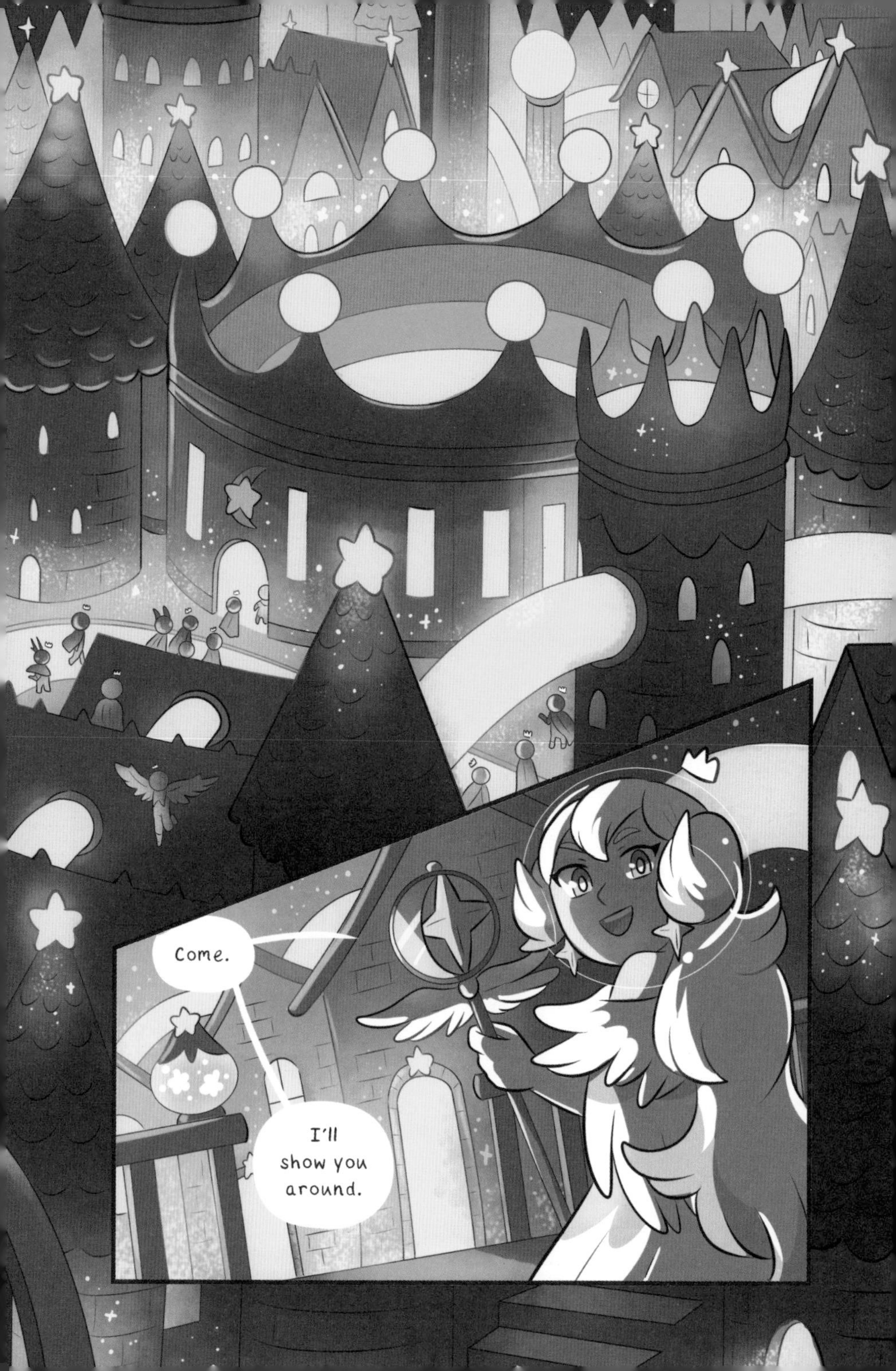
Come.
I'll show you around.

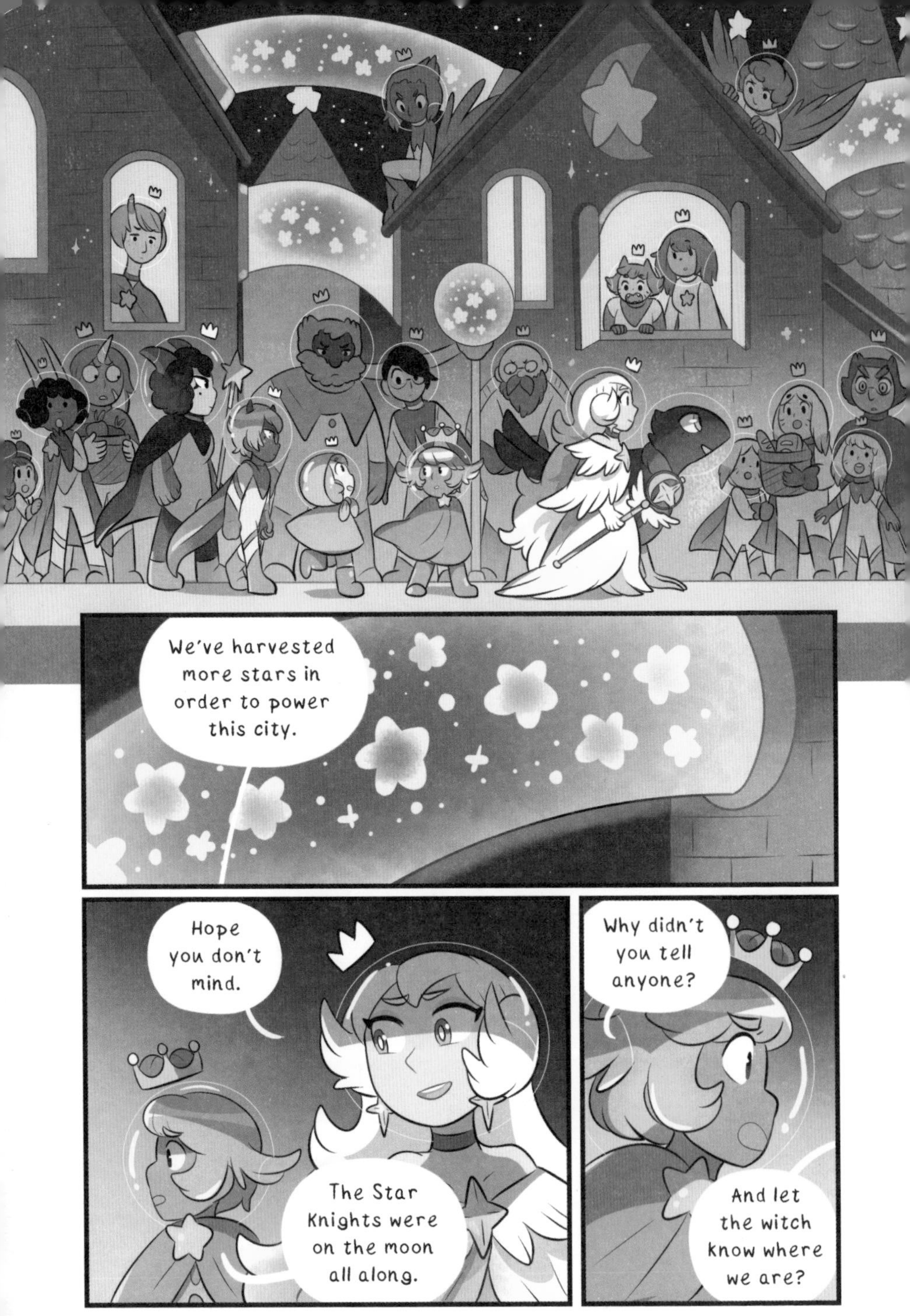

We've harvested more stars in order to power this city.
Hope you don't mind.
The Star Knights were on the moon all along.
Why didn't you tell anyone?
And let the witch know where we are?

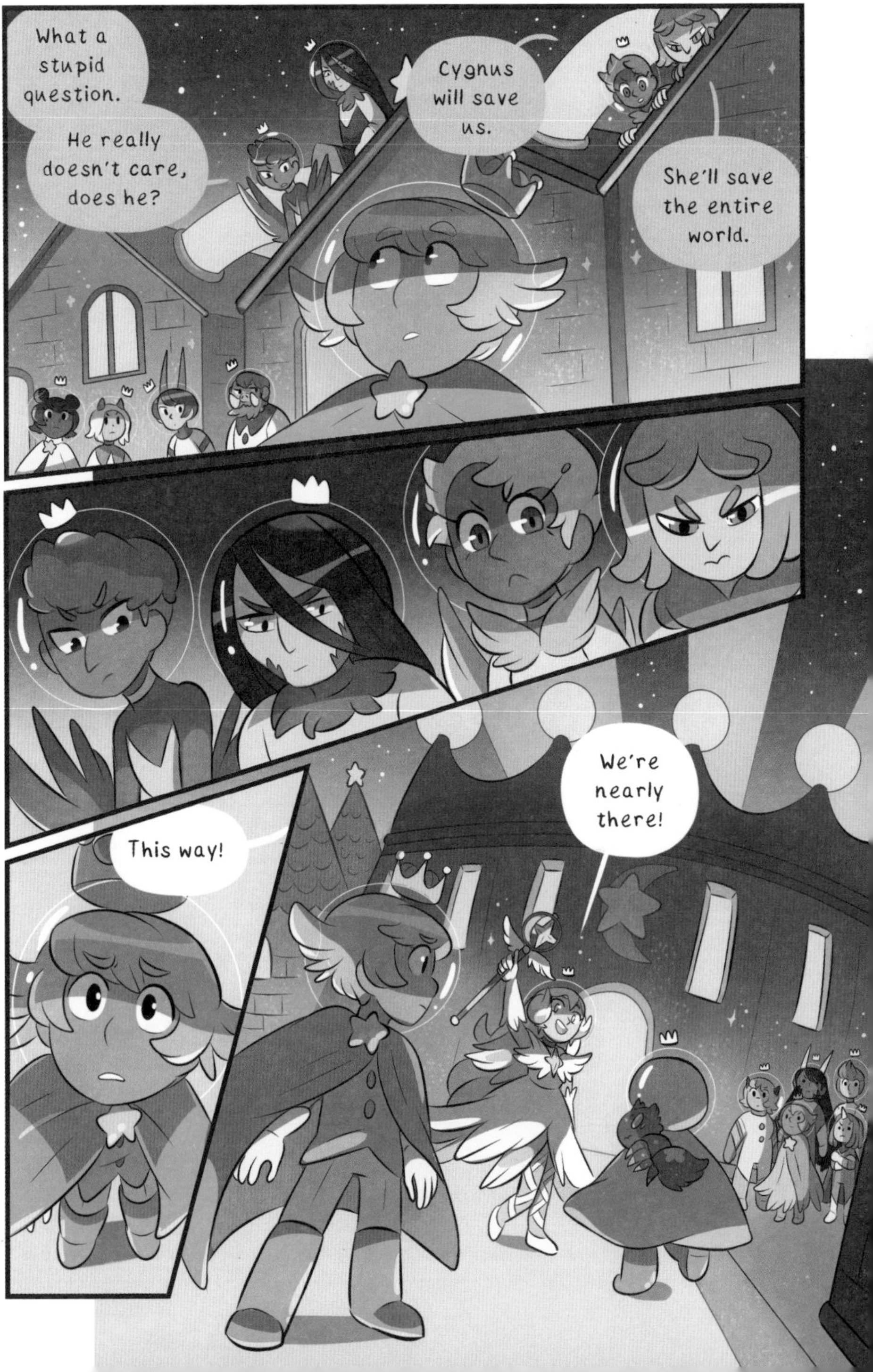
What a stupid question.
He really doesn't care, does he?
Cygnus will save us.
She'll save the entire world.
This way!
We're nearly there!

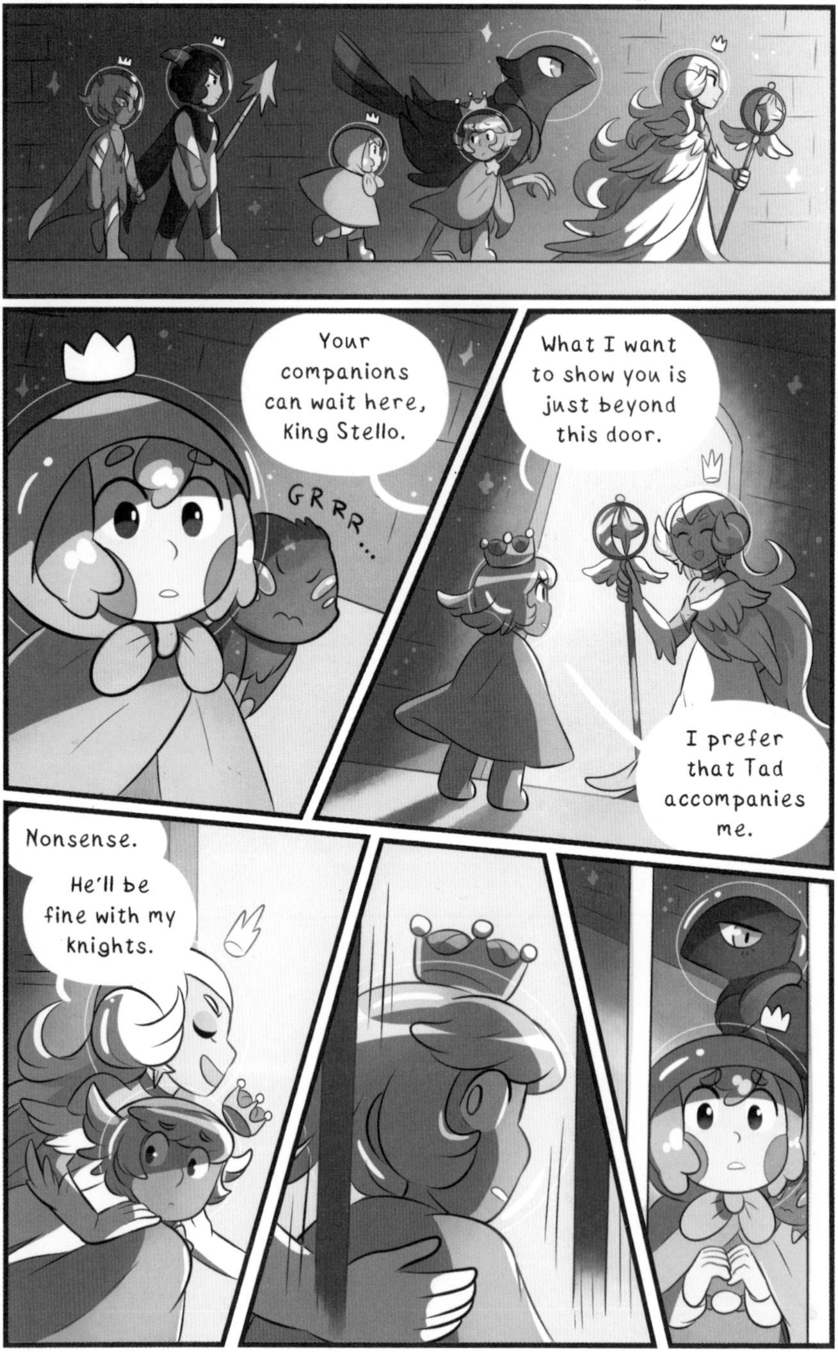
Your companions can wait here, King Stello.
GRRR...
What I want to show you is just beyond this door.
I prefer that Tad accompanies me.
Nonsense.
He'll be fine with my knights.

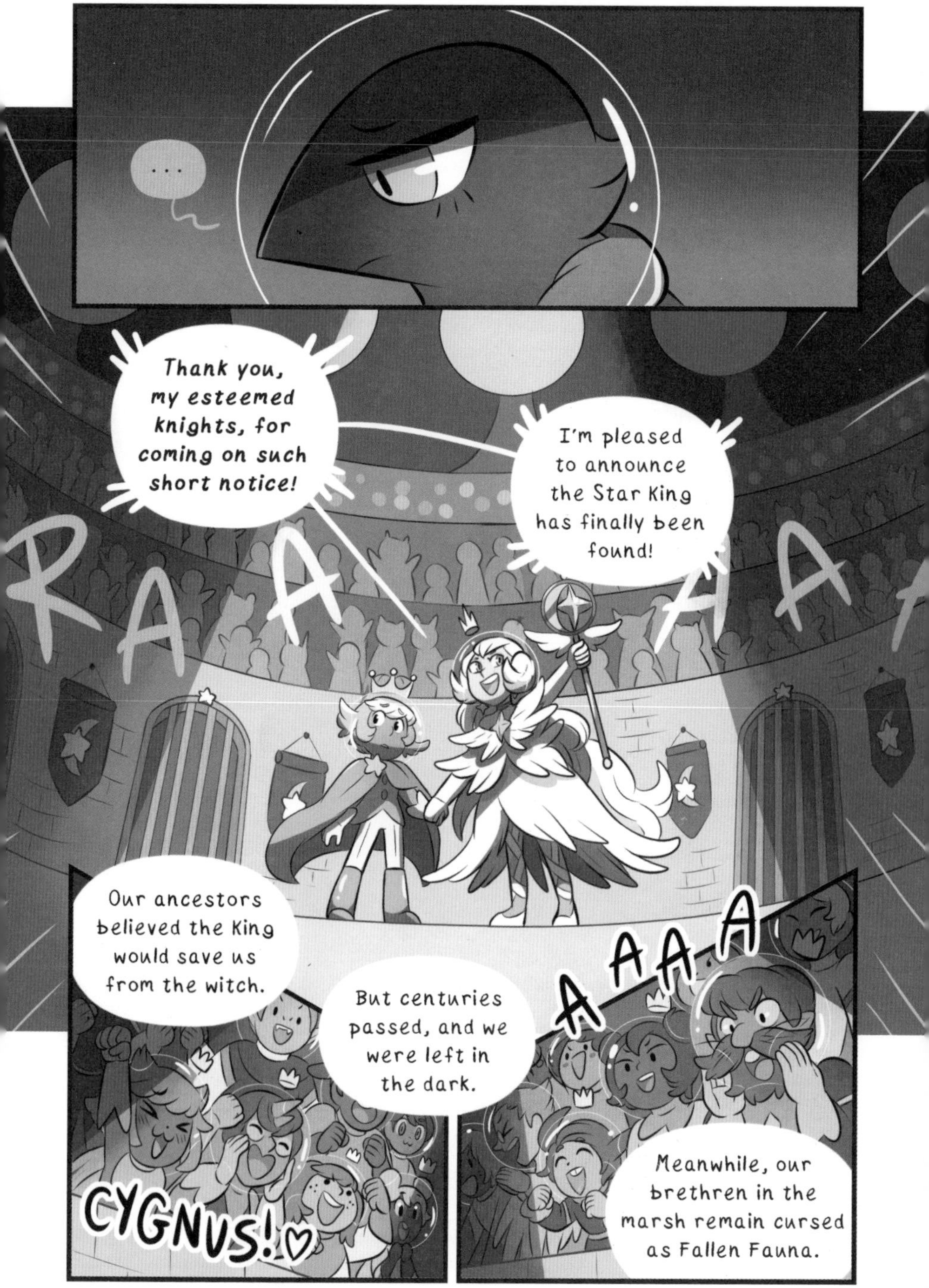
...
Thank you, my esteemed knights, for coming on such short notice!
I'm pleased to announce the Star King has finally been found!
RAAAAAA
Our ancestors believed the King would save us from the witch.
But centuries passed, and we were left in the dark.
AAAA
CYGNUS!♡
Meanwhile, our brethren in the marsh remain cursed as Fallen Fauna.

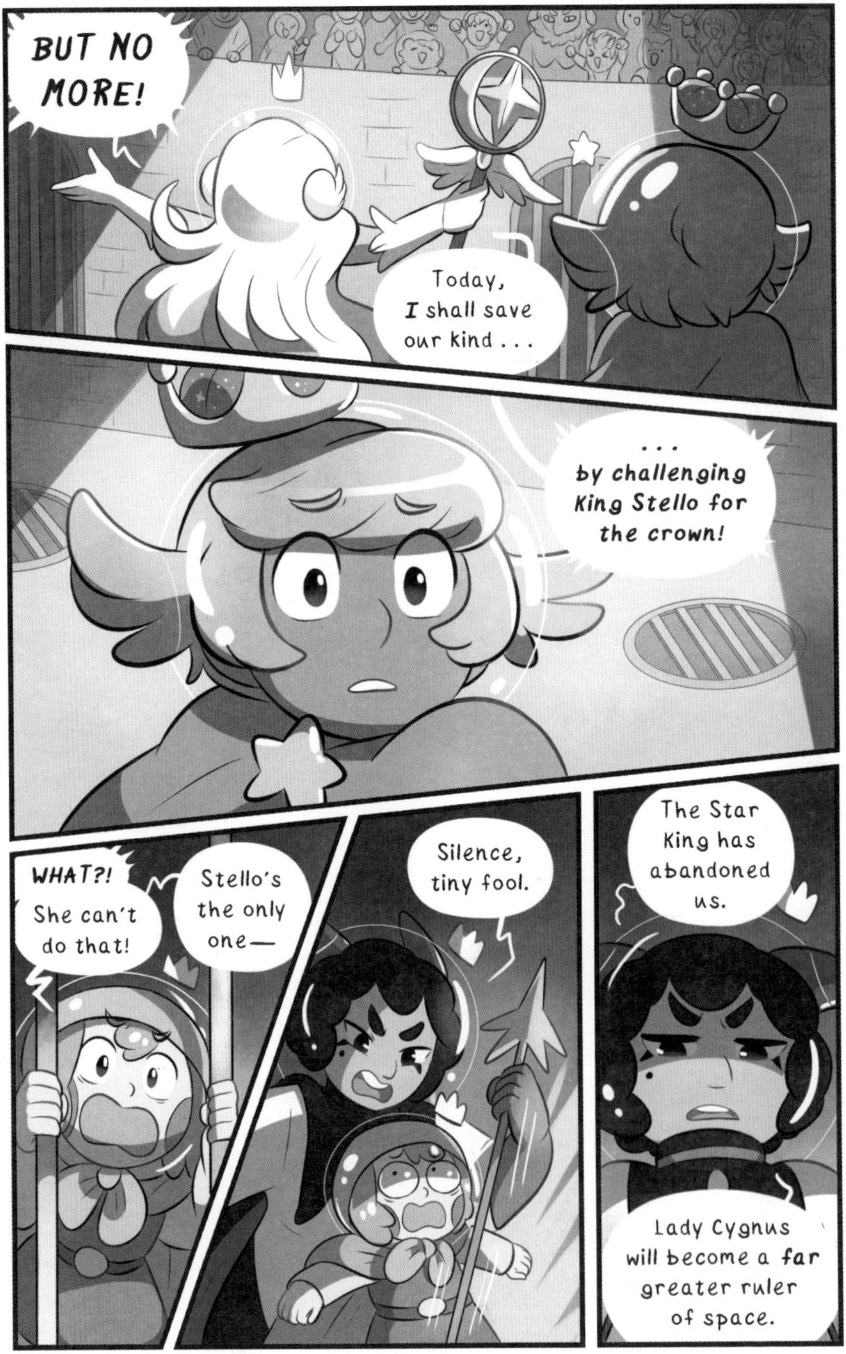
BUT NO MORE!
Today, I shall save our kind . . .
. . . by challenging King Stello for the crown!
WHAT?! She can't do that!
Stello's the only one—
Silence, tiny fool.
The Star King has abandoned us.
Lady Cygnus will become a far greater ruler of space.

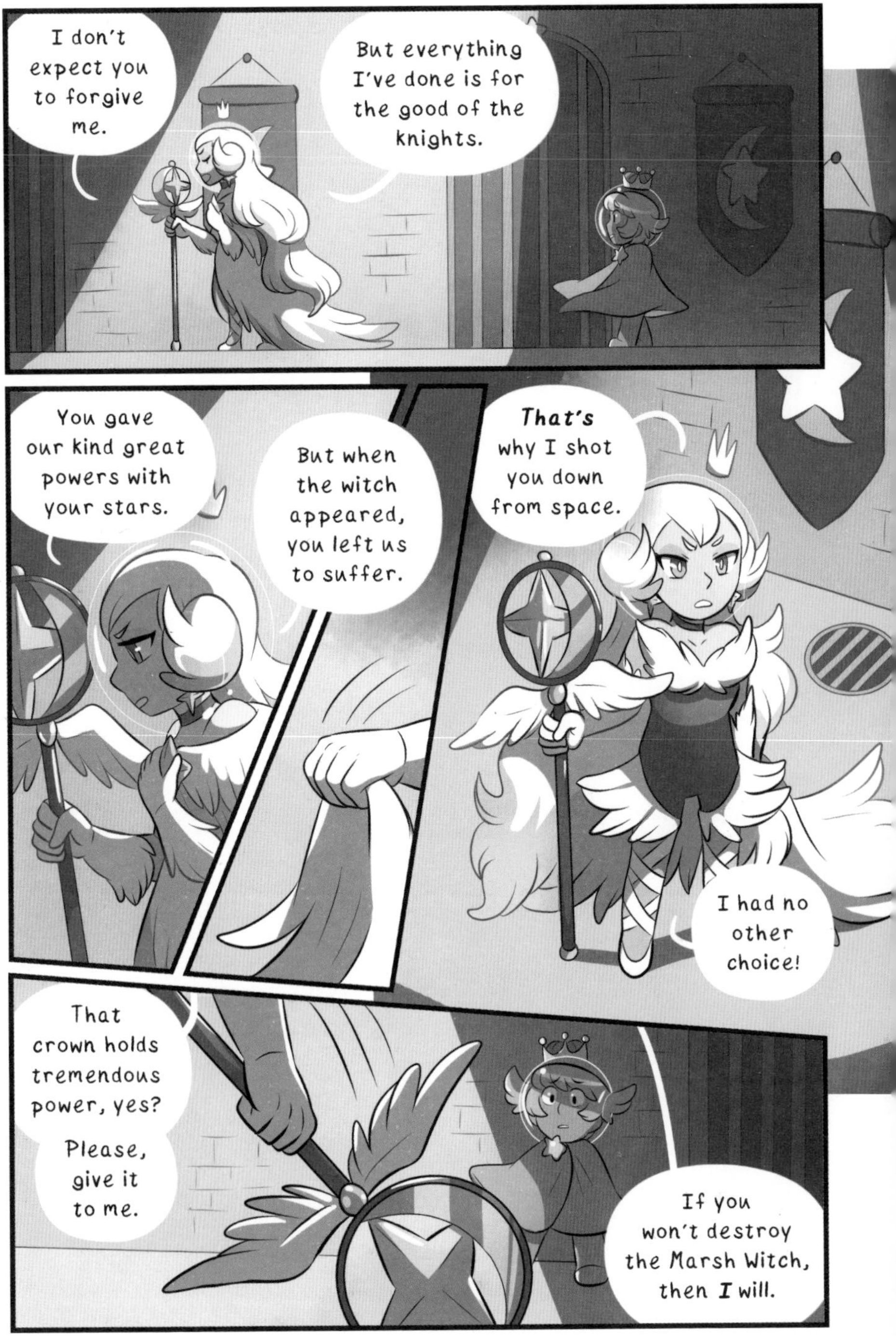
I don't expect you to forgive me.
But everything I've done is for the good of the knights.
You gave our kind great powers with your stars.
But when the witch appeared, you left us to suffer.
That's why I shot you down from space.
I had no other choice!
That crown holds tremendous power, yes?
Please, give it to me.
If you won't destroy the Marsh Witch, then *I* will.

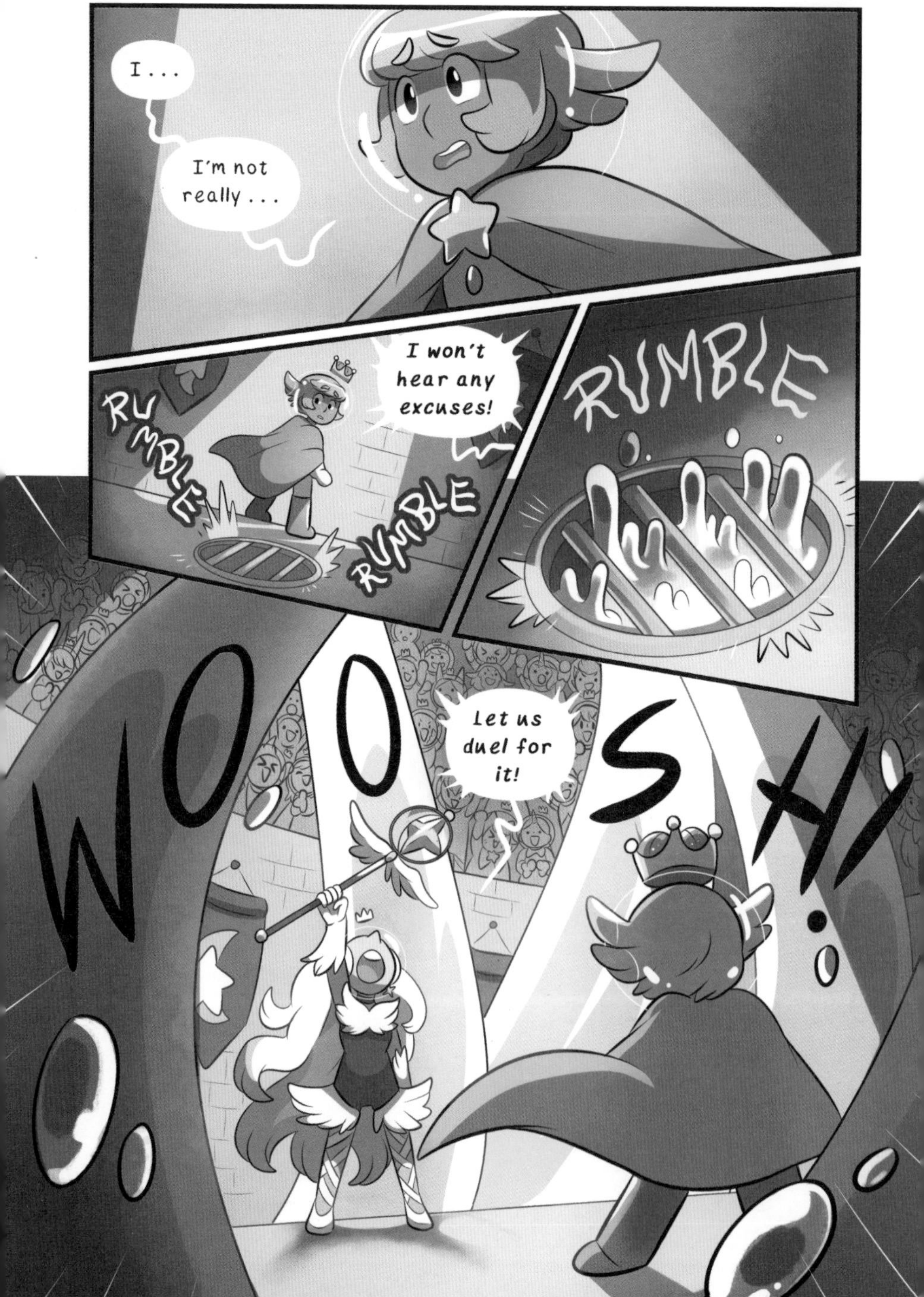
I . . .
I'm not really . . .
RUMBLE
I won't hear any excuses!
RUMBLE
RUMBLE
Let us duel for it!
WOOSH!

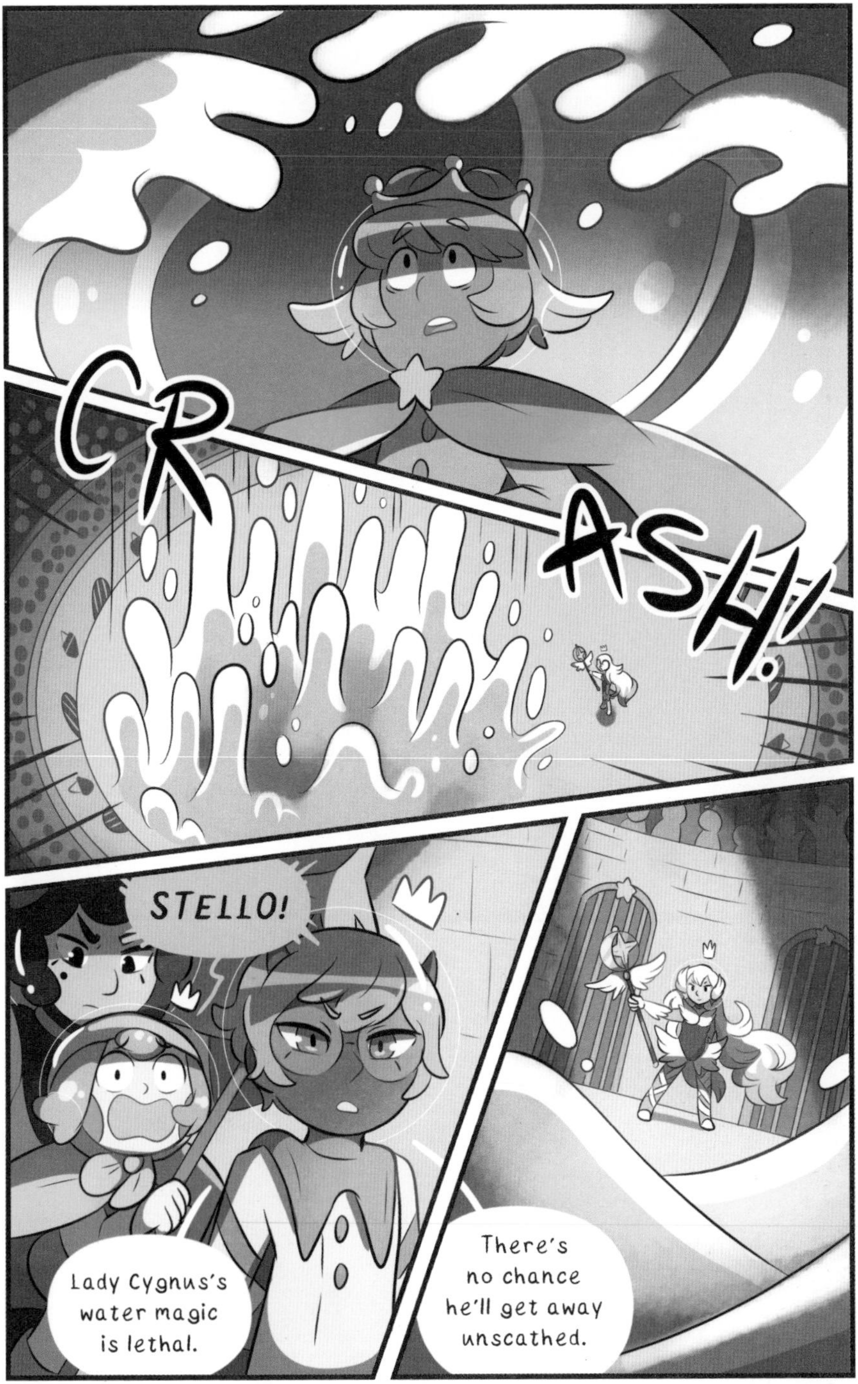
CRASH!
STELLO!
Lady Cygnus's water magic is lethal.
There's no chance he'll get away unscathed.

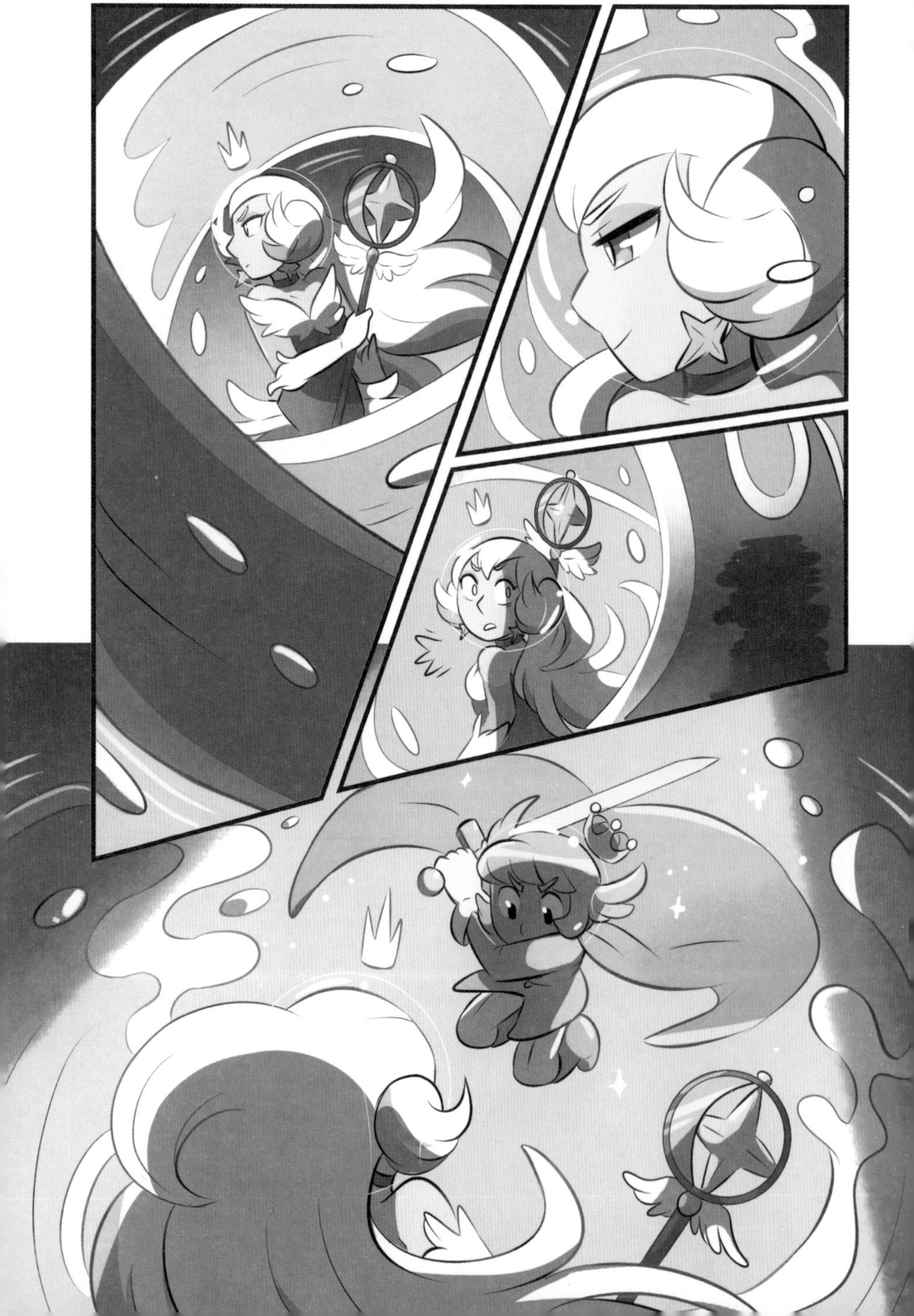

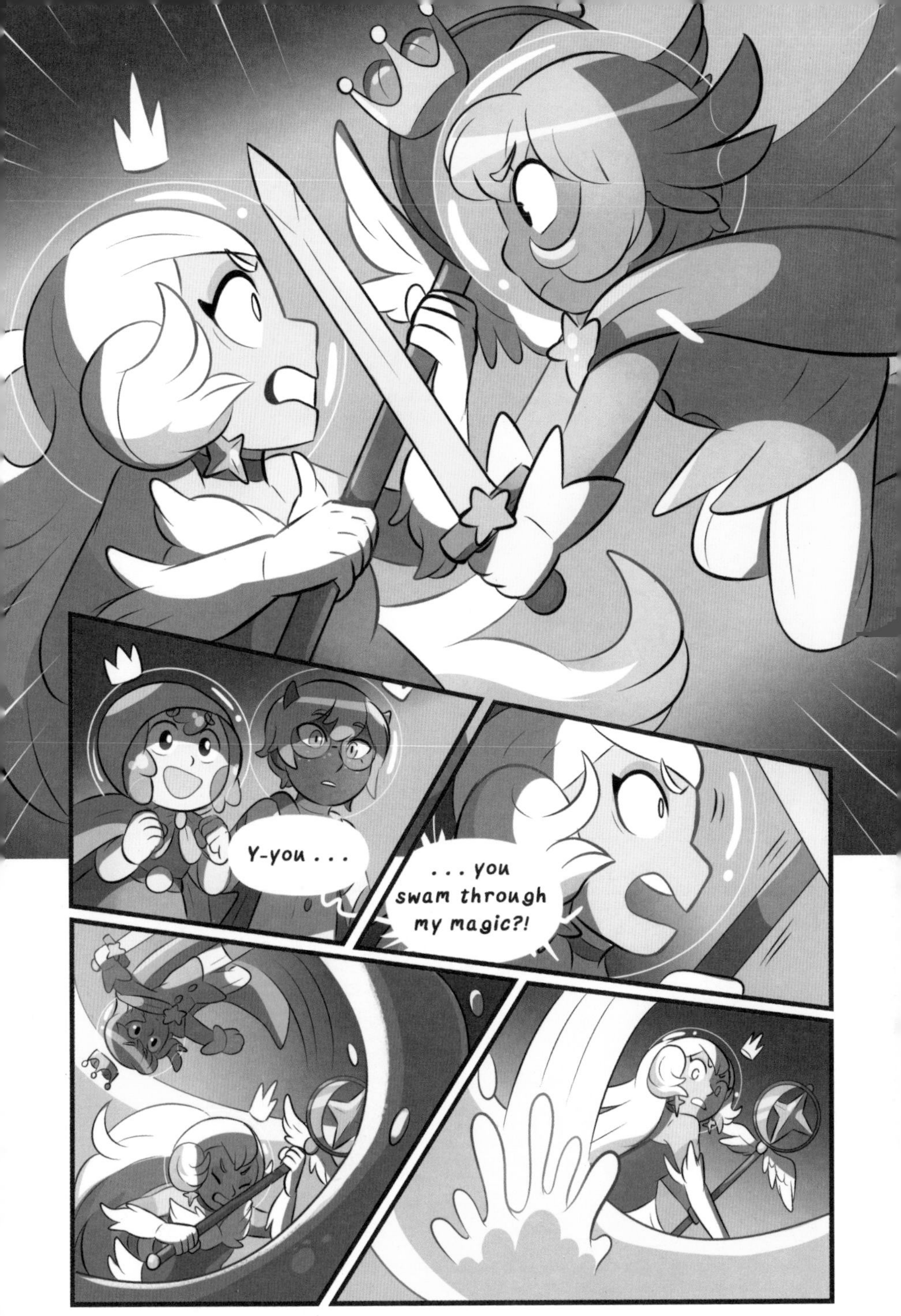
Y-you . . .
. . . you swam through my magic?!

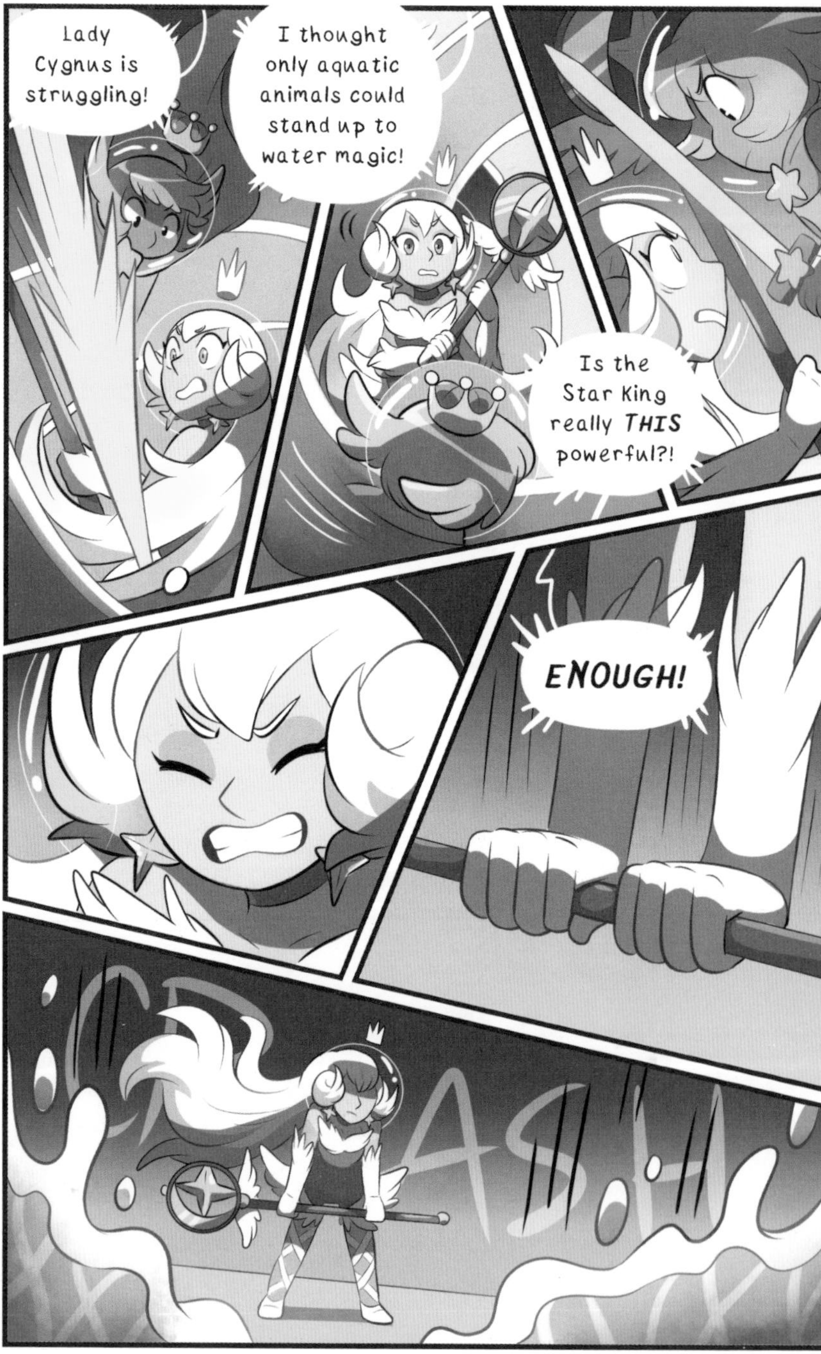
Lady Cygnus is struggling!
I thought only aquatic animals could stand up to water magic!
Is the Star King really THIS powerful?!
ENOUGH!

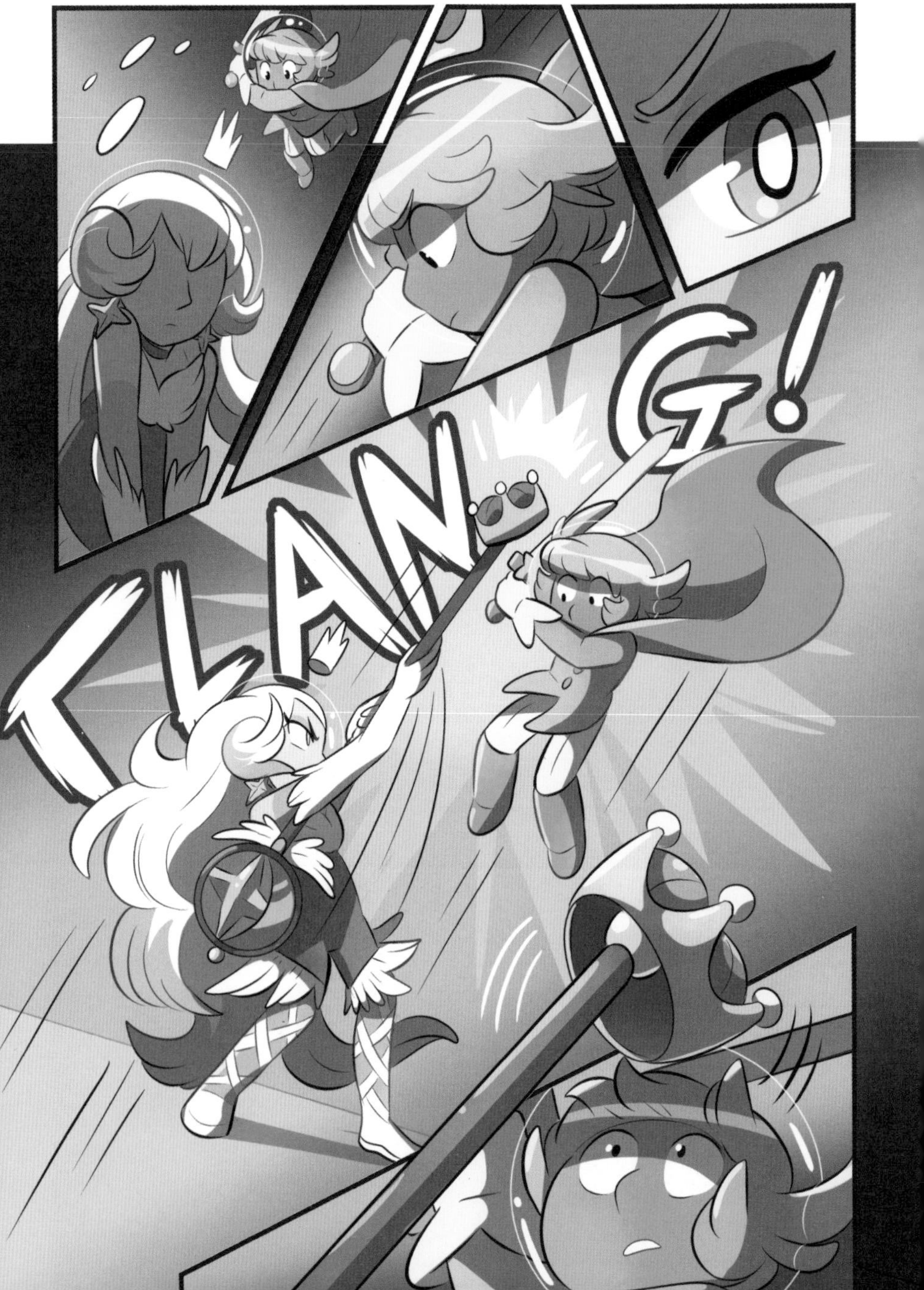
CLANG!

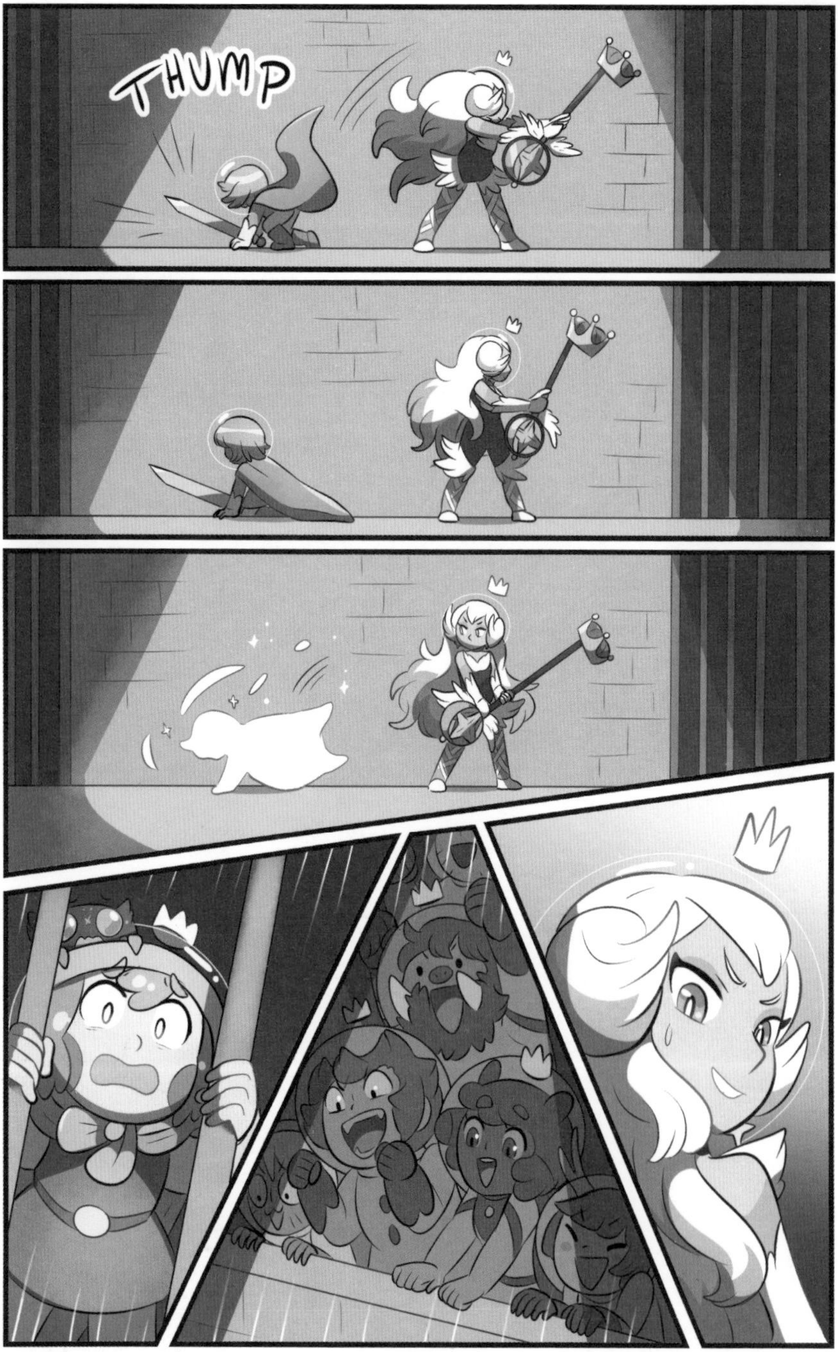
THUMP

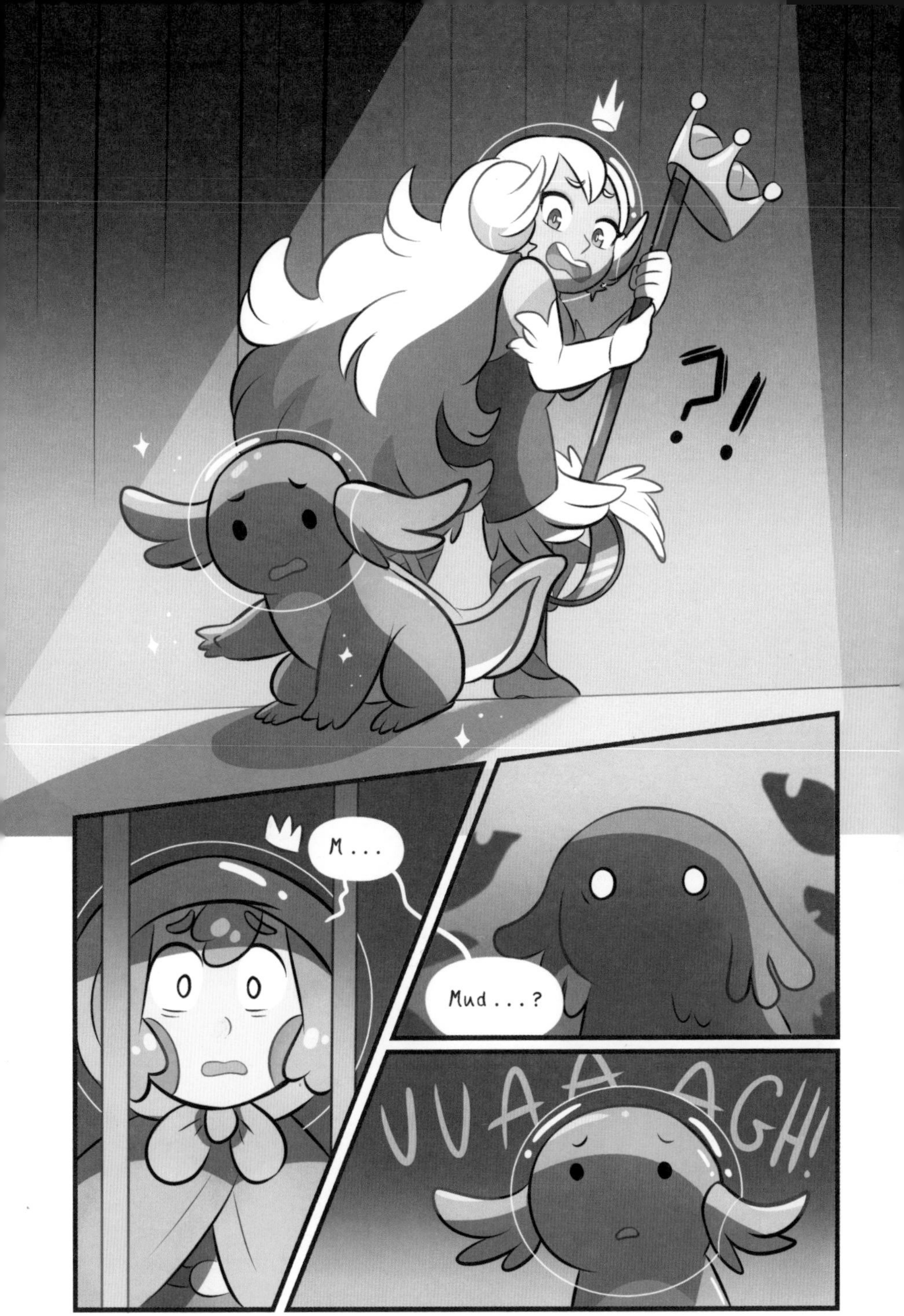
?!
M...
Mud...?
UUAAAGH!

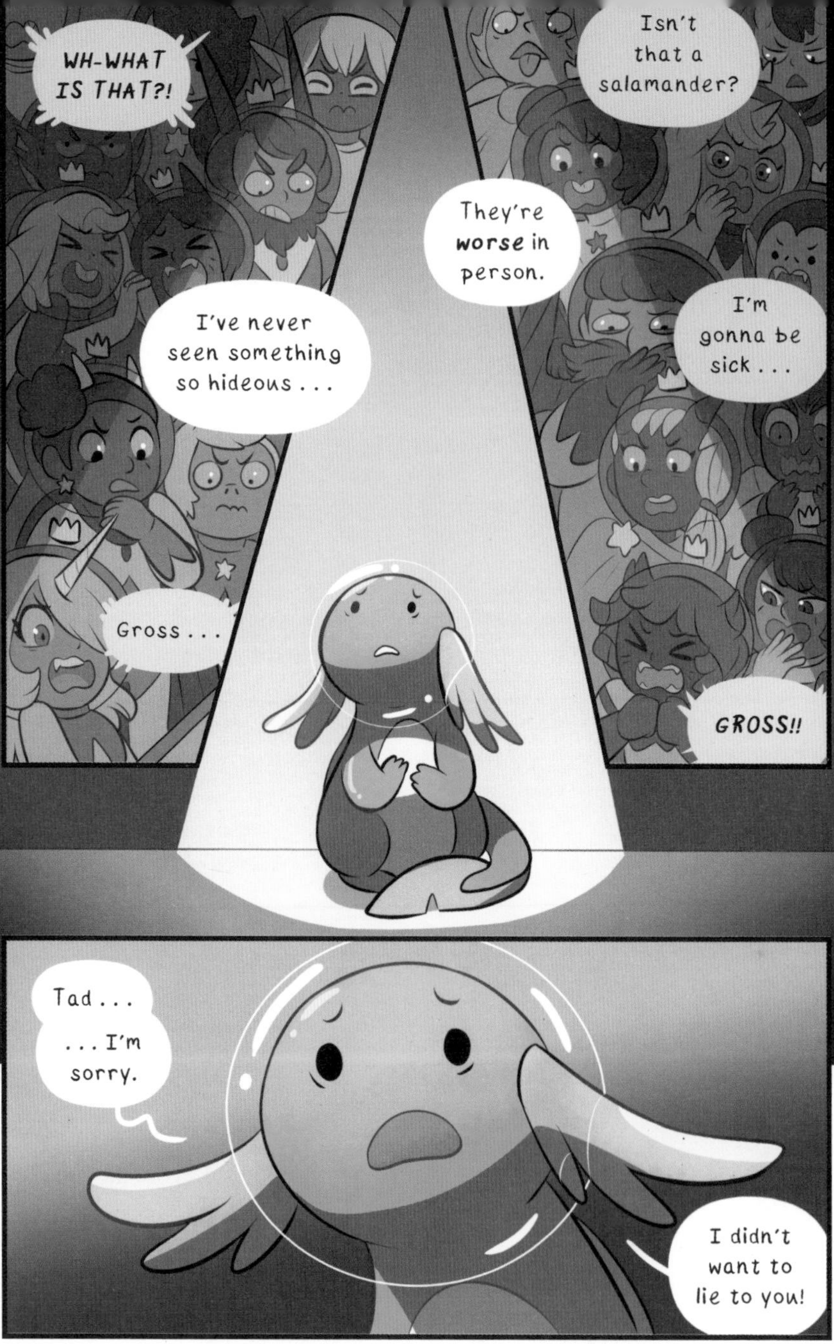
WH-WHAT IS THAT?!
Isn't that a salamander?
They're **worse** in person.
I've never seen something so hideous . . .
I'm gonna be sick . . .
Gross . . .
GROSS!!
Tad . . .
. . . I'm sorry.
I didn't want to lie to you!

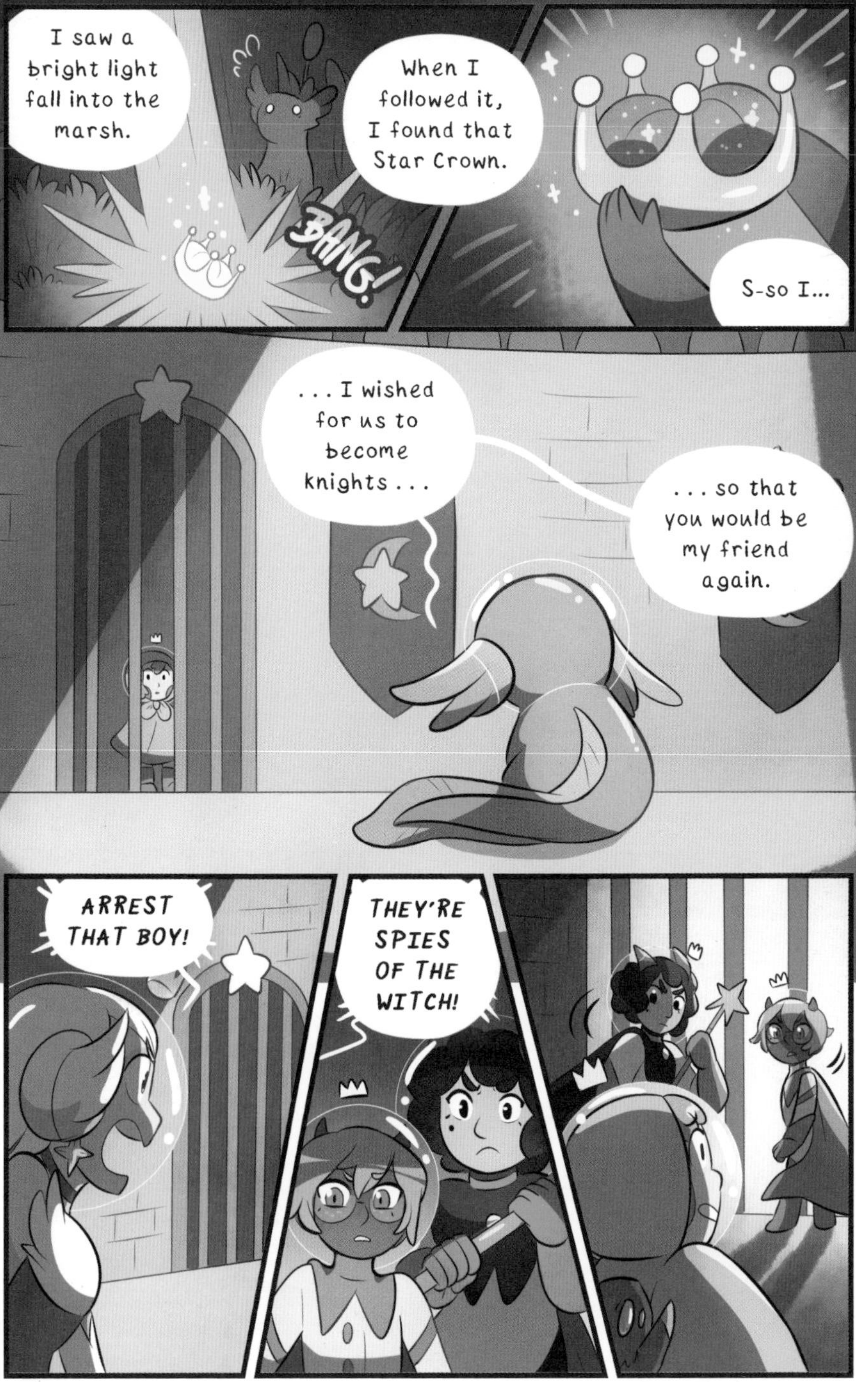

I saw a bright light fall into the marsh.
When I followed it, I found that Star Crown.
BANG!
S-so I...
. . . I wished for us to become knights . . .
. . . so that you would be my friend again.
ARREST THAT BOY!
THEY'RE SPIES OF THE WITCH!

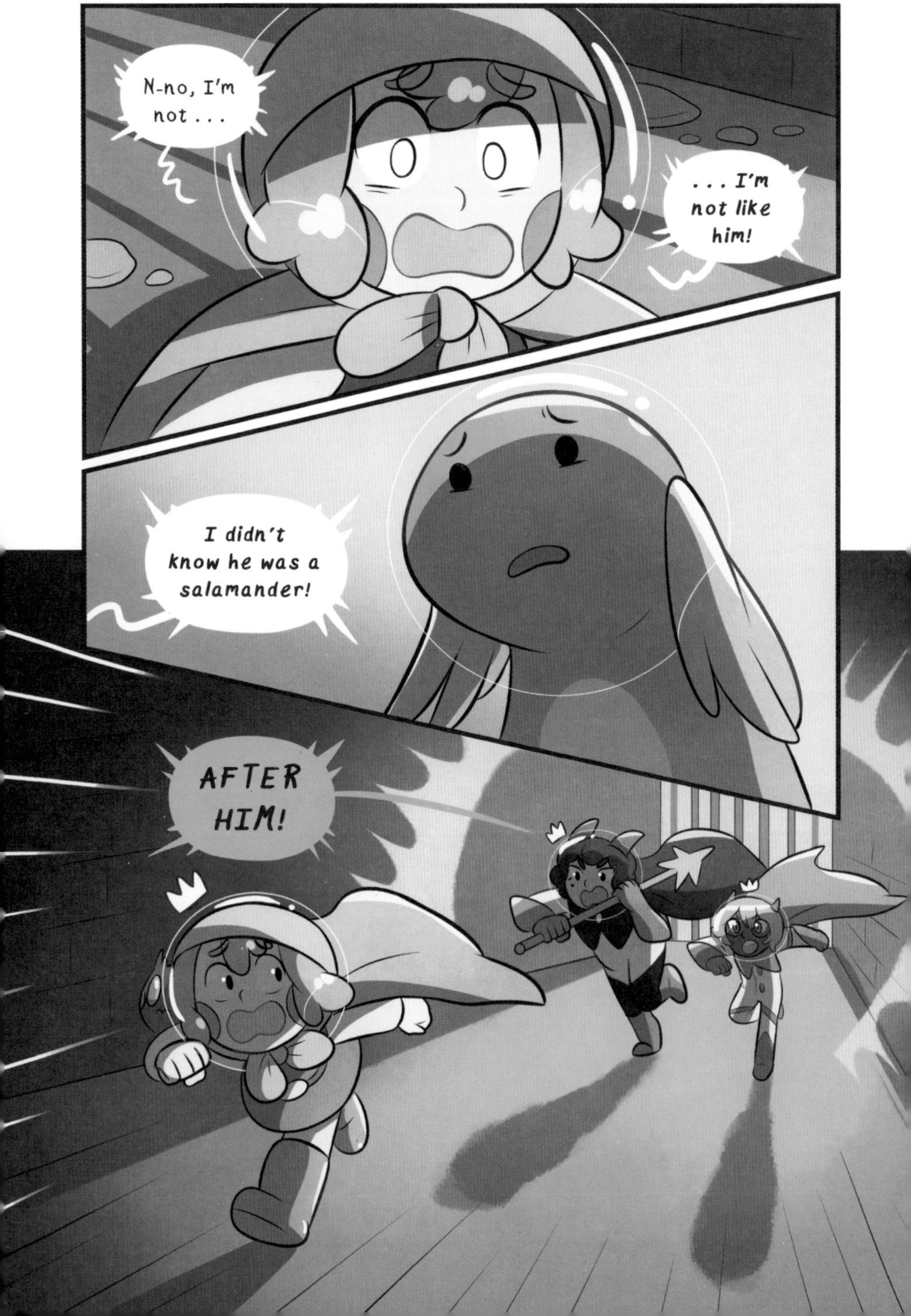
N-no, I'm not . . .
. . . I'm not like him!
I didn't know he was a salamander!
AFTER HIM!

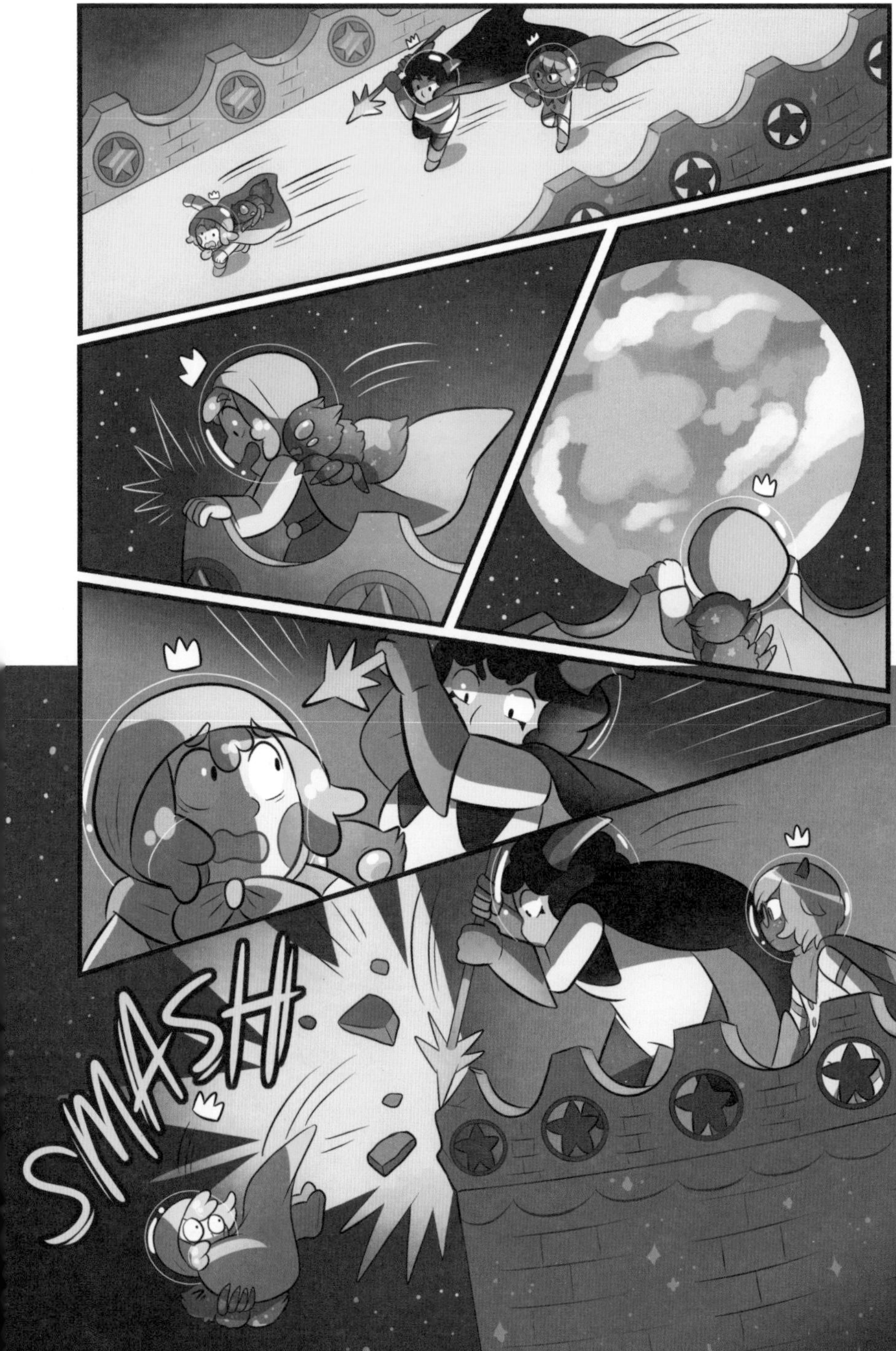
SMASH

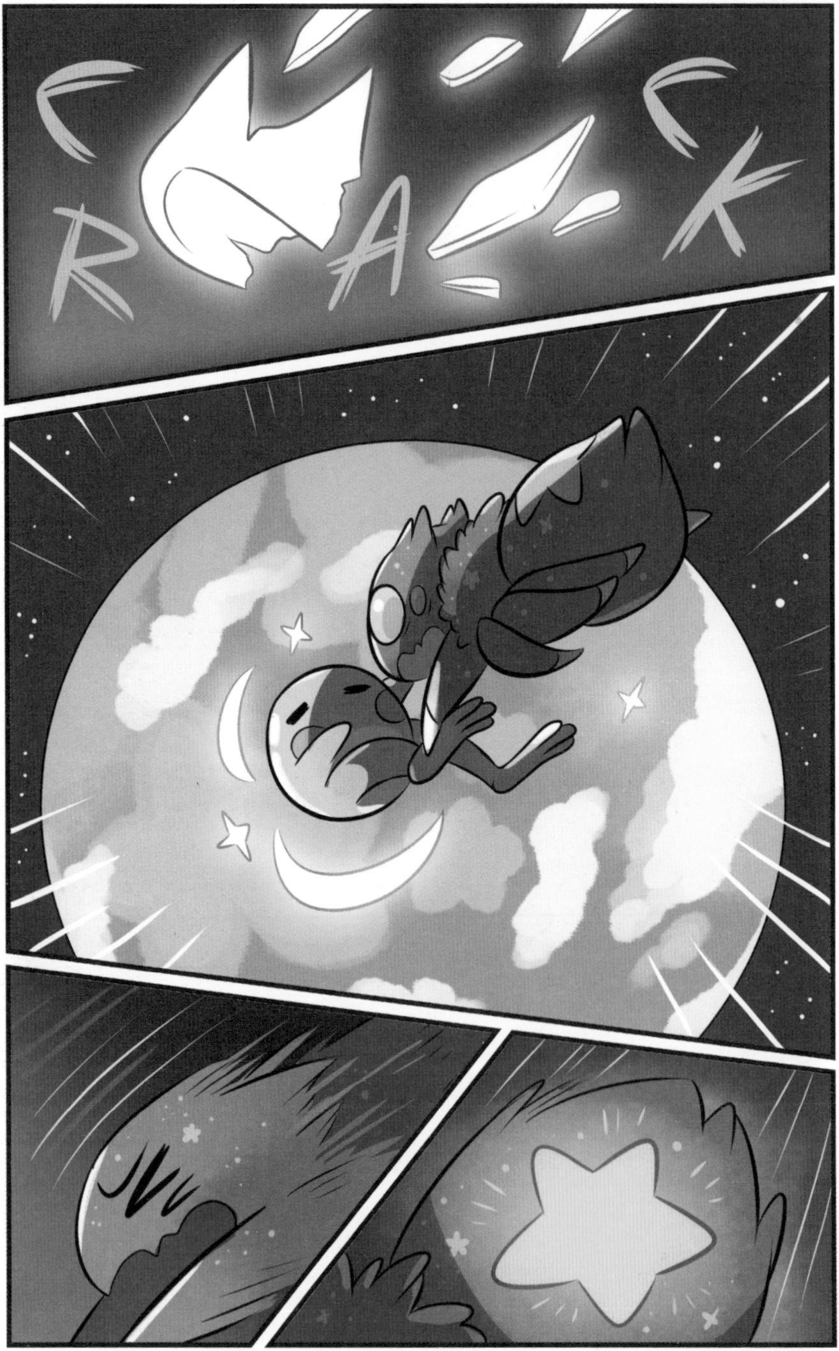
CRACK

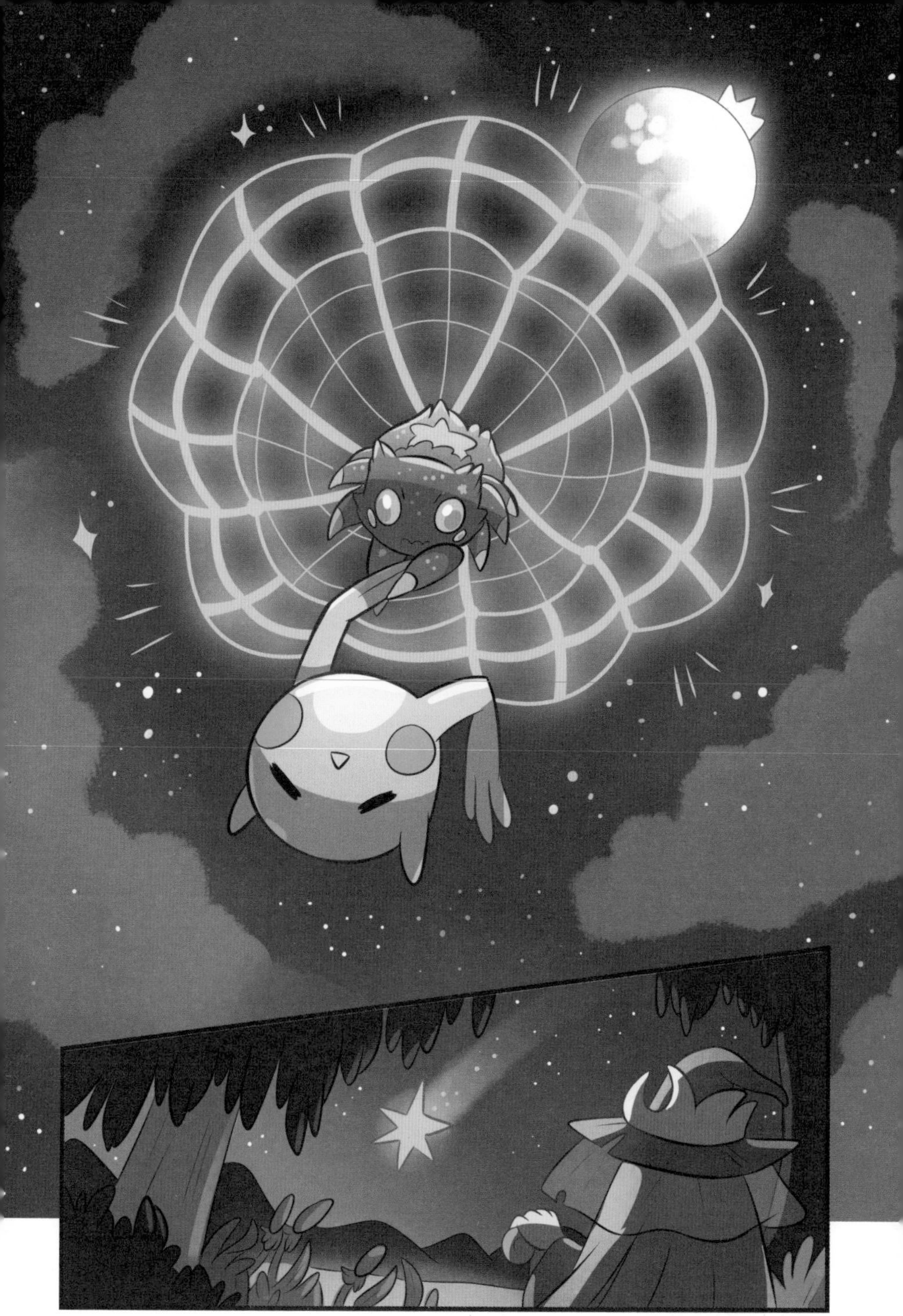

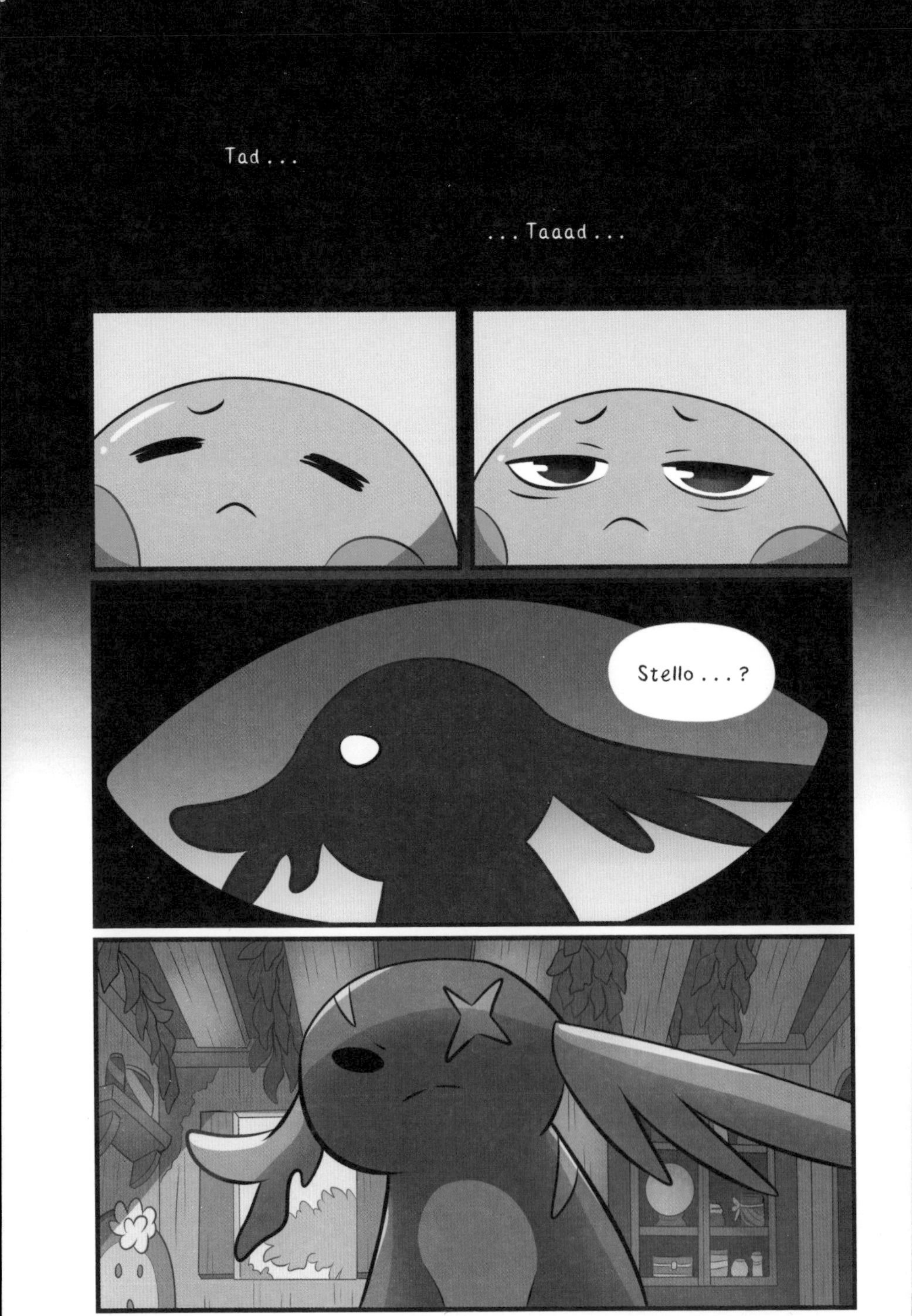
Tad . . .
. . . Taaad . . .
Stello . . . ?

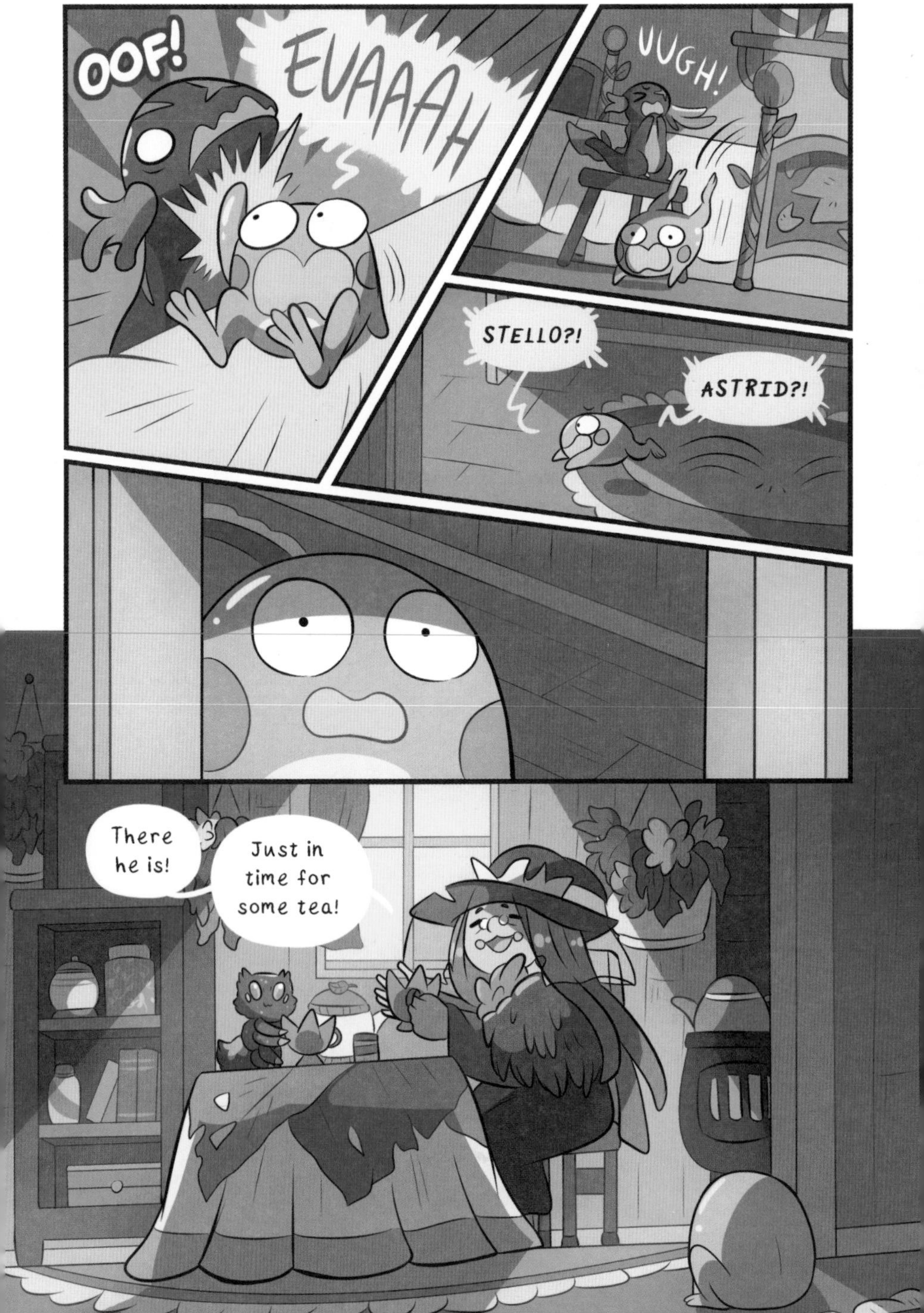
OOF!
EVAAAAH
UUGH!
STELLO?!
ASTRID?!
There he is!
Just in time for some tea!

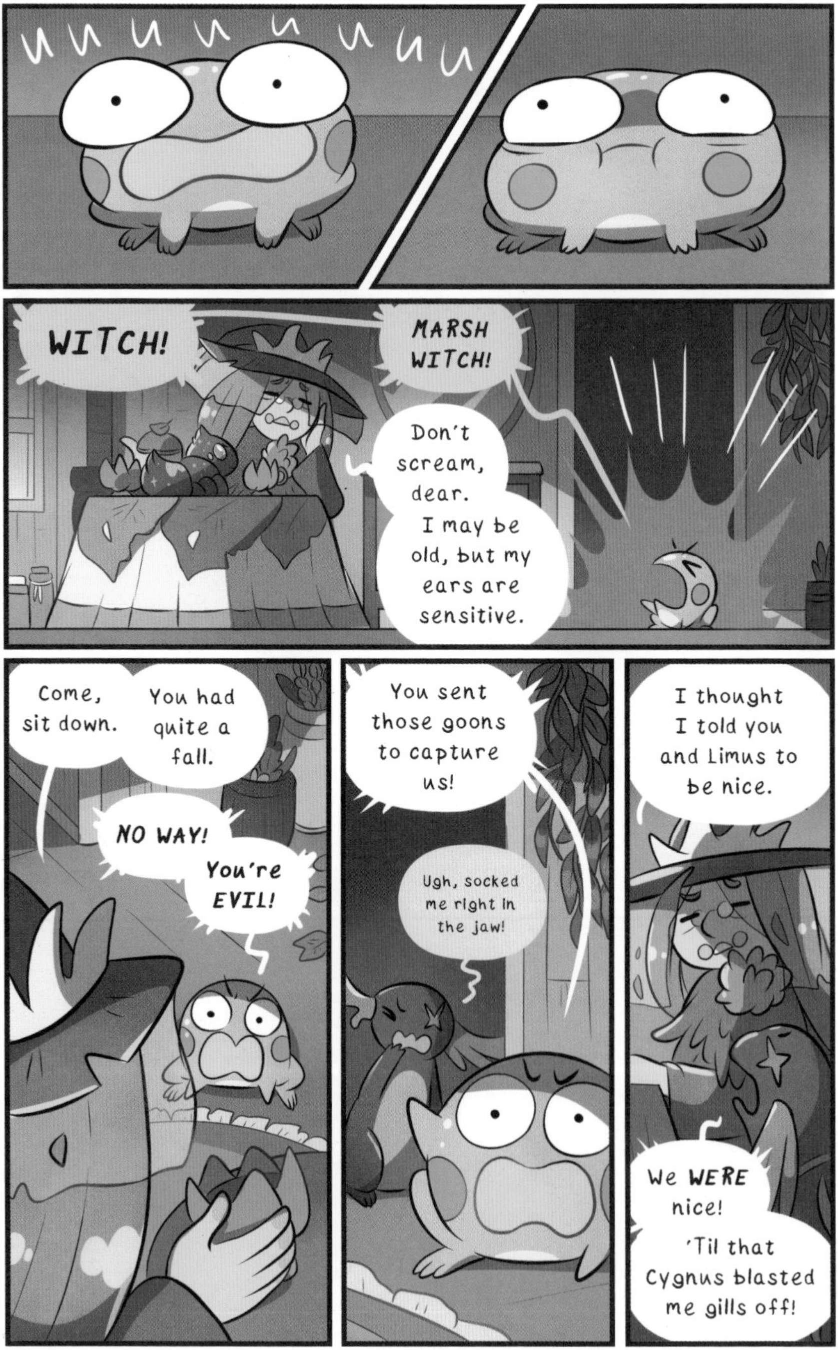

uuuuuuuuuu
WITCH!
MARSH WITCH!
Don't scream, dear.
I may be old, but my ears are sensitive.
Come, sit down.
You had quite a fall.
NO WAY!
You're EVIL!
You sent those goons to capture us!
Ugh, socked me right in the jaw!
I thought I told you and Limus to be nice.
We WERE nice!
'Til that Cygnus blasted me gills off!

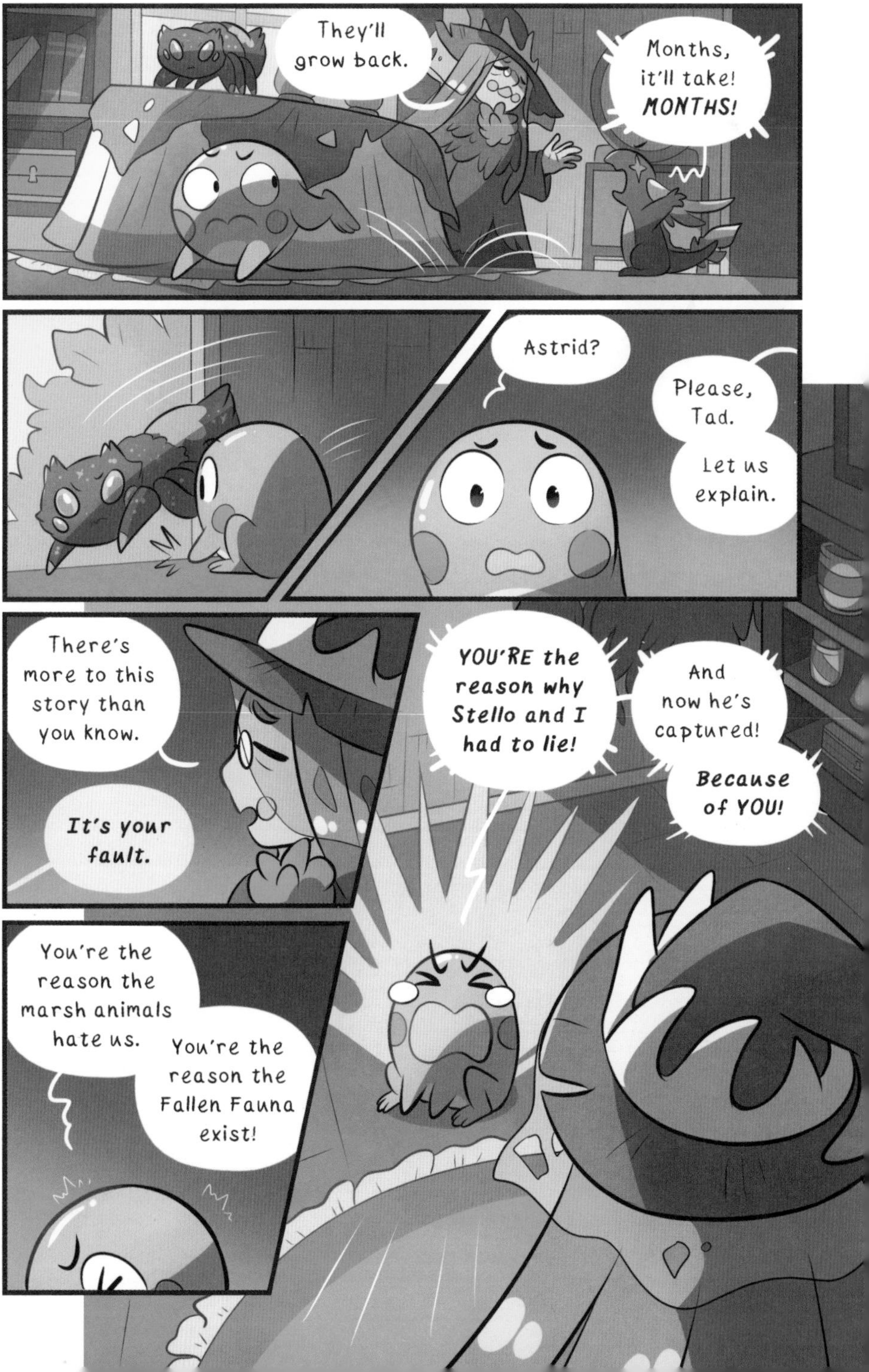
They'll grow back.
Months, it'll take! MONTHS!
Astrid?
Please, Tad.
Let us explain.
There's more to this story than you know.
It's your fault.
YOU'RE the reason why Stello and I had to lie!
And now he's captured!
Because of YOU!
You're the reason the marsh animals hate us.
You're the reason the Fallen Fauna exist!

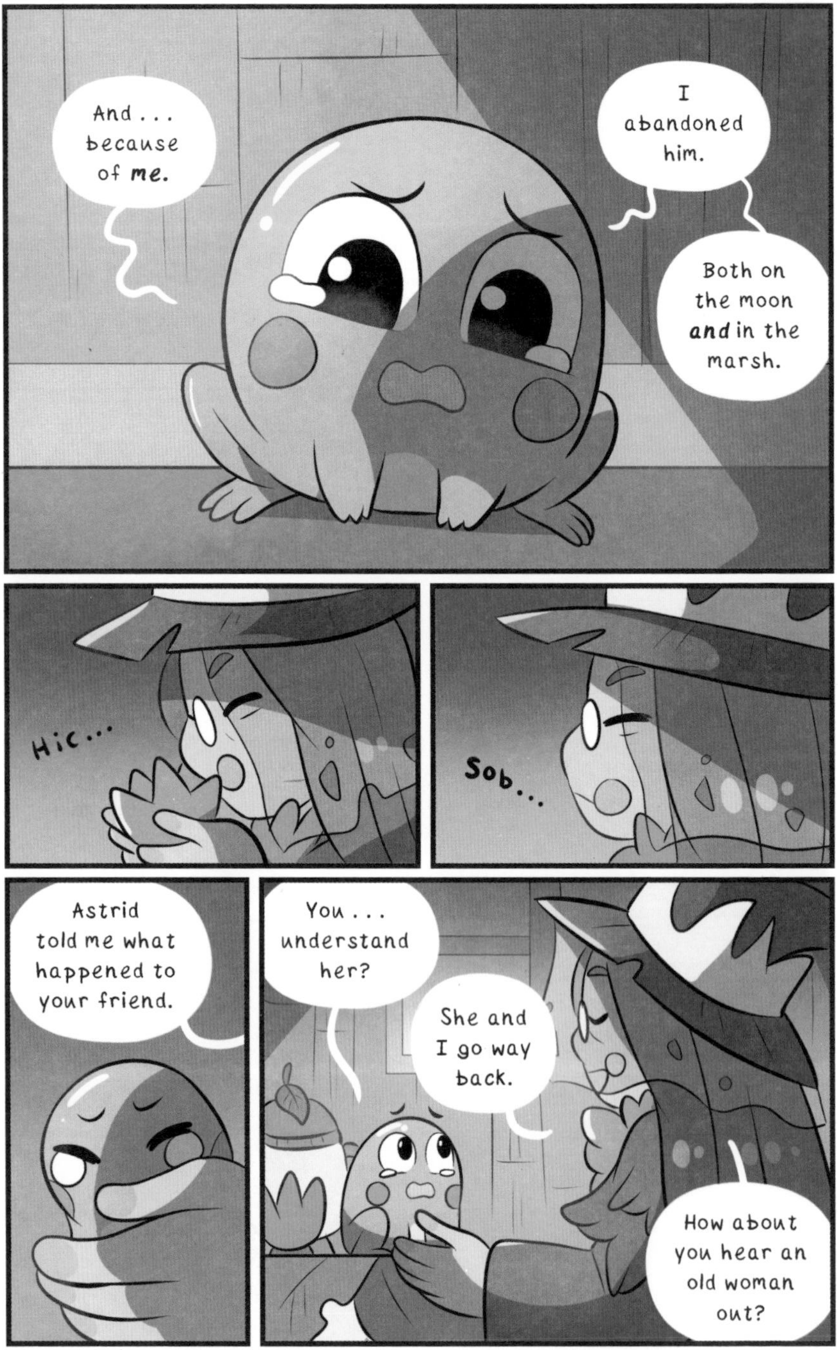

And . . . because of **me.**
I abandoned him.
Both on the moon **and** in the marsh.
Hic...
Sob...
Astrid told me what happened to your friend.
You . . . understand her?
She and I go way back.
How about you hear an old woman out?

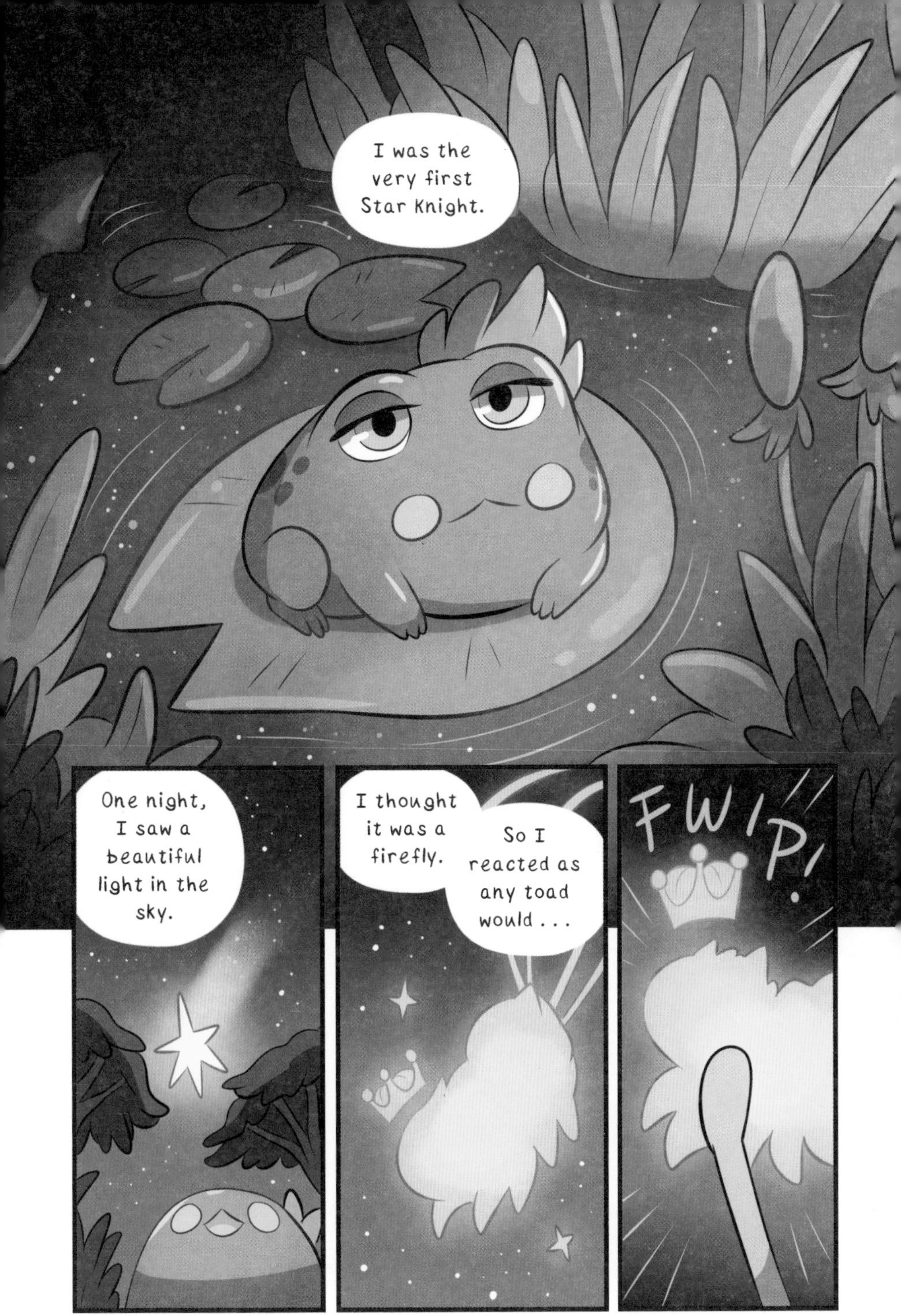
I was the very first Star Knight.
One night, I saw a beautiful light in the sky.
I thought it was a firefly.
So I reacted as any toad would . . .
FWIP!

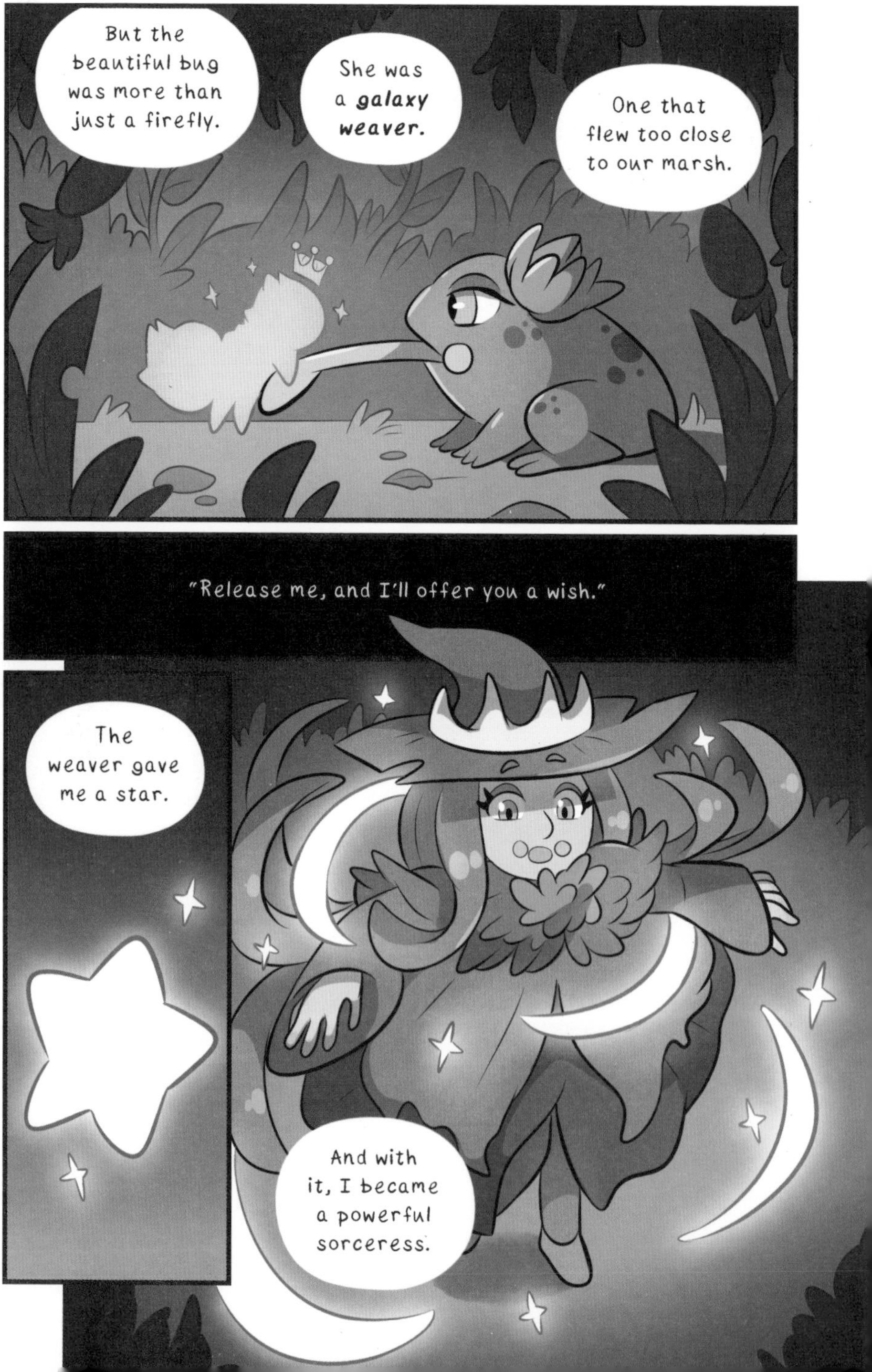
But the beautiful bug was more than just a firefly.
She was a **galaxy weaver.**
One that flew too close to our marsh.
"Release me, and I'll offer you a wish."
The weaver gave me a star.
And with it, I became a powerful sorceress.

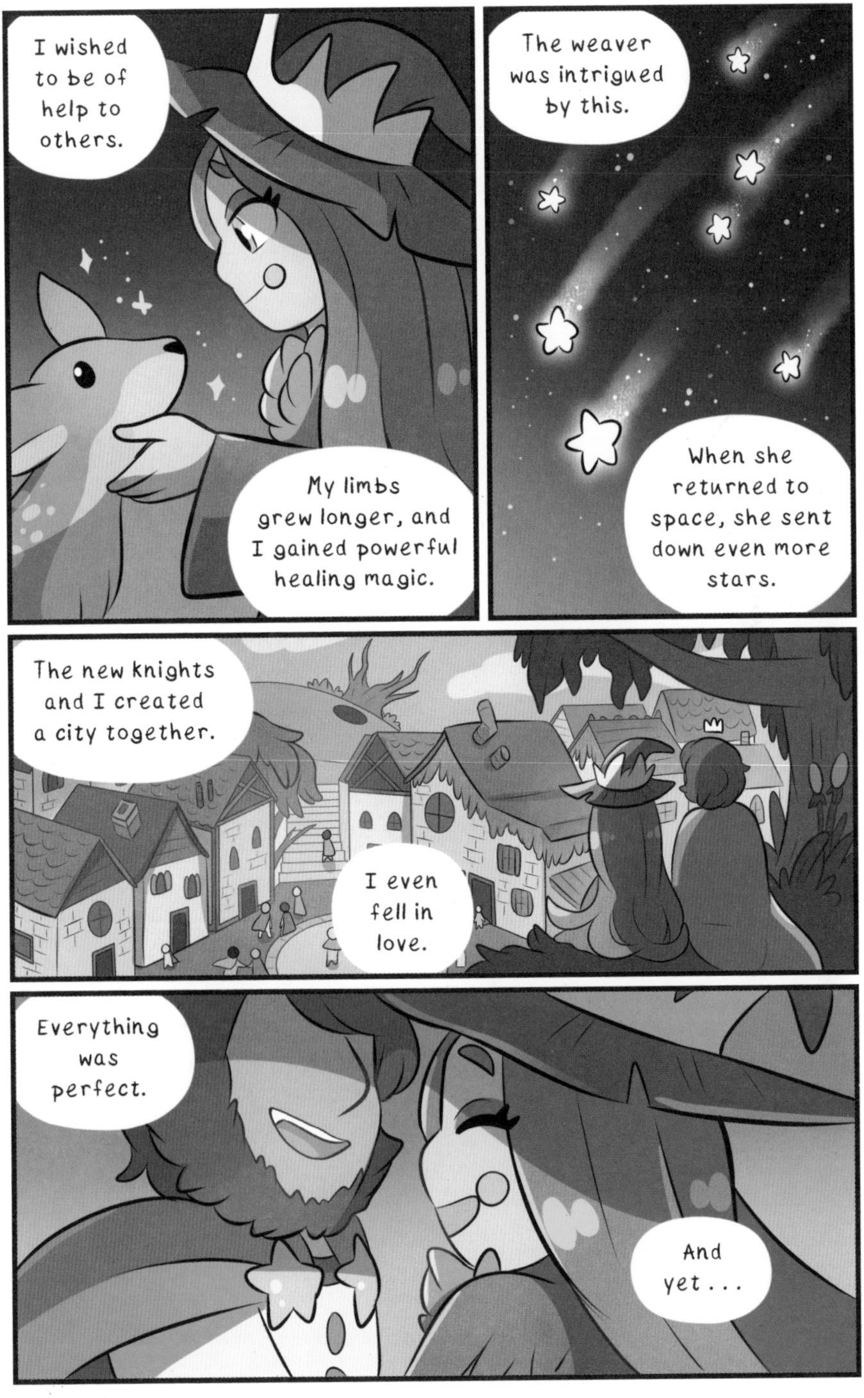
I wished to be of help to others.
My limbs grew longer, and I gained powerful healing magic.
The weaver was intrigued by this.
When she returned to space, she sent down even more stars.
The new knights and I created a city together.
I even fell in love.
Everything was perfect.
And yet . . .

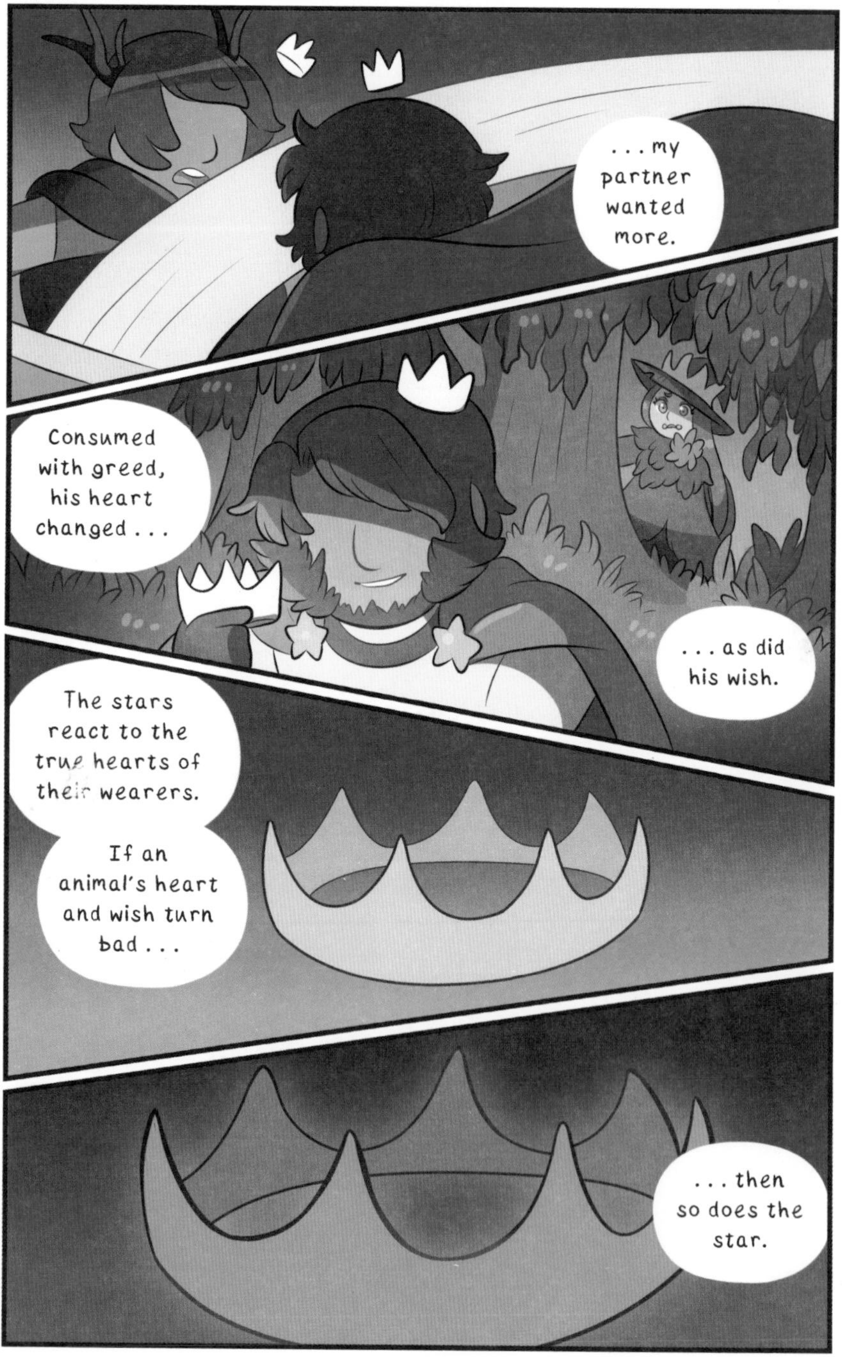
. . . my partner wanted more.
Consumed with greed, his heart changed . . .
. . . as did his wish.
The stars react to the true hearts of their wearers.
If an animal's heart and wish turn bad . . .
. . . then so does the star.

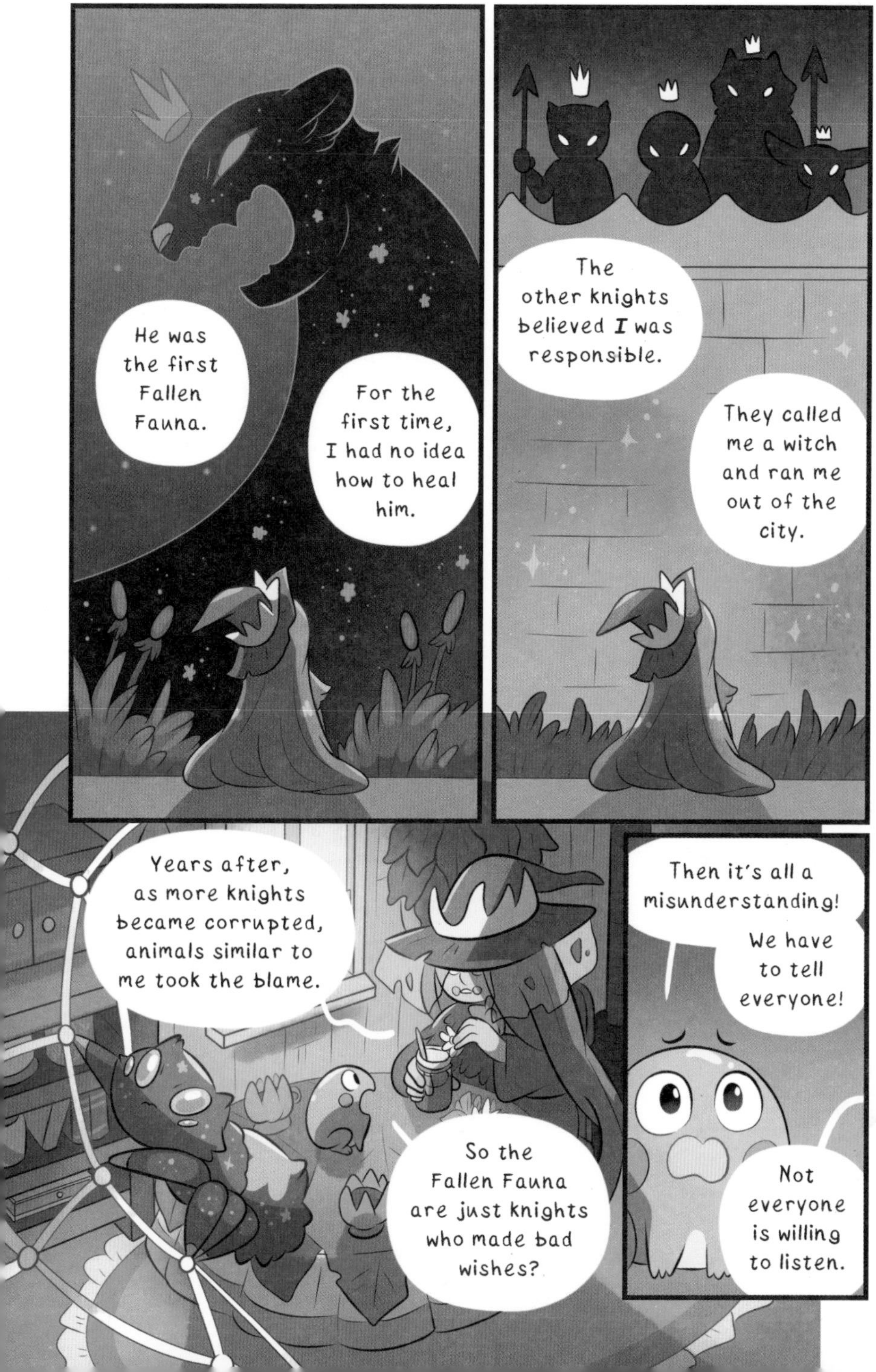
He was the first Fallen Fauna.
For the first time, I had no idea how to heal him.
The other knights believed I was responsible.
They called me a witch and ran me out of the city.
Years after, as more knights became corrupted, animals similar to me took the blame.
So the Fallen Fauna are just knights who made bad wishes?
Then it's all a misunderstanding!
We have to tell everyone!
Not everyone is willing to listen.

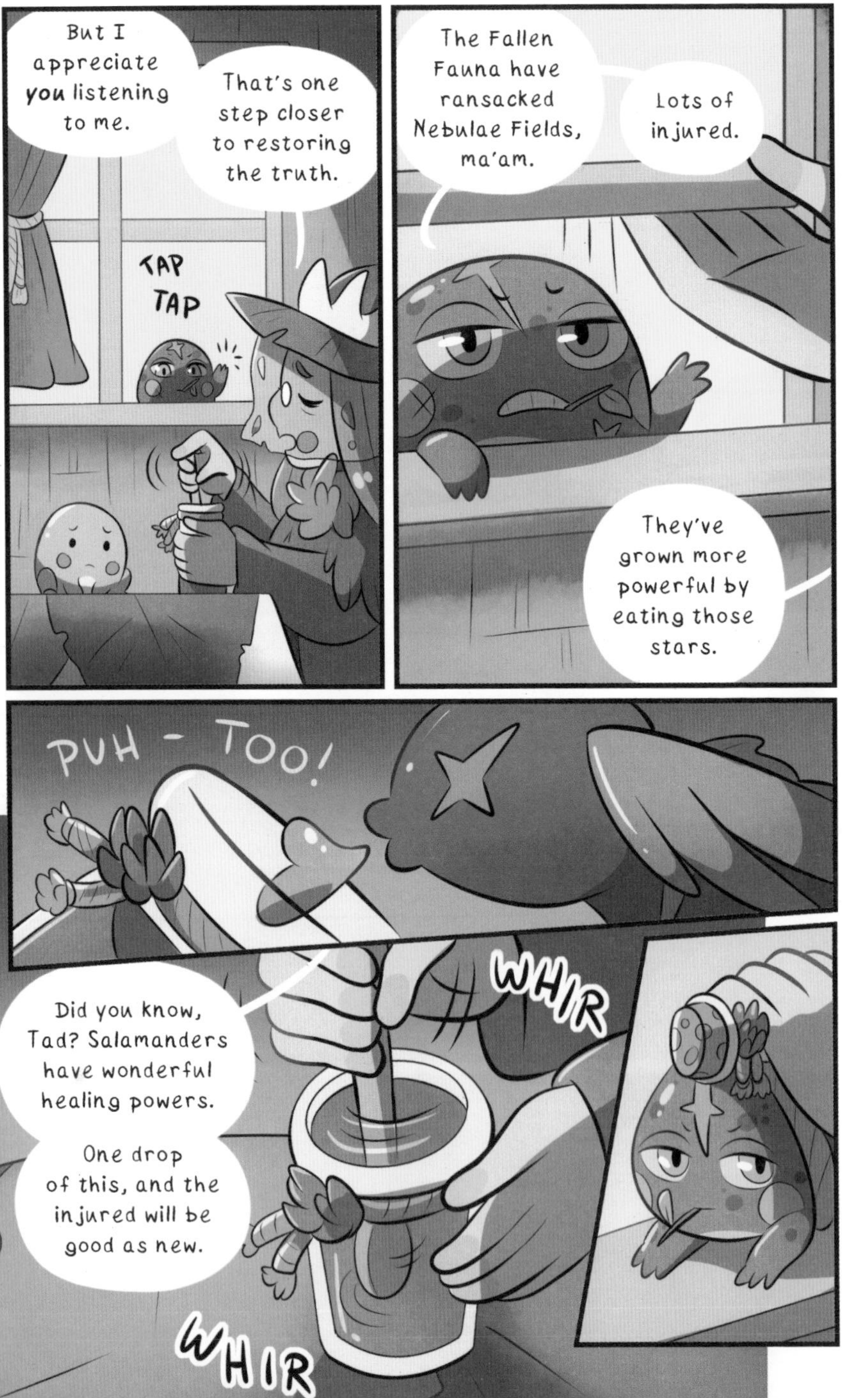
But I appreciate **you** listening to me.
That's one step closer to restoring the truth.
TAP TAP
The Fallen Fauna have ransacked Nebulae Fields, ma'am.
Lots of injured.
They've grown more powerful by eating those stars.
PUH - TOO!
WHIR
Did you know, Tad? Salamanders have wonderful healing powers.
One drop of this, and the injured will be good as new.
WHIR

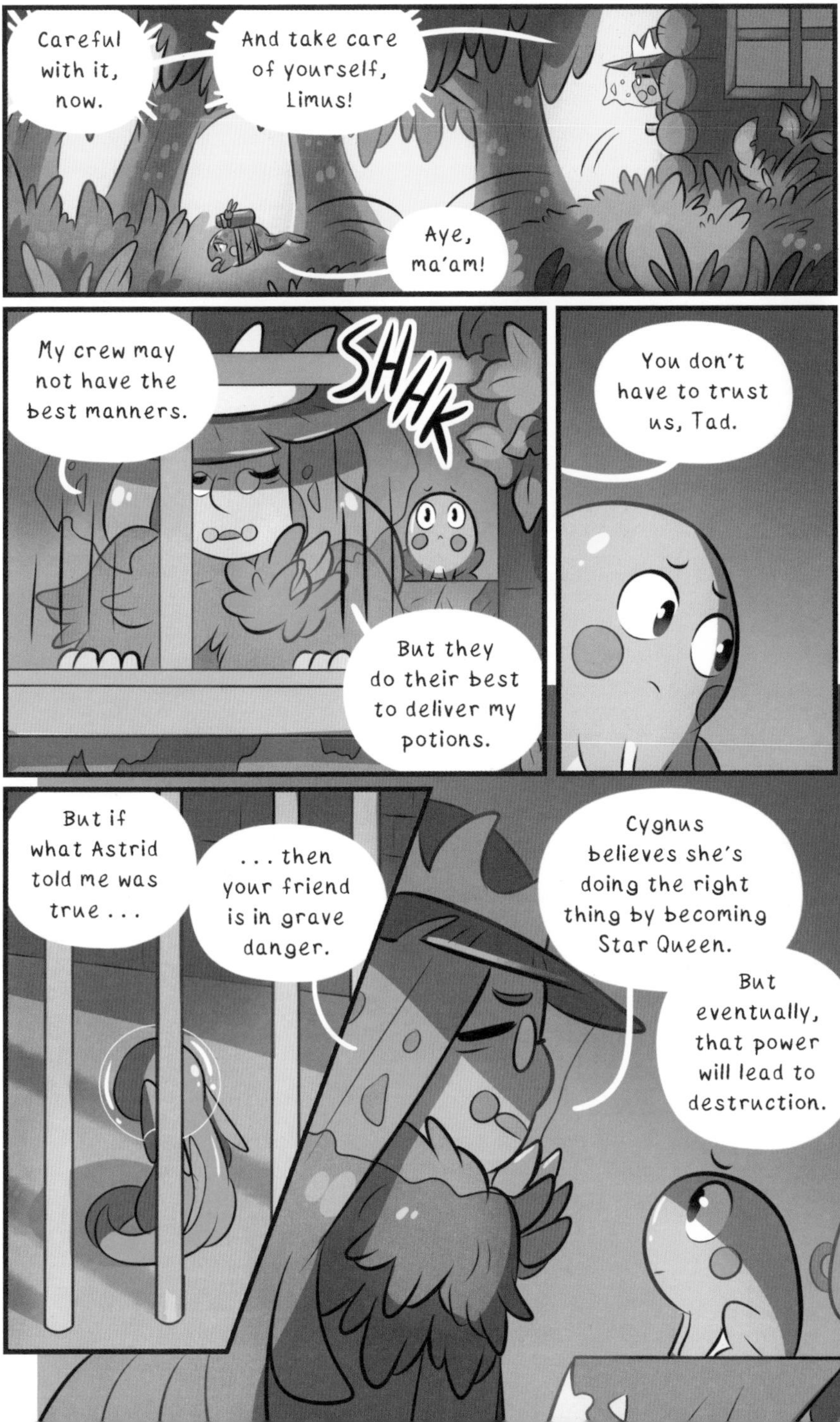
Careful with it, now.
And take care of yourself, Limus!
Aye, ma'am!
My crew may not have the best manners.
SHHK
But they do their best to deliver my potions.
You don't have to trust us, Tad.
But if what Astrid told me was true . . .
. . . then your friend is in grave danger.
Cygnus believes she's doing the right thing by becoming Star Queen.
But eventually, that power will lead to destruction.

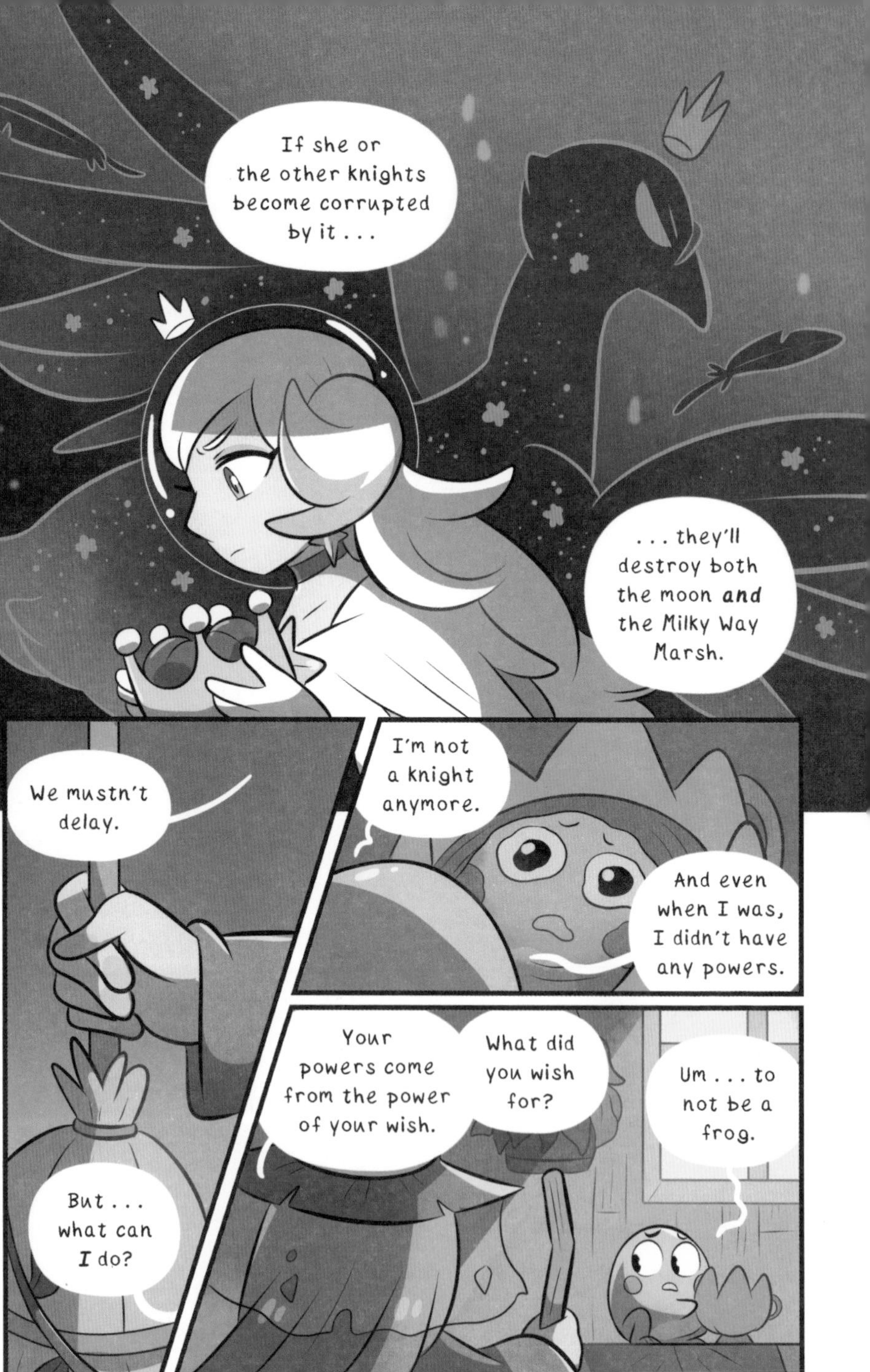
If she or the other knights become corrupted by it . . .
. . . they'll destroy both the moon **and** the Milky Way Marsh.
We mustn't delay.
I'm not a knight anymore.
And even when I was, I didn't have any powers.
Your powers come from the power of your wish.
What did you wish for?
Um . . . to not be a frog.
But . . . what can *I* do?

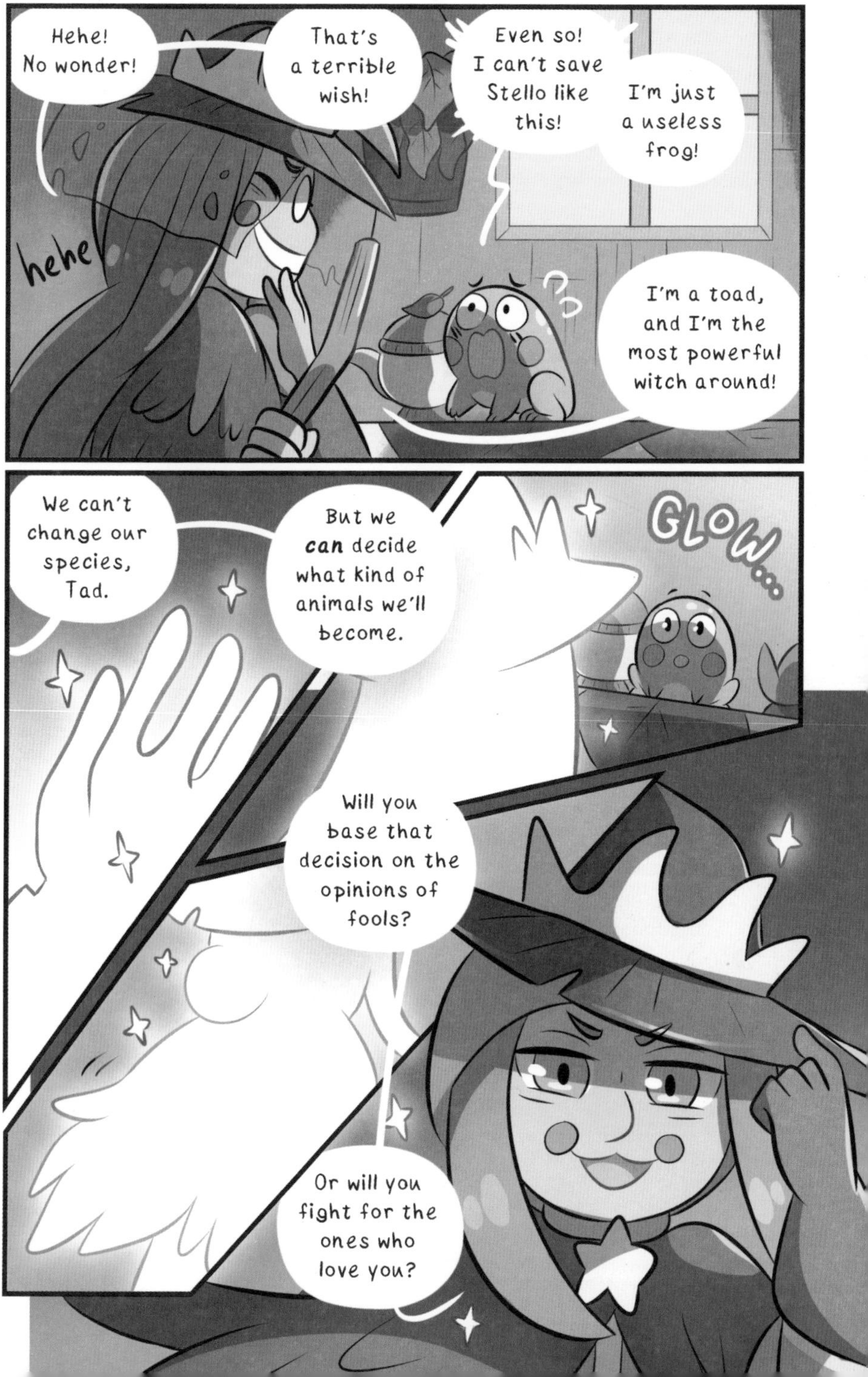
Hehe! No wonder!
That's a terrible wish!
Even so! I can't save Stello like this!
I'm just a useless frog!
hehe
I'm a toad, and I'm the most powerful witch around!
We can't change our species, Tad.
But we **can** decide what kind of animals we'll become.
GLOW...
Will you base that decision on the opinions of fools?
Or will you fight for the ones who love you?

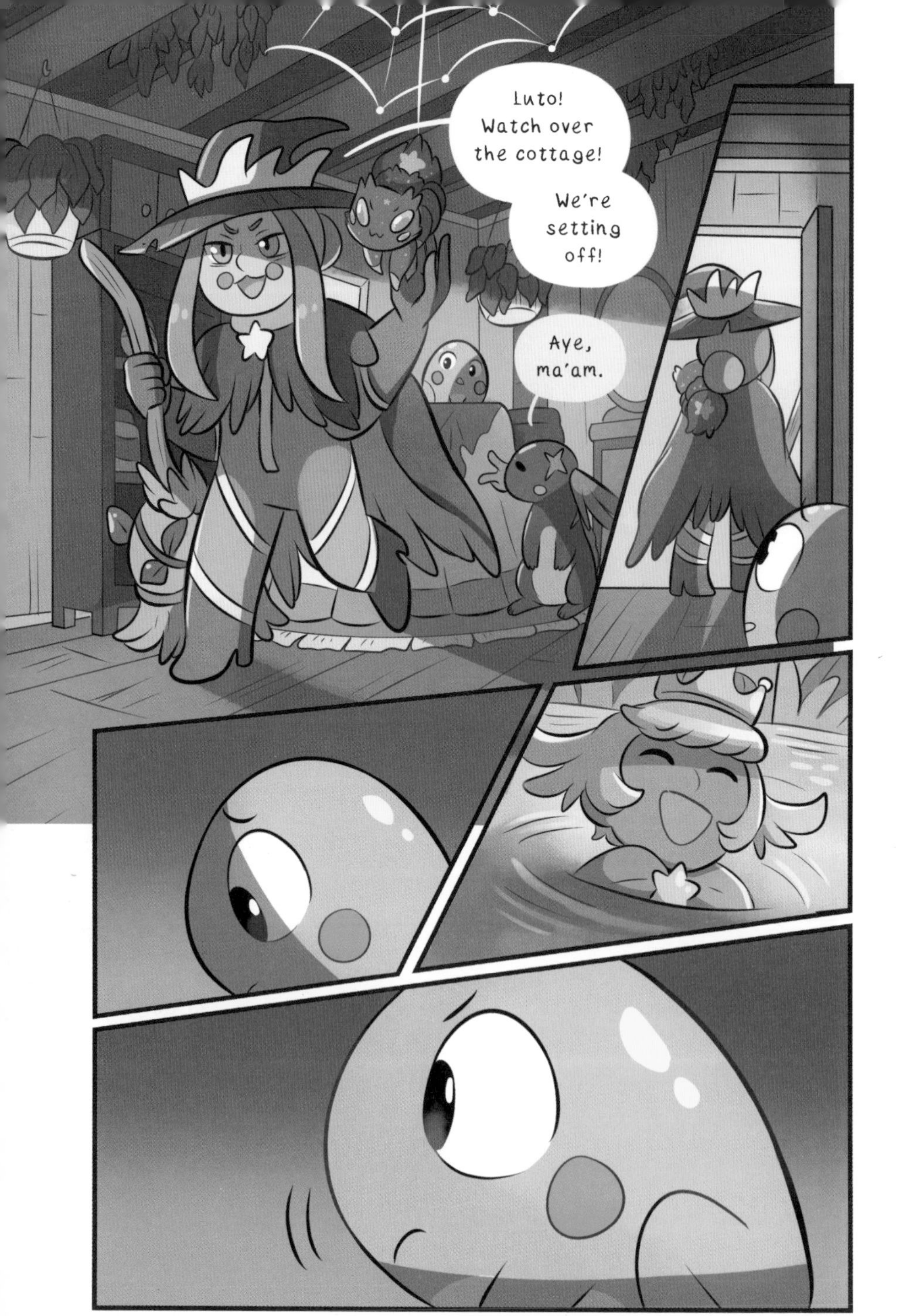
Luto! Watch over the cottage!
We're setting off!
Aye, ma'am.

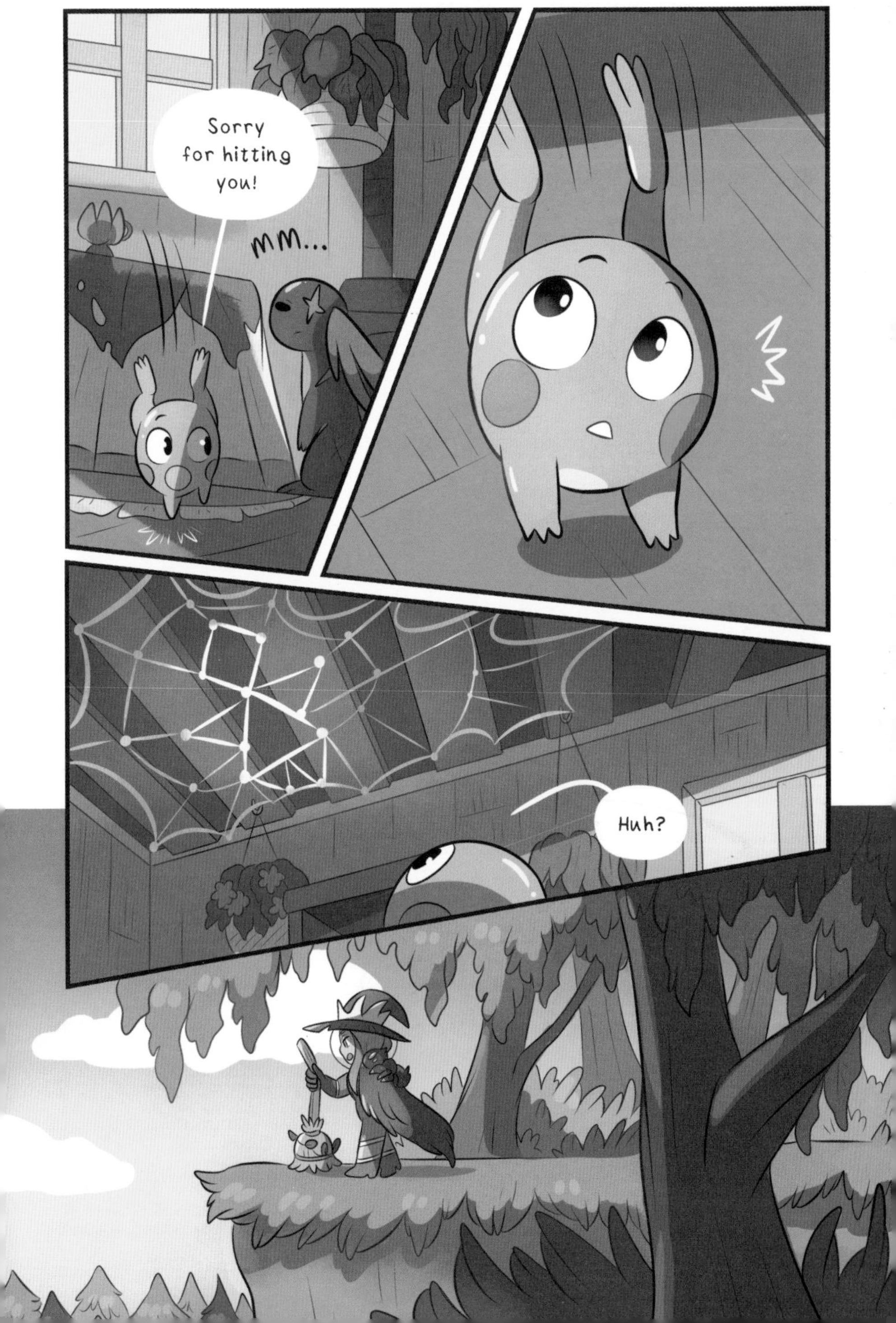
Sorry for hitting you!
MM...
Huh?

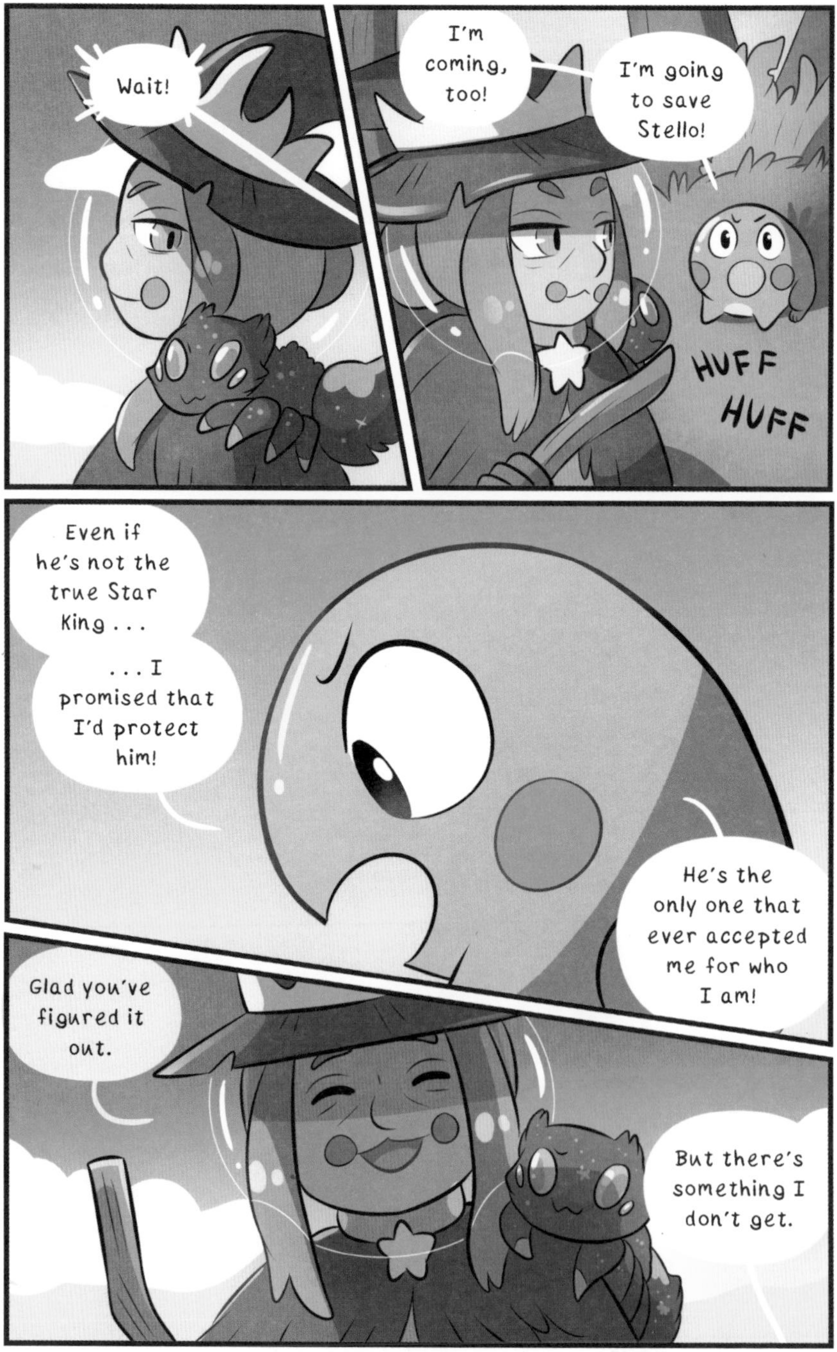
Wait!
I'm coming, too!
I'm going to save Stello!
HUFF HUFF
Even if he's not the true Star King . . .
. . . I promised that I'd protect him!
He's the only one that ever accepted me for who I am!
Glad you've figured it out.
But there's something I don't get.

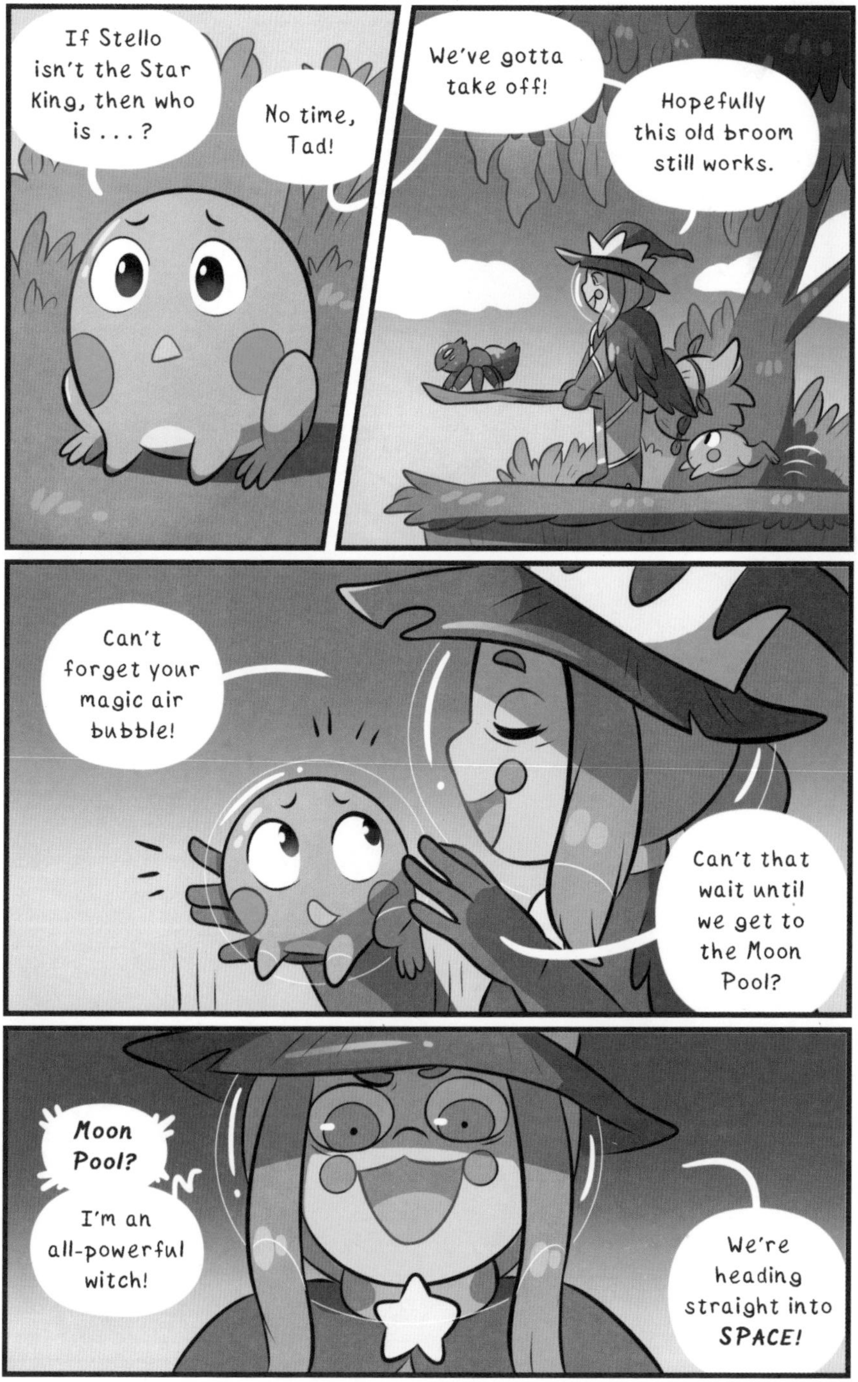
If Stello isn't the Star King, then who is . . . ?
No time, Tad!
We've gotta take off!
Hopefully this old broom still works.
Can't forget your magic air bubble!
Can't that wait until we get to the Moon Pool?
Moon Pool?
I'm an all-powerful witch!
We're heading straight into SPACE!

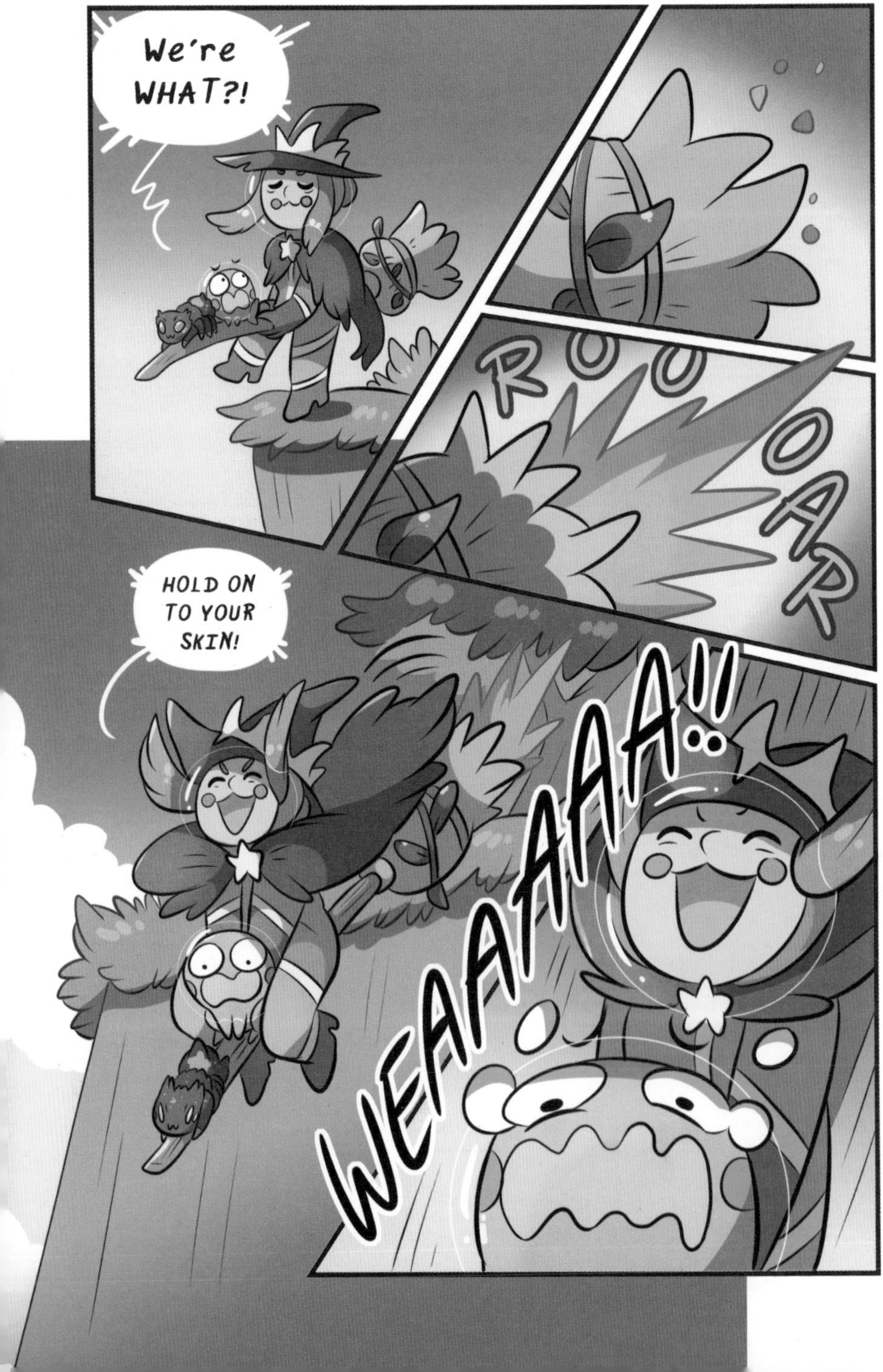

We're WHAT?!
ROOOOAR
HOLD ON TO YOUR SKIN!
WEAAAAAA!!

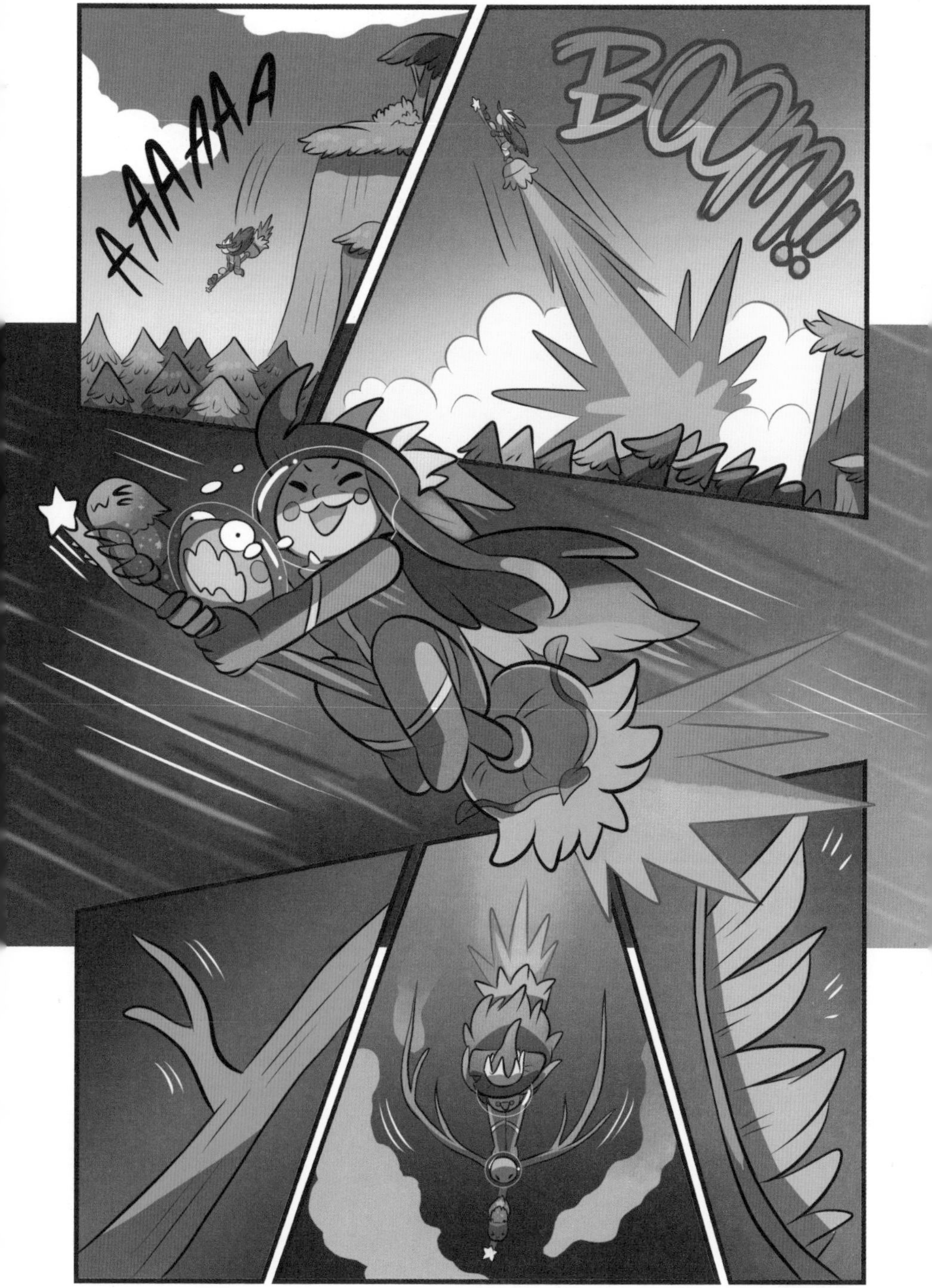
AAAAAAA
BOOM!!

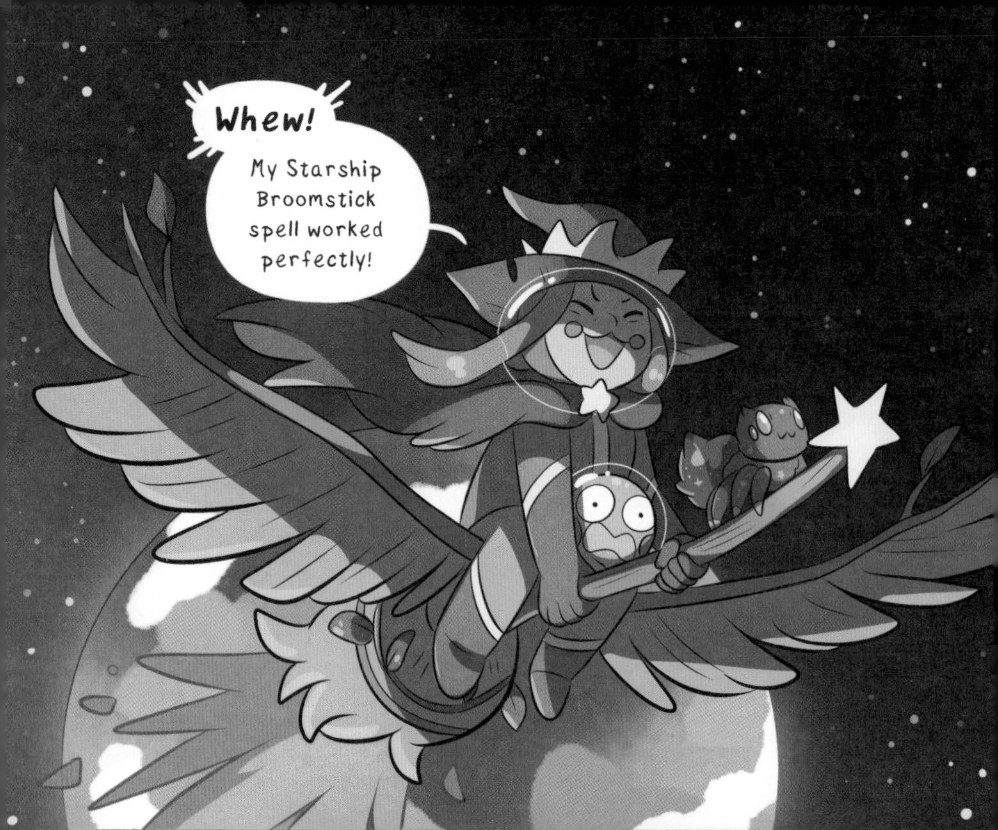
Whew!
My Starship Broomstick spell worked perfectly!

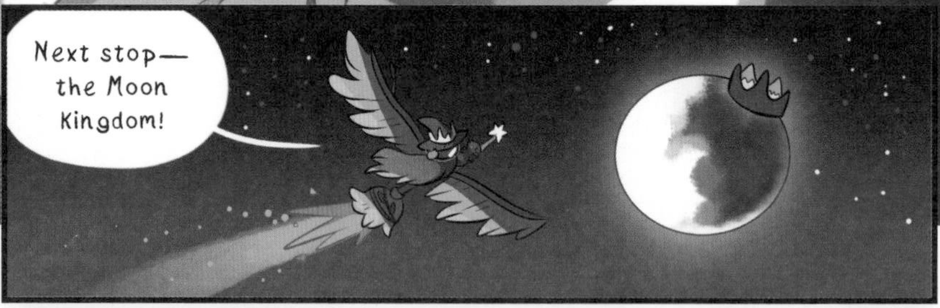
Next stop— the Moon Kingdom!

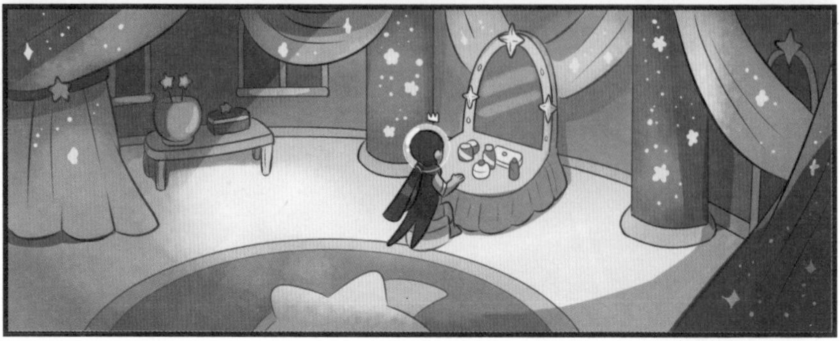

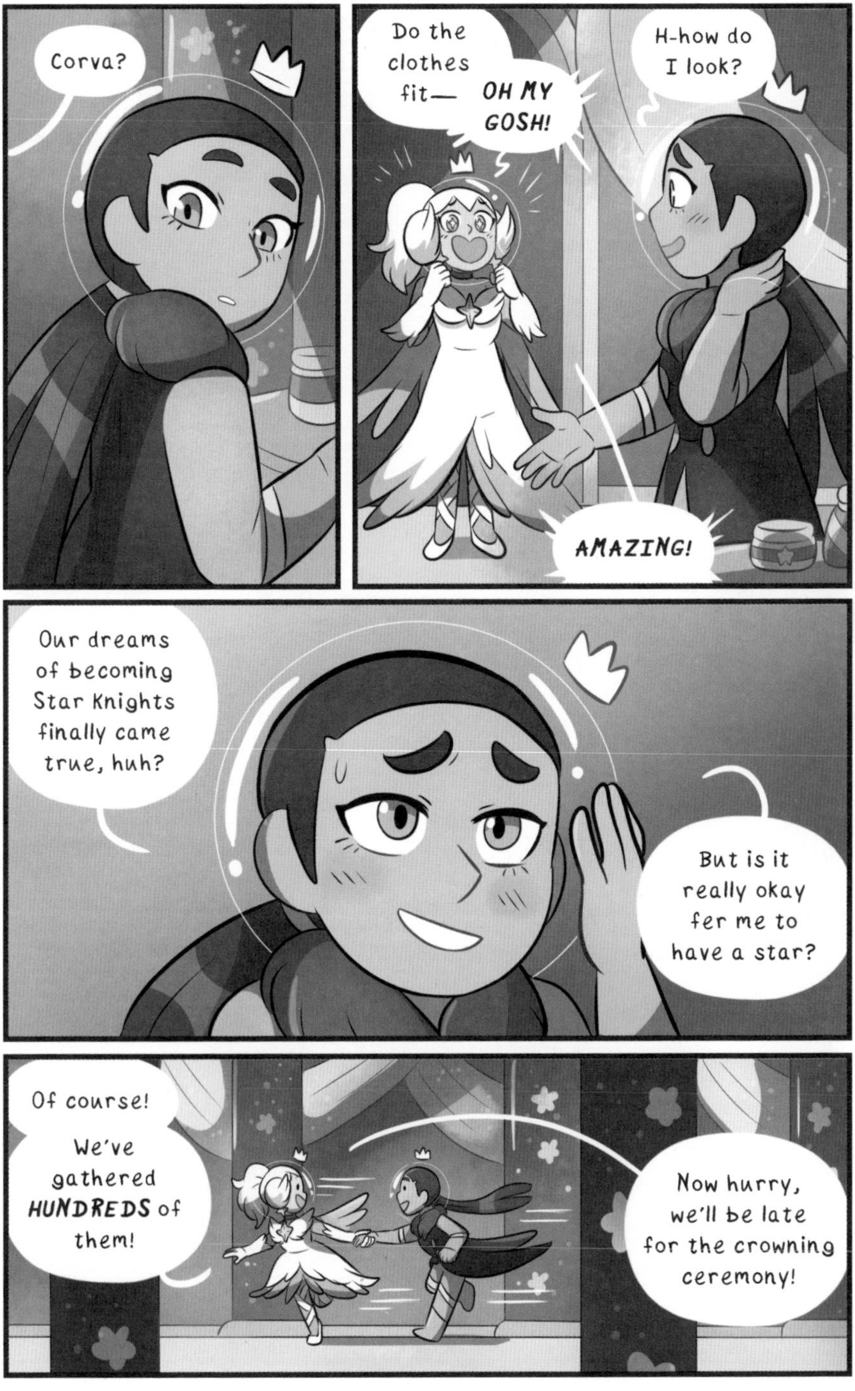
Corva?
Do the clothes fit—
OH MY GOSH!
H-how do I look?
AMAZING!
Our dreams of becoming Star Knights finally came true, huh?
But is it really okay fer me to have a star?
Of course!
We've gathered HUNDREDS of them!
Now hurry, we'll be late for the crowning ceremony!

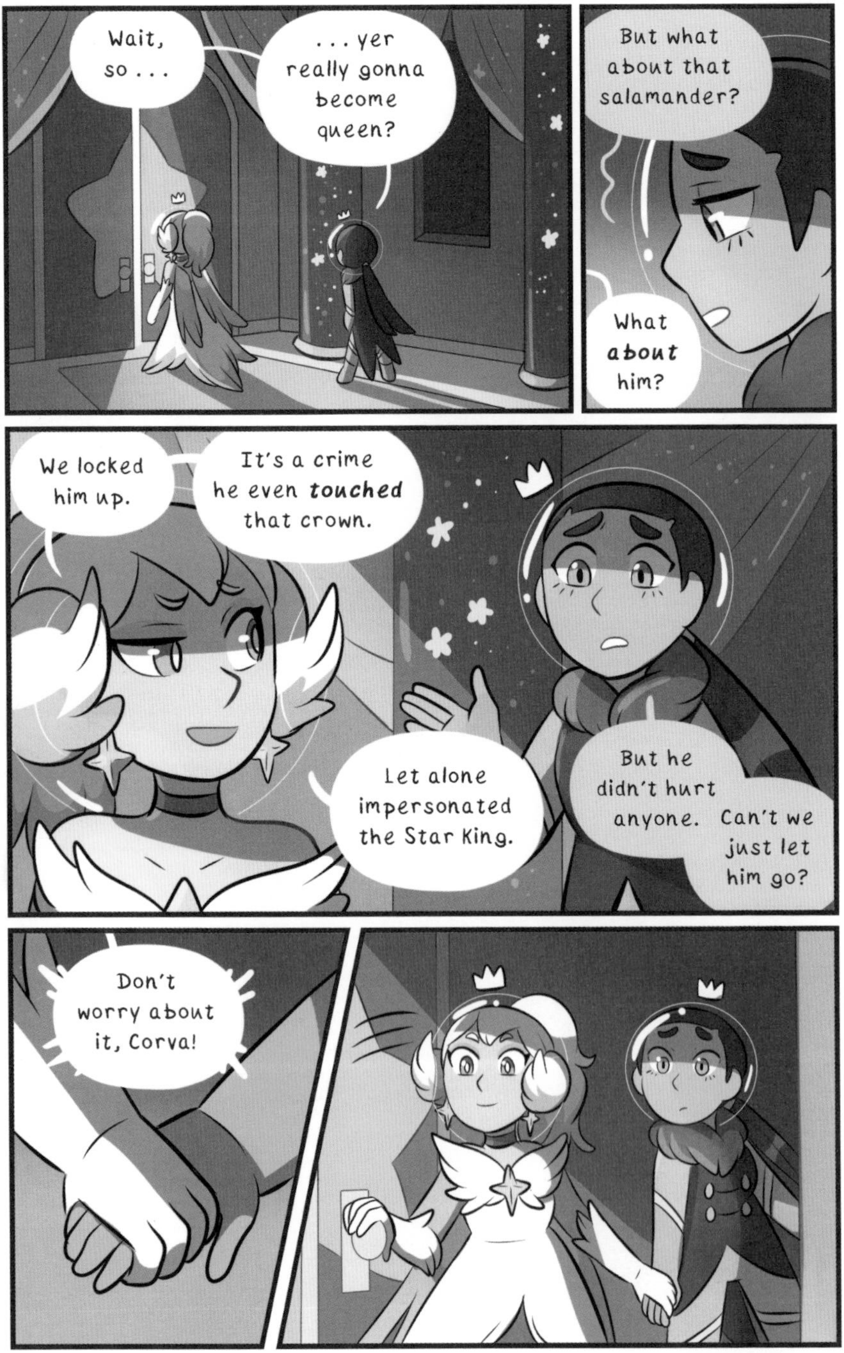
Wait, so . . .
. . . yer really gonna become queen?
But what about that salamander?
What **about** him?
We locked him up.
It's a crime he even **touched** that crown.
Let alone impersonated the Star King.
But he didn't hurt anyone.
Can't we just let him go?
Don't worry about it, Corva!

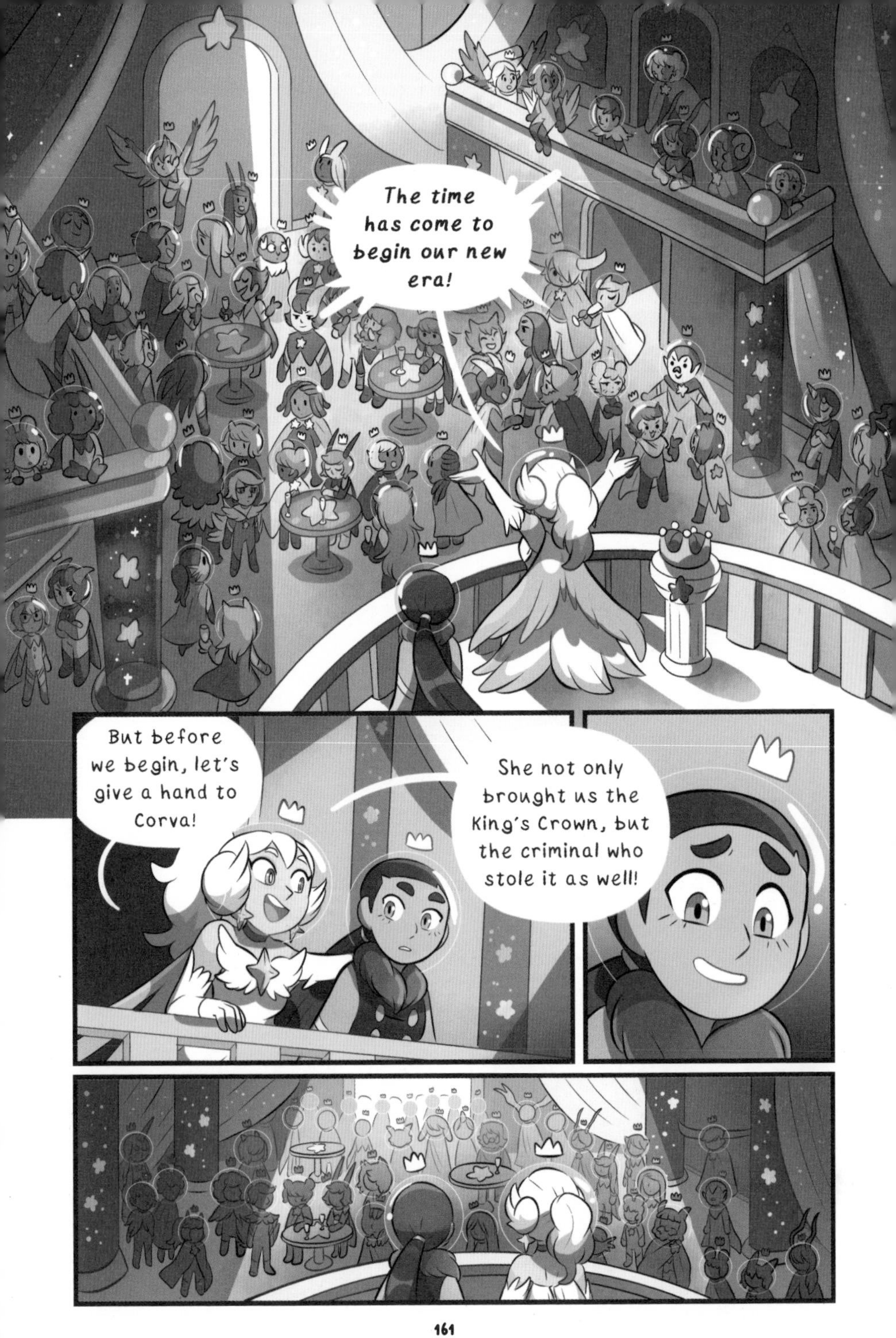
The time has come to begin our new era!
But before we begin, let's give a hand to Corva!
She not only brought us the King's Crown, but the criminal who stole it as well!

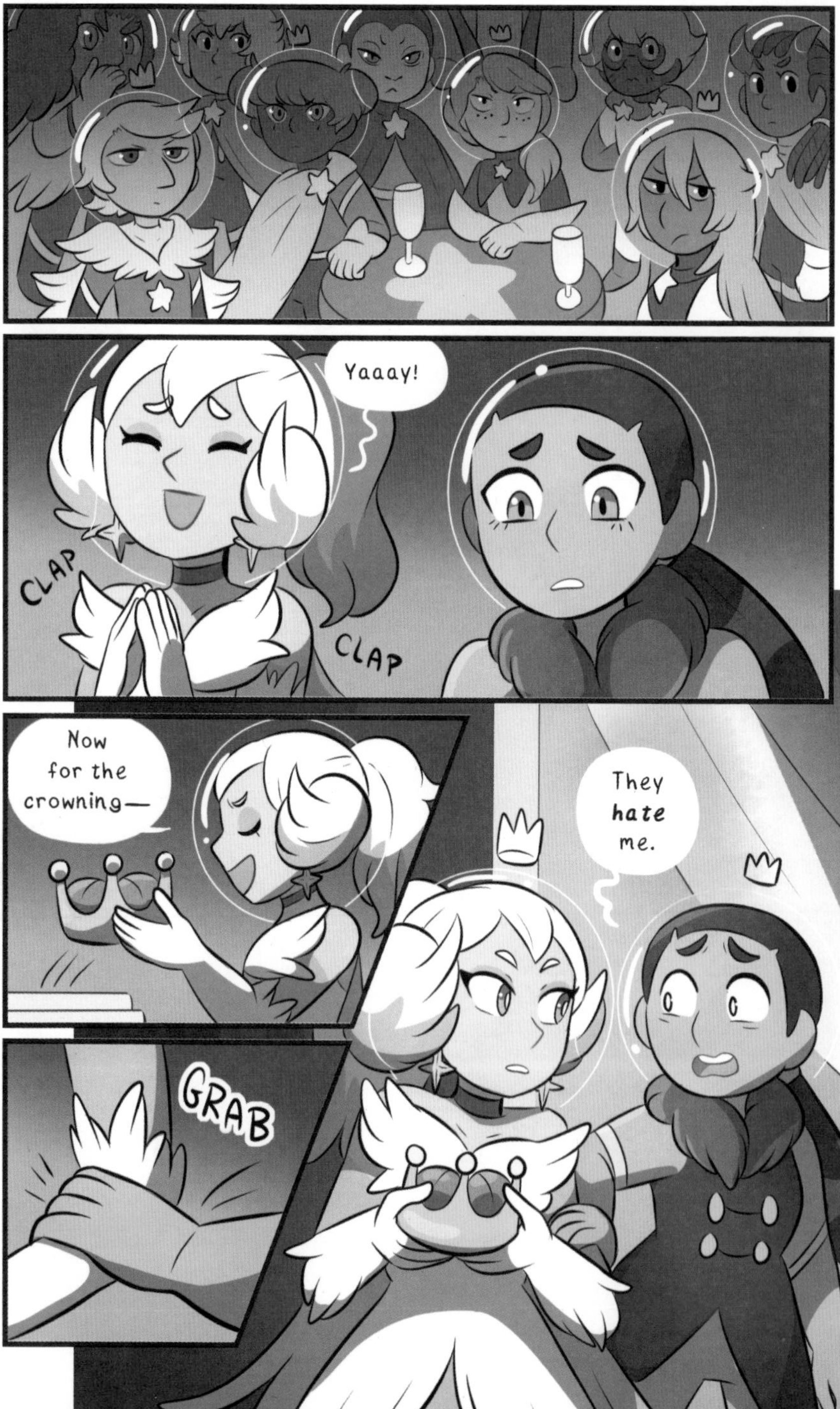
Yaaay!
CLAP
CLAP
Now for the crowning—
They hate me.
GRAB

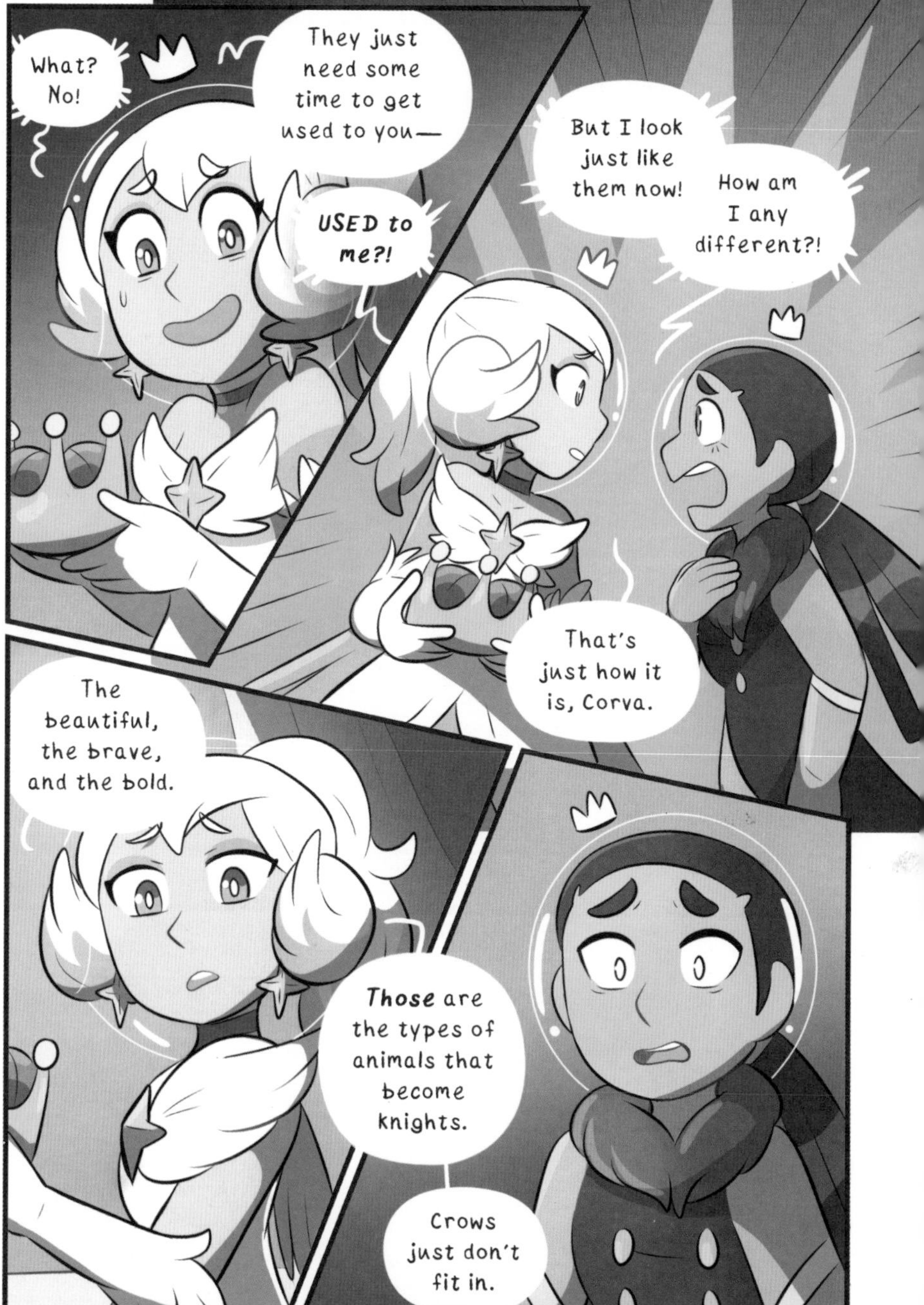
What? No!
They just need some time to get used to you—
USED to me?!
But I look just like them now!
How am I any different?!
That's just how it is, Corva.
The beautiful, the brave, and the bold.
Those are the types of animals that become knights.
Crows just don't fit in.

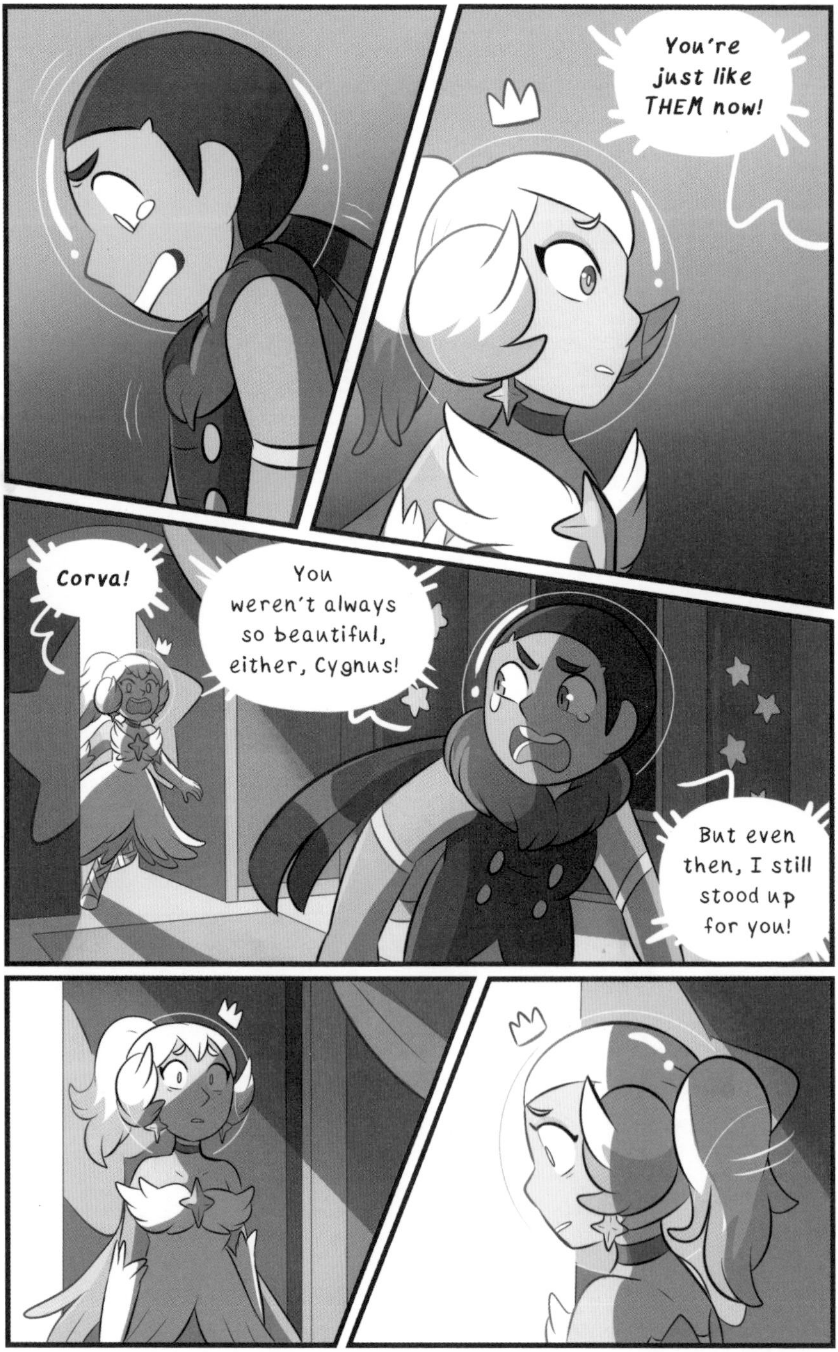

You're just like THEM now!
Corva!
You weren't always so beautiful, either, Cygnus!
But even then, I still stood up for you!

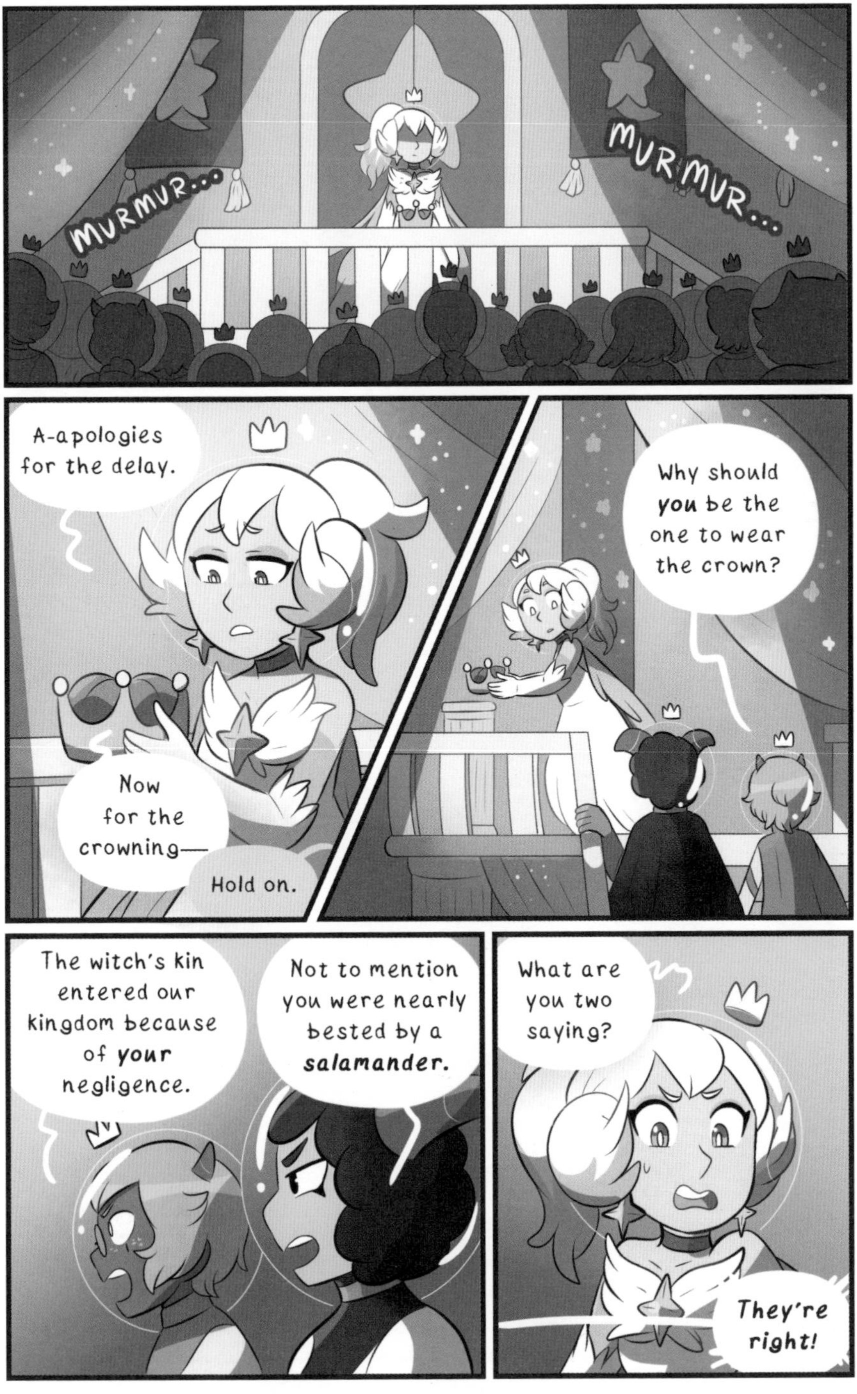
MURMUR...
MURMUR...
A-apologies for the delay.
Now for the crowning—
Hold on.
Why should you be the one to wear the crown?
The witch's kin entered our kingdom because of your negligence.
Not to mention you were nearly bested by a salamander.
What are you two saying?
They're right!

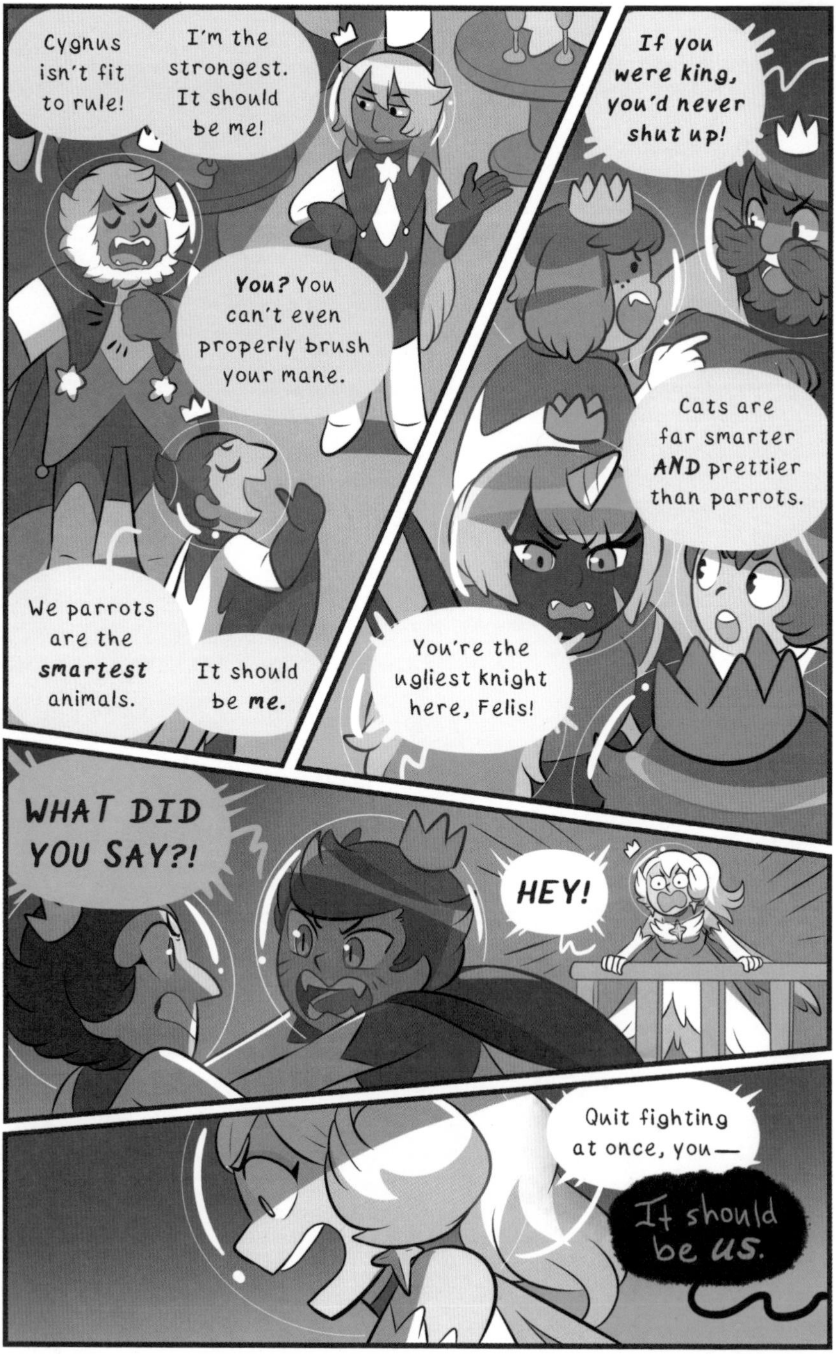

Cygnus isn't fit to rule!
I'm the strongest. It should be me!
You? You can't even properly brush your mane.
We parrots are the smartest animals.
It should be me.
If you were king, you'd never shut up!
Cats are far smarter AND prettier than parrots.
You're the ugliest knight here, Felis!
WHAT DID YOU SAY?!
HEY!
Quit fighting at once, you—
It should be US.

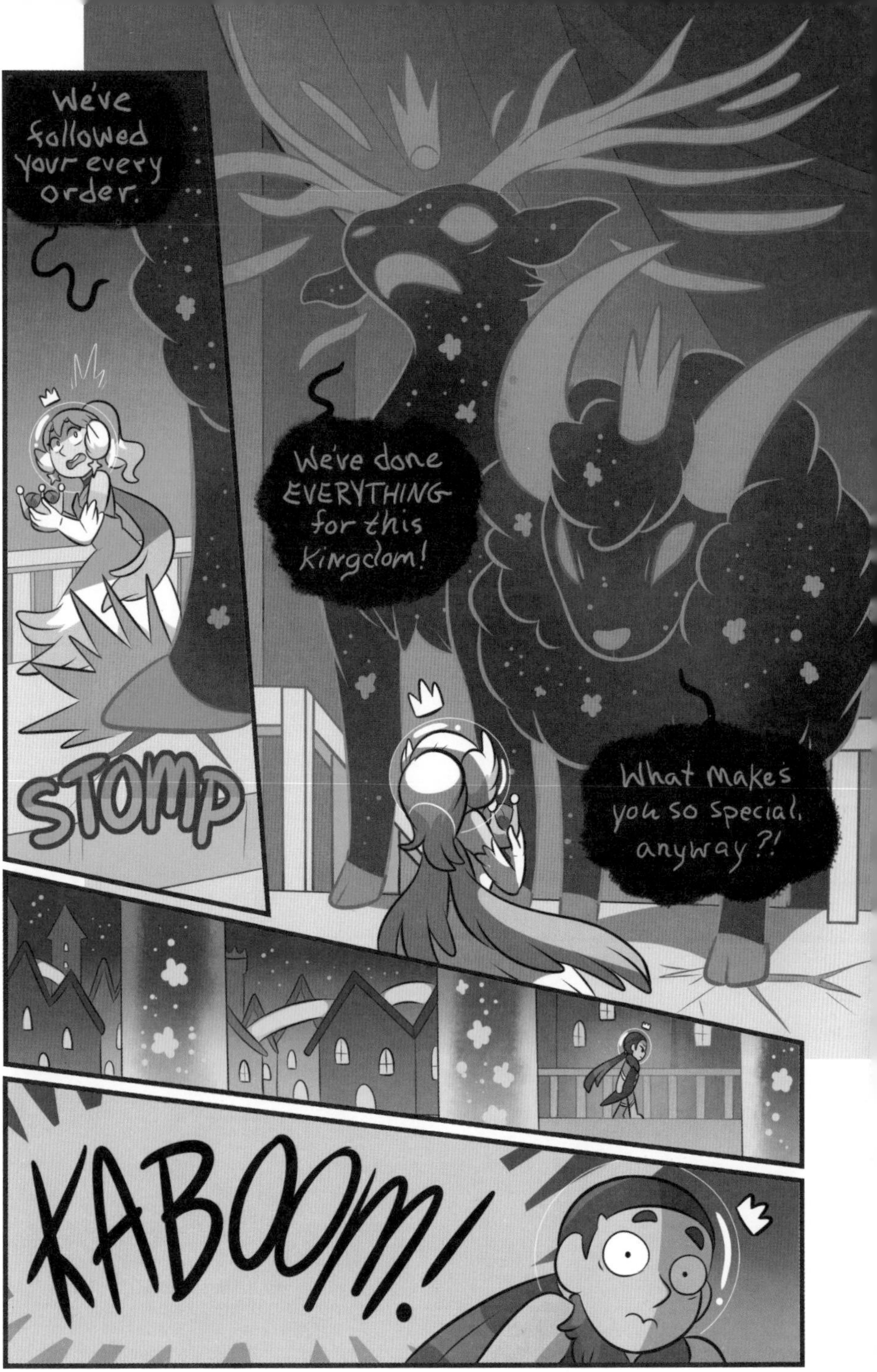
We've followed your every order.
STOMP
We've done EVERYTHING for this kingdom!
What makes you so special, anyway?!
KABOOM!

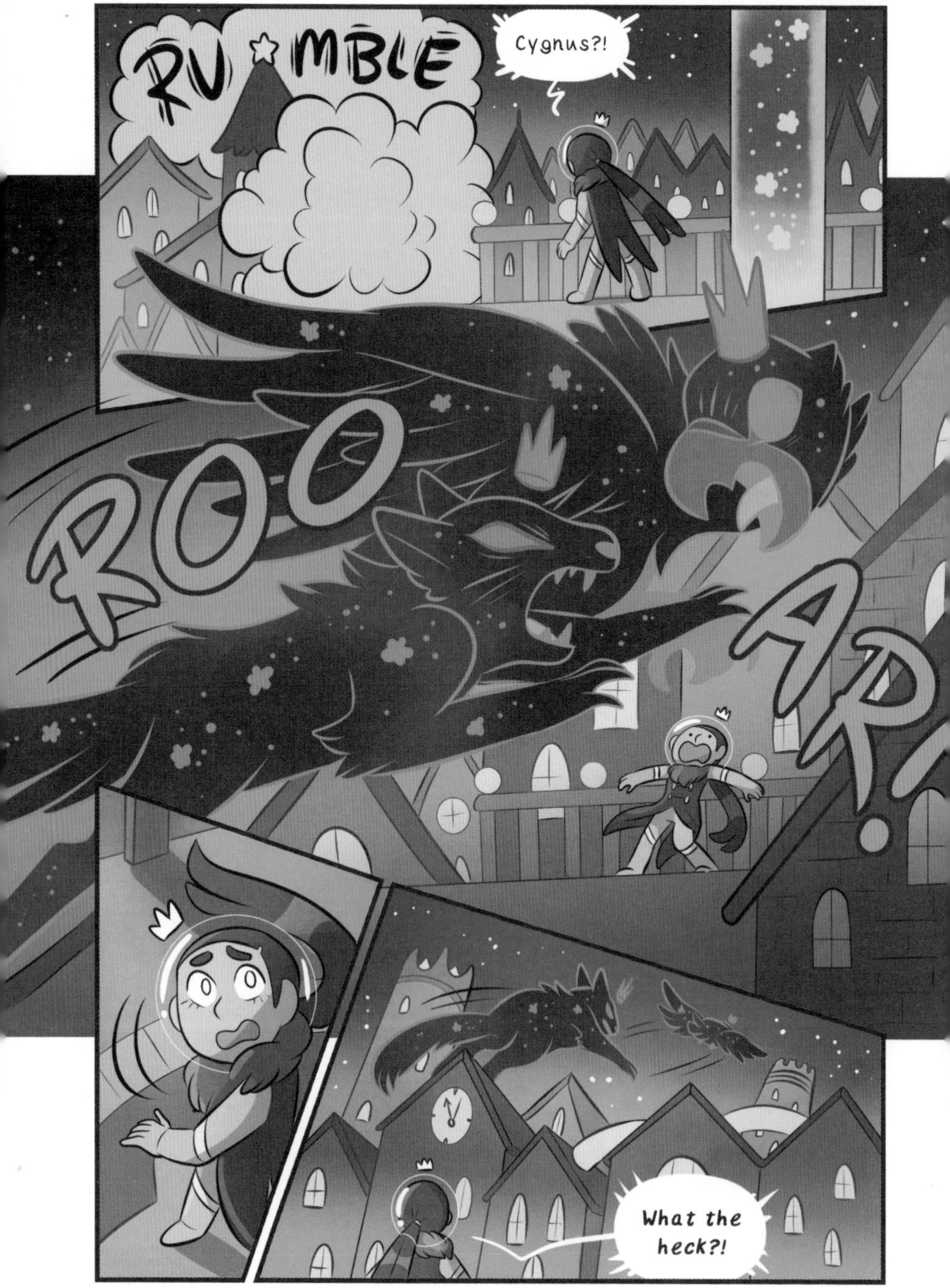
RUMBLE
Cygnus?!
ROOOAR!
What the heck?!

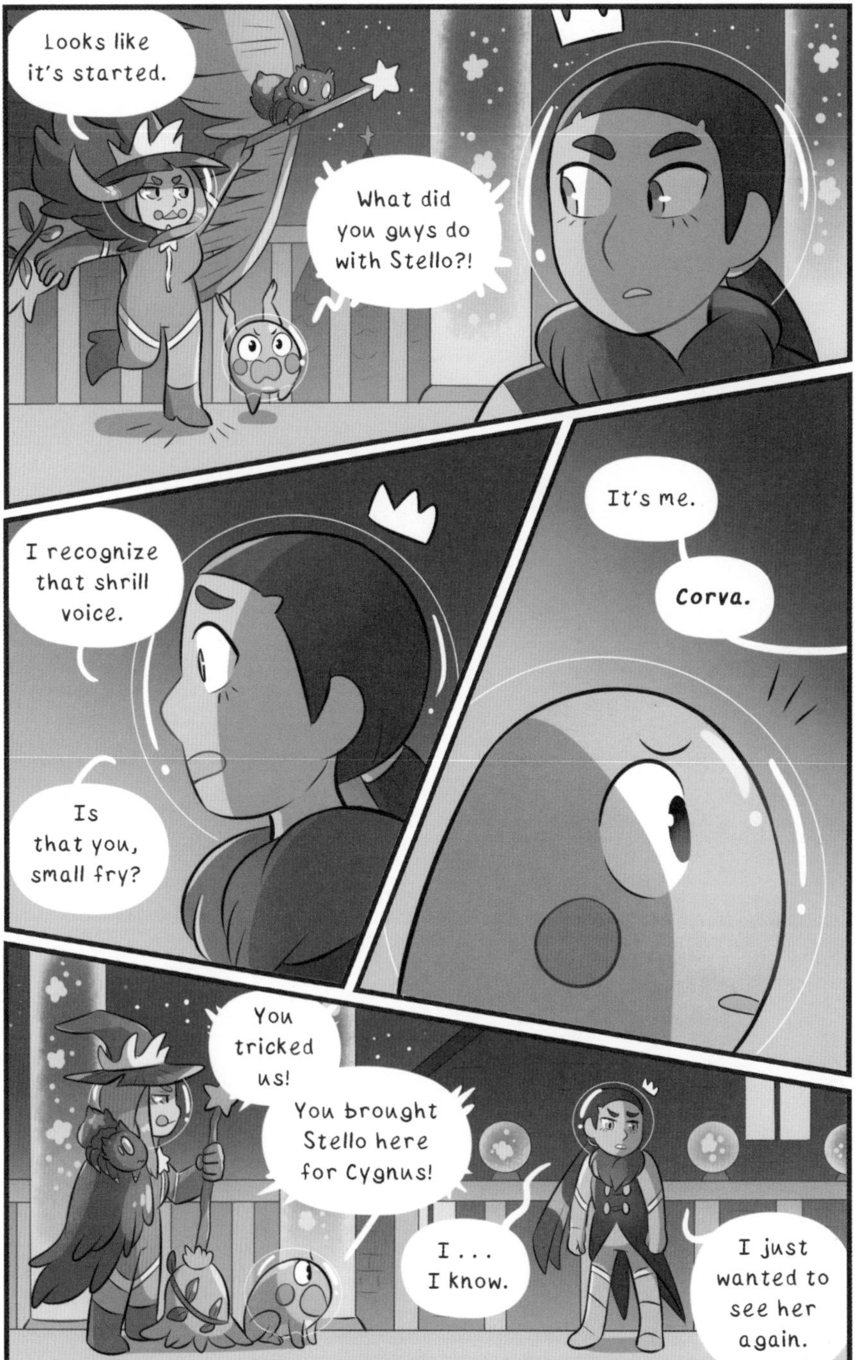
Looks like it's started.
What did you guys do with Stello?!
I recognize that shrill voice.
Is that you, small fry?
It's me.
Corva.
You tricked us!
You brought Stello here for Cygnus!
I . . . I know.
I just wanted to see her again.

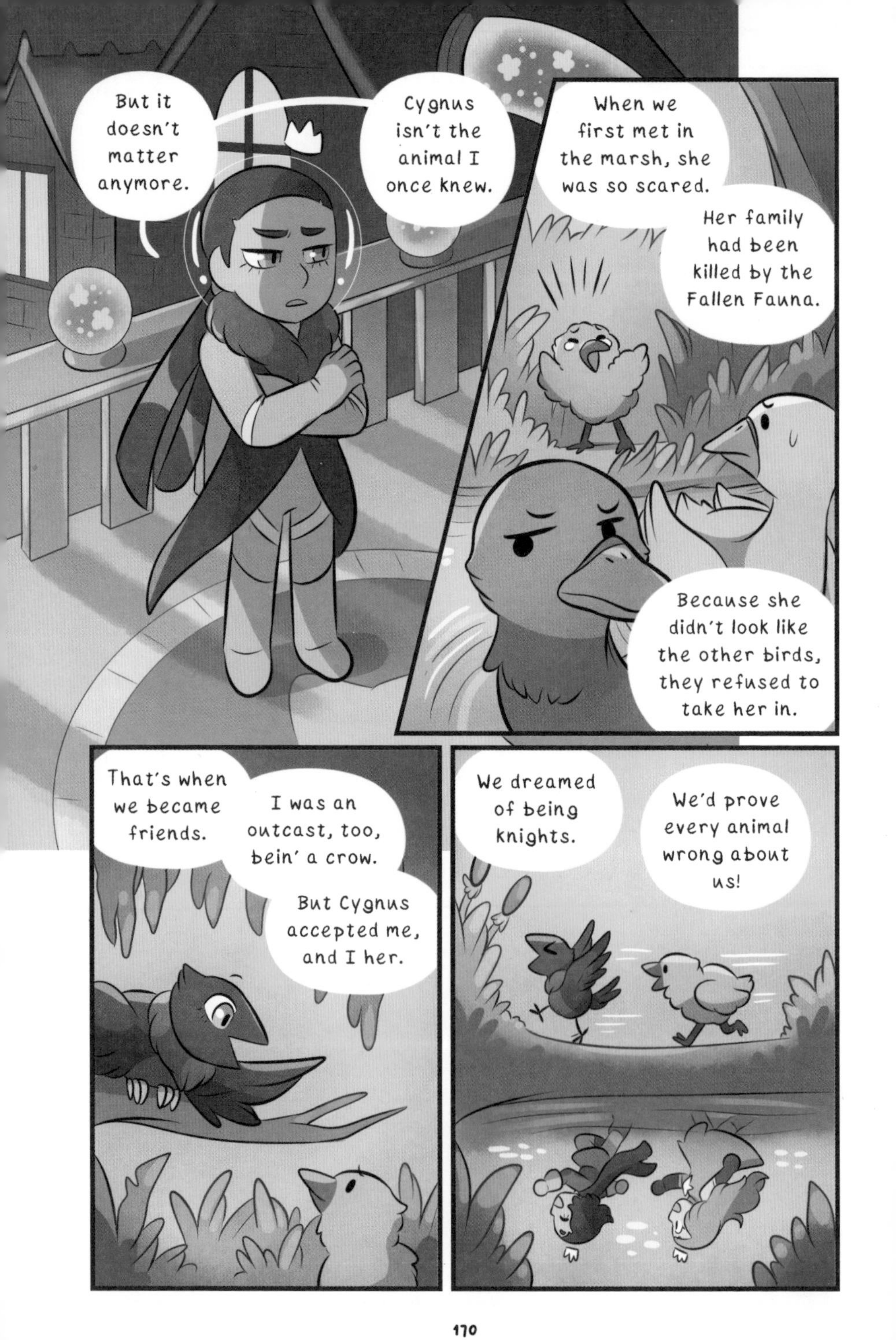

But it doesn't matter anymore.
Cygnus isn't the animal I once knew.
When we first met in the marsh, she was so scared.
Her family had been killed by the Fallen Fauna.
Because she didn't look like the other birds, they refused to take her in.
That's when we became friends.
I was an outcast, too, bein' a crow.
But Cygnus accepted me, and I her.
We dreamed of being knights.
We'd prove every animal wrong about us!

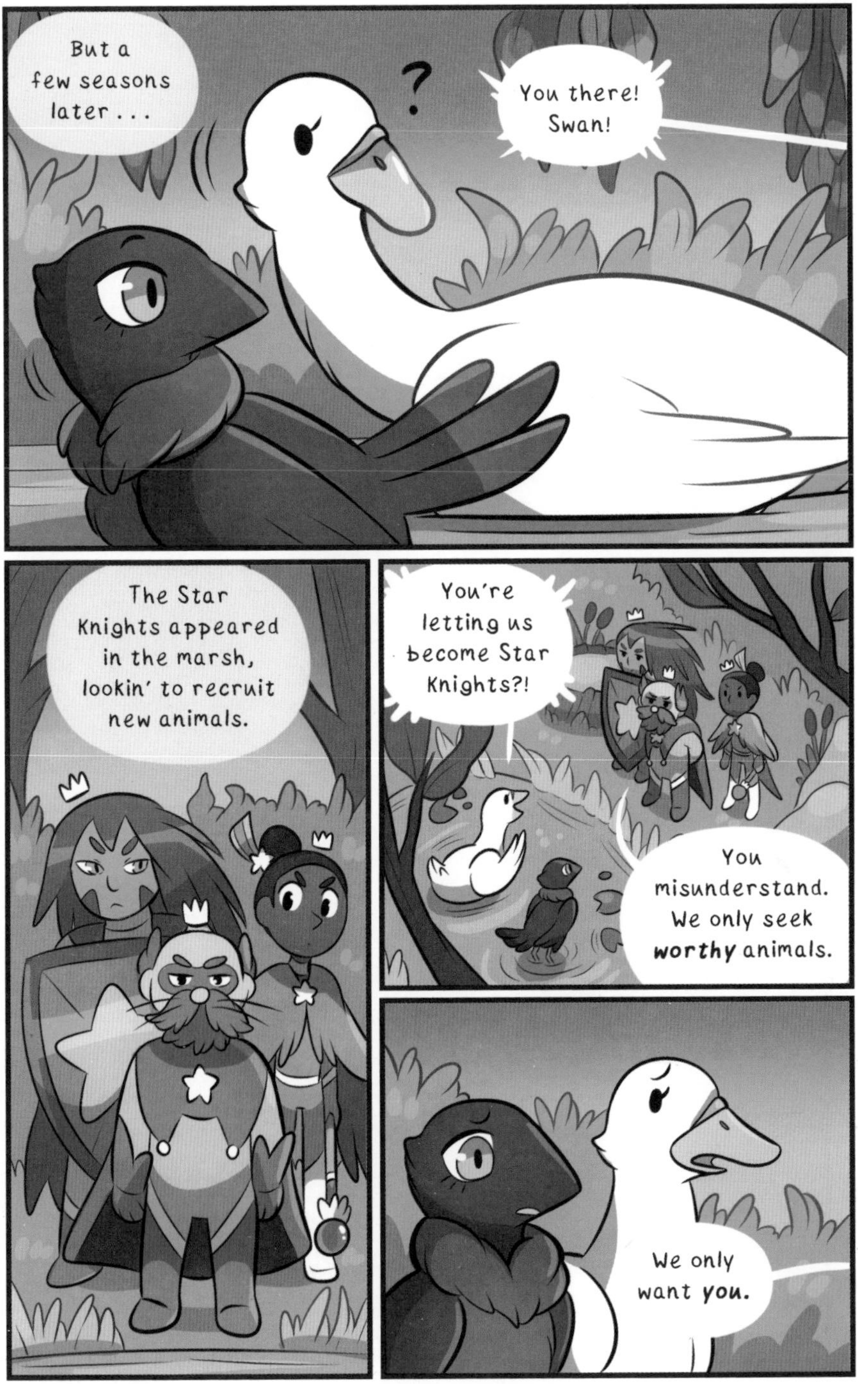
But a few seasons later . . .
?
You there! Swan!
The Star Knights appeared in the marsh, lookin' to recruit new animals.
You're letting us become Star Knights?!
You misunderstand. We only seek **worthy** animals.
We only want **you.**

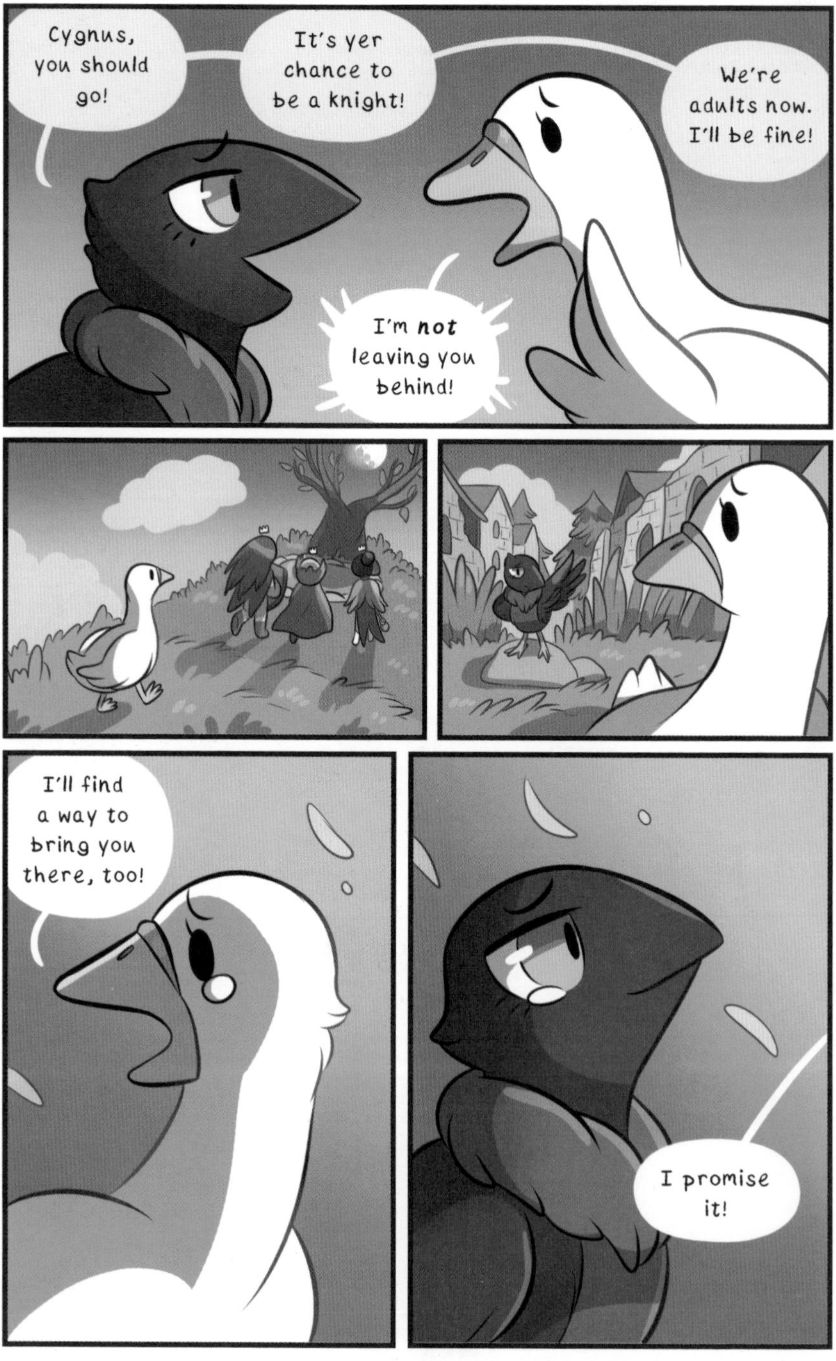
Cygnus, you should go!
It's yer chance to be a knight!
We're adults now. I'll be fine!
I'm **not** leaving you behind!
I'll find a way to bring you there, too!
I promise it!

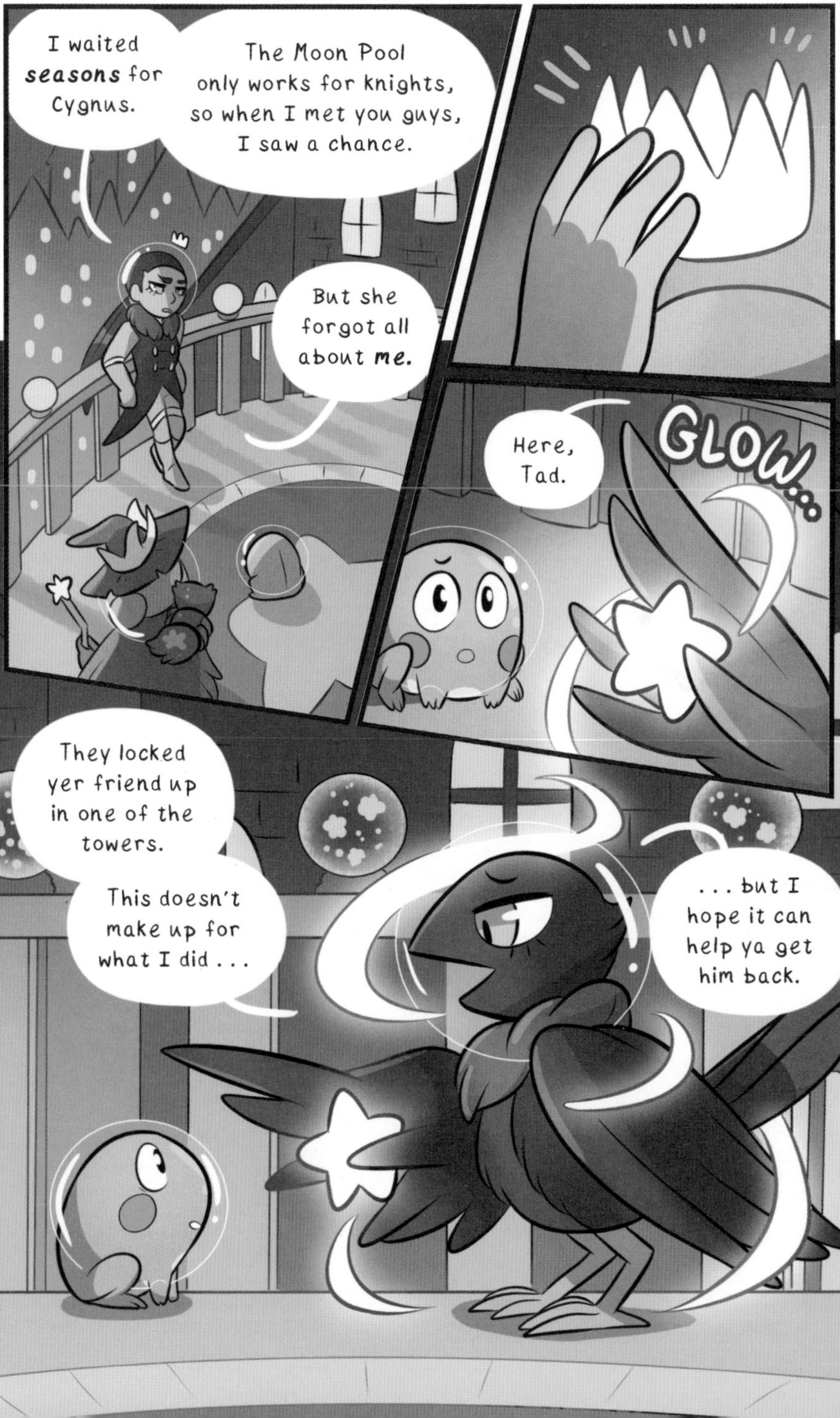
I waited seasons for Cygnus.
The Moon Pool only works for knights, so when I met you guys, I saw a chance.
But she forgot all about me.
Here, Tad.
GLOW...
They locked yer friend up in one of the towers.
This doesn't make up for what I did . . .
. . . but I hope it can help ya get him back.

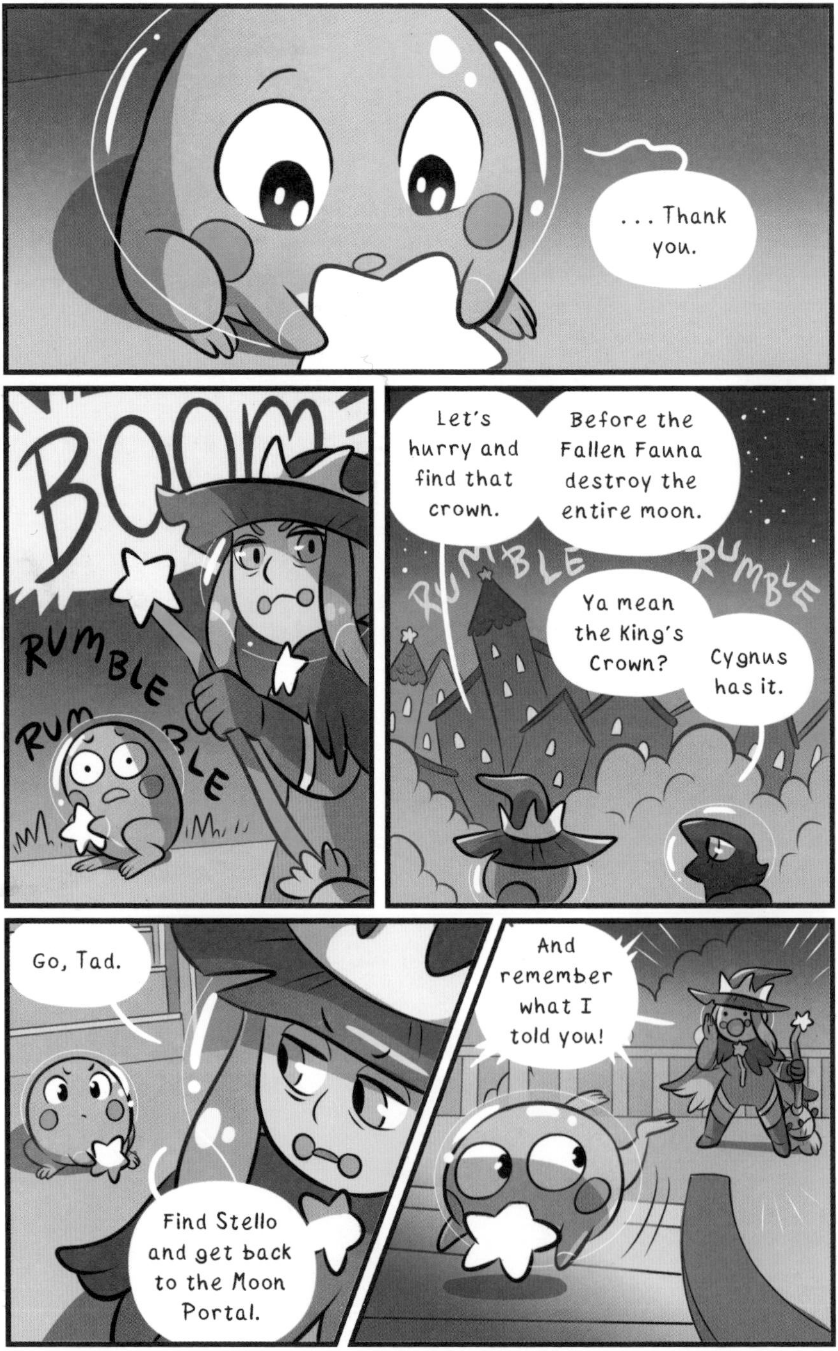

. . . Thank you.
BOOM
RUMBLE RUMBLE
Let's hurry and find that crown.
Before the Fallen Fauna destroy the entire moon.
RUMBLE RUMBLE
Ya mean the King's Crown?
Cygnus has it.
Go, Tad.
Find Stello and get back to the Moon Portal.
And remember what I told you!

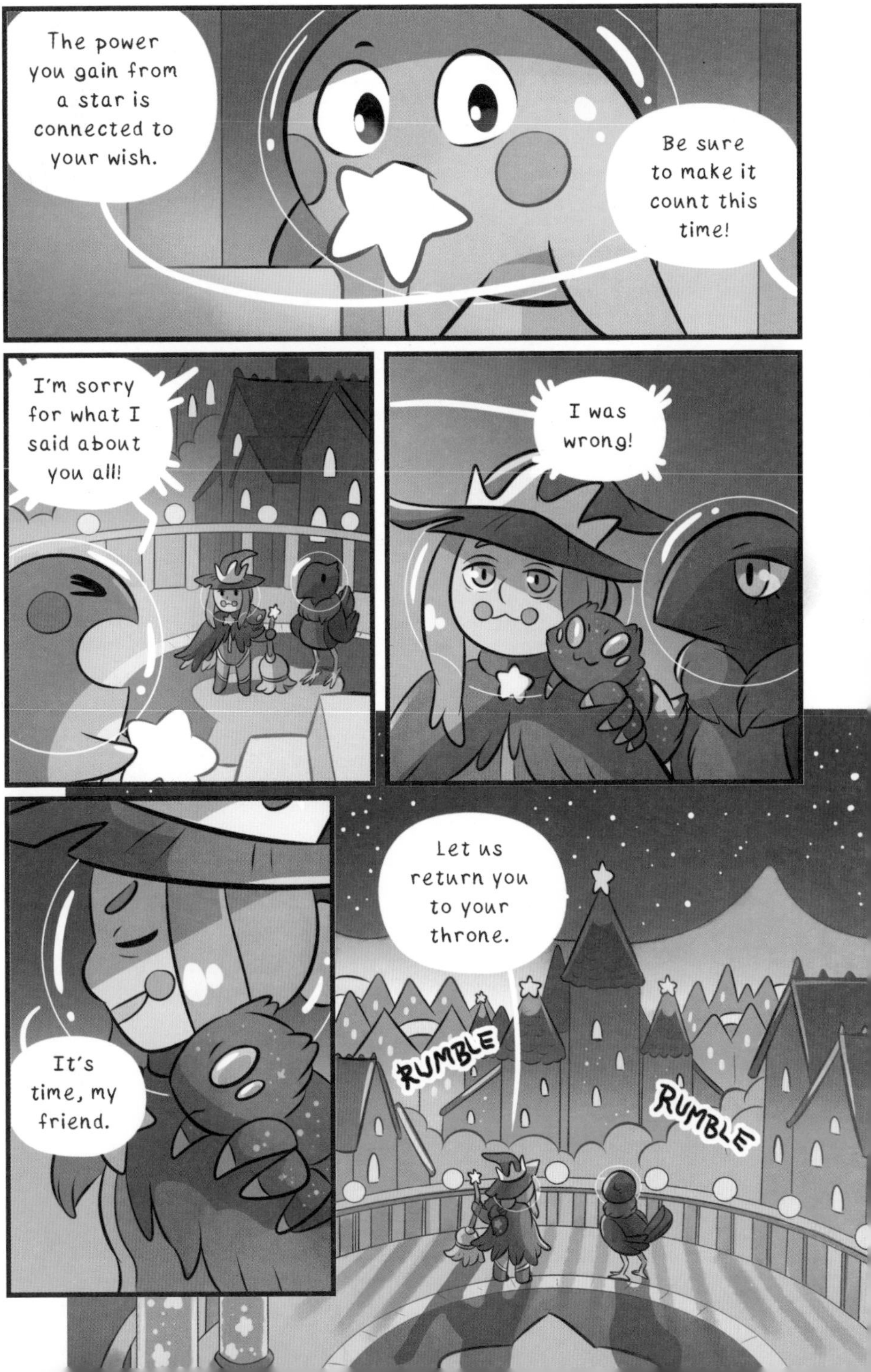
The power you gain from a star is connected to your wish.
Be sure to make it count this time!
I'm sorry for what I said about you all!
I was wrong!
It's time, my friend.
Let us return you to your throne.
RUMBLE
RUMBLE

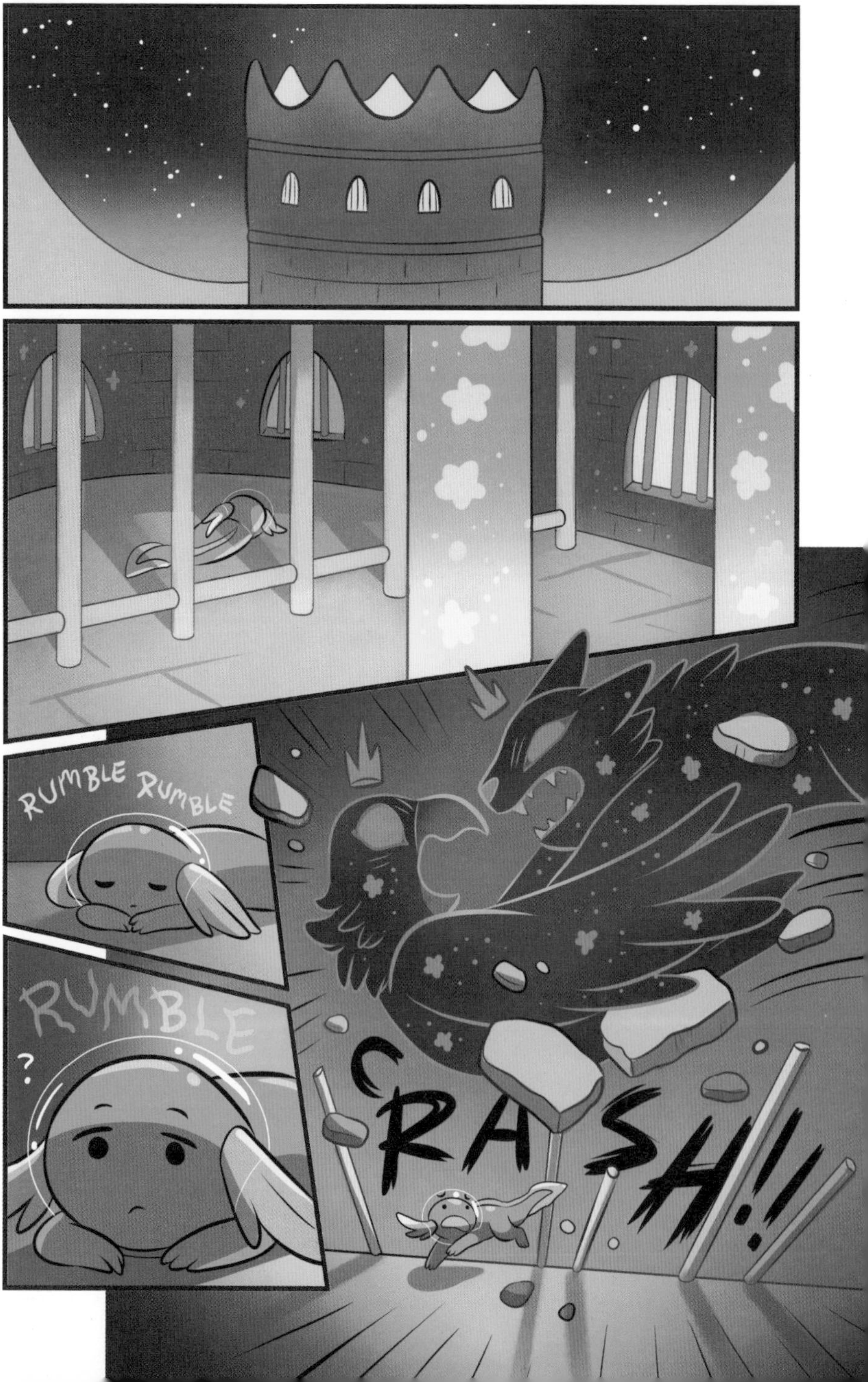
RUMBLE RUMBLE
RUMBLE
?
CRASH!!

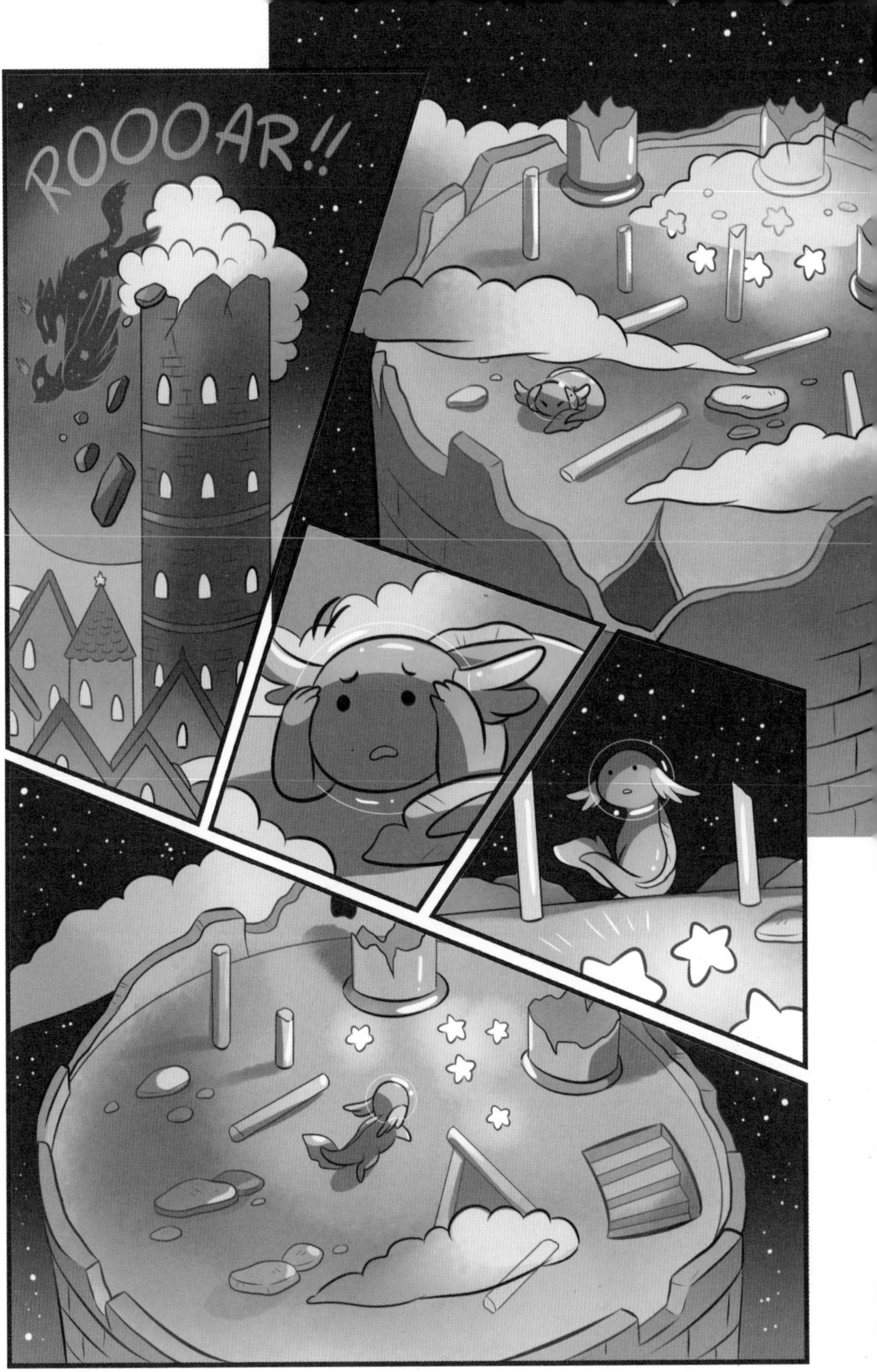
ROOOAR!!

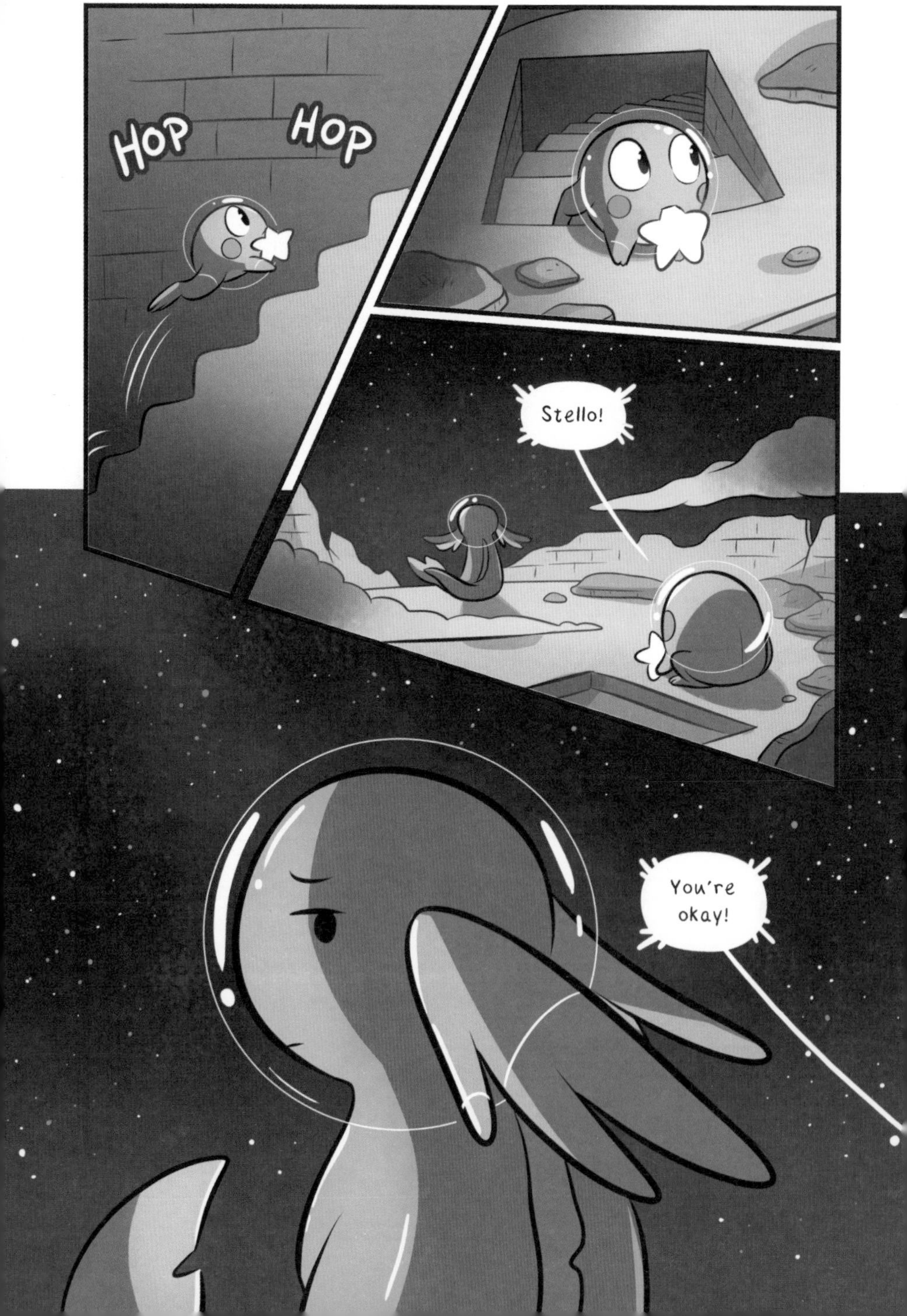
HOP
HOP
Stello!
You're okay!

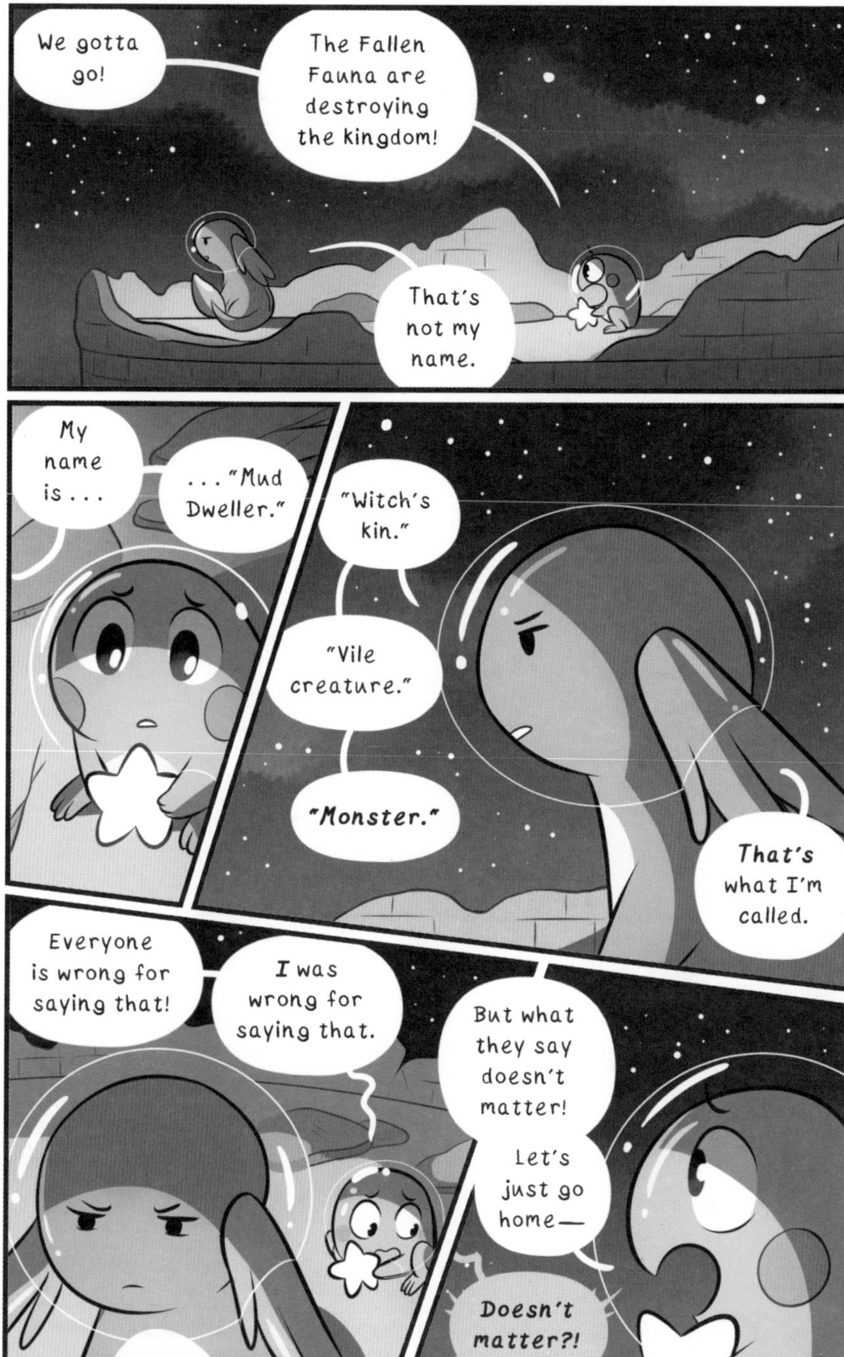
We gotta go!
The Fallen Fauna are destroying the kingdom!
That's not my name.
My name is . . .
. . . "Mud Dweller."
"Witch's kin."
"Vile creature."
"Monster."
That's what I'm called.
Everyone is wrong for saying that!
I was wrong for saying that.
But what they say doesn't matter!
Let's just go home—
Doesn't matter?!

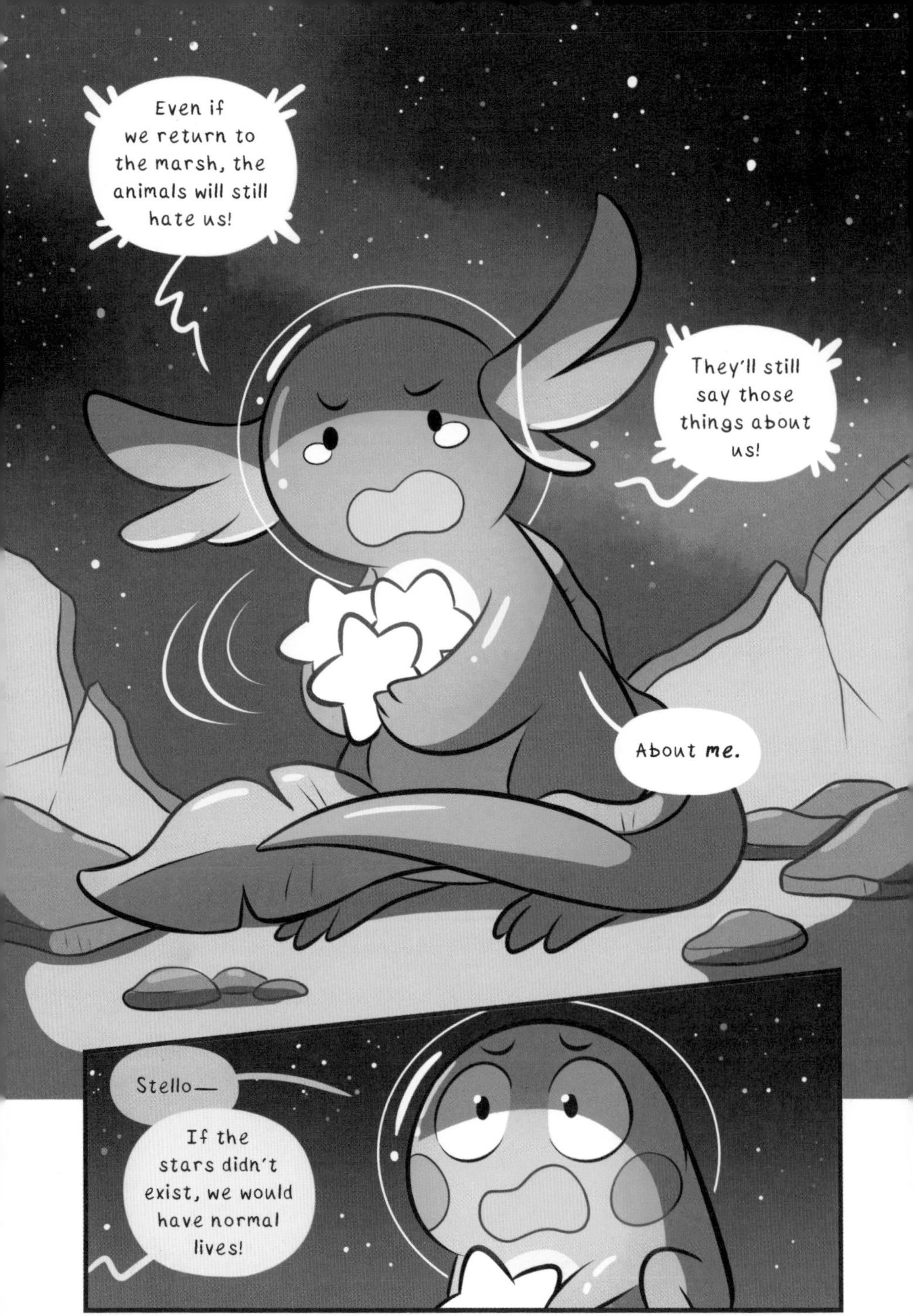
Even if we return to the marsh, the animals will still hate us!
They'll still say those things about us!
About **me.**
Stello—
If the stars didn't exist, we would have normal lives!

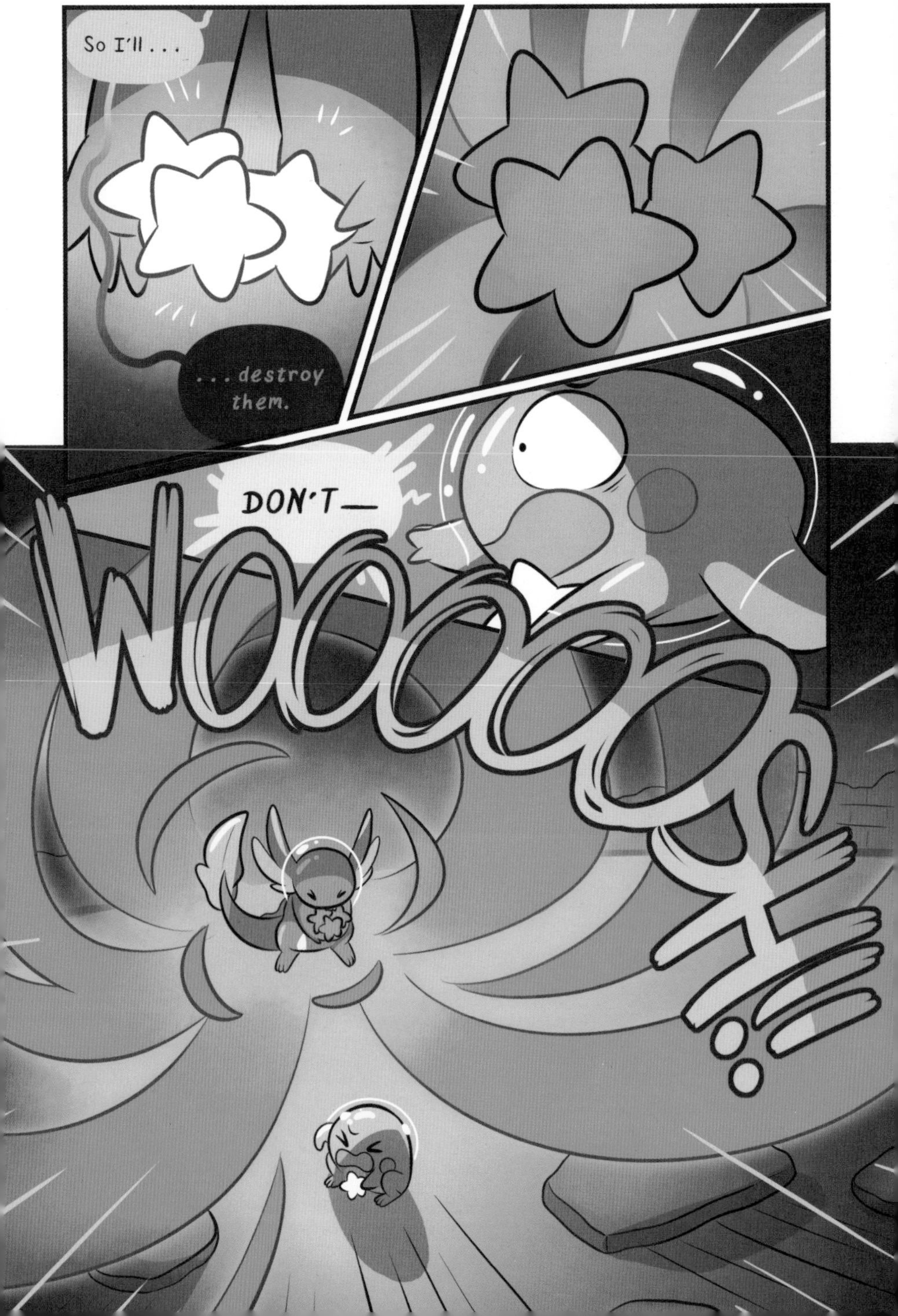
So I'll . . .
. . . destroy them.
DON'T—
WOOOOOOAH!!

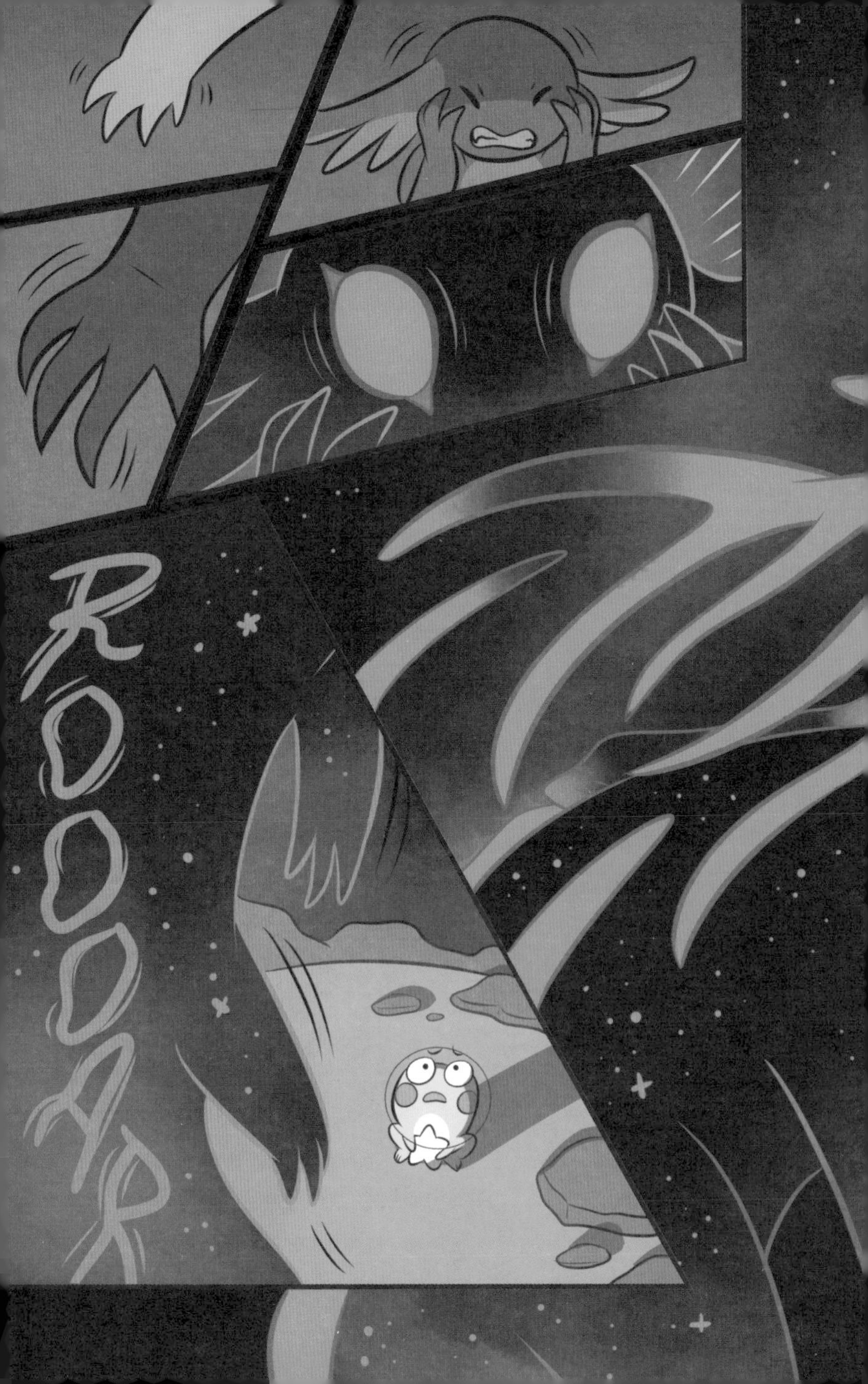
ROOOOAR

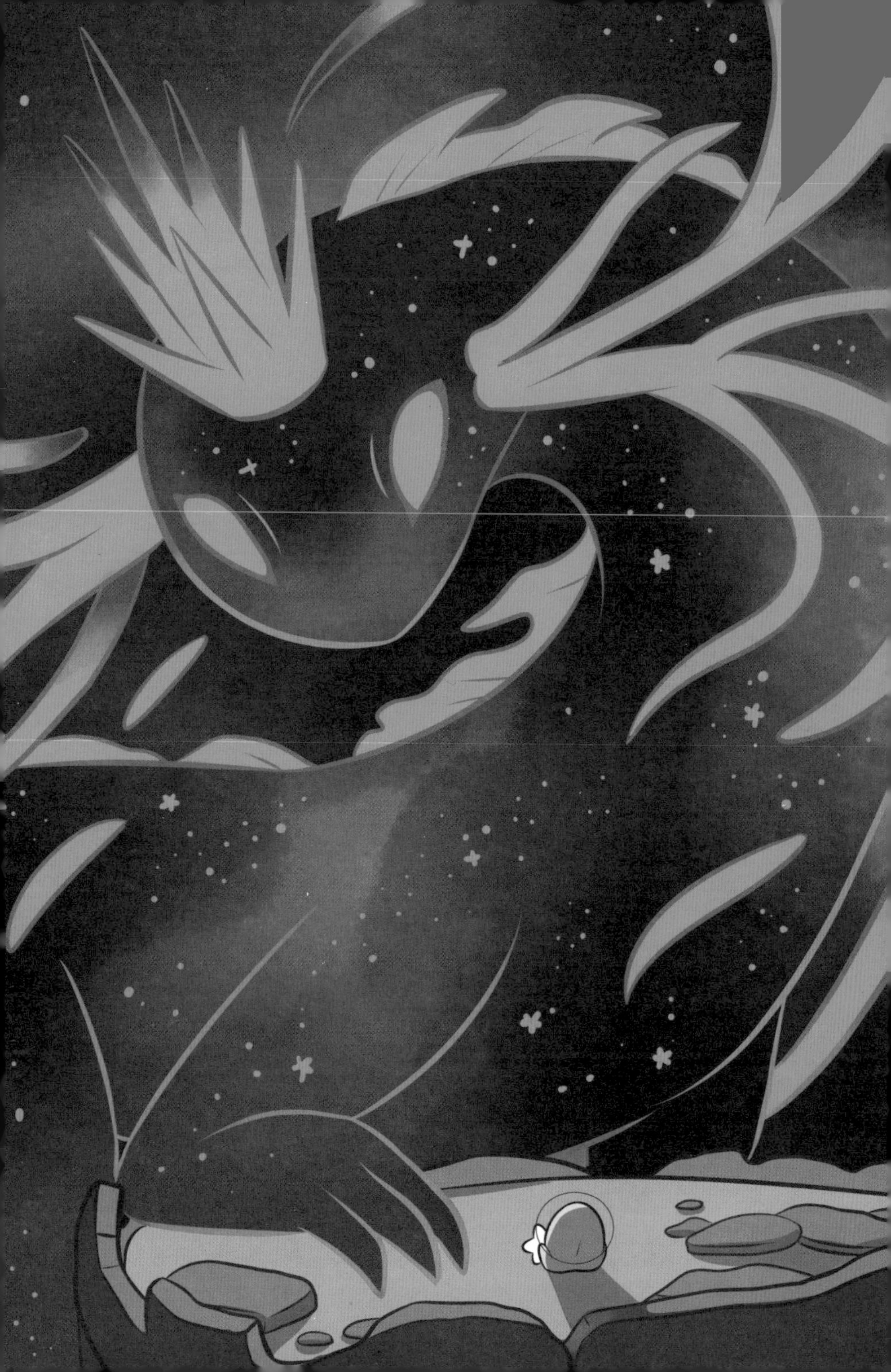

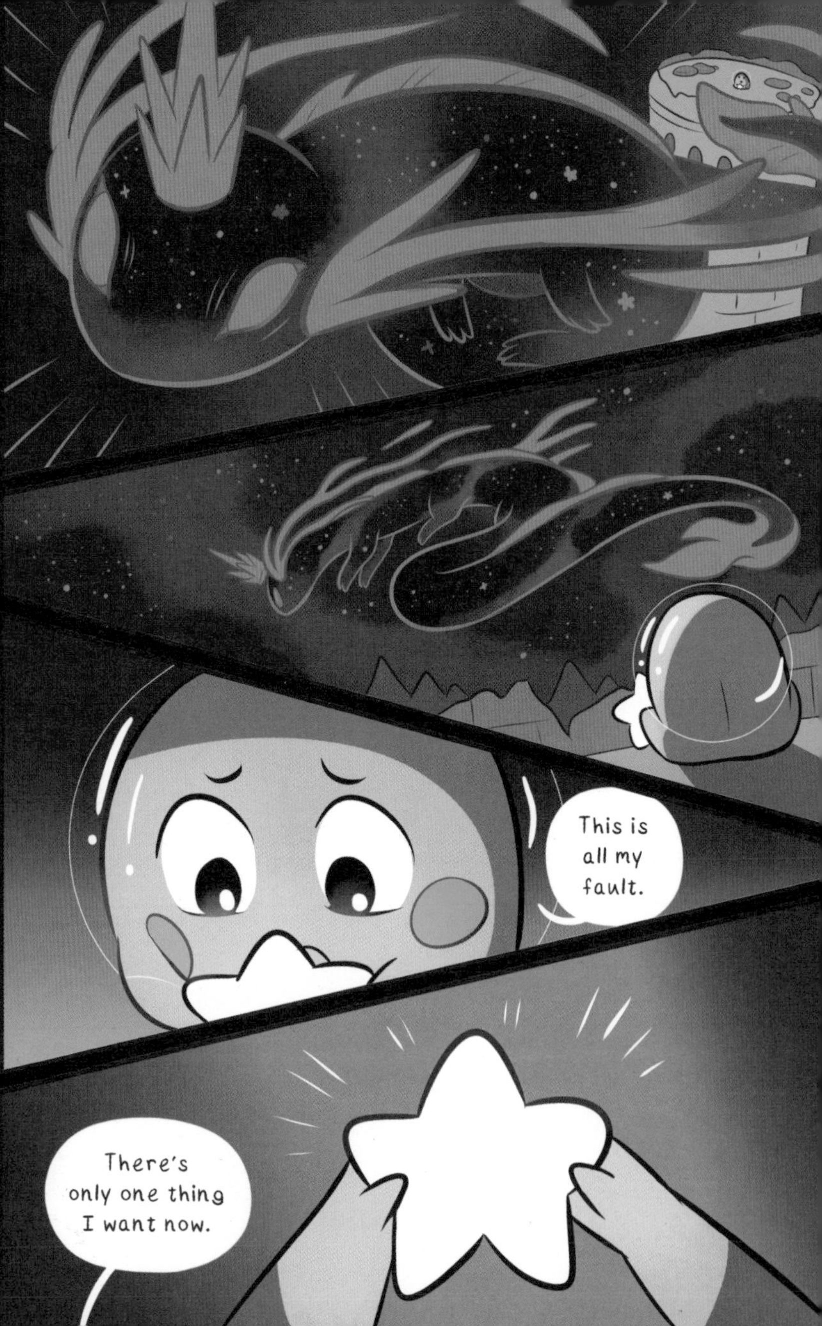
This is all my fault.
There's only one thing I want now.

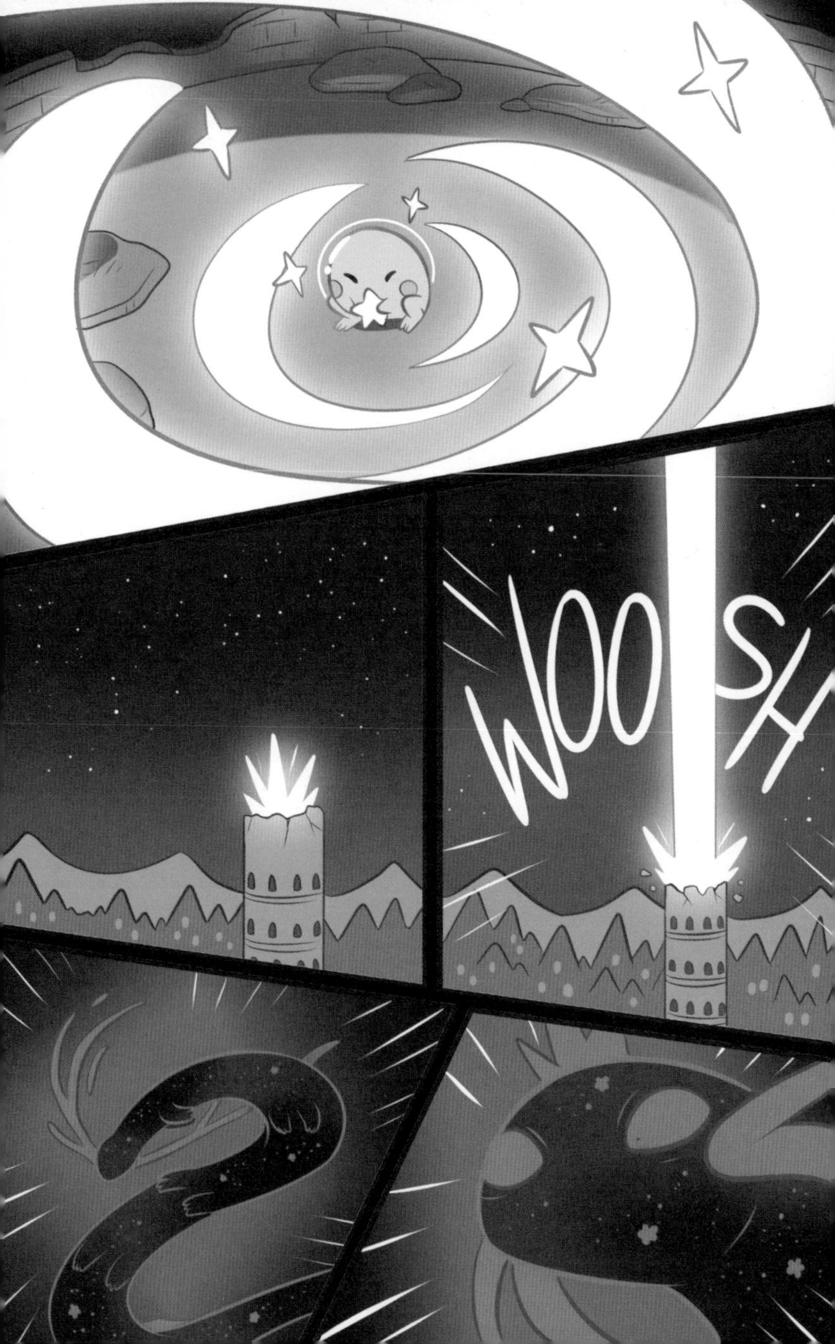
WOOSH

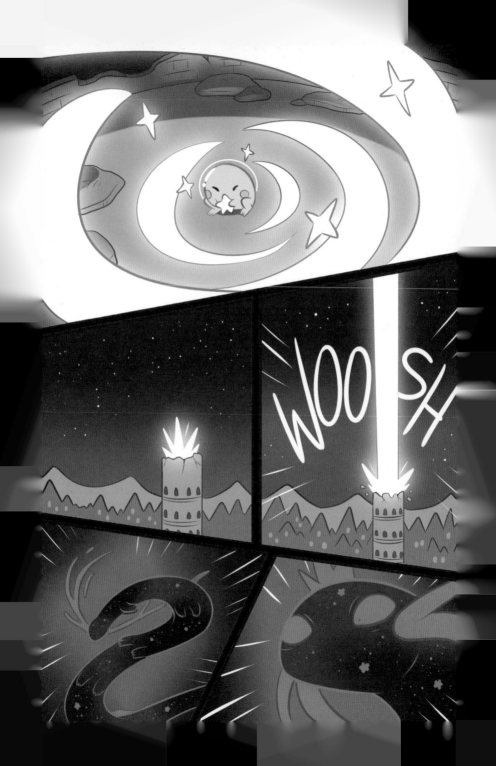

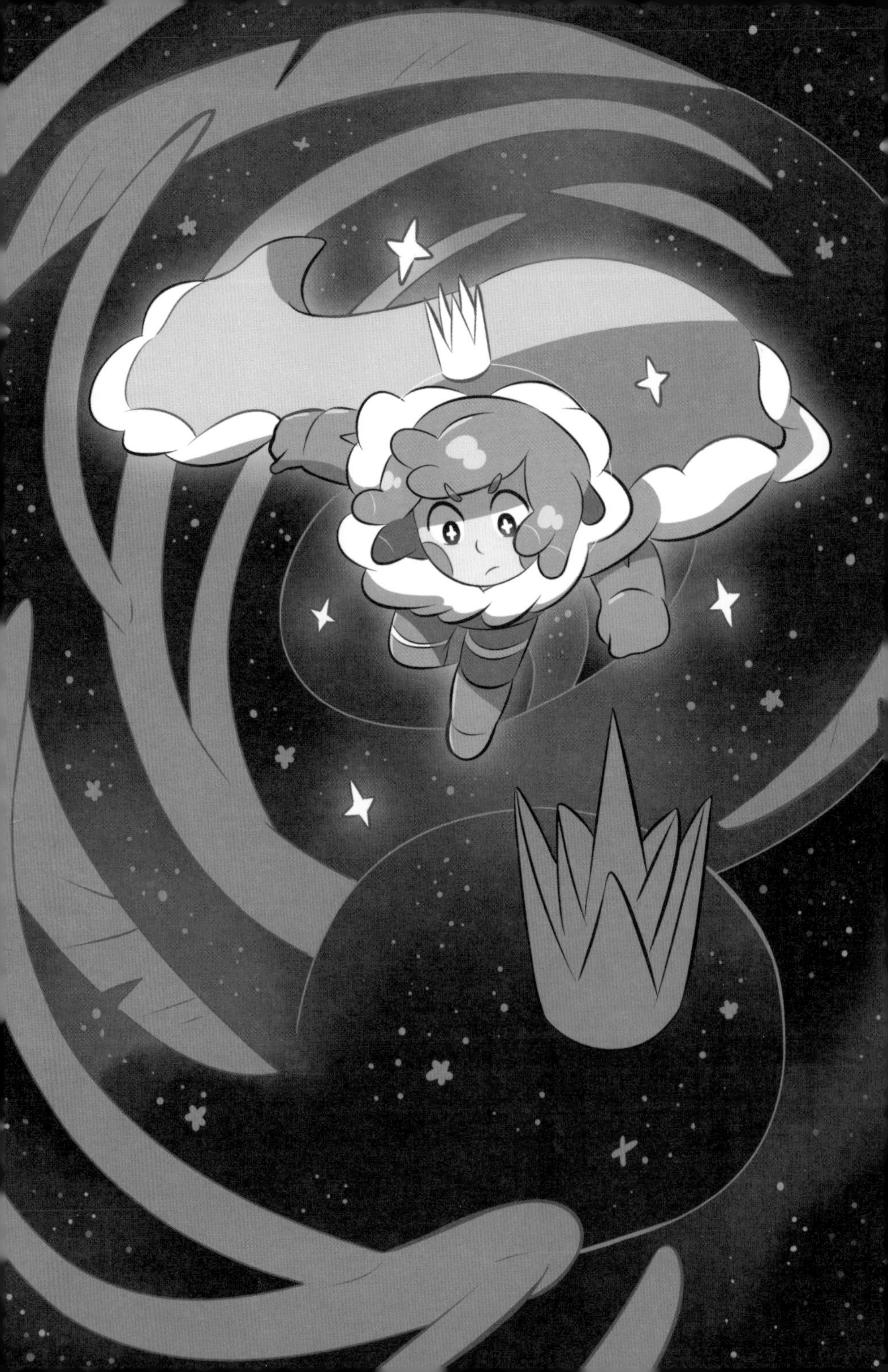

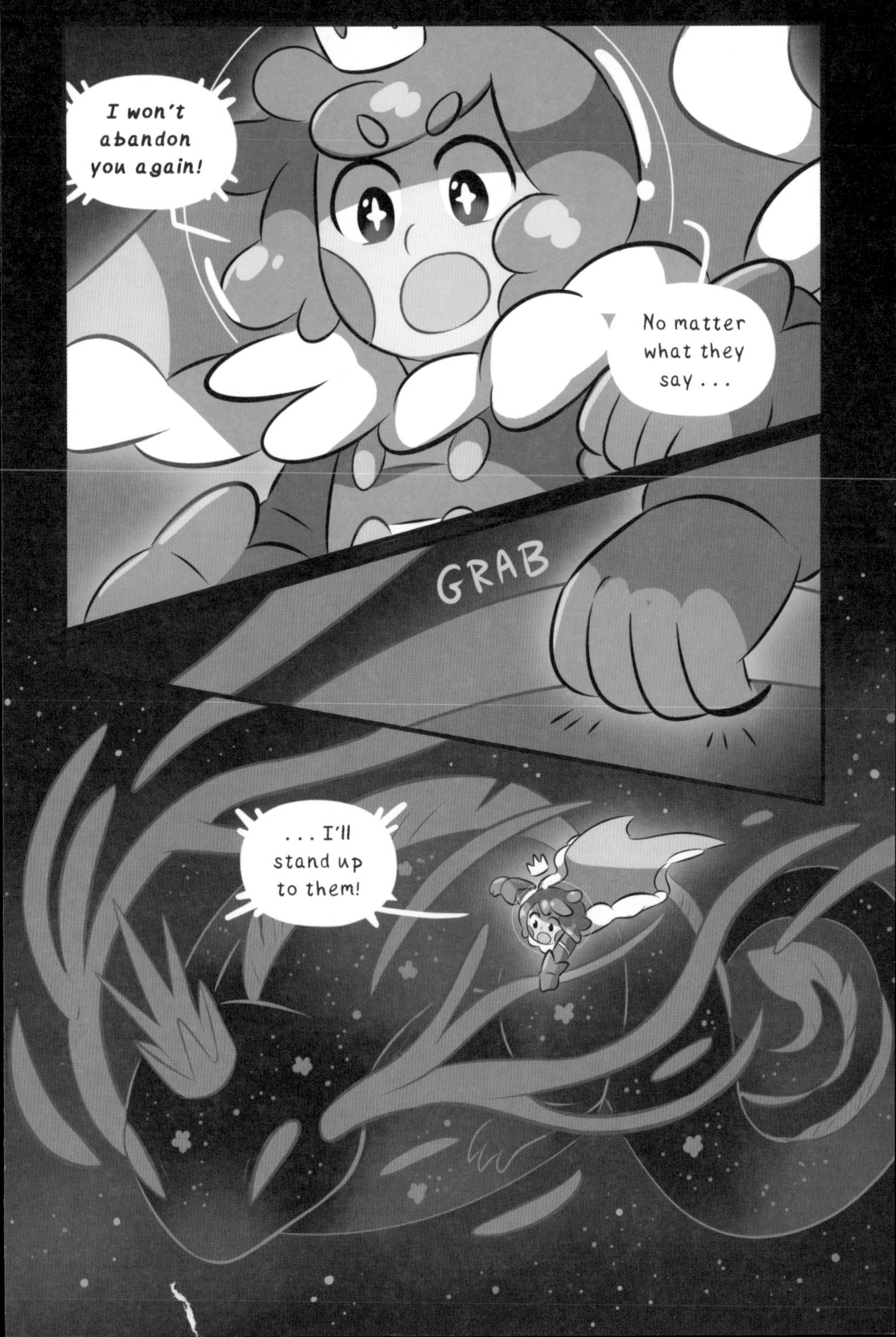
I won't abandon you again!
No matter what they say . . .
GRAB
. . . I'll stand up to them!

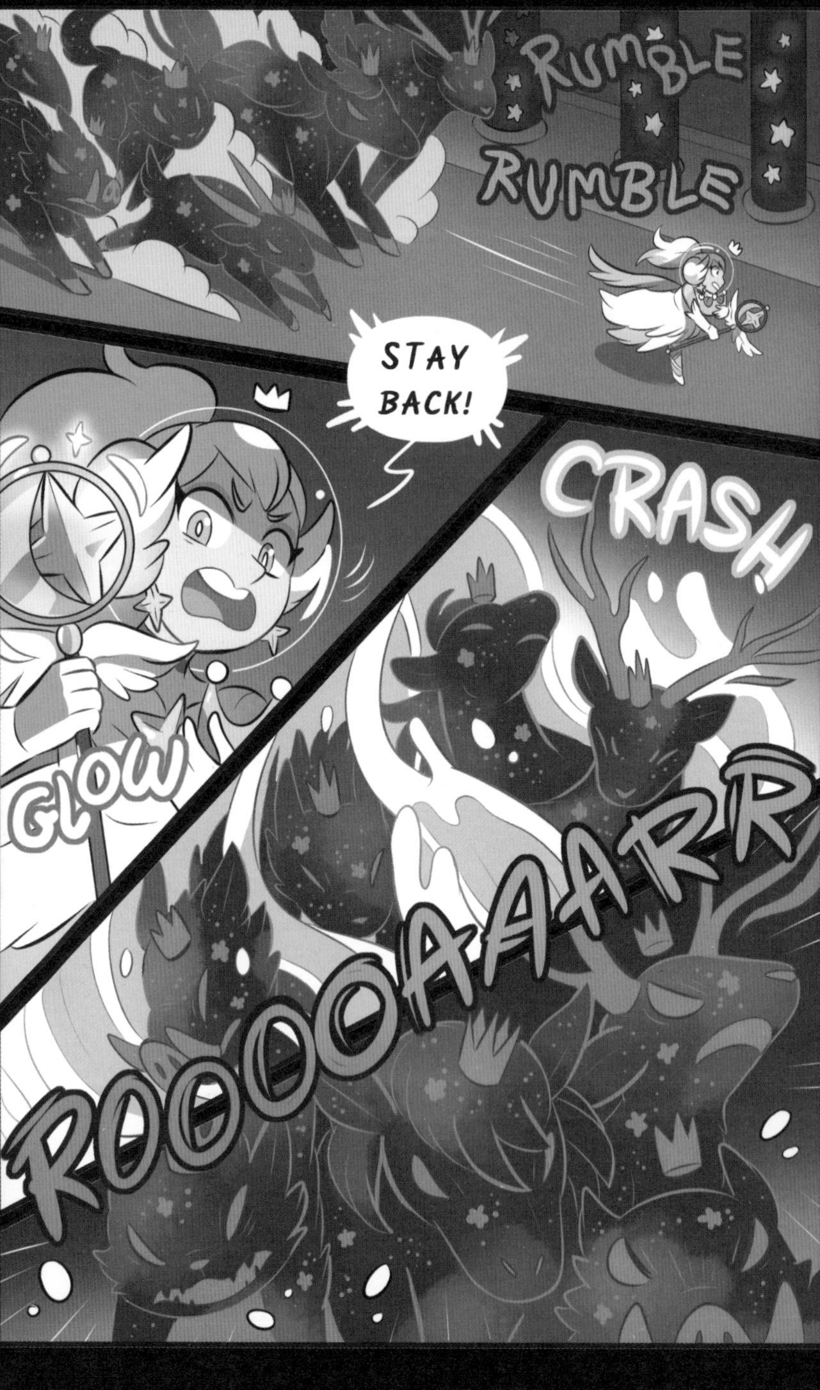
RUMBLE
RUMBLE
STAY BACK!
GLOW
CRASH
ROOOOAAARR

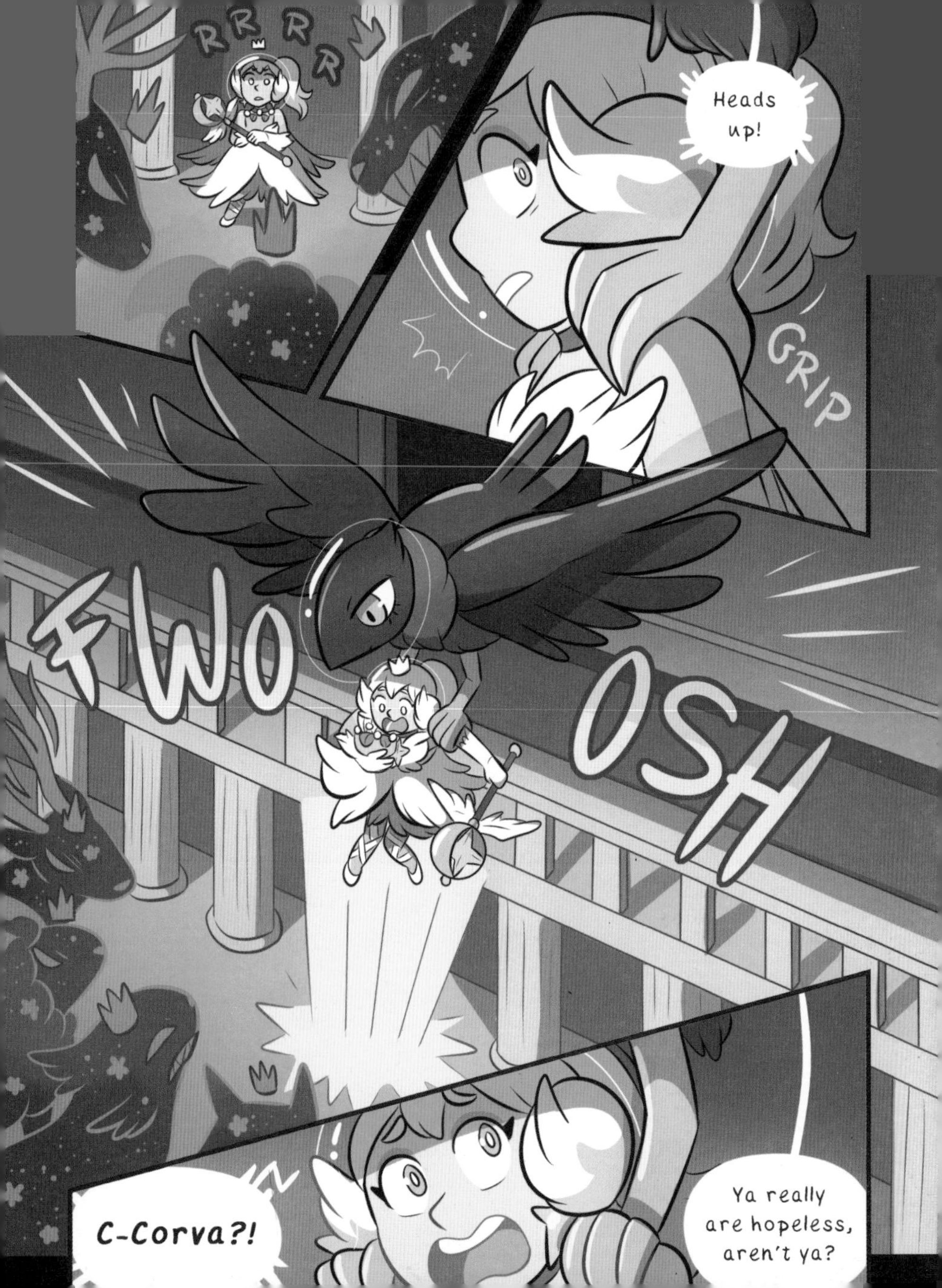
RRRR
Heads up!
GRIP
FWOOSH
C-Corva?!
Ya really are hopeless, aren't ya?

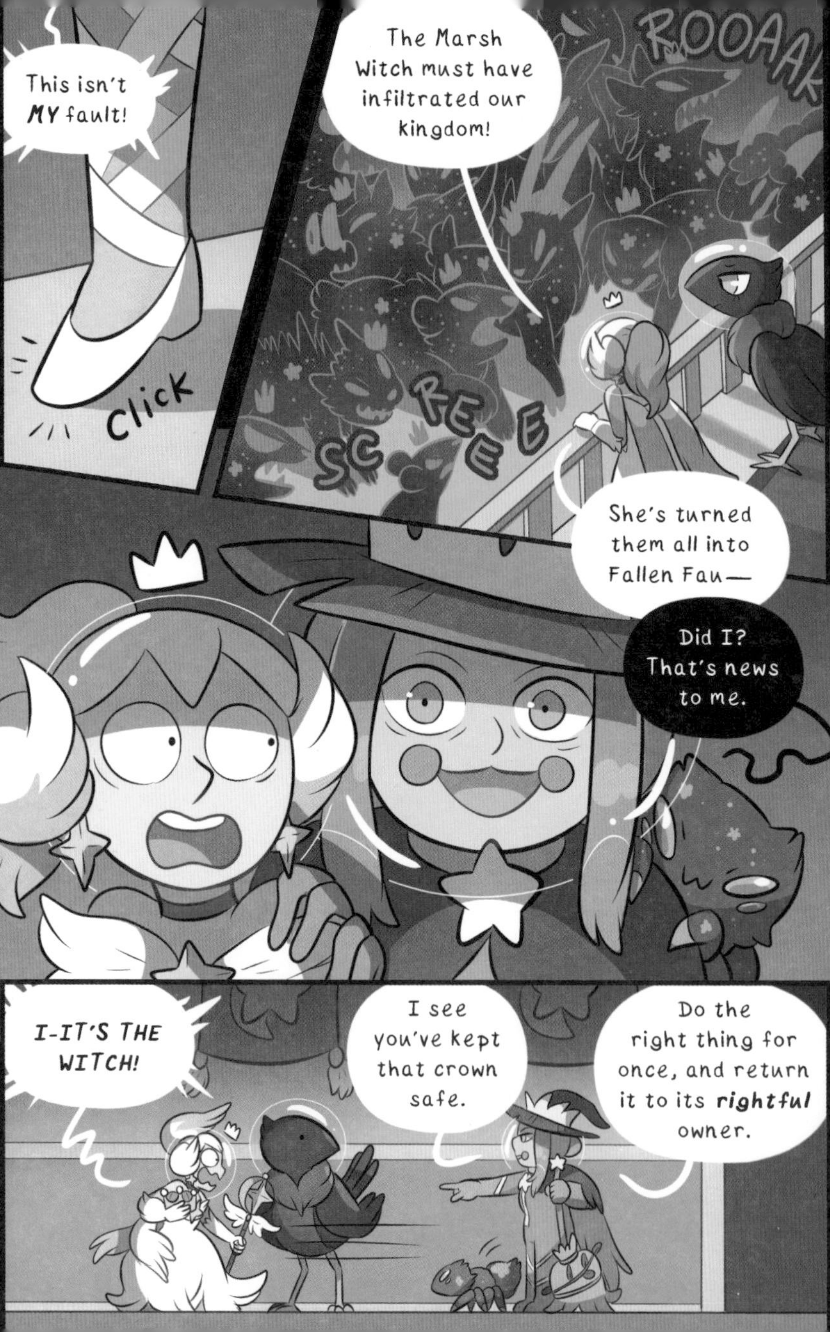
This isn't **MY** fault!
CLICK
The Marsh Witch must have infiltrated our kingdom!
ROOAAK
SCREEE
She's turned them all into Fallen Fau—
Did I? That's news to me.
I-IT'S THE WITCH!
I see you've kept that crown safe.
Do the right thing for once, and return it to its **rightful** owner.

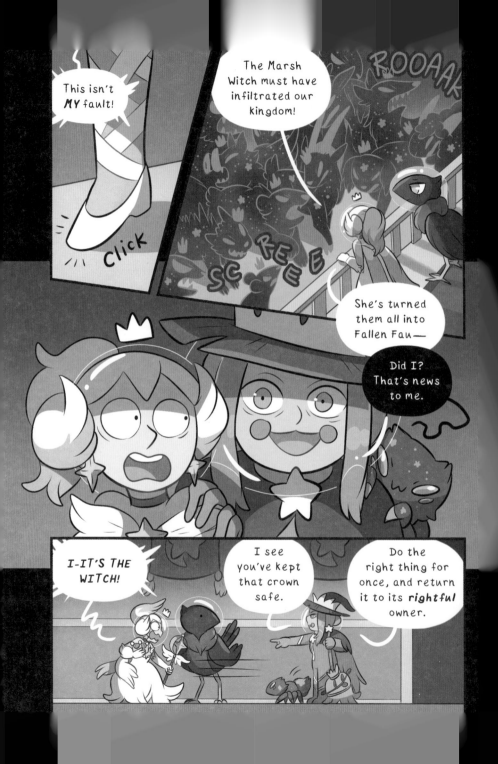

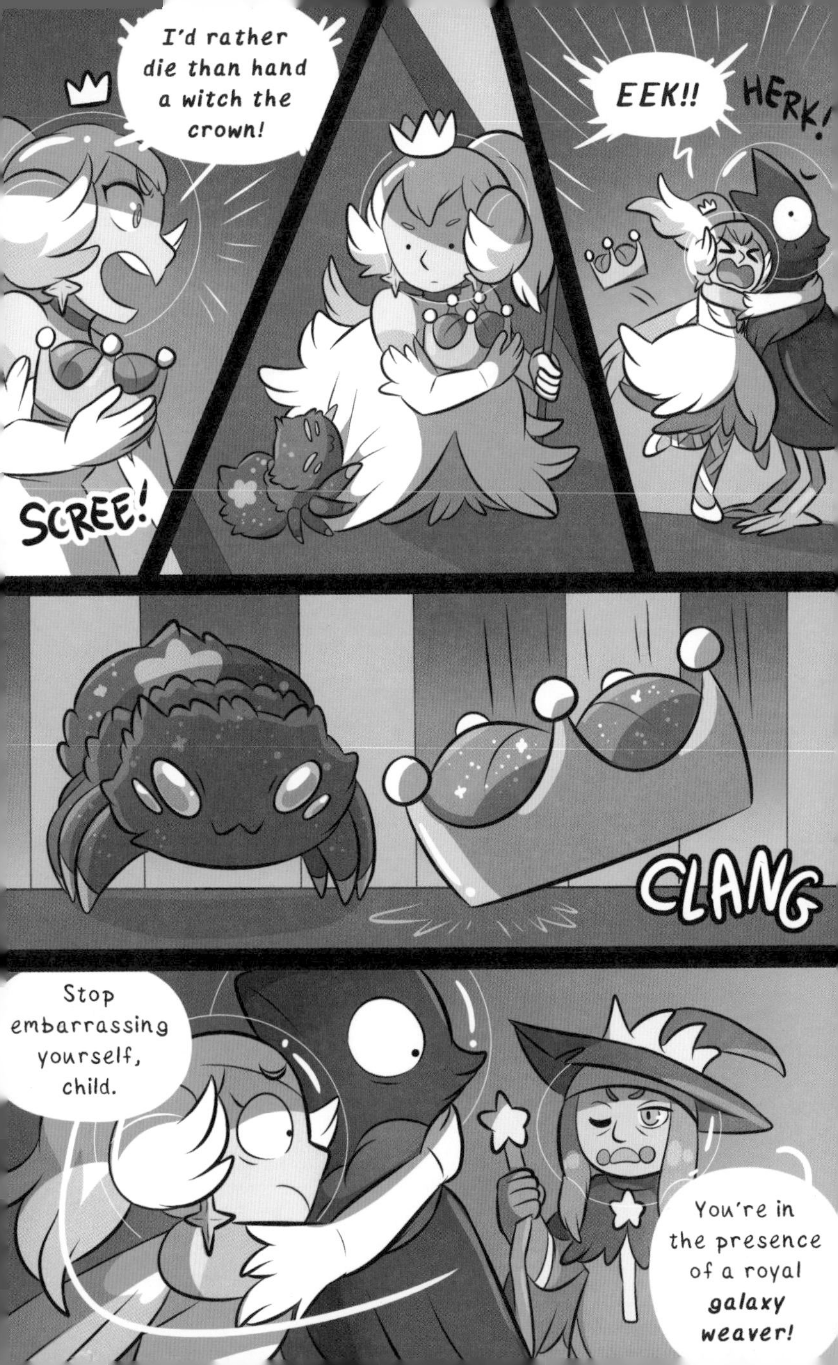
I'd rather die than hand a witch the crown!
SCREE!
EEK!!
HERK!
CLANG
Stop embarrassing yourself, child.
You're in the presence of a royal galaxy weaver!

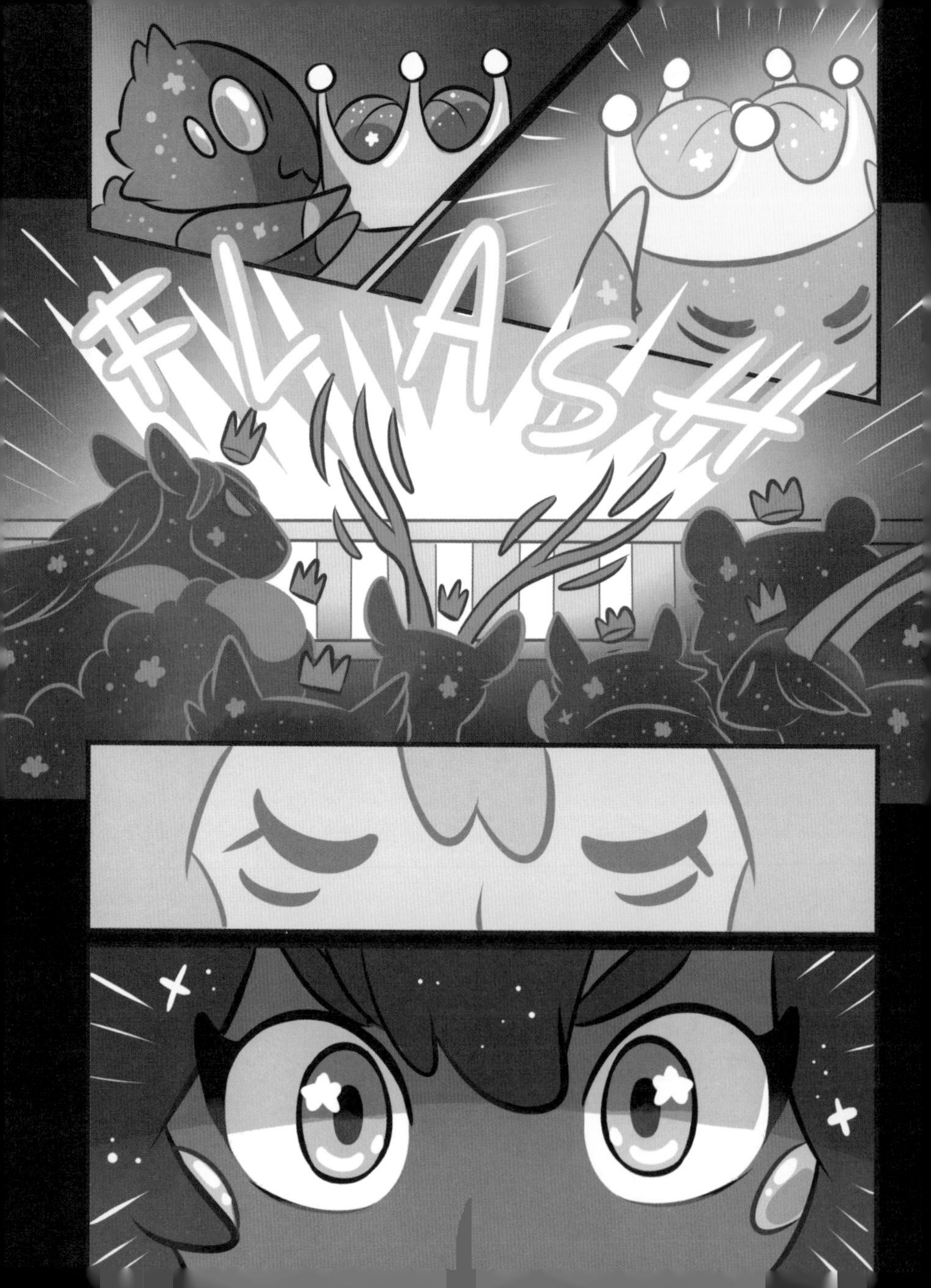
FLASH

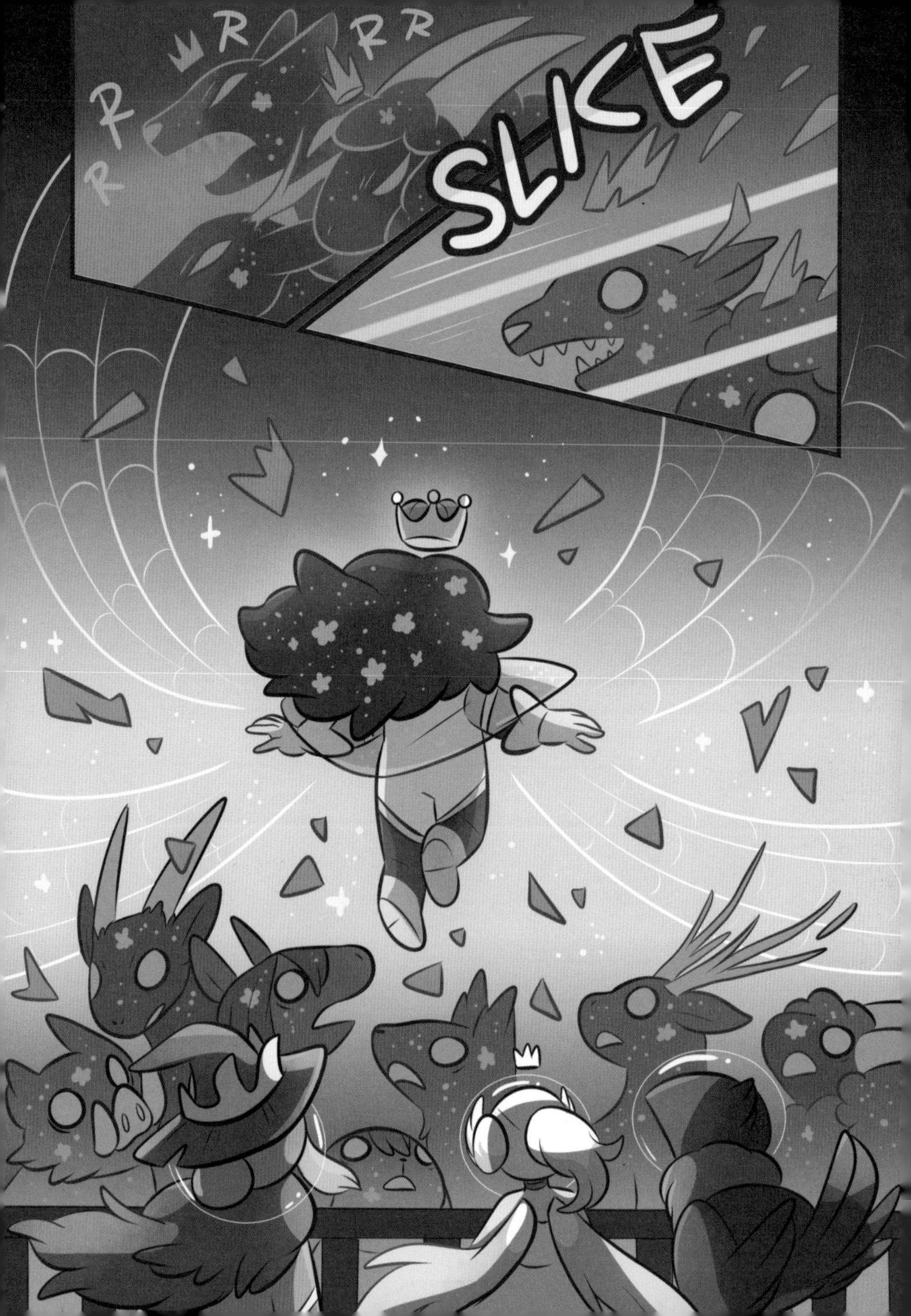
R
R
R
R
RR
SLICE

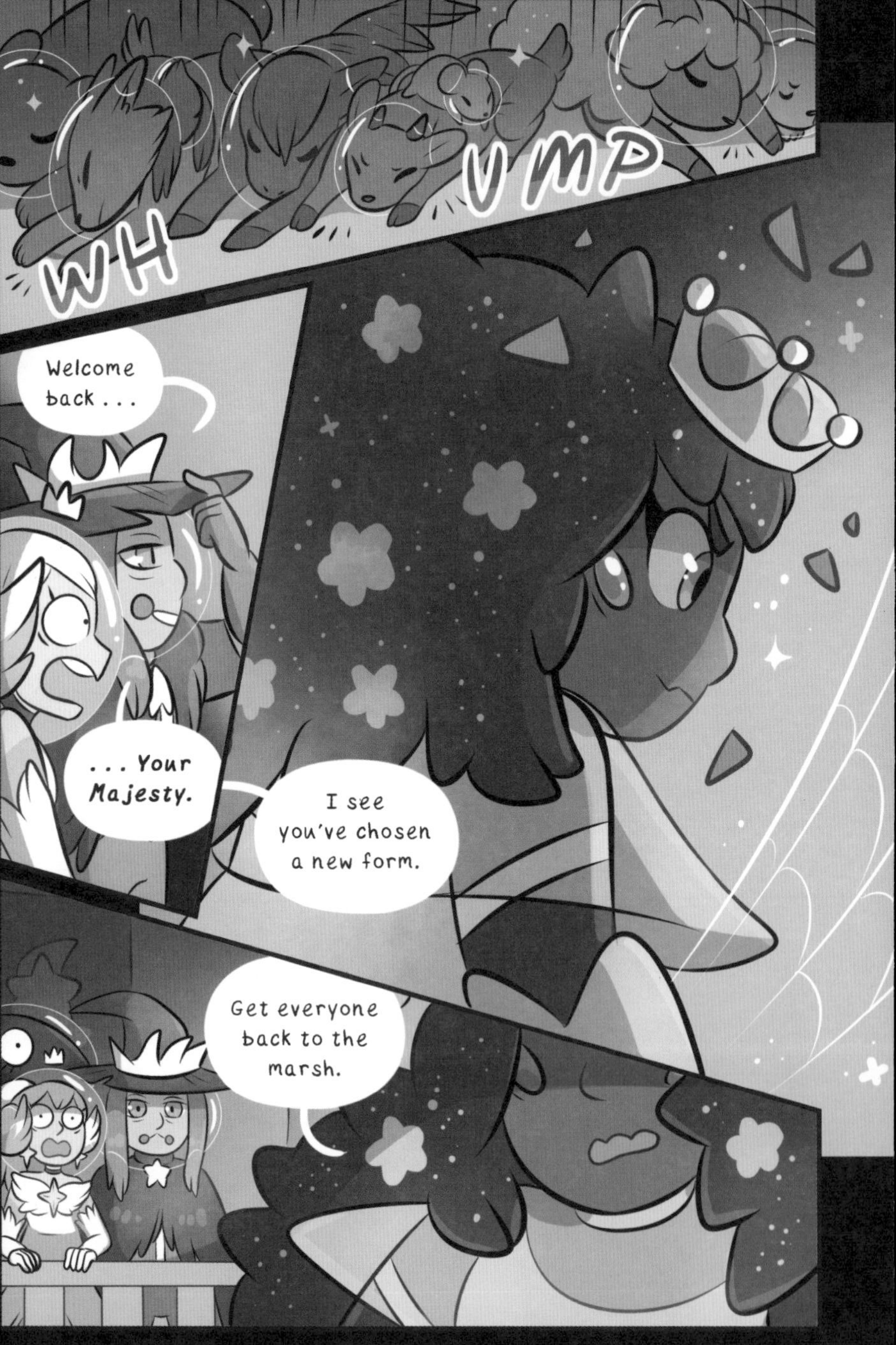
WH
UMP
Welcome back . . .
. . . Your Majesty.
I see you've chosen a new form.
Get everyone back to the marsh.

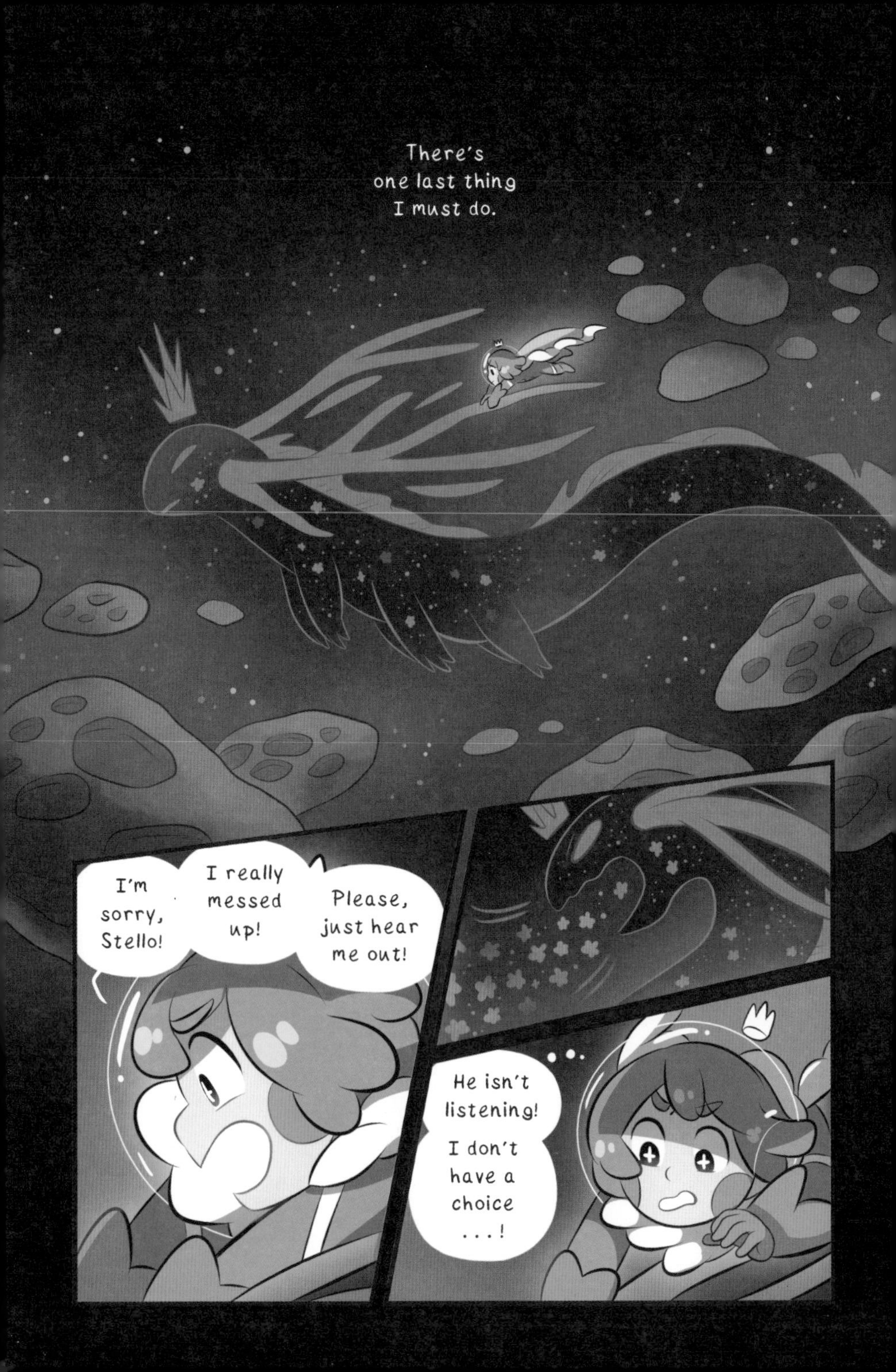

There's one last thing I must do.
I'm sorry, Stello!
I really messed up!
Please, just hear me out!
He isn't listening!
I don't have a choice . . . !

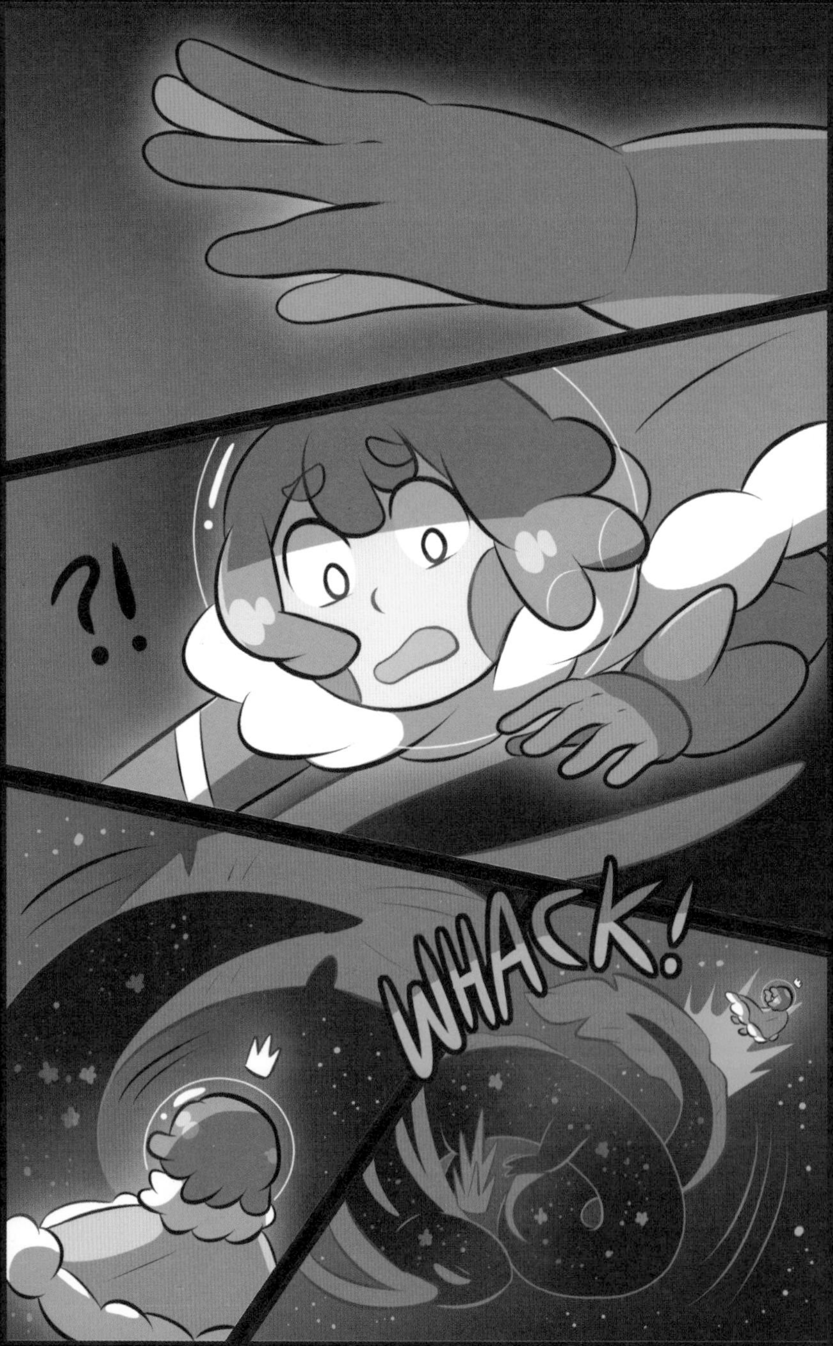
?!
WHACK!

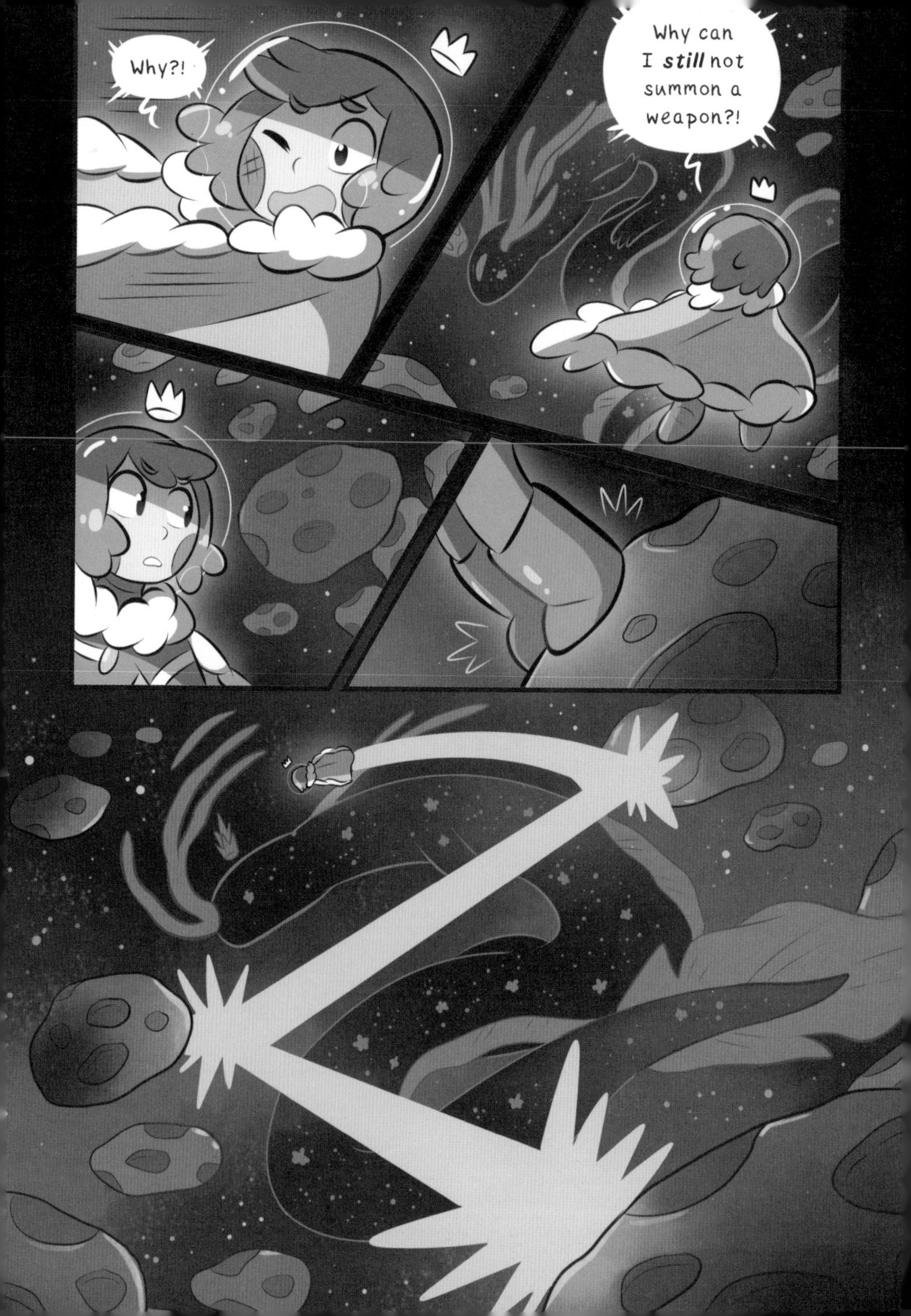
Why?!
Why can I **still** not summon a weapon?!

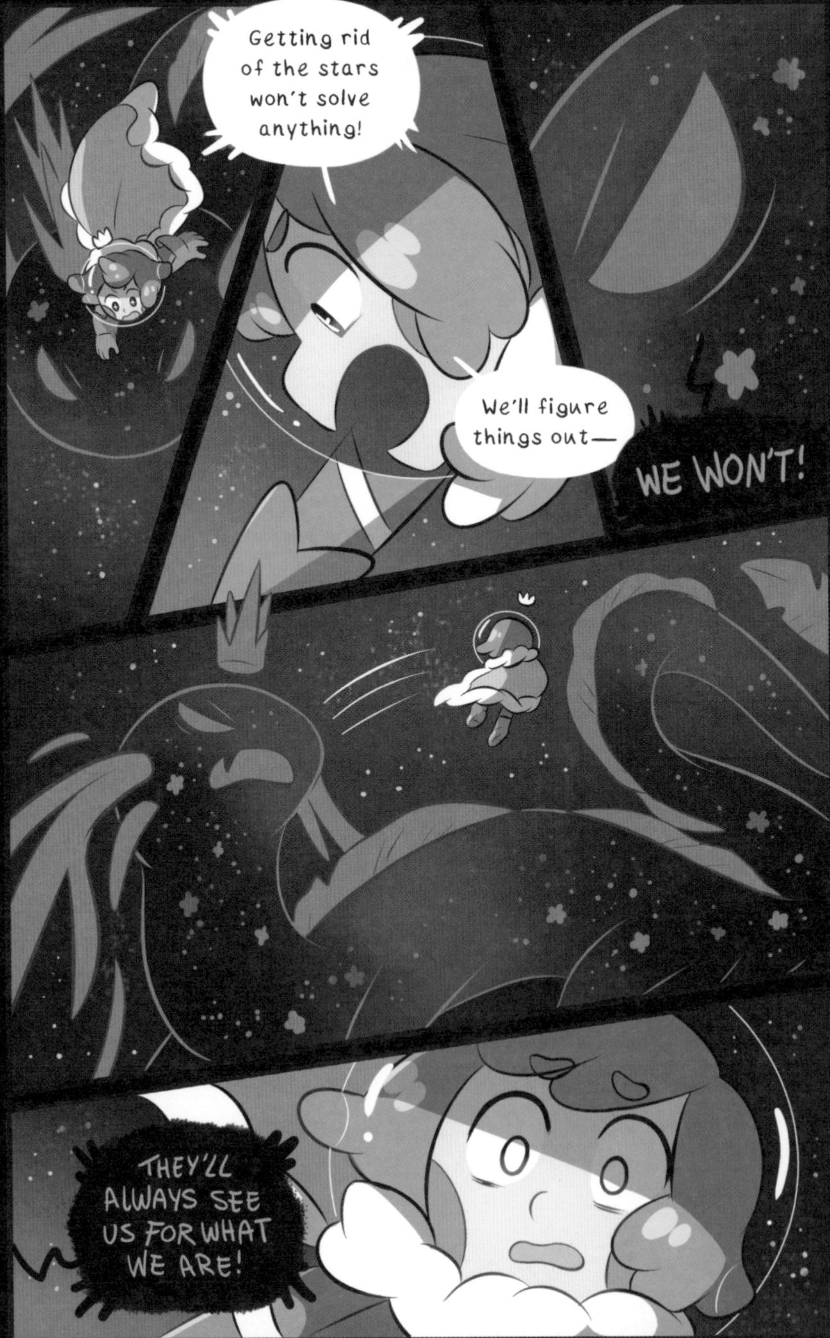
Getting rid of the stars won't solve anything!
We'll figure things out—
WE WON'T!
THEY'LL ALWAYS SEE US FOR WHAT WE ARE!

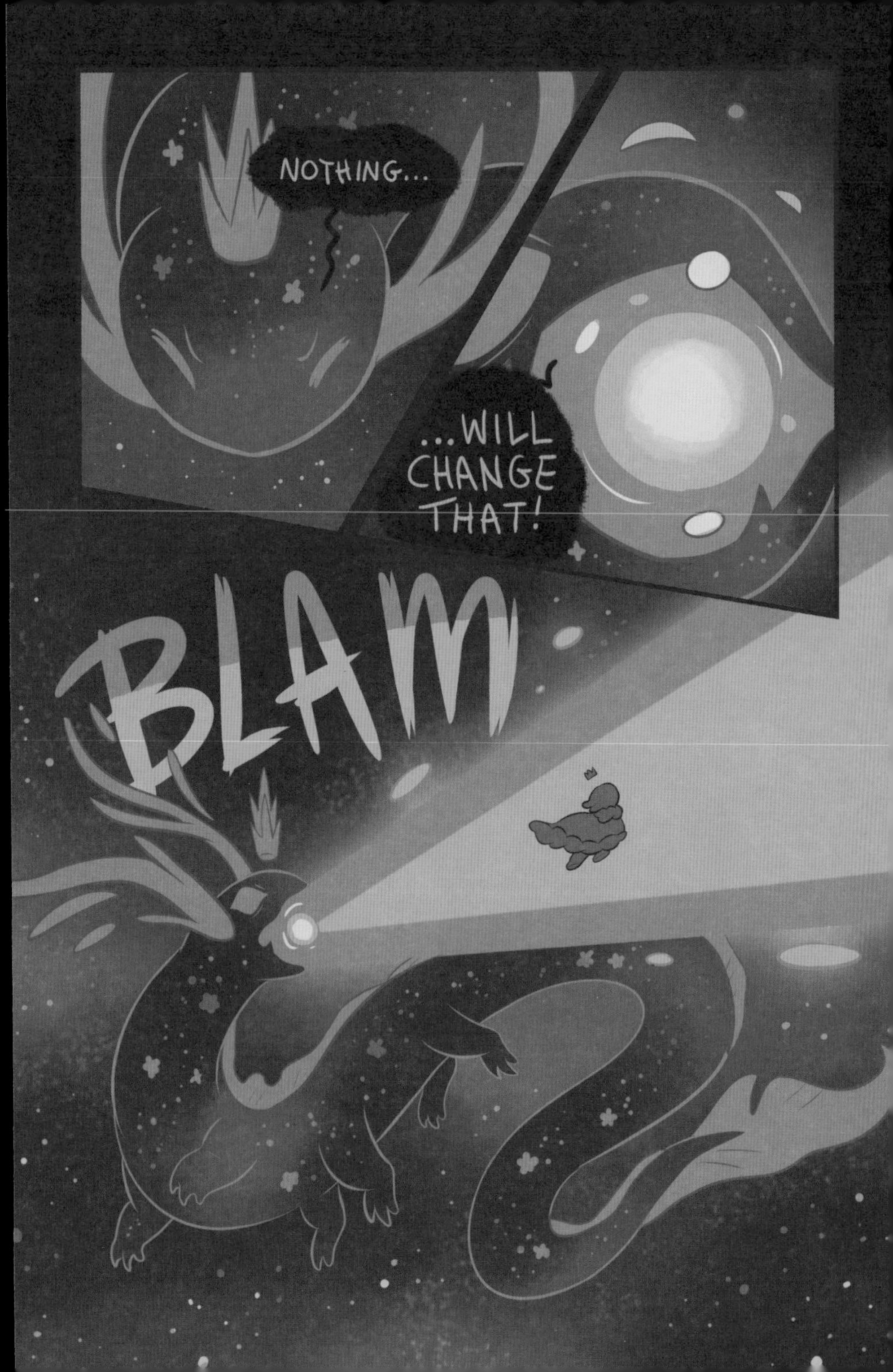
NOTHING...
...WILL CHANGE THAT!
BLAM

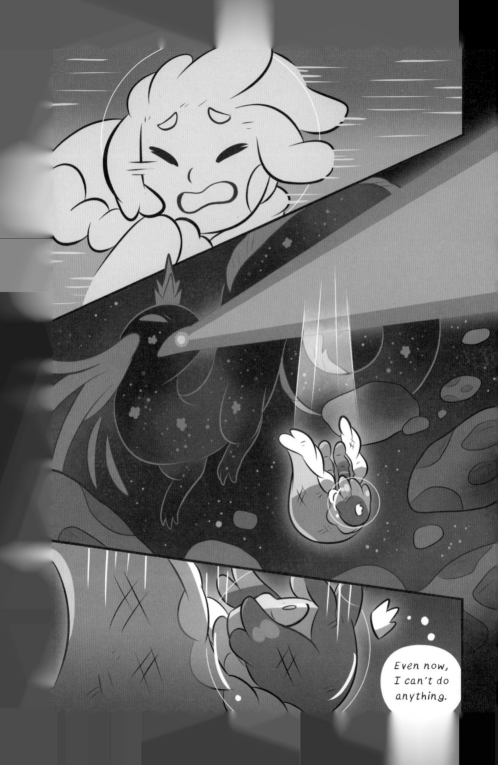

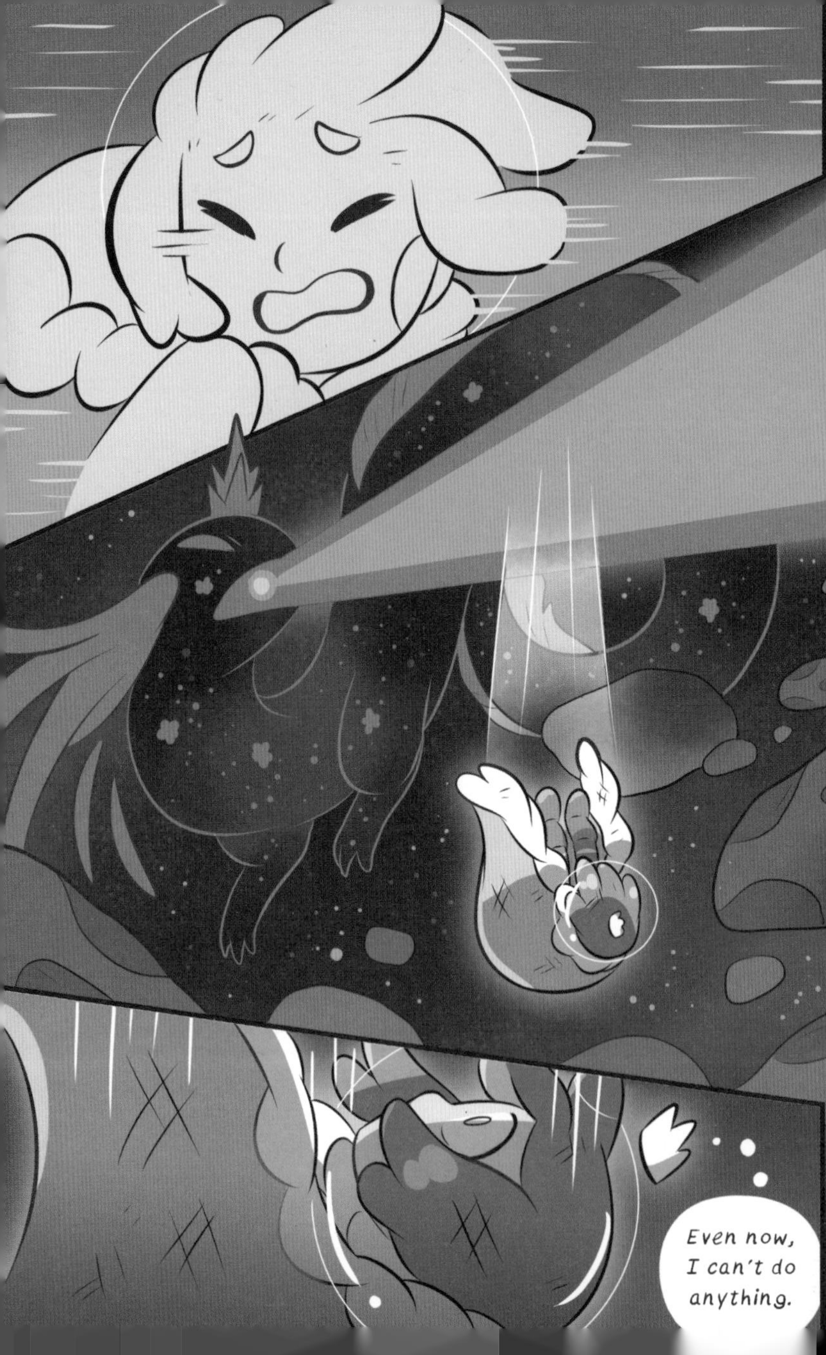
Even now, I can't do anything.

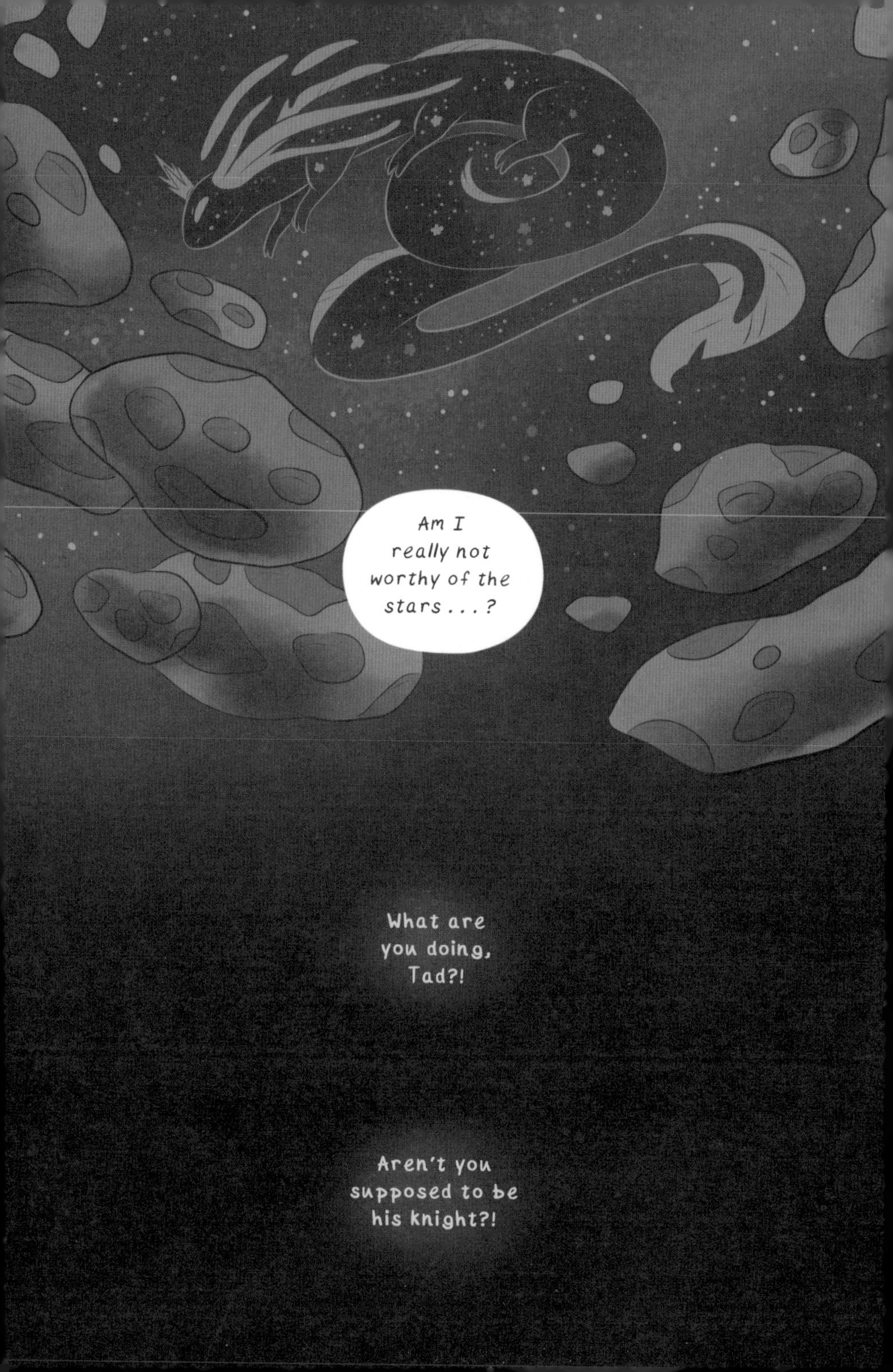
Am I really not worthy of the stars . . . ?
What are you doing, Tad?!
Aren't you supposed to be his knight?!

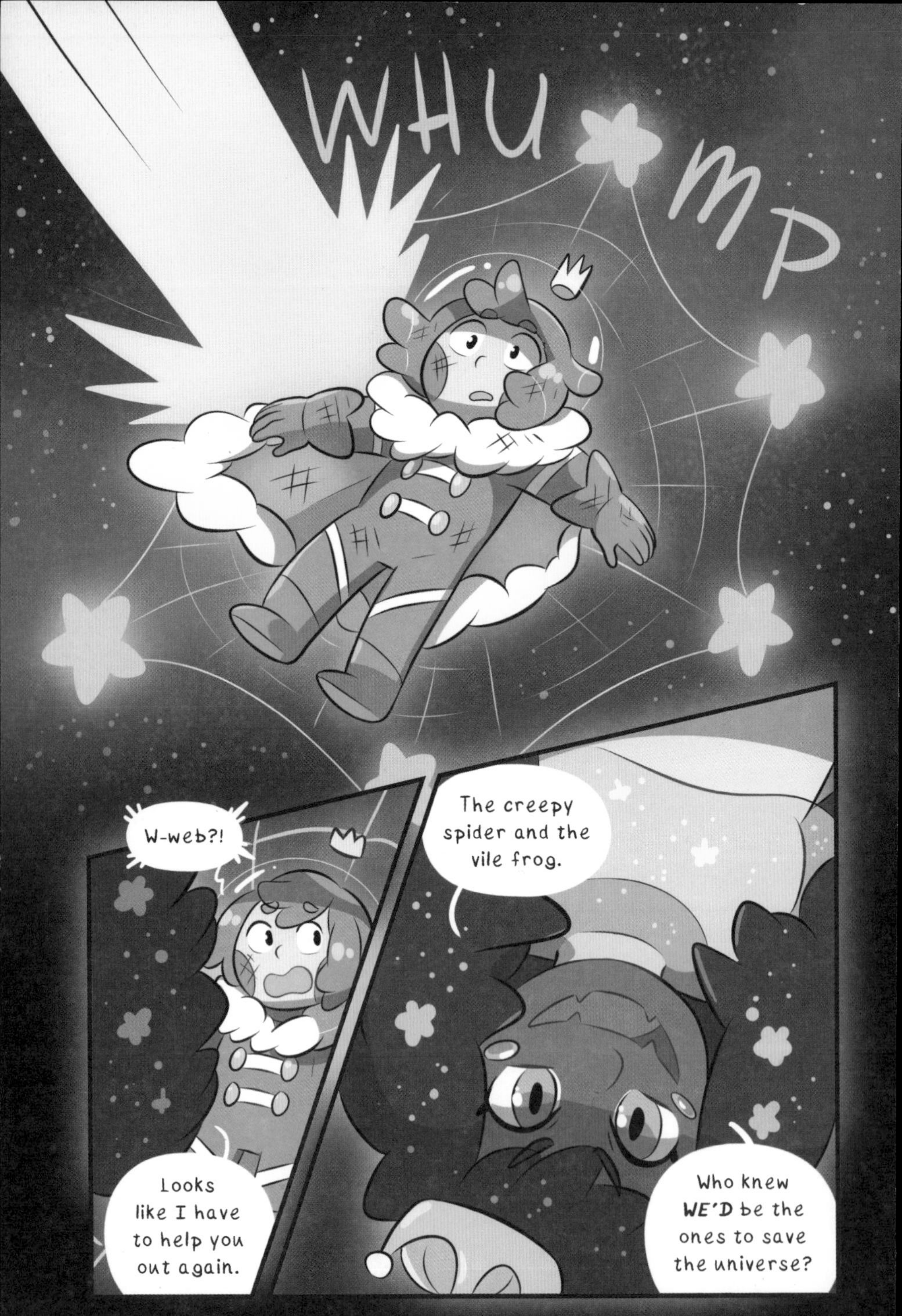
WHUMP
W-web?!
Looks like I have to help you out again.
The creepy spider and the vile frog.
Who knew **WE'D** be the ones to save the universe?

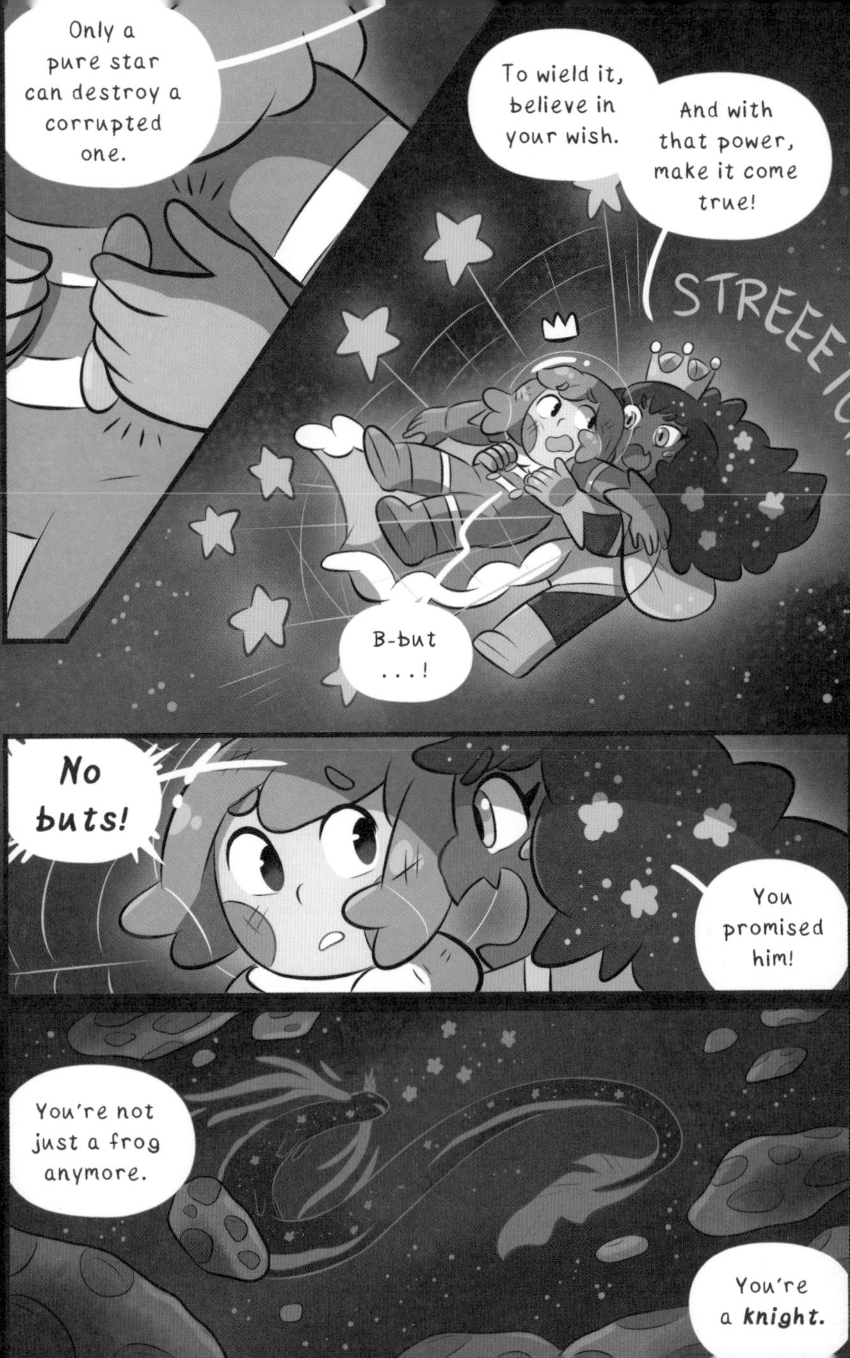
Only a pure star can destroy a corrupted one.
To wield it, believe in your wish.
And with that power, make it come true!
STREEEETCH
B-but . . . !
No buts!
You promised him!
You're not just a frog anymore.
You're a **knight.**

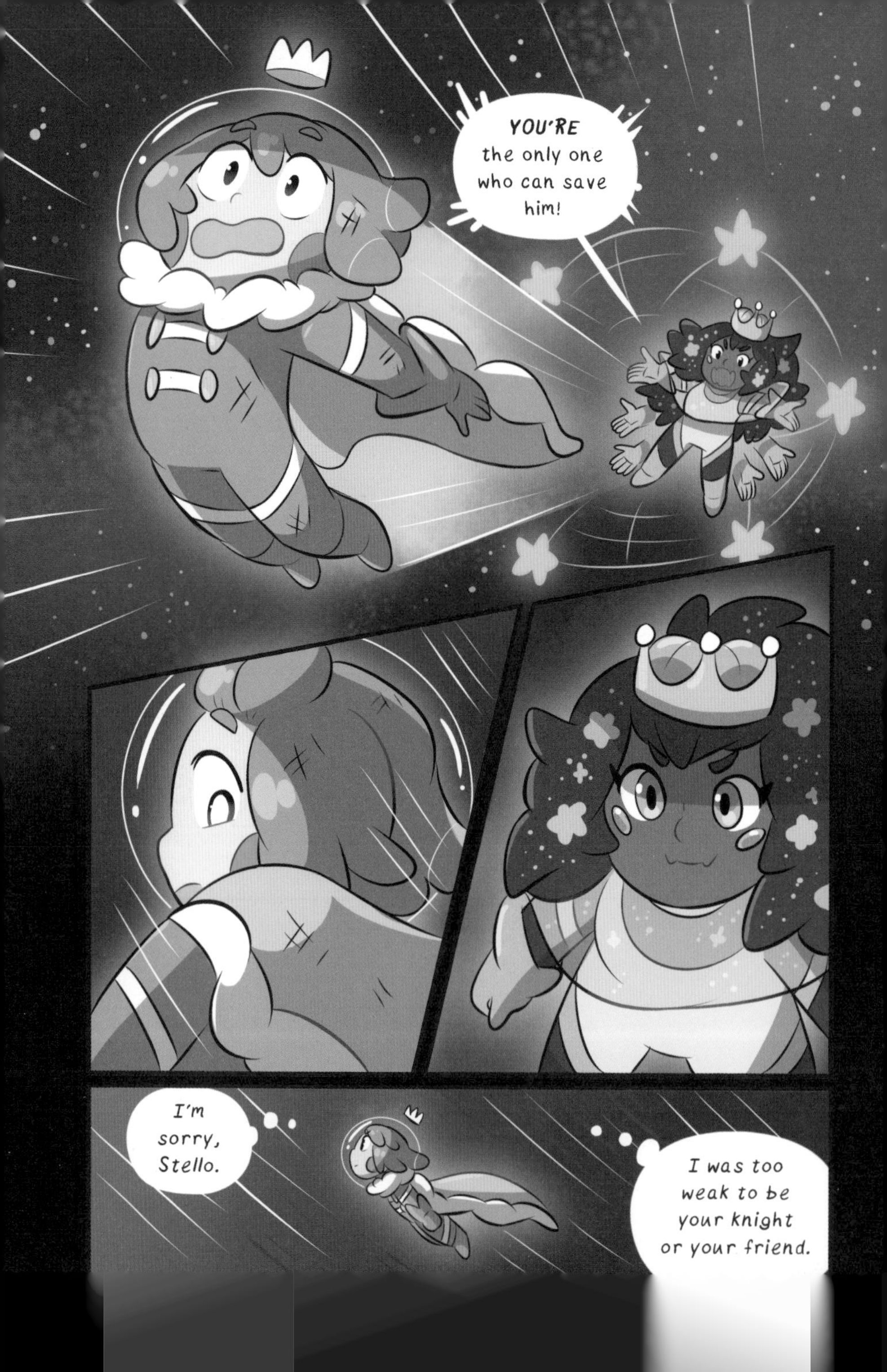
YOU'RE the only one who can save him!
I'm sorry, Stello.
I was too weak to be your knight or your friend.

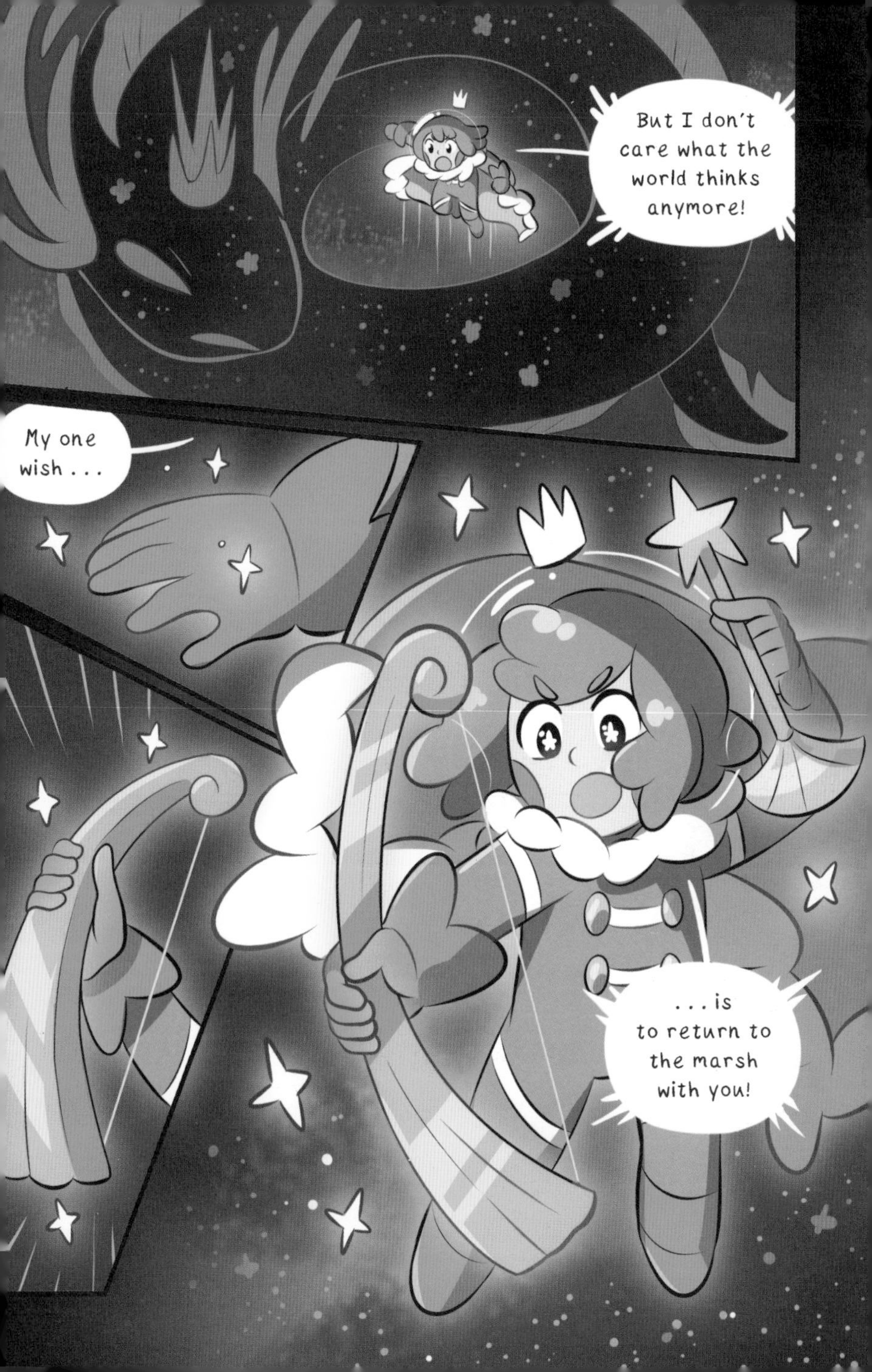
But I don't care what the world thinks anymore!
My one wish . . .
. . . is to return to the marsh with you!

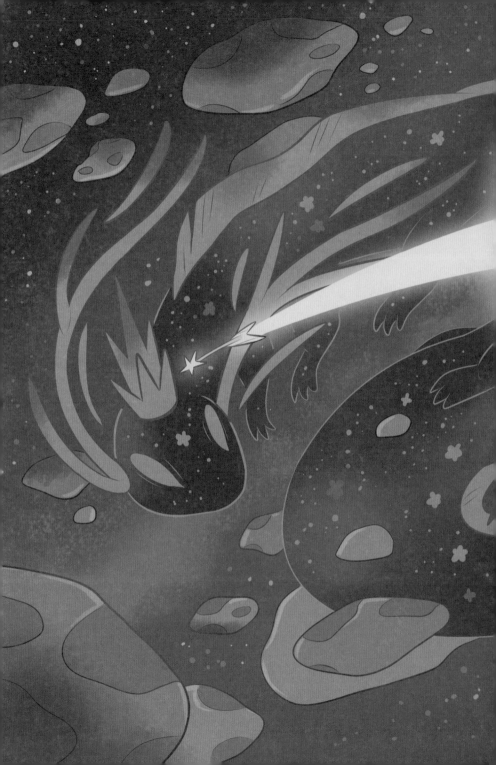

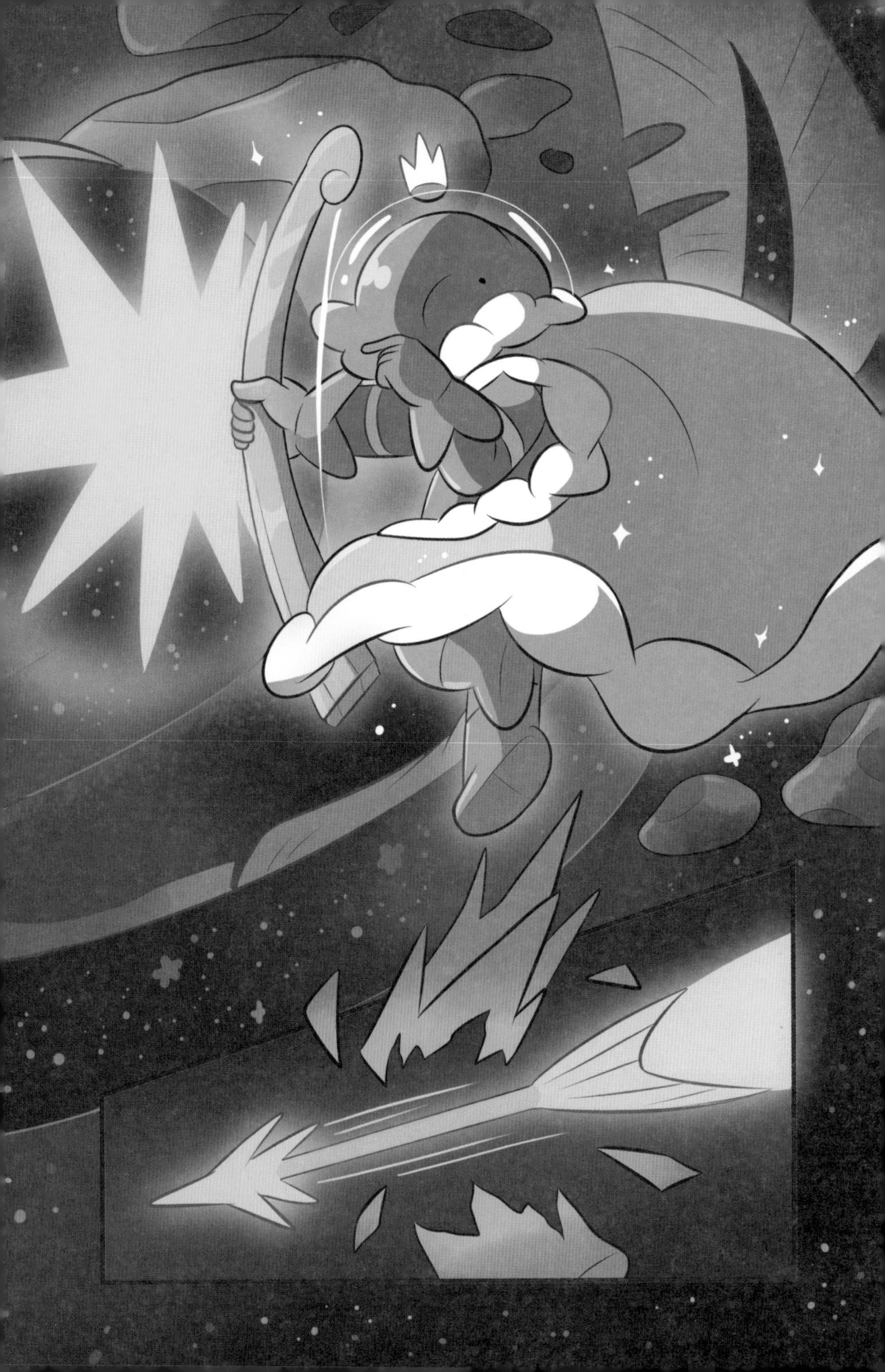

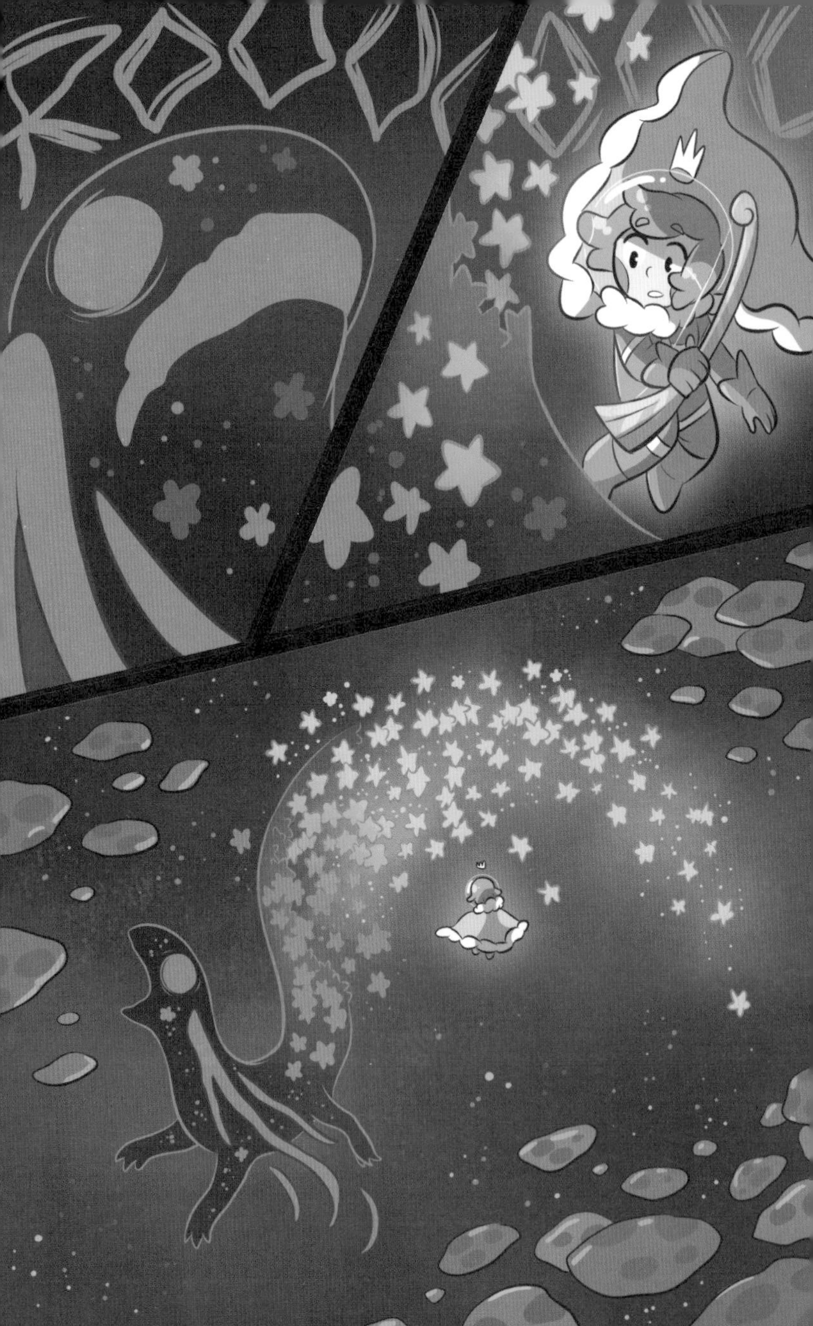
ROOOOOOO

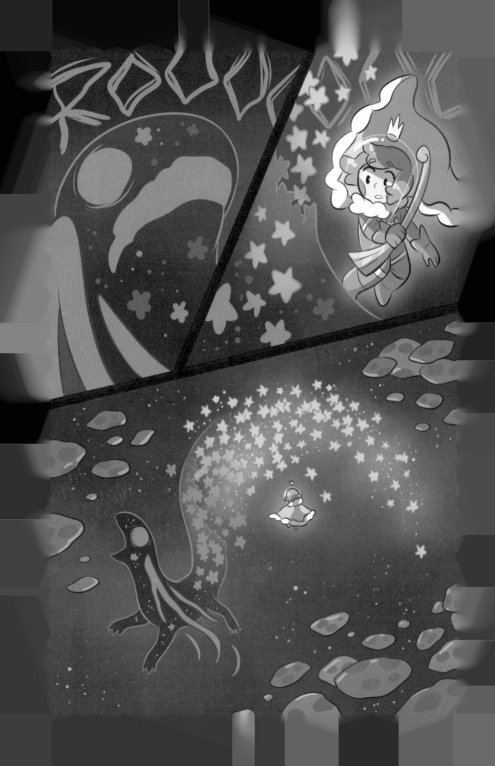

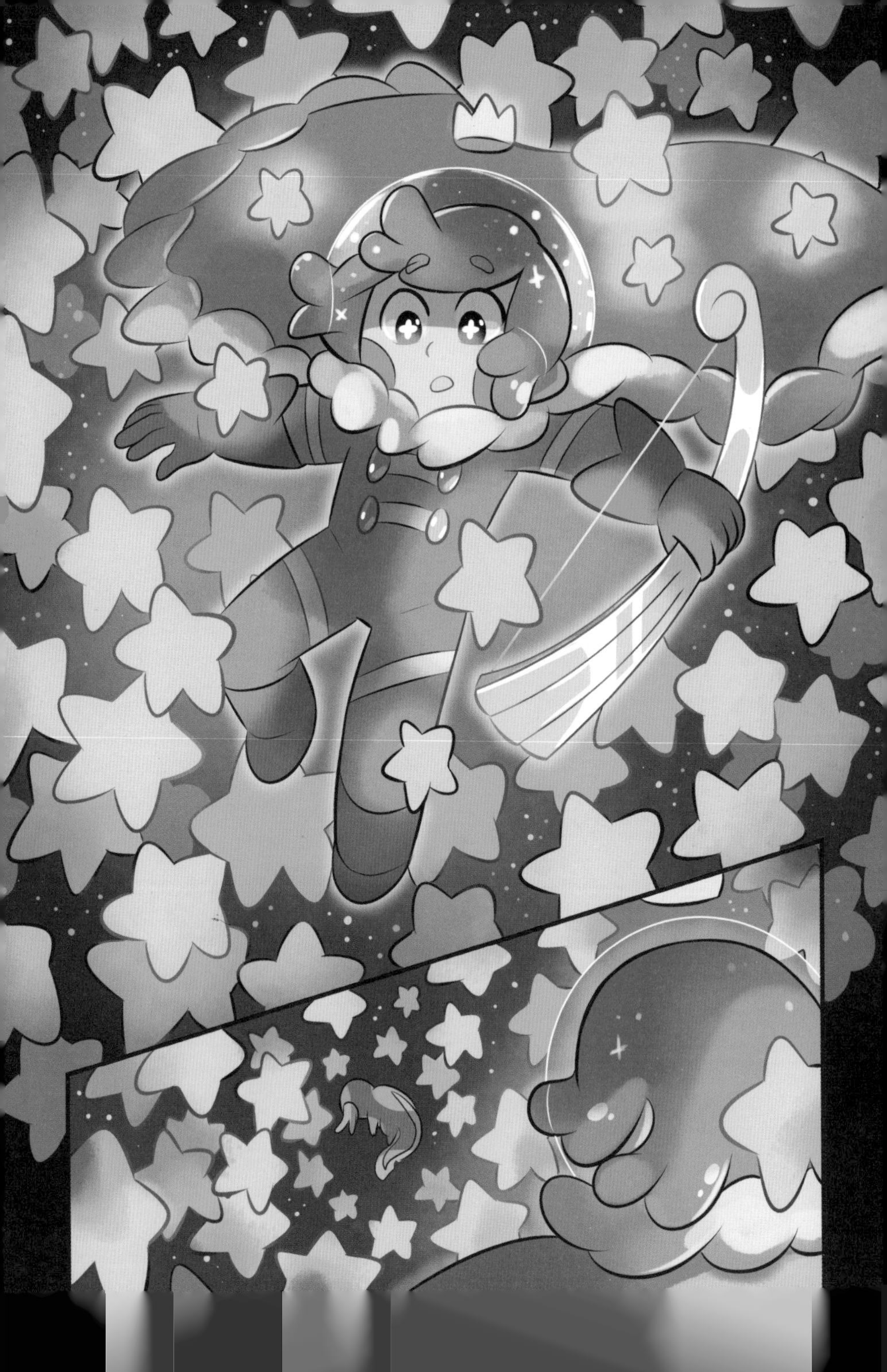

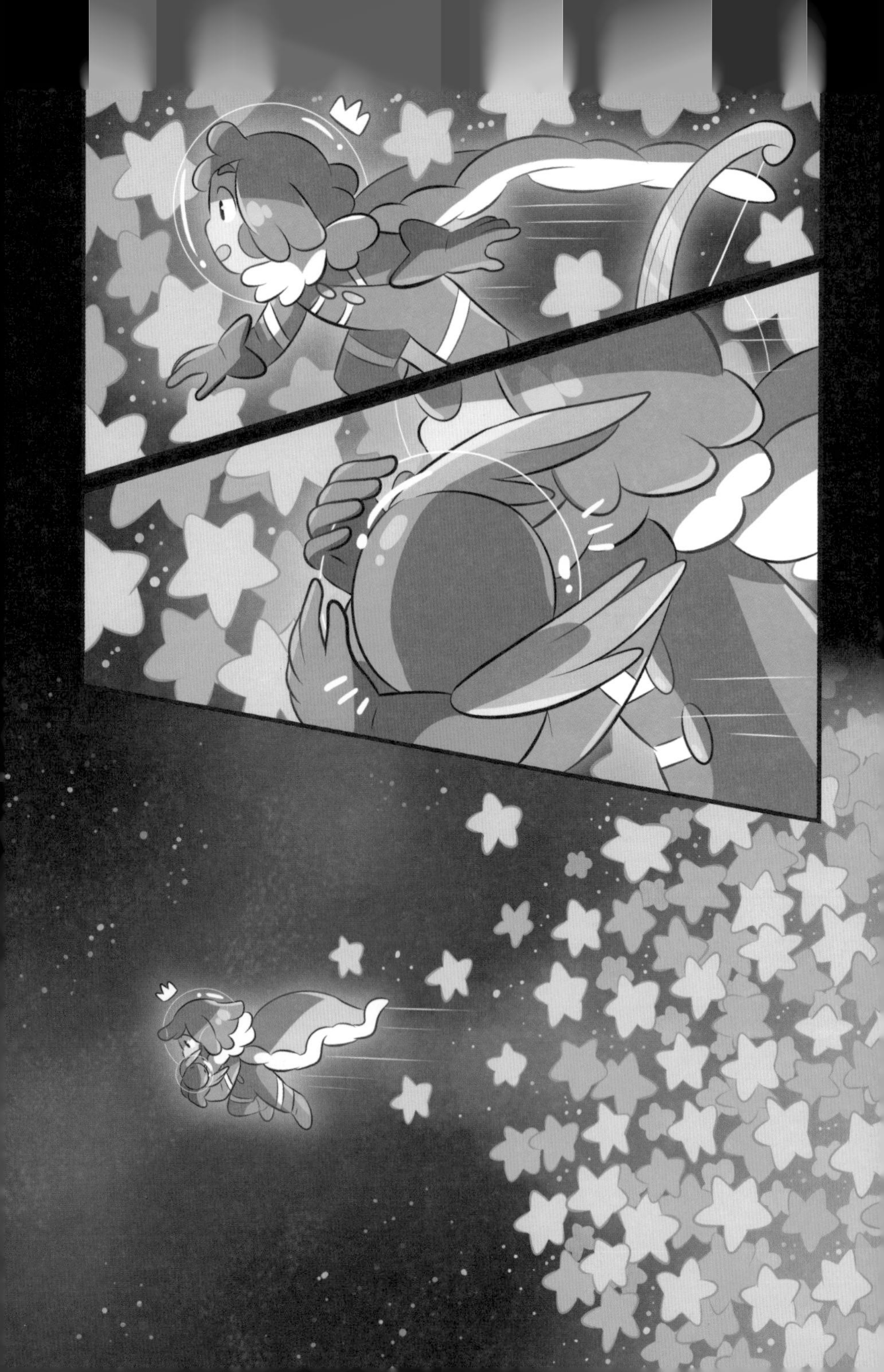

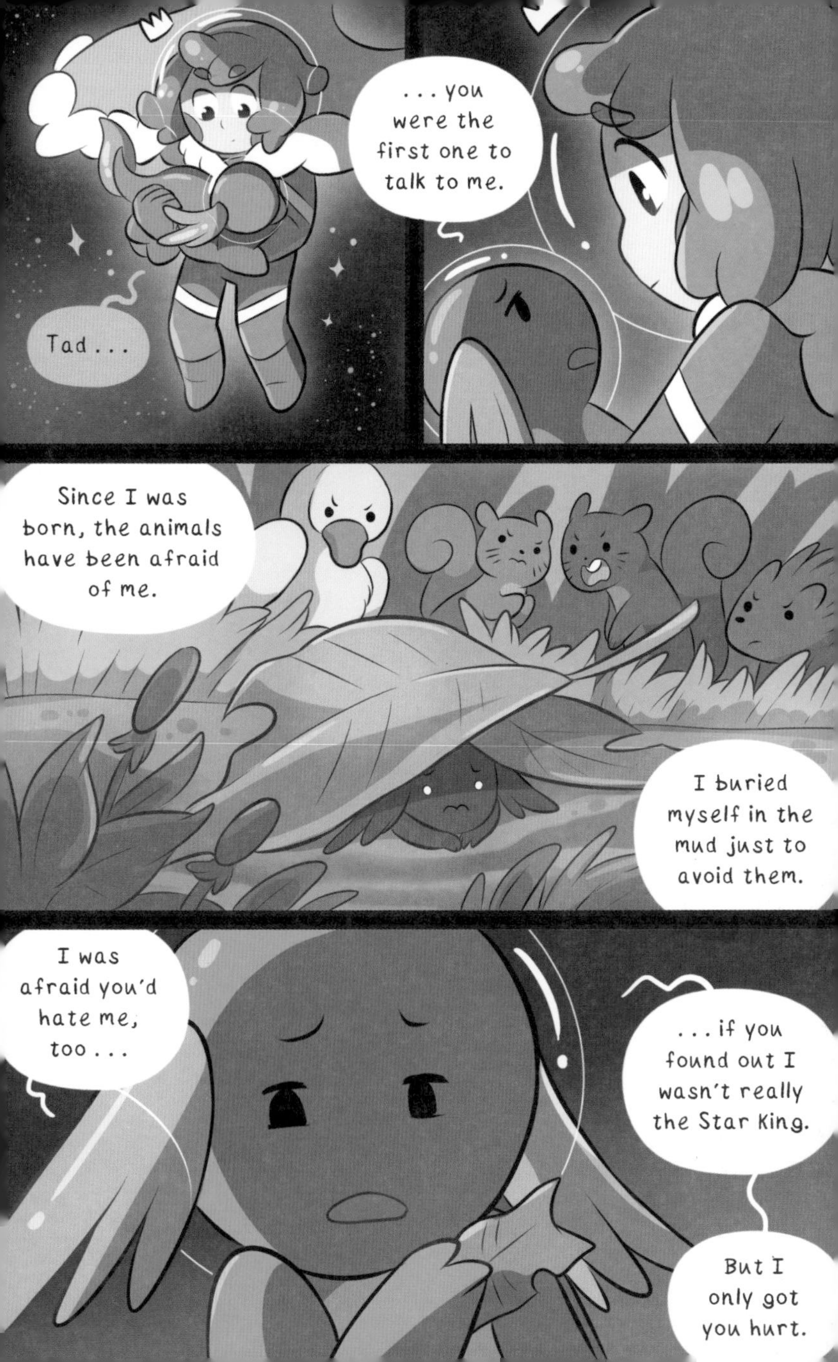
Tad . . .
. . . you were the first one to talk to me.
Since I was born, the animals have been afraid of me.
I buried myself in the mud just to avoid them.
I was afraid you'd hate me, too . . .
. . . if you found out I wasn't really the Star King.
But I only got you hurt.

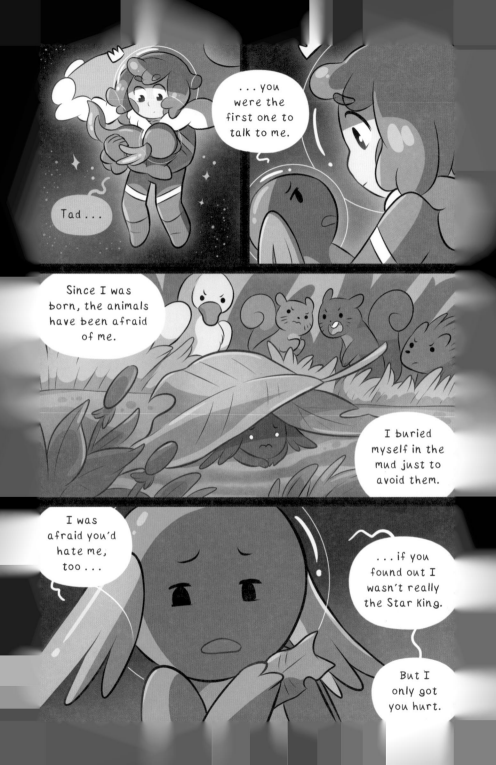

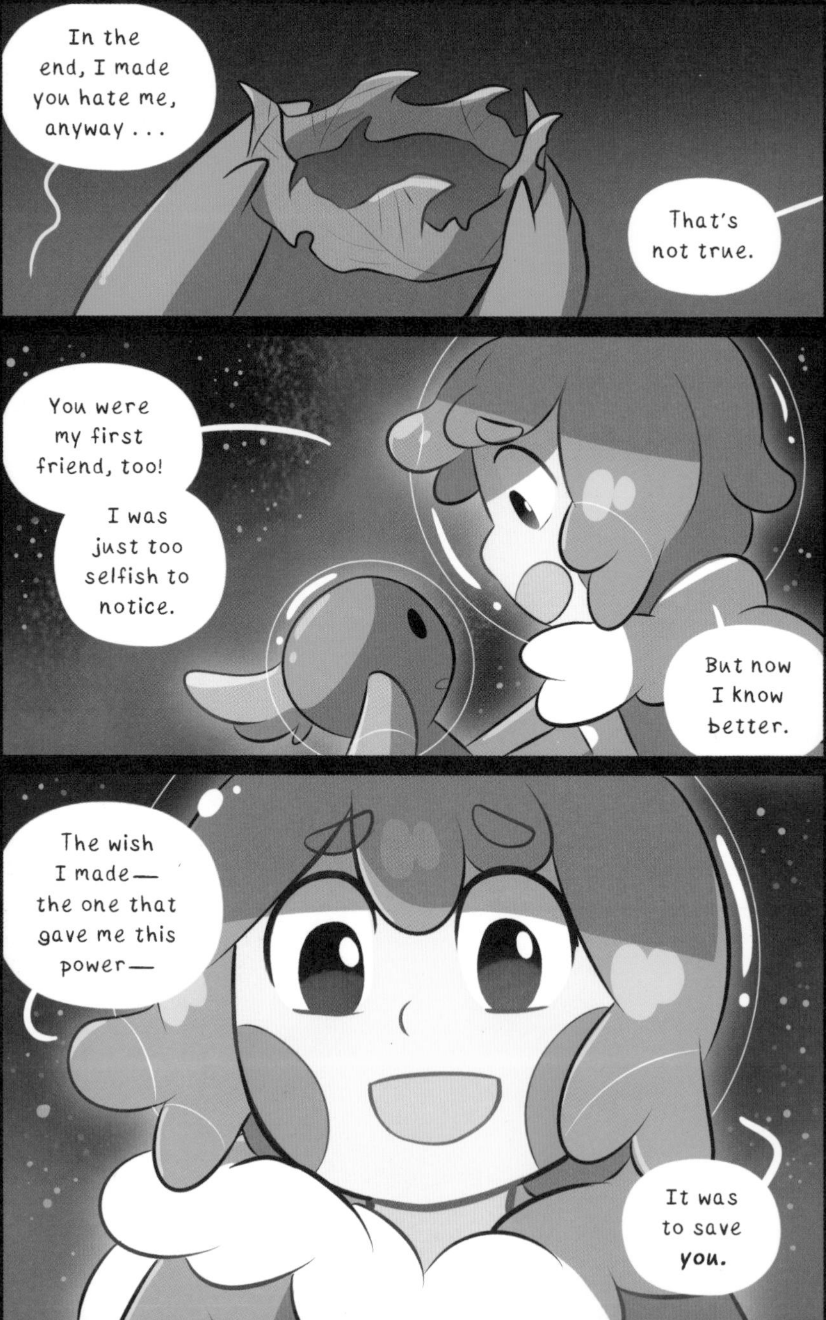
In the end, I made you hate me, anyway . . .
That's not true.
You were my first friend, too!
I was just too selfish to notice.
But now I know better.
The wish I made—the one that gave me this power—
It was to save **you.**

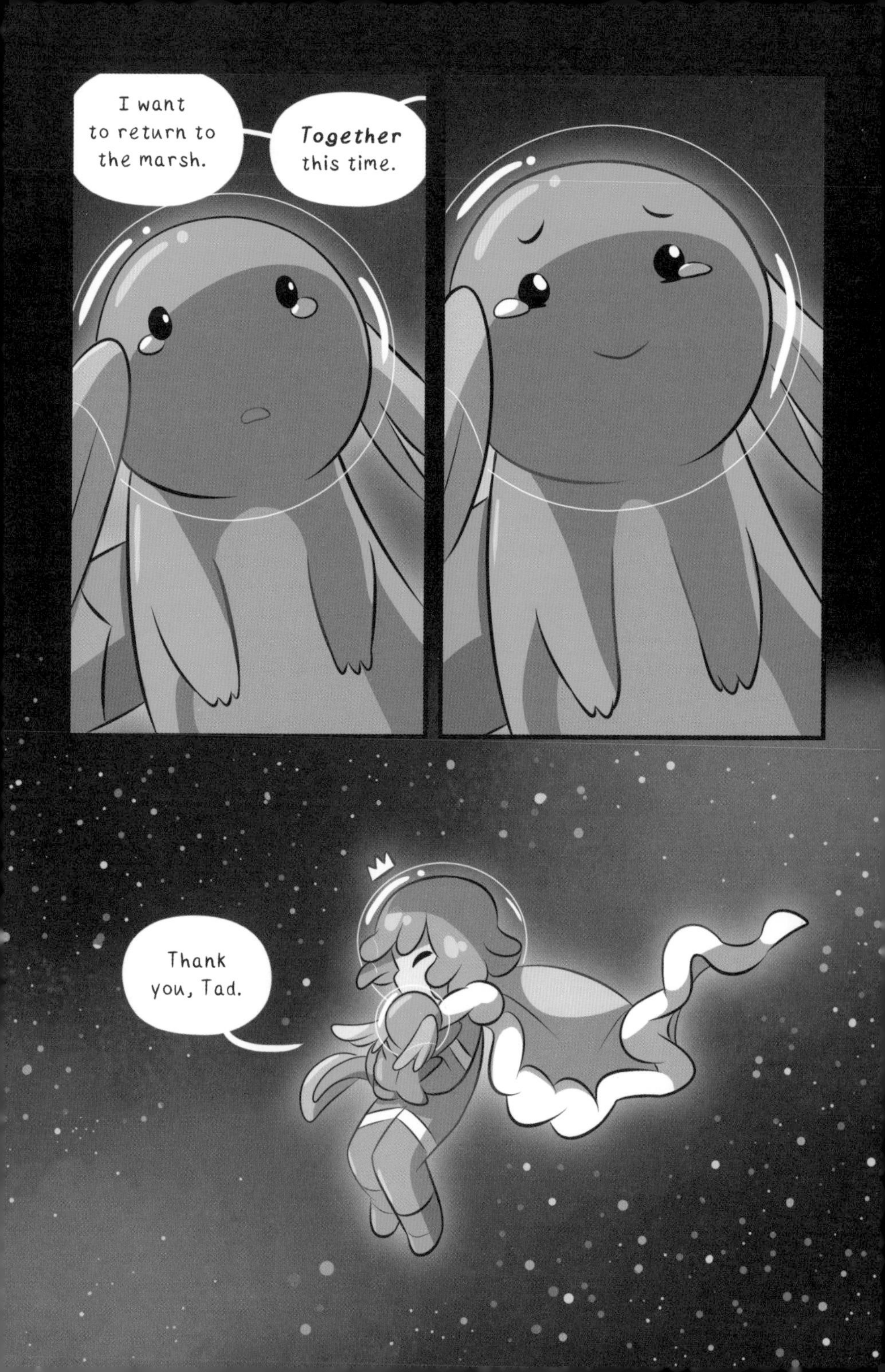
I want to return to the marsh.
Together this time.
Thank you, Tad.

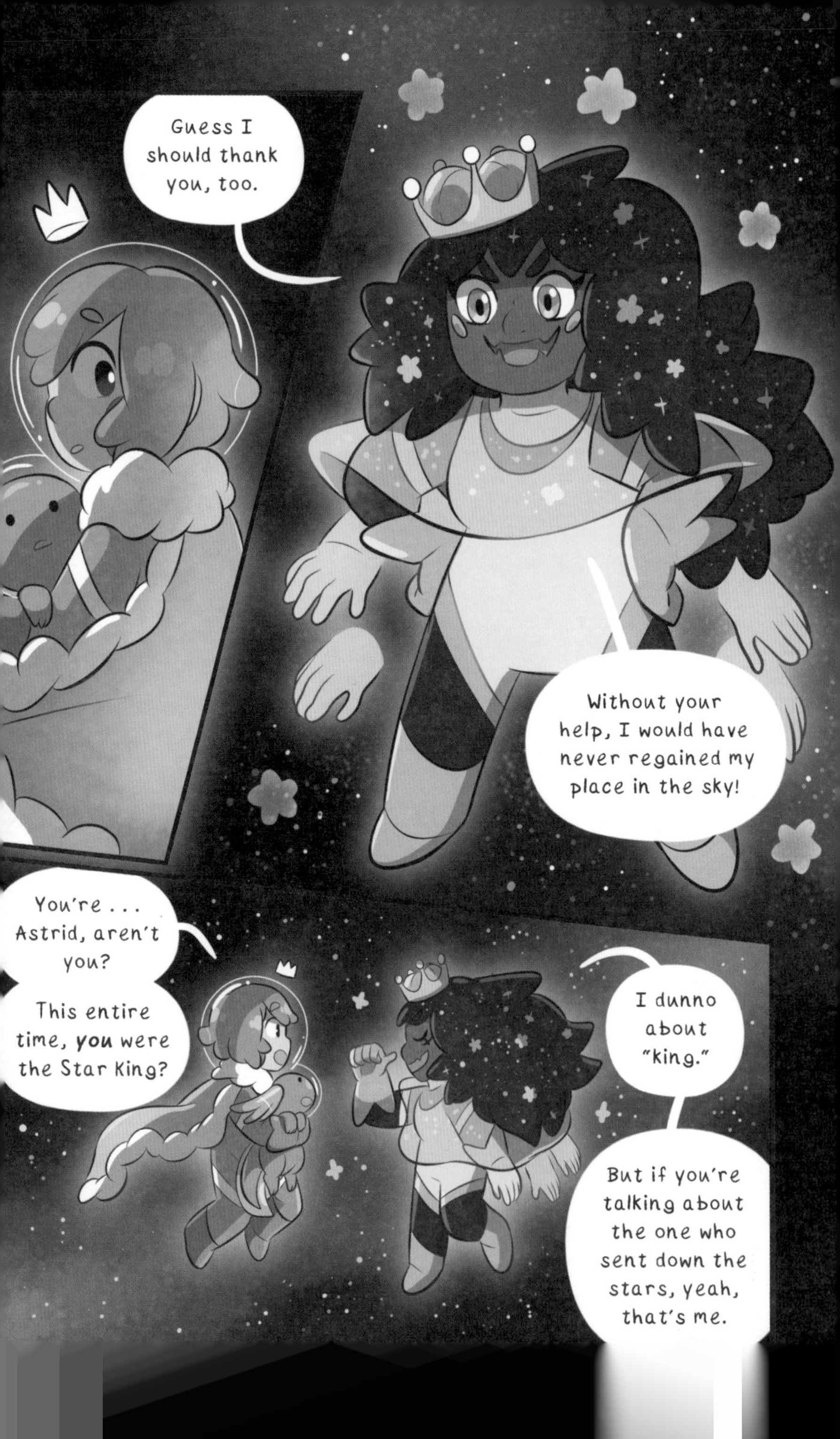
Guess I should thank you, too.
Without your help, I would have never regained my place in the sky!
You're . . . Astrid, aren't you?
This entire time, **you** were the Star King?
I dunno about "king."
But if you're talking about the one who sent down the stars, yeah, that's me.

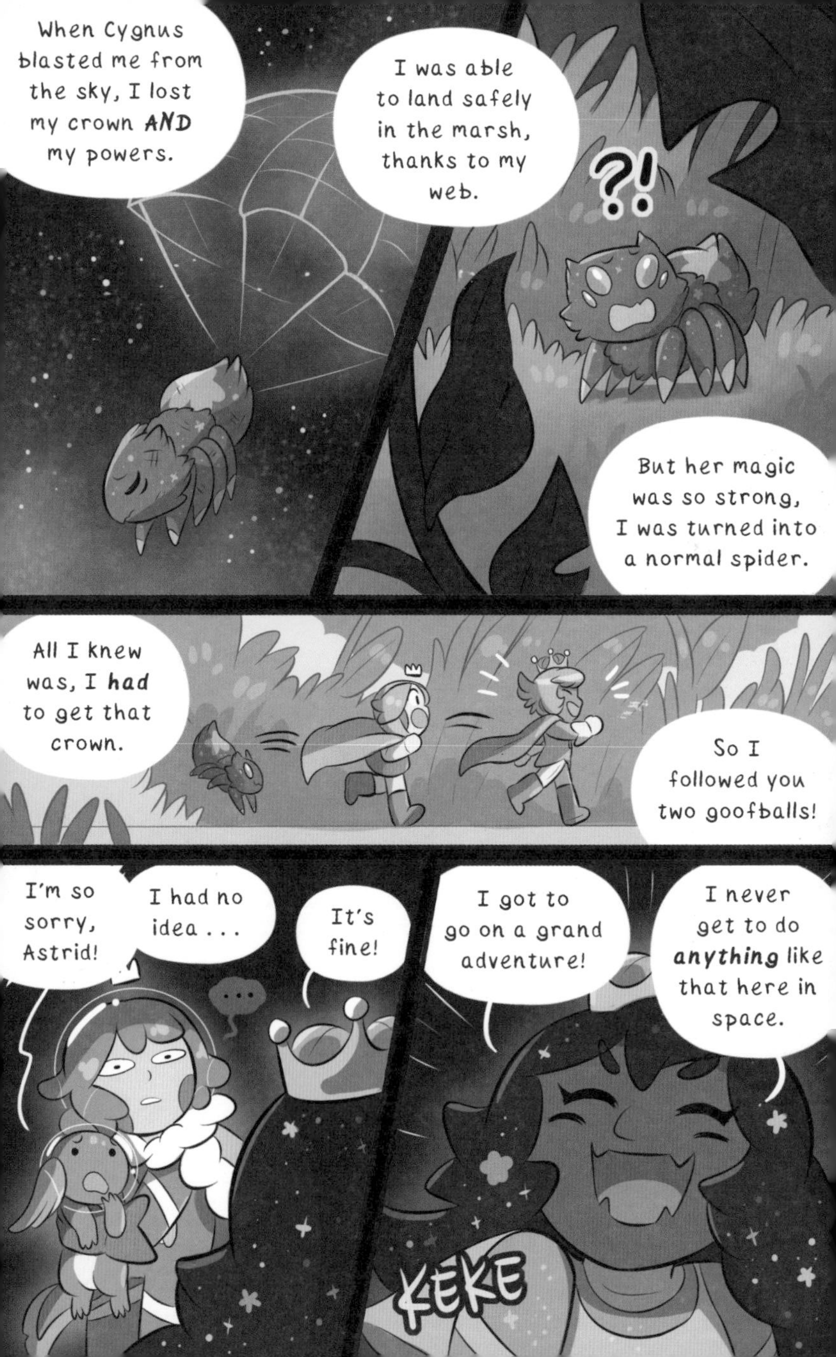

When Cygnus blasted me from the sky, I lost my crown AND my powers.
I was able to land safely in the marsh, thanks to my web.
?!
But her magic was so strong, I was turned into a normal spider.
All I knew was, I had to get that crown.
So I followed you two goofballs!
I'm so sorry, Astrid!
I had no idea . . .
It's fine!
I got to go on a grand adventure!
I never get to do anything like that here in space.
KEKE

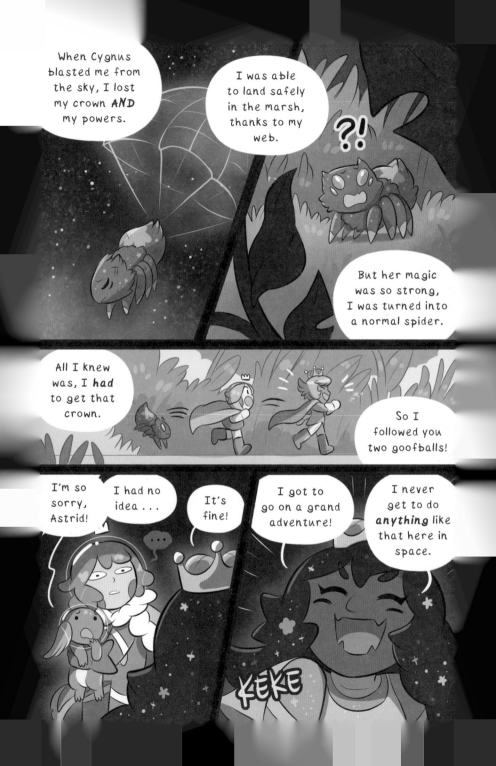

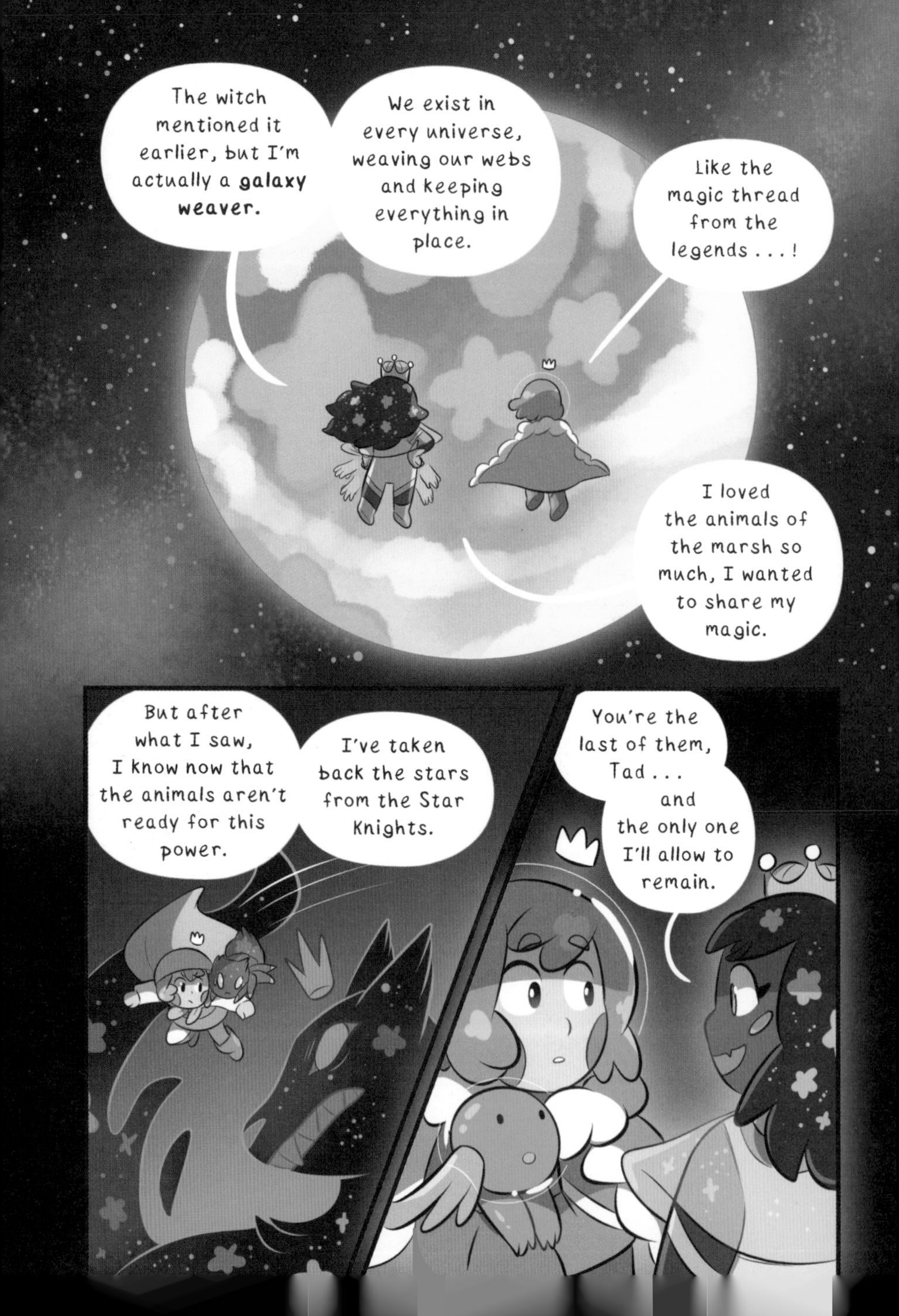
The witch mentioned it earlier, but I'm actually a **galaxy weaver.**
We exist in every universe, weaving our webs and keeping everything in place.
Like the magic thread from the legends . . . !
I loved the animals of the marsh so much, I wanted to share my magic.
But after what I saw, I know now that the animals aren't ready for this power.
I've taken back the stars from the Star Knights.
You're the last of them, Tad . . .
and the only one I'll allow to remain.

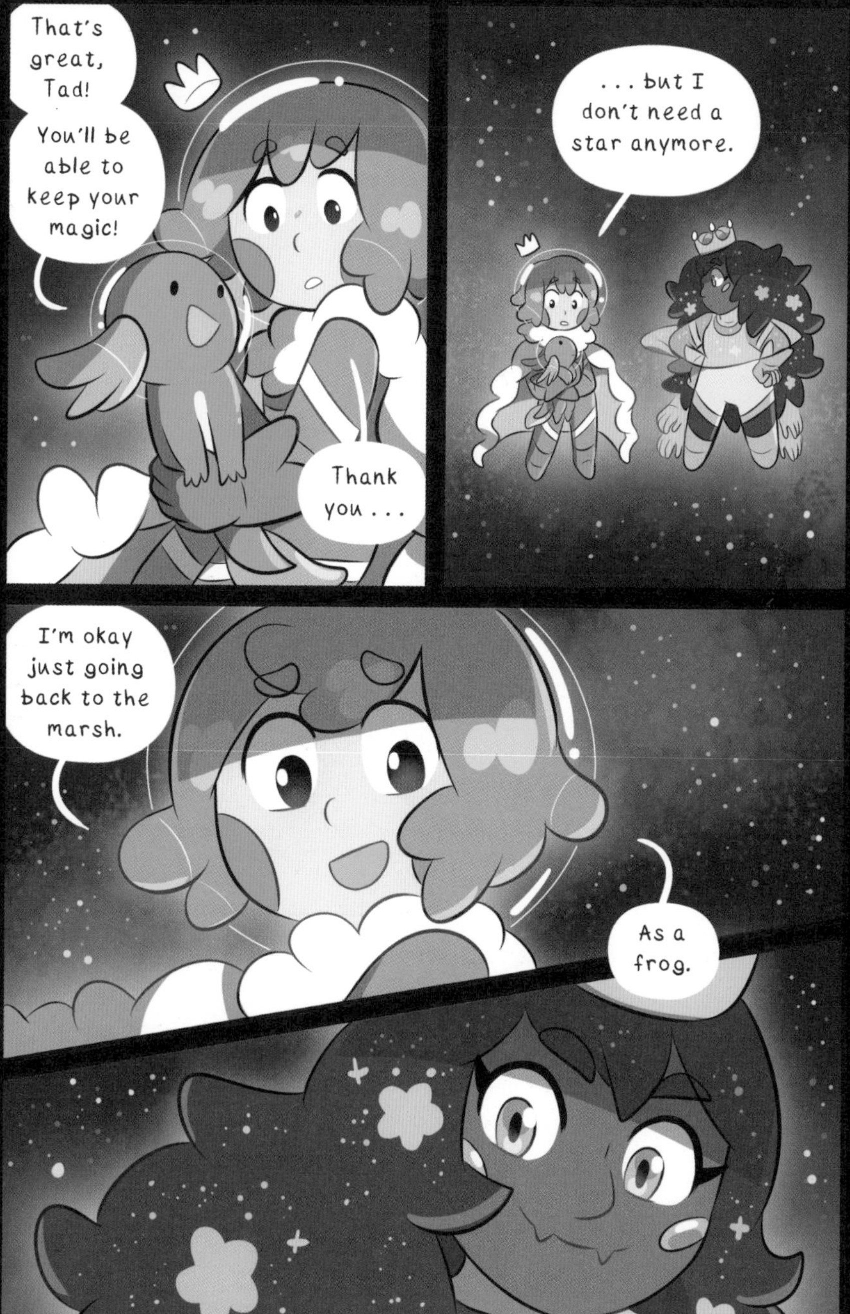
That's great, Tad!
You'll be able to keep your magic!
Thank you . . .
. . . but I don't need a star anymore.
I'm okay just going back to the marsh.
As a frog.

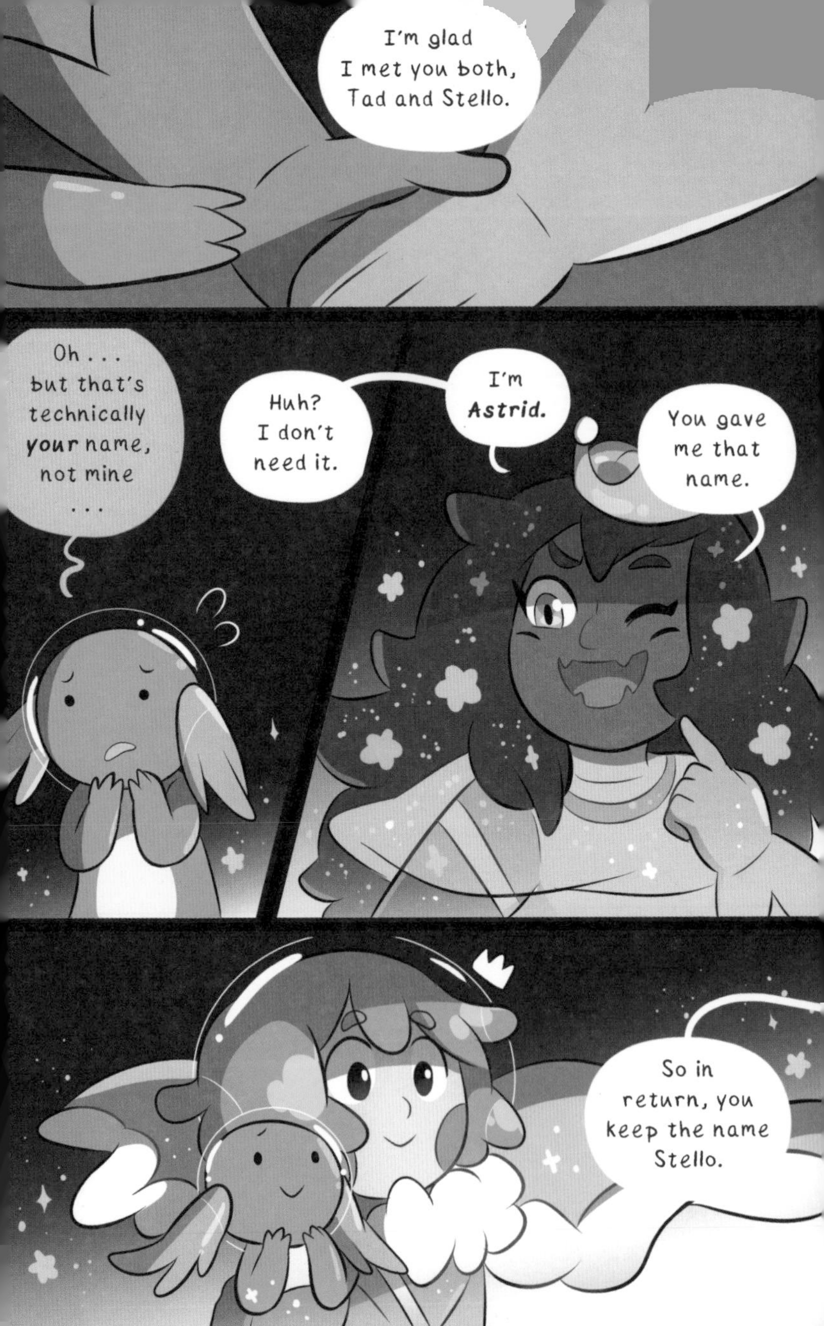
I'm glad I met you both, Tad and Stello.
Oh . . . but that's technically **your** name, not mine . . .
Huh? I don't need it.
I'm **Astrid.**
You gave me that name.
So in return, you keep the name Stello.

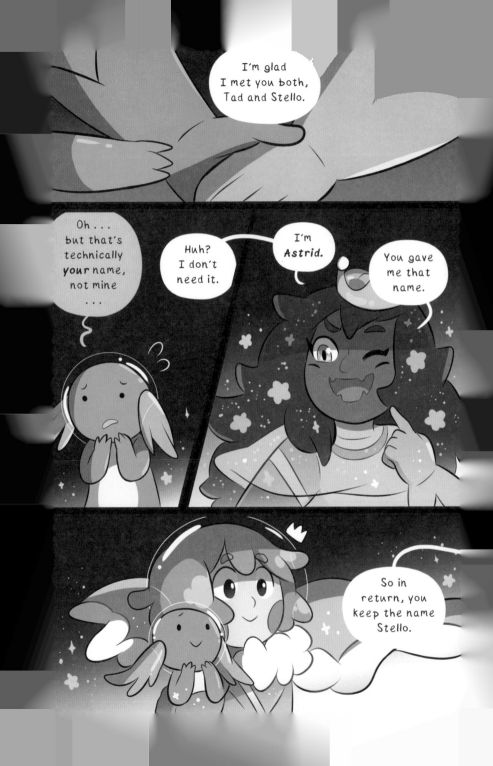

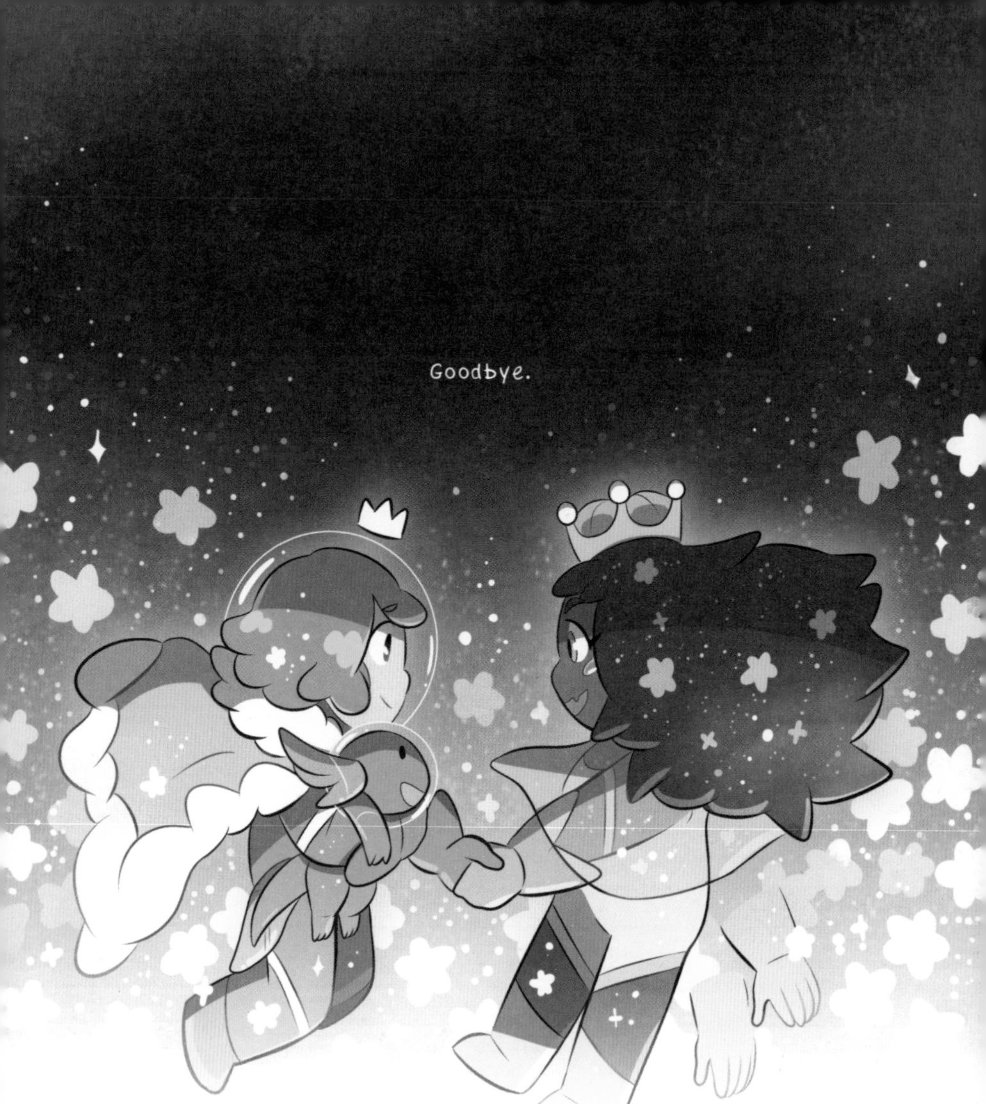
Goodbye.

For now.

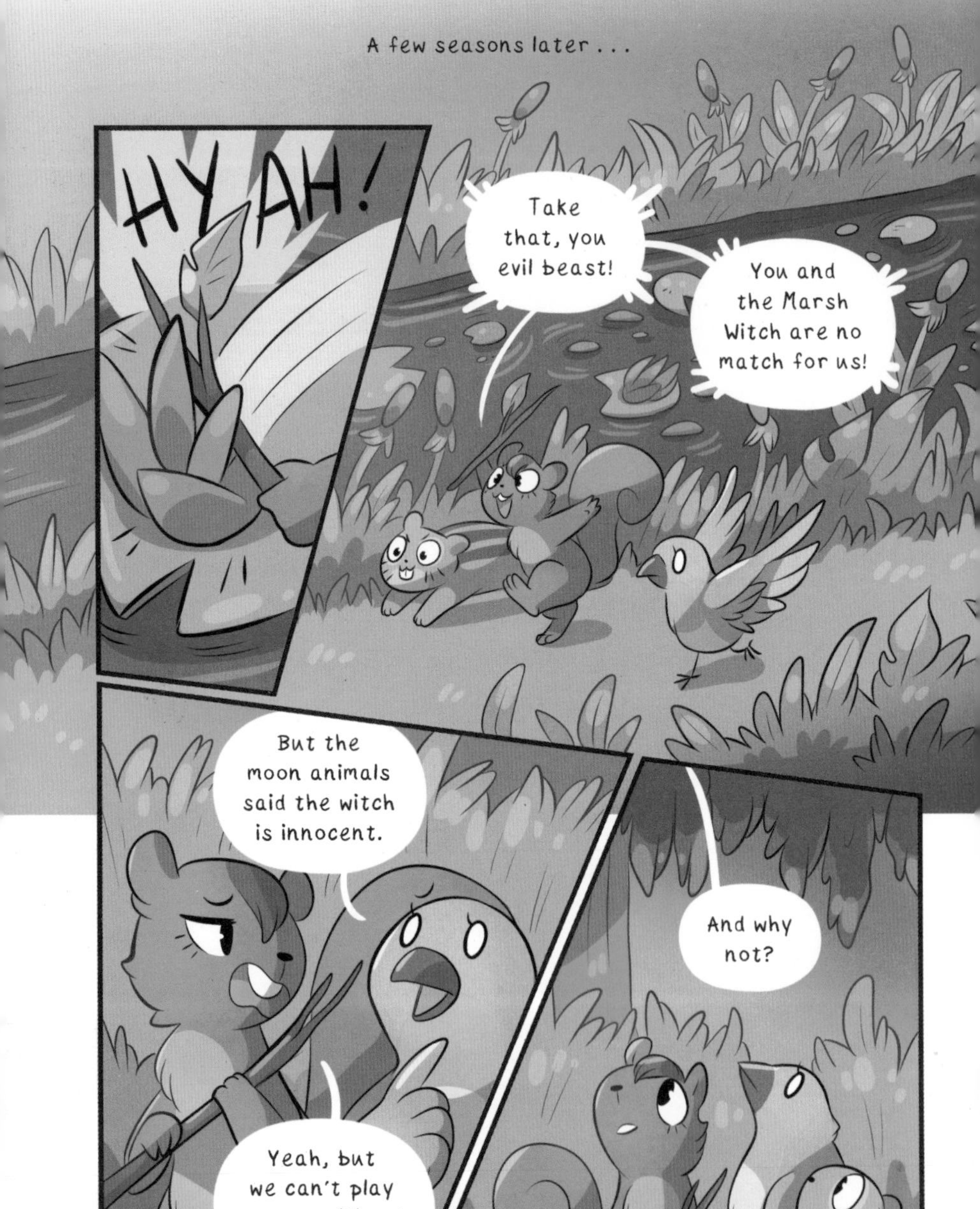
A few seasons later . . .
HYAH!
Take that, you evil beast!
You and the Marsh Witch are no match for us!
But the moon animals said the witch is innocent.
Yeah, but we can't play a game without a **witch.**
And why not?

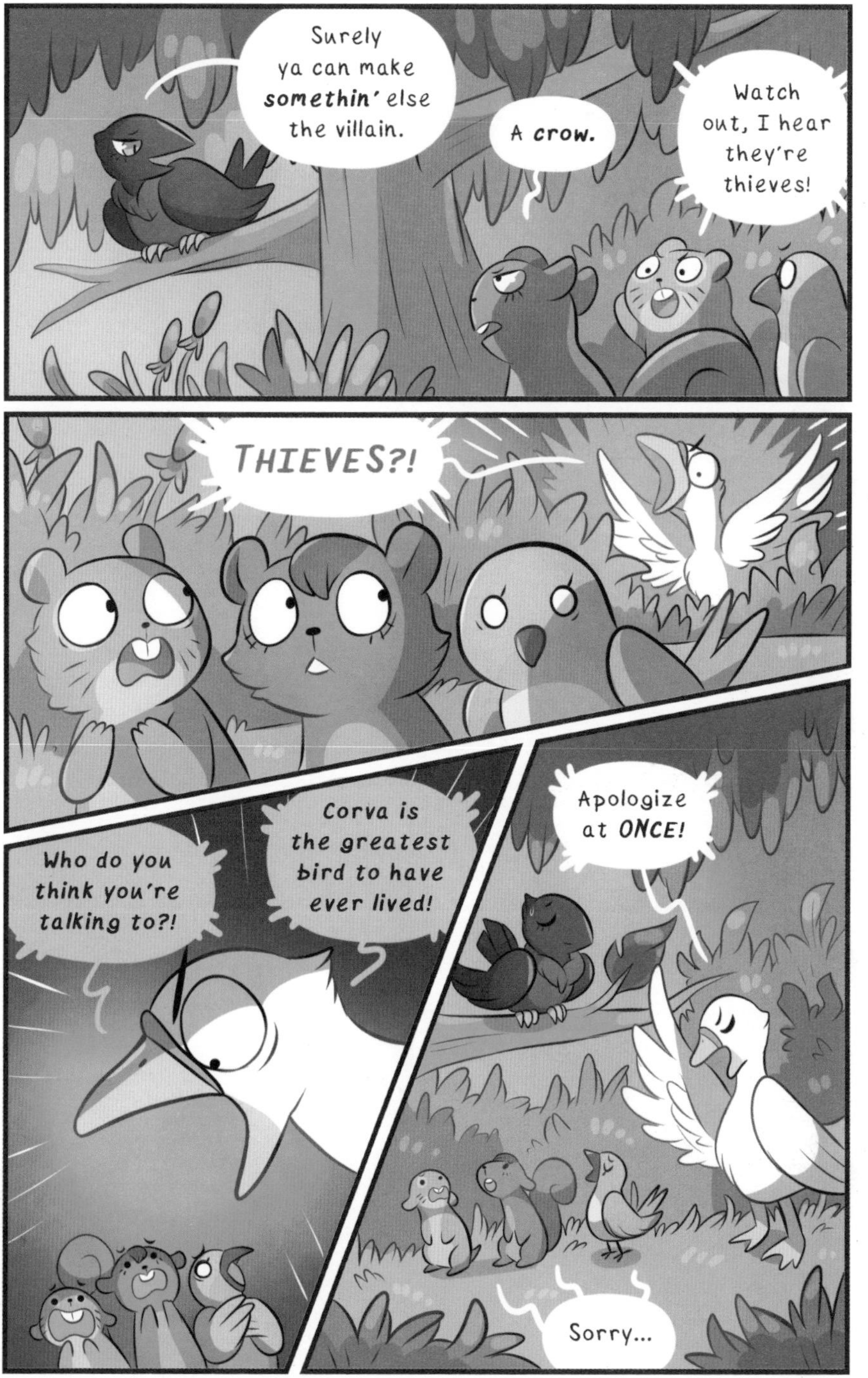

Surely ya can make **somethin'** else the villain.
A **crow.**
Watch out, I hear they're thieves!
THIEVES?!
Who do you think you're talking to?!
Corva is the greatest bird to have ever lived!
Apologize at ONCE!
Sorry...

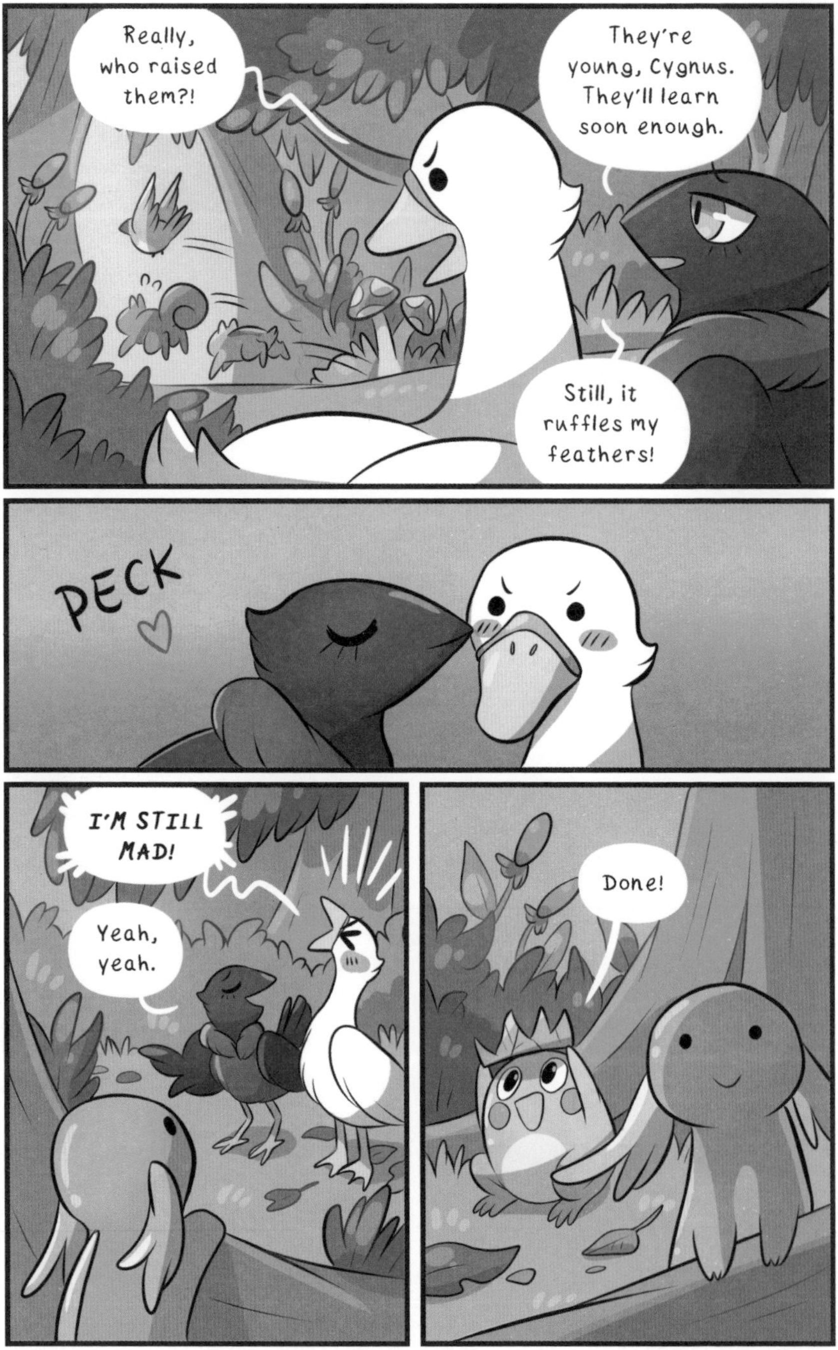
Really, who raised them?!
They're young, Cygnus. They'll learn soon enough.
Still, it ruffles my feathers!
PECK
I'M STILL MAD!
Yeah, yeah.
Done!

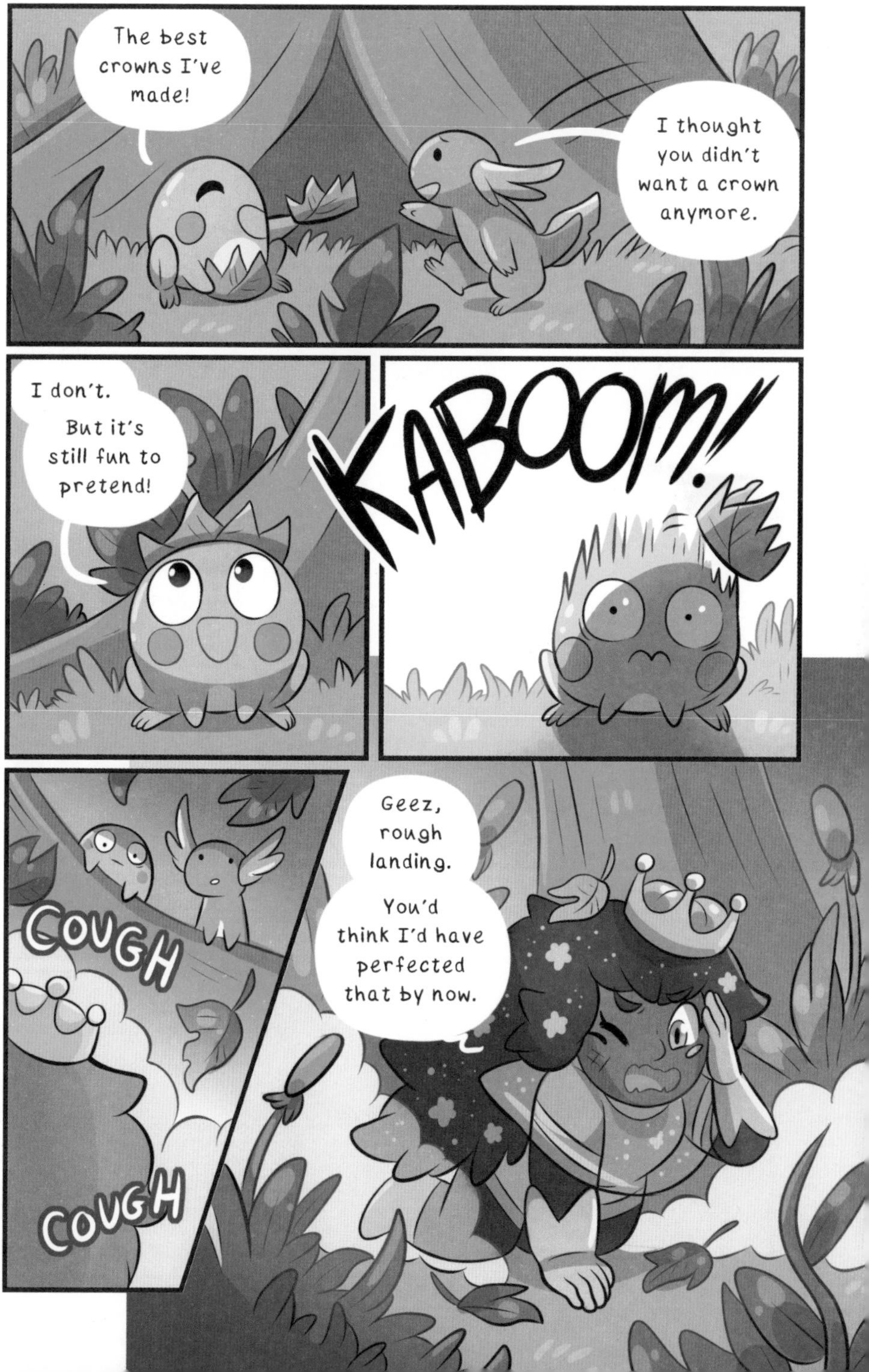
The best crowns I've made!
I thought you didn't want a crown anymore.
I don't.
But it's still fun to pretend!
KABOOM!
COUGH
COUGH
Geez, rough landing.
You'd think I'd have perfected that by now.

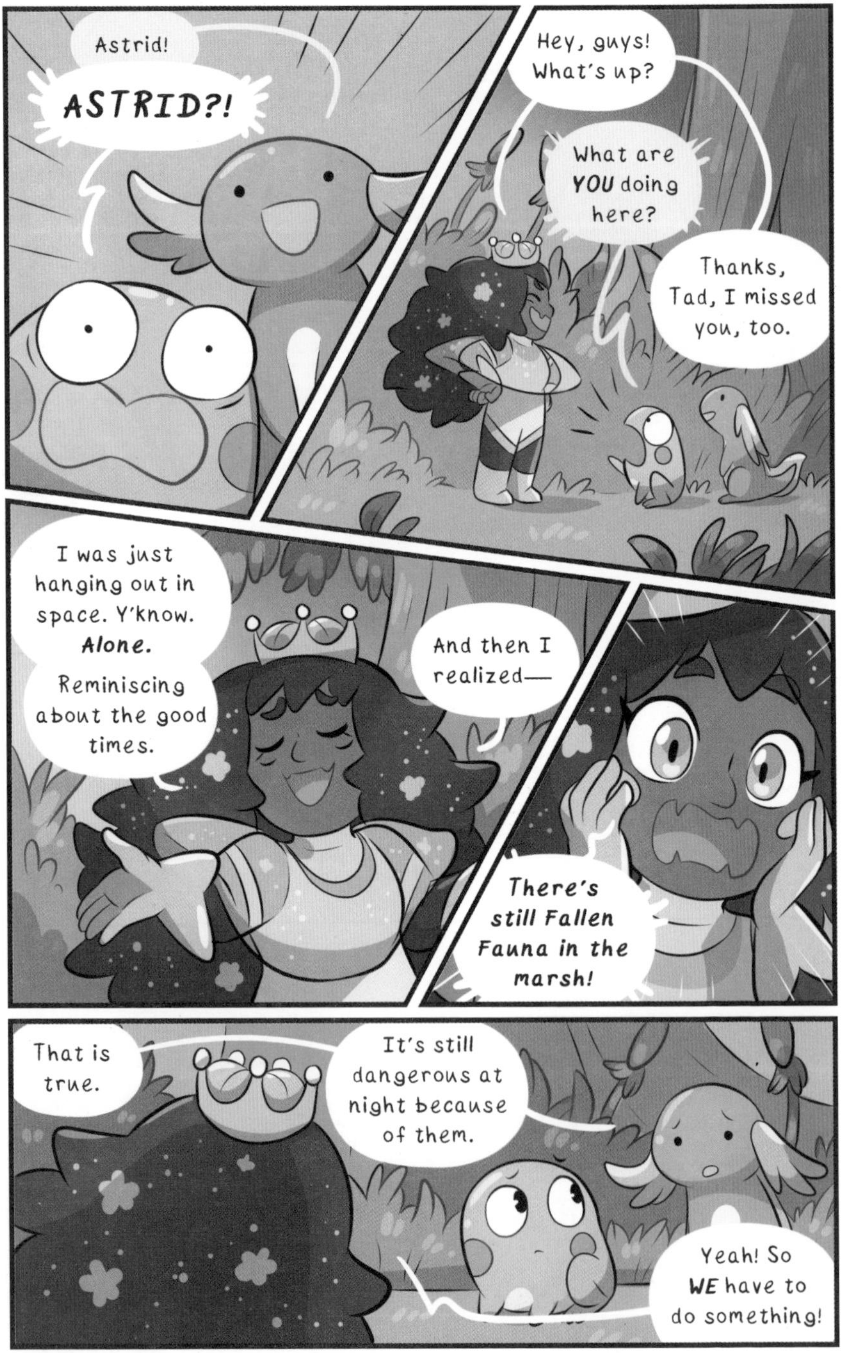

Astrid!
ASTRID?!
Hey, guys! What's up?
What are YOU doing here?
Thanks, Tad, I missed you, too.
I was just hanging out in space. Y'know. Alone.
Reminiscing about the good times.
And then I realized—
There's still Fallen Fauna in the marsh!
That is true.
It's still dangerous at night because of them.
Yeah! So WE have to do something!

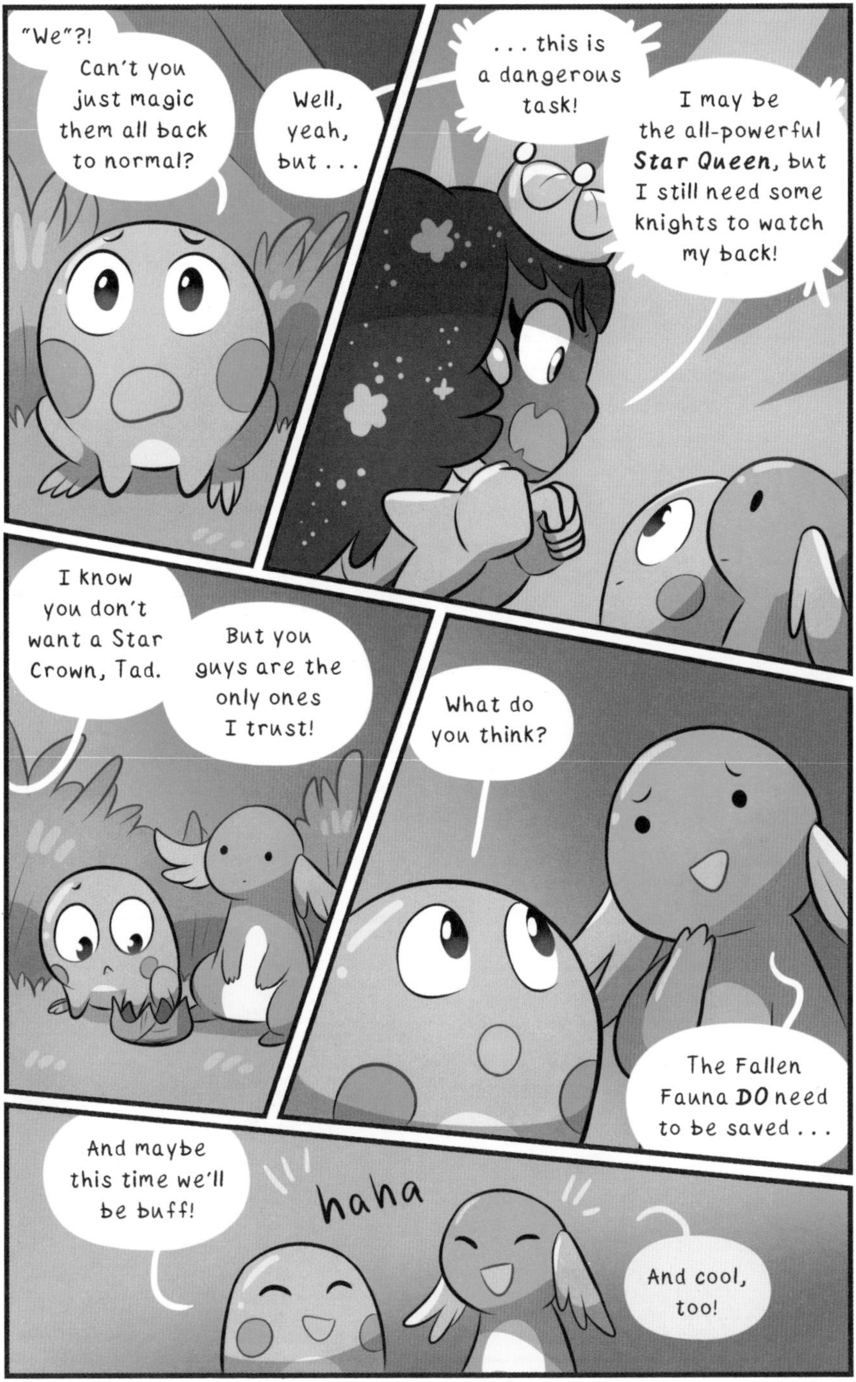
"We"?!
Can't you just magic them all back to normal?
Well, yeah, but . . .
. . . this is a dangerous task!
I may be the all-powerful **Star Queen**, but I still need some knights to watch my back!
I know you don't want a Star Crown, Tad.
But you guys are the only ones I trust!
What do you think?
The Fallen Fauna **DO** need to be saved . . .
And maybe this time we'll be buff!
haha
And cool, too!

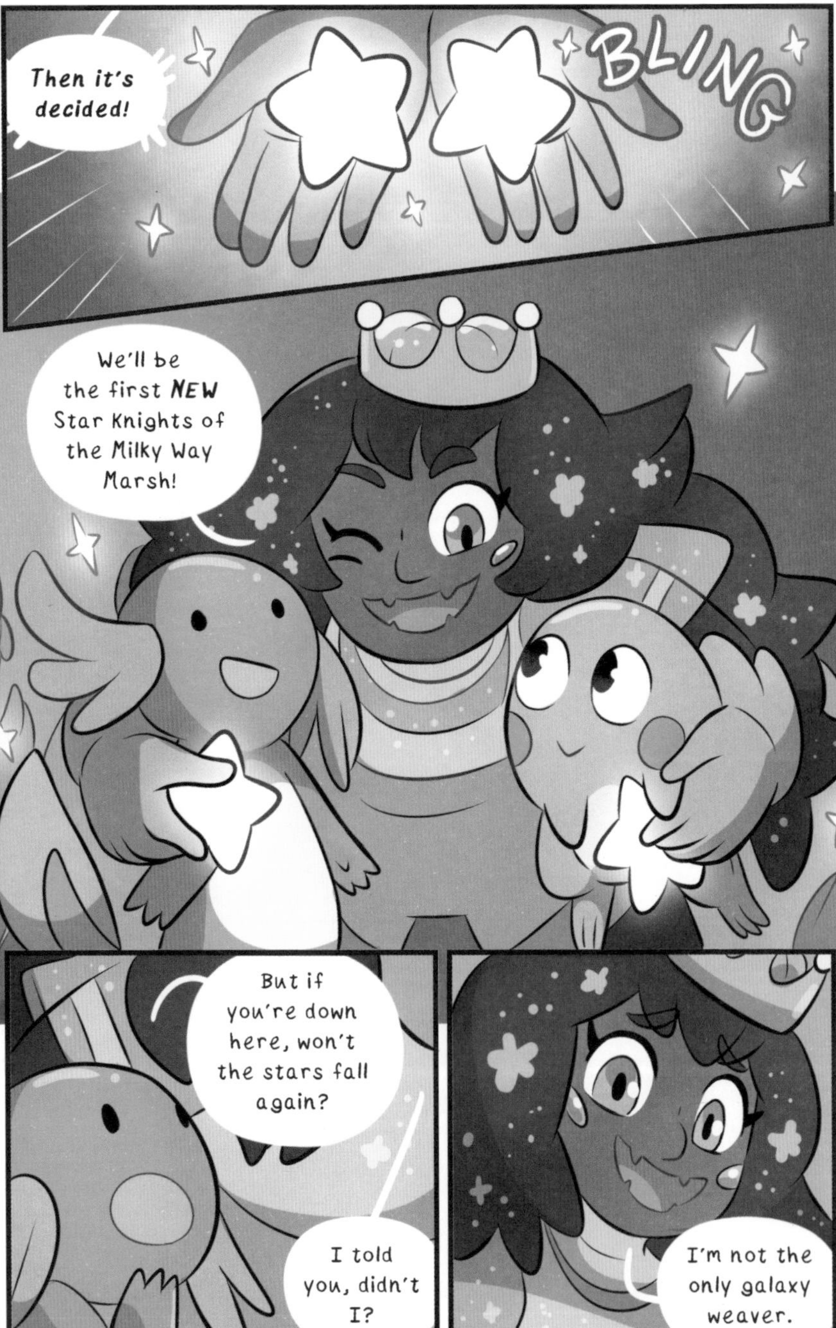
Then it's decided!
BLING
We'll be the first NEW Star Knights of the Milky Way Marsh!
But if you're down here, won't the stars fall again?
I told you, didn't I?
I'm not the only galaxy weaver.

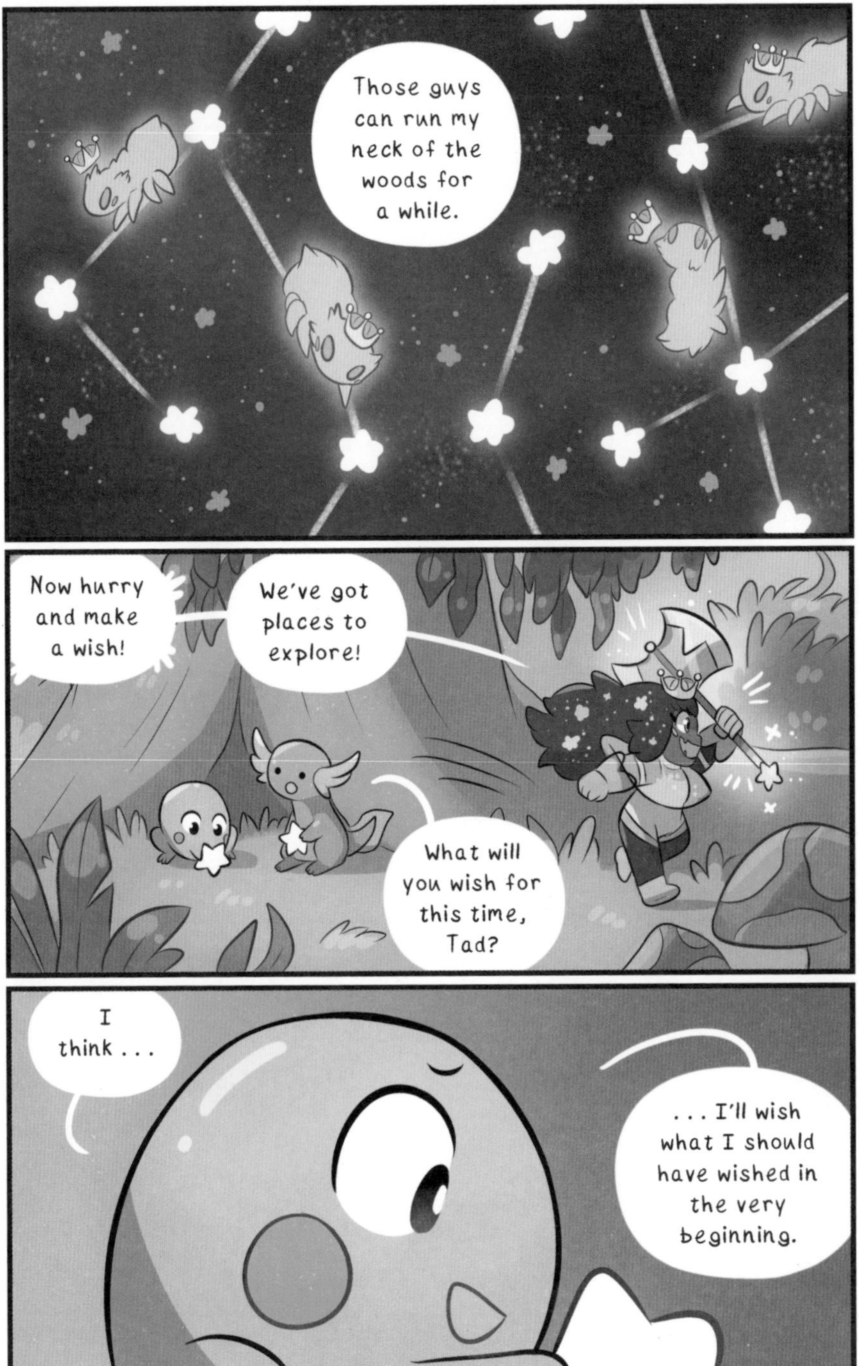
Those guys can run my neck of the woods for a while.
Now hurry and make a wish!
We've got places to explore!
What will you wish for this time, Tad?
I think . . .
. . . I'll wish what I should have wished in the very beginning.

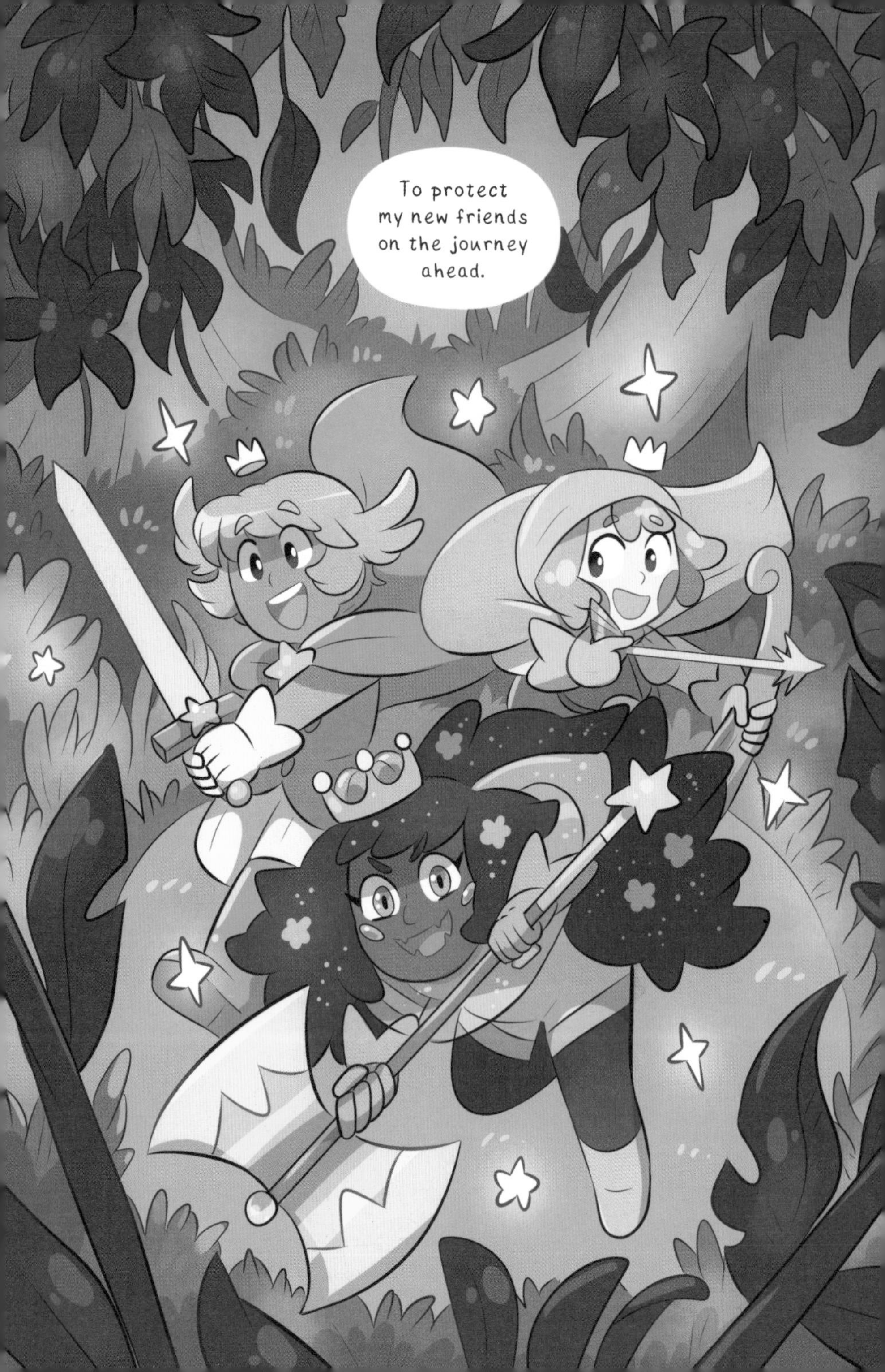
To protect my new friends on the journey ahead.

Acknowledgments

To everyone who has supported me on this journey—
thank you! It has meant the world, and whether
big or small, I could not have completed this journey
without you.

To my friends Natalie, Alicea, Vyvy, Lea, Pat, Jenny, Abi, and
Lena, for the many fun drawing sessions and games, and for
providing company during an otherwise secluded time.

My mentors Blake, Shane, and Michele, for their guidance
and encouragement over the years.

My amazing agent, Britt, and everyone on the
Random House Graphic team for helping me create
this story, as well as giving me the opportunity to tell it.

And of course, my family for their support, and my mom, who
always believed in me, even when I could not.
Thank you so much.

Kay Davault is a comic artist from Nashville, Tennessee, who enjoys drawing cute characters and scary monsters and combining the two together. Her first major work was the all-ages mystery series Oddity Woods, which kickstarted her obsession with drawing hundreds of pages of comics.

Star Knights is Kay's first published work. She hopes you enjoyed Tad's story as much as she enjoyed telling it.

@kaydavault
kaydavault.com

"Journey to Stars"

In 2017, I created a small comic about a frog prince's adventure to find the stars. Here's a look at the tiny story that eventually became the inspiration for *Star Knights*!

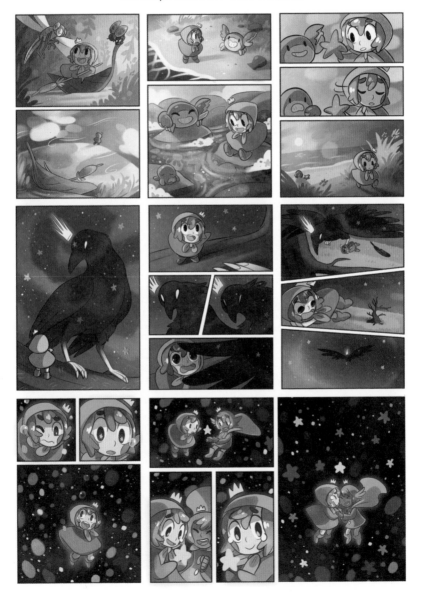

Concept Art

Tad

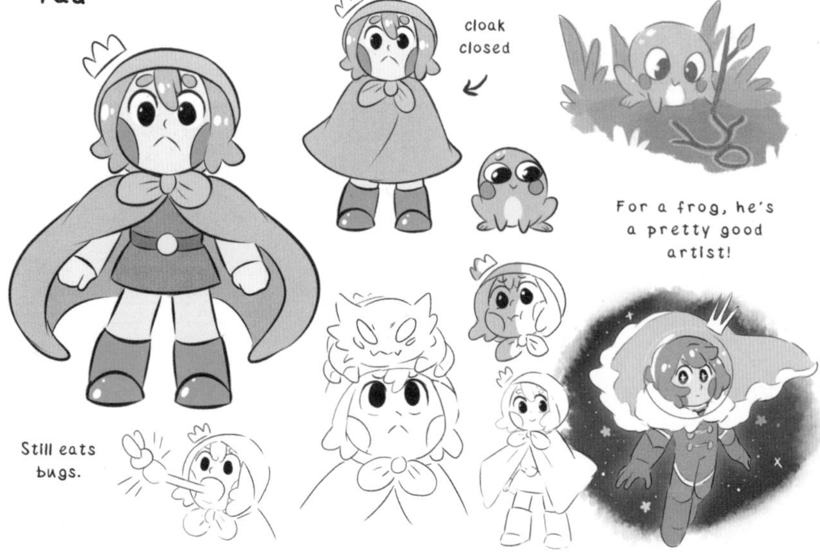

cloak closed
For a frog, he's a pretty good artist!
Still eats bugs.

Stello

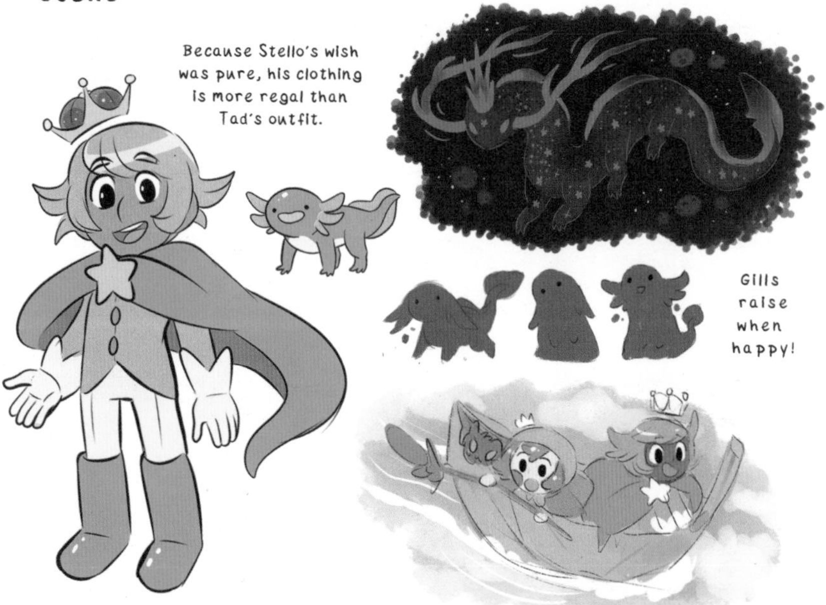

Because Stello's wish was pure, his clothing is more regal than Tad's outfit.
Gills raise when happy!

Astrid

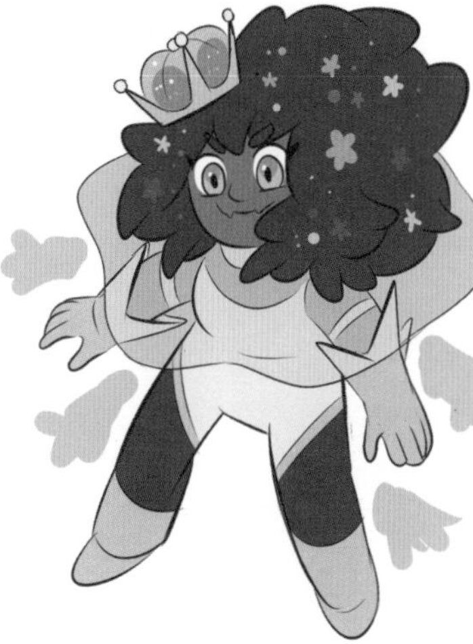

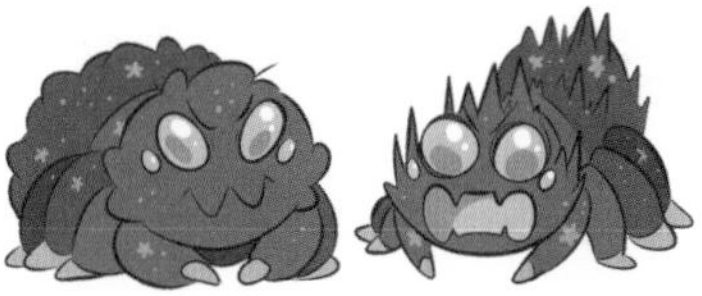

In her human form, she creates
four extra arms with starlight.

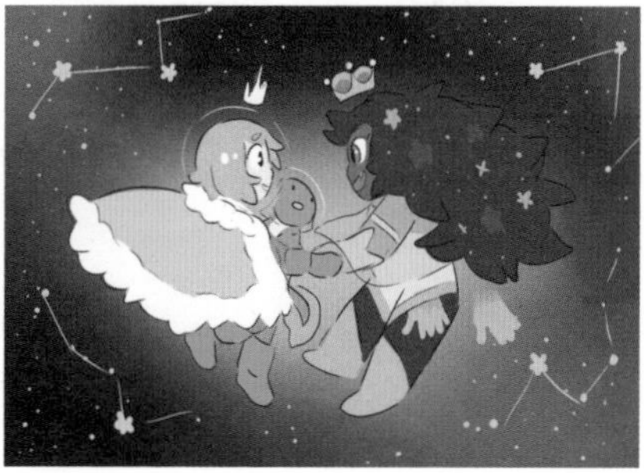

Star Knights

Their human designs are inspired by their animal
forms, as well as their own idea of what they'd look like.
All knights have special powers depending on their species!

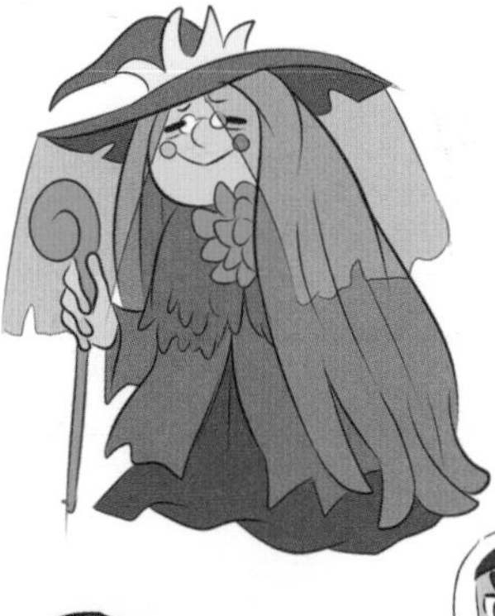

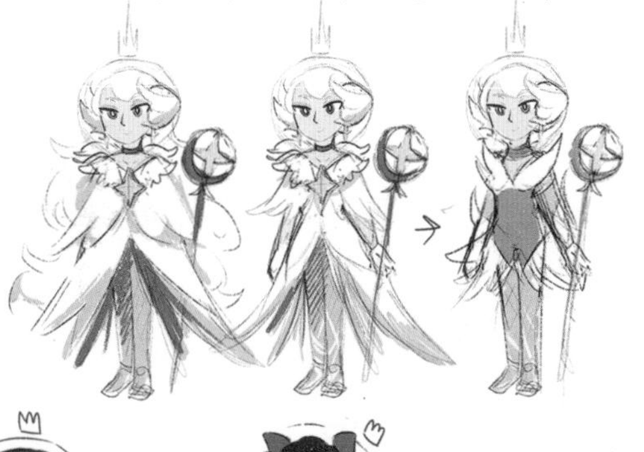

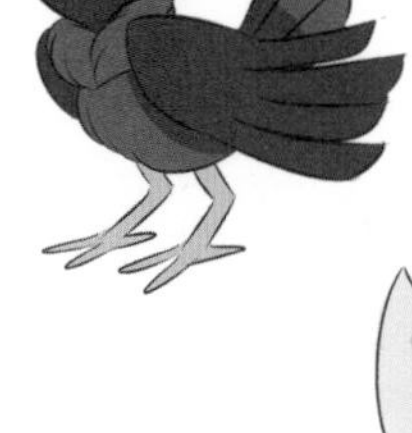

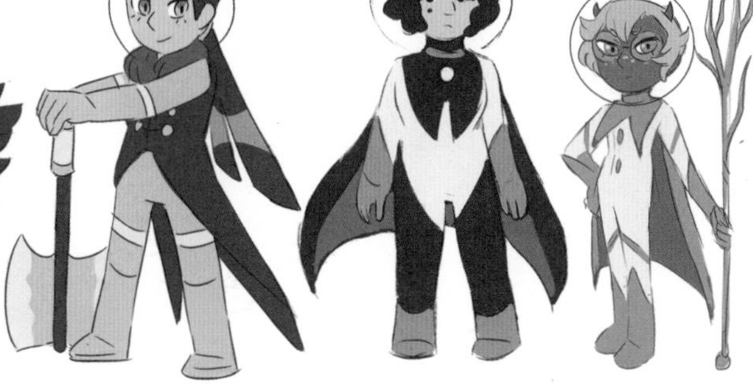

MAGIC AND ADVENTURE AWAIT

One pig's perilous journey to find purpose and friendship
Ham Helsing
VAMPIRE HUNTER
RICH MOYER

NEW YORK TIMES BESTSELLING SERIES
HiLo
GiNA THE GIRL WHO BROKE THE WORLD
BY JUDD WINICK

MAPMAKERS AND THE LOST MAGIC
CAMERON CHITTOCK
AMANDA CASTILLO

STAR KNIGHTS
KAY DAVAULT

STEVE L. McEVIL
Lucas Turnbloom

SUPER SIDEKICKS
NO ADULTS ALLOWED
Gavin Aung Than
NEW YORK TIMES BESTSELLING CARTOONIST

Sophie Escabasse
Witches of Brooklyn

5 Worlds
THE SAND WARRIOR
Mark Siegel
Alexis Siegel
Xanthe Bouma
Matt Rockefeller
Boya Sun

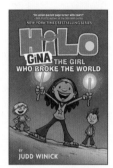